# Mountain Time

# Mountain Time

Bernard DeVoto

Little, Brown and Company · Boston · 1947

*Tarquin, suspecting the messenger's loyalty, made no answer. But he took the fellow into his private garden and, in his presence, under his very eyes, lopped off the heads of the tallest poppies with his sword.*

*My friend, we are simple, idiotic people.*

# 1

## New York 1919

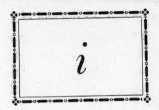

*i*

THE HOUSE officers of Mercy Hospital ate dinner when and where they could. Some of them could get as much as twenty minutes free and eat in the dining room. Some carried a plate from the kitchen to a ward desk or a lab table and came back to it when they could. Some phoned the kitchen to put something on a tray and they'd get to it sometime. But at six-thirty every afternoon all who were on the surgical service, six assistant residents and eighteen interns, were supposed to meet in the head resident's suite to discuss the day's job. At least half of them were always able to get there for at least part of the twenty or thirty minutes it took.

Most of them lived in the west end of the Nurses' Home, in the corner of the grounds nearest Tenth Avenue. It was a rose-brick building that had been built for the indigent poor of New York City in 1844 and called Paupers' House, a useful name still. The head resident had not only a cell but a cubicle too, fully twelve feet square though one corner was cut off by a main steam line. Its plaster walls had presumably been painted tan and there were a desk and four chairs that had come down the ages. On the wall over the desk was a row of framed photographs, former residents.

These photographs were eight by ten and tradition said that they were not hung till the subject moved up out of Mercy into the great world of surgery. Cy Kinsman, who in March 1919 had been surgical resident for just over three months, was violating tradition; he was hanging his at the end of the row and it was ten by twelve. It showed him in his uniform as a captain of the

3

Medical Corps, which would make it doubly offensive to the juniors.

Pete Estey, senior assistant resident and in charge of the Emergency Ward, got there first. At the end of any day the state of a house officer's clothes made him resemble a street cleaner but the University of Virginia gave Pete an air even in whites and he had natural advantages too. He was not the only one on the service who admired Cy's hands but he was the only one whom Cy felt free to call a friend. Pete comprehended the photograph at once. "Buildin' a back fire, Cy?"

"Applying a counterirritant."

"Counter-counterirritant."

"I don't want to let the boys down. Don't they count on me to be snooty?"

"I'd say they generally use two *t*'s. Nice piece of serge. Cam Steele says you look like a lopsided left guard. I don't think you're a bit lopsided."

"You should have seen me in His Majesty's uniform. And by God I had a striker to keep it clean. Batman, we King's men said."

"Make a useful innovation at Mercy."

"What suit would he keep clean?"

Pete sat on the floor. It was nothing to Pete Estey that Dr. Alexander McAllister, the deity of Mercy Hospital, had brought back a stranger from Base 98 in France as his assistant and heir, and had passed him over everyone's head to make him resident. To others it meant a good deal and the affront was not diminished by the fact that Little Mac had brought back a man who was not only very good indeed but behaved with due consciousness of his talents. Kinsman? you were supposed to say on the service, oh, he's a brilliant bastard but he's a bastard.

They came in by twos and threes now, more than usual for they were going to get some of their own back tonight. Reynolds —in charge of Obstetrics, crammed with medical intelligence, a man who would permit himself no problems, married—Reynolds glanced from the photograph to Cy and said, "Leaving us?"

"Just revising the procedure."

4

You needed no clairvoyance to perceive that Reynolds disliked Cy in the self-contained way of a man who was sure of himself and knew where he was going—or to understand that he would behave correctly toward any man who had the power of a head resident. But Cam Steele openly hated Cy's guts and Cam crowded up to the photograph. "Damn if it isn't Kinsman in a soldier suit. Did you get to France, Cy?"

That was good for a general laugh and Cam played for another one. "Get a chance to operate over there? Be a good idea to tell us about it sometime."

Cy said, "Happy hour first."

Steele looked happy at once. "Was there something about a carcinoma?" he said, and various faces lighted up.

Cy cooled them off. "We had a drunk in Ward C today." The intern who had been brought up from the dog lab just four days ago turned pink and squared his shoulders. His name was Woodard and he looked ready to take it. Somebody would damn well have to. Cy had got there in time to stop the brawl before any harm was done, but the episode was an indignity to medicine and a slur on the honor of Mercy Hospital.

"Okay, Woodard," he said. "I can't say it was your fault. I didn't, either, for it was mine. Mercy pays me two precious dollars a day to make sure that our noses are all clean. France is a big laugh, but in France you'd be in quarters now and headed for a general court. You'd be lucky if they ever let you paint another tonsil. A patient gets a pint of liquor and gets drunk. No. It won't happen again—not if an archangel tries to bring it in. He might have killed someone. Or himself. We don't like surplus deaths at Mercy." Cy let sweetness seep into his voice. "You see, they show in the weekly report. The Old Man might have been vexed."

Nobody was looking at him. Pete Estey asked from his corner by the steam pipes, "Found out how he got it?"

"Part of the ward service of Mercy. He got it from an orderly —Rizutto." That compounded the shame, which might have been tolerable if it had come in under a visitor's coat.

5

"That does it," Pete said. "I guess you had to make a report."

"Rizutto is fired. So is Swenson, out of the kitchen. The Superintendent couldn't prove it on Swenson but he's fired. The Old Man will hist my tail up between my shoulders tomorrow."

Cam Steele was impatient. "What about today's miracle of surgery? Or is diagnosis the word I mean?"

Cy nodded. They were entitled to their fun. "Did you bring the plate, Charlie?"

Charlie Moss—in charge of Private Wing—propped a large X-ray plate up on Cy's desk and the boys crowded round it. "Patient lives at Gramercy Park and today was a precious privilege for Charlie and me. We'll never see the inside of his house but we're well acquainted with the inside of patient."

Steele said, "What we hear is, there was a carcinoma there all the time."

"That's right."

"You mean, now we've got to wrestle with the idea you could be wrong, Cy?"

That was what they had a chance to ram home. The Old Man had rammed it home this morning. Dr. Alexander McAllister and his assistant had disagreed about that carcinoma, of which not the faintest shadow showed on the X-ray plate and about which the clinical indications had been contradictory. Little Mac said there was a growth there; Cy said he didn't have enough to go on. At this time yesterday Cy had advised the juniors that intuition was an untrustworthy instrument of diagnosis.

If it was a cancer, it had so impressive an owner that Dr. McAllister did not bother to throw the preliminary tantrum in the scrub room that was one way of getting the focus he liked. He came in peacefully and started scrubbing up in silence. He even smiled at the nurse who held his gown.

"Did you pack a lunch?" Cy muttered to Charlie Moss. "The McAllister Excavating and Marching Club is off down the bay. All day inside a millionaire."

Charlie played them close to his chest. "Want to bet Mac is wrong? One dollar there's no cancer?"

6

"I didn't say there wasn't. I said the Little Giant doesn't know."

So, with the incision made and the stomach in view, Little Mac paused and turned a poker face toward Cy. "Don't see it, Cy?"

"No, Colonel."

"Moss?"

"No, sir."

Mac said over his shoulder to the dozen-odd medical students in the high seats, "Indications of carcinoma were yes and no. We X-rayed it. Didn't show on the plates. My assistant couldn't see it. Neither could I. Can't see it now. Obviously can't be there. Means nothing that patient was losing weight like a punctured balloon. Means nothing that the digestive habits of a lifetime had gone haywire." He thrust a hand into the incision and brought up the pylorus. There it was on the back, a round hard mass. The old devil! He became McAllister the Great with an aura of wisdom at a thousand watts. "Feel it, Cy." Cy felt it, though he had no doubts. "Feel it, Moss." Charlie felt it.

"Science said it couldn't be there," Mac told the medical students. "Is there, by God."

"Wait a minute, Colonel," Cy said, too low to be heard up above. "What I said was, you weren't sure."

Mac explored inside, talking as he worked. "That's right, Cy. If I'd waited to be sure, that would have been science but the patient would have died. As it is we're probably in time. Patient practically sure to live."

That's the intuition of the master too, and furthermore your genius will rise up and persuade you to stay in too long. Cy refrained from saying it. What he did say was, "Going to send a specimen to Pathology?"

"Before I go on in? Trying to tell me it's not m'lignant?"

"No. Still, you don't know if it is."

"Oh, hell, Cy." To the seats, "My assistant wants me to wait while Pathology tells me it's cancer. . . . Nothing on the dome of the liver. . . . Nothing on the mesentery. . . . No metastasis. We're in time. . . . Science is a pretty thing, Cy, but a surgeon has got to think with his fingers."

7

"I remember. A surgeon thinks with his fingers. A surgeon has the infallible reflex."

Getting apprehensive, Charlie Moss muttered, "Shut up, Cy."

Mac heard him. "Yes, do shut up, Cy. And don't be a theoretical surgeon. It couldn't be there, only it was. I will now operate."

He did so for well over two hours, radically, according to a technique and with instruments he had invented, all named for him. He took about two thirds of the stomach and the upper part of the duodenum, then hooked up the intestine. Cy placed clamps, tied bleeders, used sponges, following those gifted fingers with fingers just as gifted. He vigilantly watched his master, aware that Mac was watching him just as critically. No need: neither would catch the other off base. Alexander McAllister had been called the best operator in the AEF and was certainly the best abdominal man in the United States. He was, all five-feet-six of him, a great surgeon. And he had picked Cy on the principle that a great man's assistant had to be an apprentice great man.

At Base Hospital 98 there had been no occasion to think of Mac in any way but just that: a superb workman, a man who walked up to the job, who stood all the pressure that might be put on him. In the four months since that simple time ended Cy had come to understand that Mac was a prima donna, a grandstander, and the spotlighted tyrant of Mercy Hospital. And none of that mattered at all when the chips were down. When Mac walked out on the operating floor he put on greatness.

He was a great man now. Rose Stine, the redheaded Jewess who would go on running the pathology lab till her chief got back from France, came in to get her specimen and stayed to watch the master workman. She glanced at Cy and her eyes over her mask derided him—excellence in others is a mortal pang, isn't it, Kinsman? She understood Cy too well but was doing him an injustice. Little Mac was Caruso singing an aria, he was Christy Mathewson pitching to the Cubs, and above all things else Dr. Kinsman admired perfection of skill.

Afterward Mac was too pleased by his performance to bawl Cy

out for impudence on the floor. "Didn't show on the plate, huh? There is no substitute for clinical experience, Cy."

"Your ace took it, Colonel. And still you didn't know what was there."

"The hell I didn't. Your fingers think. You may not know how you know but you know. When you've worked at it as long as I have, you don't question what you know. You tear up the tests and go ahead, if your fingers say so."

That was what the juniors found enjoyable now. Cam Steele whinnied. "That limb you climbed out on, Cy—you still want us to string along with science?"

"The great surgeon guessed right," Cy said equably. "He thought it all out with his fingers. My point is, you people fall, oh, say half a millimeter short of being the great surgeon. And you can't read Braille. Better hold to the tests."

"We like to think you're a great surgeon too," one of them said.

"Sure, must have forty pounds on the Old Man," Steele agreed. "But you'd say Mac's got a future in surgery, wouldn't you?"

Cy said, "Dr. Kinsman's point for the eager mind is just this: if you guess that something's there and find it there, that was still a guess."

"Or maybe if you say it's there and then you find it's there, that's surgery."

"Surgery is so many things. Evisceration, for instance. The Old Man's job this morning was a fine poem, only it was twelve dozen poems. When something shows up in front of the thinking fingers, it just has to come out."

Charlie Moss confirmed him. "No five o'clock whistle at all. He just went right on."

Pete Estey could be trusted to keep his grip on the point. "I declare, you're a hard man to follow, Cy. Which point are you making? That we ought to wait till the X-ray shows it even if the patient dies—"

"I say nobody should be allowed to hack away the trunk till Pathology says what it is—ten years from now nobody will be allowed to."

9

"Sure, but you're also bellyaching that we mustn't do things in too big a way or the patient will die. I say that's two points and they ain't the same."

"Cy's point," Cam Steele said, "is it's time to talk about the X Point."

That got a laugh too. The X Point, called everything from the Kinsman Crossroads on down, sometimes a long way down, came close to being Cy's obsession. It was the great divide. On one side of it the patient lived, on the other side of it he must infallibly die, and medicine ought to know more about it.

Charlie Moss said, "Want to try another limb, Cy? What's the prognosis on our millionaire?"

Cy shook his head. "The odds would say he's a long way past Painted Post this minute. We spent at least three-quarters of an hour too long inside him, just for the view. But he's a McAllister miracle and it's bad judgment to bet against a miracle."

A summons had arrived for Reynolds. At the door he said, "How are we to know how near we are to Painted Post, Cy? Are we supposed to smell it?"

Reynolds could not know it but his cool voice had stopped Cy short. For it brought instantly into his mind the big, bearded face of Wesley Wales Kinsman, M.D., of the Rocky Mountains. Old Doc Kinsman, the sagebrush GP, dead these eight years. Old Doc Kinsman, who had been the science of medicine and the healing art in Custis for so many years. Old Doc Kinsman, who believed that he could smell death the moment he came into a patient's house, if death had an appointment there. . . . "How'd you know he was going to die, Doc?"—and that rumbling voice, "I knew—I can smell death."

"You know," Cy said, "my old man believed that. He thought he could smell death."

Reynolds asked, "Could he?" and went out.

"I bet your old man was a humdinger too," Steele said.

Cy was still seeing that bearded face. "He could not. He couldn't smell it. No, and the Little Giant can't feel it with his fingers, either."

The annunciator bell was ringing for Pete Estey. Cy waved them out. "Better get back to a million dollars, Charlie. He'll need a lot of blood out there at Painted Post."

Cy sat down to write up the miracle for the weekly staff conference where Little Mac would discuss it—if the miracle were still in town on Friday. He was called to Ward B, where a scared intern had some blood coming through a dressing. "Change the dressing, everything's okay," Cy said. But Dr. Epstein had specifically said not to change it. "Change it," Cy said. At the ward desk he read rapidly through the day's records. A third-day appendix had shot up a temperature spike and Cy called the intern, but the boy had been on the job and the spike had already begun to go down. He had them by heart, anyway; the other pictures were all right. He wrote a series of directions—Mrs. Christopherson won't need so much saline from now on, Mrs. Peticic can go on solids tomorrow, I don't like Mrs. Smalley's urine, run another series of tests right away. Medical Wing got him on the phone and his opposite number said they were only six hours late on that alleged backache, would Cy be so good as to come now or go to hell? He crossed the court through a March slush storm and the head medical resident was dressed in store clothes and his wife was waiting downstairs. God almighty, they got time off in Medical. They decided that the tests said it was just a backache but let's try all over again and be sure. Cy said he'd like to apply for the first vacancy on the service, and went back to his kingdom.

His kingdom from noon on, anyway, when the staff were mostly gone and there was nobody to say sir to. It was the best of all as the night quiet welled through the Wing and a man could feel the tiller rope ride easier in his hands. He began his evening rounds. In Private Wing Charlie Moss was coming out of the carcinoma's door. He whispered, "He's practically eating at Delmonico's now—I'll take a dollar for a dollar-ten," as they went in. The nurse stood up and the three of them gazed silently at that elderly, withdrawn face in the dark. Old Doc Kinsman's nostrils would have known. Old Doc Kinsman's son had no way of knowing. "I've been known to be wrong," he whispered and Charlie nodded quite seriously.

The six big rooms of Ward A were spokes of a wheel and Cy heard a rasping breath. He stepped in, glanced at the first bed, stepped out. The floor nurse and an intern came out of the linen closet. "Put your cap on straight, sweetheart," Cy said, "and get in and take a look at that first bed." He stood in the door till the intern thrust out his hands for "safe." Well, the pleasures of the brotherhood of St. Luke were frugal enough at best, and his mind veered for a moment toward Rose Stine.

Just off the rotunda an assistant resident—Vince Moriarty—was gesturing with an intern. They swung toward Cy in a single motion and said together, "Dr. Ewald's lung abscess—"

Cy nodded. It was in a four-bed room and the nurse knew, if the boys didn't. Cy looked and listened, leaned over, nodded to her, and drew the boys outside.

"He'll be a statistic in five minutes. Hemorrhage. Nothing to be done. What was the argument?"

"I called Vince. He had you paged," the intern said. "He phoned Dr. Ewald. I said he ought to wait and leave it to you."

Cy said sourly, "Why not get him started upstairs and let a nurse phone?" He caught himself. Think you're Little Mac, Kinsman? "Actually there was no point—he'd have died in the elevator. As for procedure, you're right—" to the intern. "I get paid so the staff can take in a good show. Go phone Ewald I said as you were."

Moriarty's eyes had a look that they'd forget about before the year was out. A big Pennsylvania fullback with a Holy Cross brogue. He hadn't had those years of advanced dressing station, Mobile 48, and Base 98. Cy put a hand on his shoulder. "Some of them die, Vince."

"Yeah. I'll go stand by."

And that was right and Vince had instincts. Cy headed toward home. But even if you could smell it, there still ought to be better ways to get in between, and oftener. Dorothy Sponberg came out of her office, bony, stooped, her nondescript gray hair raddled, her cap falling off, and handed him tomorrow's operating schedule. Her title was Superintendent of Nurses but a more accurate one would have been Mercy Hospital. Maybe Cy ran the surgical service but Sponberg ran the little world, and maybe there were those who hated his guts but Sponberg didn't.

"Don't you ever sleep, Dorothy?"

"Don't you ever get tired, Cyrus?"

"Never have yet. Mac's only got a gall bladder? I ought to watch Smith do that splenectomy."

Dorothy sniffed. "You ought to help with that gall bladder. Then you've got an appendix and a hernia."

The stair well at Paupers' House had warmth, dim light, and a high tenor singing "Lord Jeffrey Amherst." Pete Estey was at Cy's desk, his shoes off, with a clipboard of notes. "Rest easy, I'm on call," he said. "I just got me some temperature curves that maybe make sense but not where I went to school." They batted them round for a while. The tenor tried "Far Above Cayuga's Waters" and quit. It was the hour when Mercy fell asleep: getting on toward a quarter to ten.

Pete stood up. "Have your batman lay out my mauve silk." He yawned. Even yawning he looked like the fifth generation at the University of Virginia and doubtless was.

"You sleep sometimes, what more do you want?" Cy said. "Mac promised you that he and St. Luke and us, we're all one together."

"Monks of the modern world."

"I'd trade my rosary for a seat at the Follies. Second balcony."

There was in Pete something admirable and strong. "Maybe for both your lungs, you mean. You got a fine talent for makin' folks mad, Cy, but you don't fool my daddy's son about the healing art. I'll have your calls piped through me. Get some sleep."

"Good night, Pete."

The room was chillier when the lithe, quiet man went out of it. Cy fussed some more with the notes for the staff conference. Ask Mac if he wanted slides. Beef to Mac about how long it took the chem lab to get a report back. Beef to the Superintendent about the lights in Ward C, about Vince Moriarty's losing his afternoon off, about the kitchen's differential in the temperatures of soup. That did it. Another day, another dollar. He started to undress and the wind was slapping sleet against the window.

He would go to sleep the moment he lay down, so he stood for a moment trying to catch something that went glimmering ahead of his mind. Something about St. Luke and the healing art? About a talent for infuriating people? Or was it something about Old Doc Kinsman—and just what? He lay down and his telephone was ringing. It was two-forty. Another dollar coming up.

"This is Emergency," the nurse was saying. She giggled. "Dr. Estey says to tell you he wouldn't wake you for a seat to the Follies. An appendix came in but he's found it's perforated. Dr. Estey says on the run, please."

"Those are my feet you hear," Cy said.

*ii*

THOUGH A Park Avenue cyst and therefore precious to Dr. McAllister, this was only a cyst after all. But there had been an earlier one and the scar tissue began to present difficulties. Mac showed the quickening wariness that means tension disciplined to use, a signature of surgical skill.

Cy placed a hemostat, stood back, and said curtly, "Hold it, Colonel." Mac froze, his eyes snapping. "Hold out your left arm." Cy turned to the nurse at the instrument table. "Get a sterile sleeve and put it on Dr. McAllister's left arm. . . . Dr. Grubner's gown brushed against your back and elbow."

Dr. Grubner, the patient's physician, was present for the patient's reassurance. He wore a gown but he wasn't sterile and knew it. Mac walked to the permanganate basin, dipped his hands, turned, and exploded in a series of high-pressure obscenities. Charlie Moss shifted hands on the retractor he was holding. The anesthetist stood up till he could look over the sheet that screened off the patient's breathing. Mac swore till he had restored his inner equilibrium. Nobody misunderstood or blamed him; you had to have some release. When the new sleeve was fastened on he came back, said "Number 3, nurse," held out his hand for the scalpel, and went tranquilly to work.

At nine-thirty Cy scrubbed up again to do a simple appendectomy. Vincent Moriarty and Cam Steele were his team. He was supposed to teach Steele something by precept and example, but it was a question whether a man with Steele's hands could be taught. "Cam," he said, while the nurse who was giving the anesthetic still said no, "for God's sake don't leap on the bleeders. You don't have to get a sack over them." That probably made things worse, for Steele was at a high pitch already.

Only a small triangle of skin was exposed but as he took the scalpel from the nurse Cy remembered the shrunken, half-withered body under the sheets. A sudden pity seized him. One of Mercy's innumerable clients from the docks and slums, and he had been terrified last night. One of the poor who did not trouble the awareness of McAllister the Great. He would get a couple of weeks in clean sheets, then be sent back to his daily stupor in flophouses. As he made the incision, everything else dropped out of mind. He had done several hundred operations at Mobile 48 and Base 98 and this one was routine, a stereotype. He was sure and economical, concerned only to get in and get out with the least time.

His easy serenity had the room relaxed too, though it would have been less stiff anyway since no staff man was here. The nurse at the patient's feet—she had nothing to do except be there —was Ginny Fortier. She had contrived to make even a sterile cap flirtatious and her blue eyes were mostly on Vince Moriarty. That must be why Vince had howled so loud when he lost his night off. "Can the big ox get round a dance floor, Ginny?" Cy asked. Ginny giggled. What would Mac have done if a nurse had giggled? "If he doesn't get his hand out of my way I'll cut it off," Cy added. Vince, holding a protractor carelessly, didn't get his hand out of the way in time, so Cy rapped it with the butt end of the scalpel. Vince turned red and beatitude showed in Cam Steele's eyes, for that was a supreme insult and it had not been directed at him. A few moments later Cy evened matters. "Hang on to the railing, Steele, or you'll fall in the incision."

Vince visibly wanted to close the incision but Cy, the job finished, stepped back and said, "Sew it up, Cam. Don't break Mercy's needles and try not to get a flap of the liver at the same time." The edge of Steele's cap was sodden with sweat and his forehead was corrugated. Cy watched with incomprehension and his hands twitched in his gloves; on Rocky Mountain trout

16

streams at fourteen he had tied leaders with a deftness Steele would never have. The man had ten thumbs and none of them an expert thumb. There was no cure for stupidity and no help for it among McAllister men, who had to think with their fingers. Afterward Cy said, "Look here, Cam, you've got to do better than you're doing. You're awkward—and you're not allowed to be. People have nervous systems. You can't jangle them with bad hands."

The tension that merely made more careful workmen of Dr. McAllister and Dr. Kinsman had Steele higher than a kite. "Christ almighty!" he shouted. "I do the best I can. What do you want, what are you looking for?"

That would not do, either. What good was a man who could not face the job coldly? "Maybe another trick in the dog lab would help." But Steele's eyes flashed a repudiation of such demotion that he just succeeded in holding back. It was astonishing how easy people found it not to love Cy Kinsman.

Since it was Friday and he would have to stay for staff conference anyway, Dr. McAllister made the grand rounds. There was a touch of the parade that used to open a Buffalo Bill show—and Cy's mind snatched at something that came almost within thought but slipped away. Mac looked every bit of his five-feet-six, and with such elegance of brown worsted, starched and striped blue cuffs, gold links, thin gold chain across the waistcoat that had white facings, and the manner of Napoleon. There were several visiting Elks on hand from Chicago, Detroit, and other provincial towns. Twenty-odd medical students. Dorothy Sponberg. A sprinkling of interns, and Cy as top kick from the old army or the drum major of Bill Cody's cavalcade. They went through the wards the way the First Division had gone down the Champs Elysées.

It was here that tact and sagacity with ward nurses paid a house officer dividends, for they could make or mar his part in the performance. They had everything so dressed up and the information so readily available that Cy could not miss. Part of the act was to toss questions at the resident so fast that he must surely

fumble but Cy never did. And he bore himself with unimpeach-
able respect, even a seemly awe, toward his chief. Clearly thyroid,
I think, Dr. McAllister, and I've had one consultation with
Medical and they'll send a man to run some more tests. This is
Mrs. Lipschitz, Dr. McAllister; there's blood sugar we find it hard
to explain; Dr. Thorwald will see her this afternoon. Why, no,
Dr. McAllister, I hadn't thought glucose necessary for Mrs.
Cohen but I'll order it.

Mac stopped at one bed and the nurse whisked off the sheet
as if she were unveiling a portrait of the chief. Mrs. Scipola, of
the Tenth Avenue Scipolas, a kidney case of Dr. Thorwald's, the
staff member on duty this month. Mac studied a sheaf of reports
and was moved to lecture on renal inadequacy and renal storm.
Everyone craned forward. Napoleon was talking, or an arch-
bishop, and with the audience so tuned who wouldn't have a
tongue of fire? The Old Man was good, though out of his field
and far from revolutionary, but even the Chicago visitor, who for
all Mac knew might have invented the kidney, seemed spell-
bound. The medics were rapt, the nurses worshipful, though Cy
noted with satisfaction that Dorothy Sponberg was checking off
items in her notebook. Mac finished; in the silence you expected
to hear the choir standing up. "Keep a sharp watch on her," Mac
said and strode on. Out in the hall he stopped, pointed a finger at
the ward intern, and peremptorily demanded, "Why did I say
that?" The intern knew perfectly well but awe choked him. "Dr.
McAllister is thinking of the picket-fence curve on the patient's
chart," Cy said. Everyone nodded: picket-fence curve, that means
the patient is going to die. The parade moved on.

There was another lecture in Ward A, this time on the diagnosis of thyroid. A reflex of protest stirred in Cy. There should
be no sanctities in this world and especially there should be none
in medicine, but hospitals were organized for the adoration of
their staffs. They walked through incense before acolytes on their
knees: no wonder they grew pompous, tyrannical, and infallible.
In another room Mac summoned everyone round him with a nod.
He picked up the clipboard of reports and checked them aloud,

slowly, with emphasis, tapping his finger. He gestured and the nurse uncovered the patient, a scrawny woman with beady, suspicious eyes. Mac methodically probed the upper abdomen, asked one of the visitors to do the same, then Cy, then Moriarty, then an intern.

In the corridor he barked at Cy, "What's the picture, Kinsman? M'lignant or b'nign?"

No thanks. "I'd prefer to explore and send a specimen to Pathology, sir."

That sufficed for Mac's purpose. "Where would you send a specimen if you were in the Maine woods?" He said "B'nign," and strode down the corridor. In the transepts of Mercy you could hear faint strains of the "Magnificat." Or of Caesar's trumpets.

He was superb at the conference. There had been a peritonitis death—not Mac's—and he nosed down every scent, tireless, ingenious, bent on fixing the responsibility. What had been done? What hadn't been done? He had Dr. Spicer, the operator, in a cold defensive rage. Nothing could be determined and Mac ordered them to think it over for a week, for by God he would have no unexplained deaths at Mercy. He closed the session with an unexpected gift.

"Dr. Kinsman stopped me in the middle of an operation this morning. He had seen a damned numbskull contaminate my sleeve. Dr. Kinsman was on his toes. Never hurt anybody at Mercy yet to be on his toes."

Look at the title: Doctor Kinsman! Cy went off to Mac's office with him, three rooms in green tile and green leather at a thousand dollars a square foot, and a view of Eighth Street with Dr. McAllister's fourteen-foot limousine and Negro chauffeur at the curb. Also view of the endless March rain. Napoleon was in the mood to relax with his marshals. He held out a cigarette case, the gold gratitude of a patient.

"Thanks for the tip, Colonel," Cy said. "But it won't make the boys love me."

Mac laughed. "None of them in a mood to ask your hand in

marriage, I hear. By God, I don't pick a staff for lovableness. Do your job. Sponberg says Steele was a mistake."

Cy nodded, dust at his heart. "Better bring him up to be a Superintendent. . . . That peritonitis case had a right to live. What's your theory?"

"Hell," Mac said. "Spicer probably nicked a bowel."

It fed a faint resentment, a resentment familiar but not quite clear. "He had a right to live," Cy repeated. Perhaps it was just too much elegance in Napoleon's clothes.

"I'm operating on Dr. Feinman Tuesday morning," Mac said. "Stomach ulcer."

Dr. Feinman was chief of Obstetrics. But also, "Tuesday is my afternoon and evening off."

Mac said, "Just see to it that you're not scheduled anywhere at eight o'clock."

A gust swept heavy rain across the window. "Remember how it rained at Toul?" Mac said suddenly—and brought blue rainy dusks and a thousand unreplaced emotions into Cy's mind.

Even the afternoon of Armistice Day. They had operated all day long, and at dusk he and Mac in the garden behind the château, trench coats over bloody whites, walking up and down between ilex hedges, and singing in the wards. Mac had said, by God what was the use of having a brother-in-law who was a United States Senator if you couldn't go home now, and he was going home, and in a dozen sparse words offered Cy the residency of Mercy. They went through rain and blue dusk and singing to find the champagne Mac said he had. You and me and Mercy Hospital and the future.

Something twisted and ached. Cy should have felt a surge of remembered comradeship, an older and a younger man doing a job with the same sureness. He didn't. Someone had laid some dry twigs on that faint resentment.

"It was a better hole than we knew," he said.

"Gripes you to square up and salute a lot of stuffed shirts you'd have been giving orders to in France, don't it? Damn good for you, Cy. You're an undisciplined cub. Somebody's got to curry you below the knees."

"You'll take care of it, Colonel. Well, I've got to go run my pushcart." He was scrutinizing Mac's chin. "You never wore a Van Dyke, did you?" he was impelled to ask.

Mac laughed. "By God, now you've got me looking like Rothweiler." At Mercy references to Dr. Rothweiler, the surgical chief at Presbyterian, were humorous.

Back on the job, Cy shook off a vague discomfort and the illusion that for a moment Mac really had had a beard. As he passed the chem lab a technician beckoned him in and held forth tiresomely about a tissue section that was in dispute. Cy cut it short by picking up the slide and the plugged test tube that held the rest of the specimen and saying he would ask Pathology to check again.

Pathology was just down the corridor. Cy came through the door on rubber soles. Rose Stine was peering down a binocular microscope and Cam Steele was standing back of her, unable to break in on her concentration. Cy grinned. Rose was an ambitious gal, she was going to conquer cancer. The obvious difficulty was that her ambition was at war with her hormones, and the body round which her white gown was wrapped sagaciously was sure to sabotage her career.

Steele was medicining his deep hurt. "I saw you ease in this morning for a glimpse of the Kinsman effect. Too bad, sister. He never even knew you were there."

Blue light from a condenser made a half circle on her cheek. She said absently, "He did a sweet job."

"You'll never make it, Rose—better lower your sights. Try Woodard, try Moriarty, hell, try me. I'll say this, though, the bastard has got genius in his hands."

Rose looked up from the mike. Her lips parted. "You're telling me?"

The white gown rippled and would have caught anyone's interest as it assuredly caught Steele's. Cy said, "Mercy has no endowed bed for Miss Stine, Cam. Miss Sponberg has been paging you for twenty minutes."

Steele said "Okay," between his teeth. But he went out.

"Smoke by all means, Rose," Cy said. "We have no rules that an attractive woman need observe."

She lit a cigarette and swung round on the lab stool. "It's your delicacy that has us all loving you," she said. "I run this lab, Cy, and maybe you'd better stop short at the door. Can I do something for you?"

He laid the slide and test tube on her bench. "I wonder," he said.

She looked at him; their eyes met and held. She let one foot find the floor. Cy said, "So he needn't tell you about my hands?"

"It's this way." Rose picked up the test tube, said, "I reported on that," put it down. "There are so many Cam Steeles in the world. Don't blame a woman who has to associate with them if a daydream gets the upper hand. Especially when the reality can smash the daydream all to hell."

He laid a hand on her shoulder. A hand that was said to have genius in it and a shoulder warm under the sleeve and softer than one would have supposed. Rose said, remotely, "Cam Steele wants to make me, he really wants to. That's flattering, a little, and—human. You're a little like a man making an experiment in the dog lab." Her voice softened. "Kinsman, I wonder if you know this battle you're fighting is really with yourself."

"There isn't any battle." He dropped his arm to her waist and lifted her off the lab stool. Her lips were warm and welcoming. "Sooner or later, I suppose," she murmured and her arms tightened. When she thrust him away her breast was high and her cheeks splendid.

"That's what I promised Virchow's statue I'd never do in the lab," she said. "No!" when he closed in, and the girl who was smiling was certainly not Dr. Stine. "Haven't the boys got enough on you? Damn you, Cy, you wouldn't know my address. You can always get it at the office. Get out of here."

At seven o'clock Tuesday morning Emergency received a stevedore who had fallen down an open hatch and was no better for it. Pete had Cy on the phone at once. He was working on a ruptured spleen when Little Mac, in his shirt sleeves, was at the door of the operating room and swearing at him for not turning the case over to someone else. "I didn't shove him in," Cy said, without looking up, and did not hear whether Mac had any more thoughts. He and Pete worked hard, they worked long, and they worked to no avail. They had the wreckage cleared up and the stevedore on his way out of the operating room when he died.

Cy remembered Dr. Feinman's ulcer for the first time and began to swear. "That's what was on Mac's mind. Hellish presumptuous of the poor not to wait, with the Little Giant working out on a colleague."

"You're mad because we lost him. I've heard you say some of them have to die."

Cy went straight to the room scheduled for Mac's job. It was over and Mac had gone—in a miff, Dorothy Sponberg said. Charlie Moss had taken Cy's place and they had called Reynolds from Obstetrics to help out with his own chief.

The nurses had all the ward windows open, for March had requisitioned a day from the end of May. Sun and softness drove the residual shame from Cy's mind and he went about his chores with intensifying impatience. He ate lunch with a chap from Medical who wanted the paradoxes of the kidney settled forthwith, then ran through corridors and across the grounds to Paupers' House. He had bought the blue serge suit in the fall of 1915 for twenty-two dollars at the Harvard Coop—he had been newly raised to senior intern, which was what they called the resident at Peter Bent Brigham, and it had had just a few days' wear all told. He owned three neckties, too.

He went back to give Pete Estey some final, quite unnecessary directions and they walked to the main entrance together and out to the gray stone steps. Smells of salt marsh and plowed Jersey fields were blowing up Eighth Street and the sunlight was shot with powdered gold. Years ago some benefactor had given Mercy a statue, a six-foot stone bird of no determinable species. It stood outside the door and generations of interns had called it the Pregnant Auk. Cy put an arm round it and gazed down the long vista of Mercy's architecture, which was of all periods and all begrimed. Moist, warm air, a wind whipping papers along the street, a sheen on pavement and on glass—contentment overspread Cy Kinsman. It was not in the least what he had envisioned that rainy dusk at Toul. But it was a good place, it answered to the competent hands of Dr. Kinsman, it was his nickel's worth and it would do.

An ambulance came clanging out of the areaway and turned eastward. "There goes your bright boy in a fireman's hat," Cy said. "He'll make trouble for you if trouble can be made. You run Dr. McAllister's hospital pretty while I'm gone."

"Your hospital will still be here when you get back. I declare, you do look odd in clothes." The Virginia drawl ran liltingly. "You got a nice day for it, Cy. I reckon you aim to waste it consortin' with harlots."

"I aim to get my girl and buy her some jelly beans."

"Deborah?" Pete had not seen Deborah but he had met her mother a month ago when Cy got her a job singing at the Trustees' tea that opened a drive for funds. "Make my compliments to Mrs. Willard. Do girls average that pretty in the Rocky Mountains?"

"Just in our home town. You should have known her sister."

"Sure it's Deborah you want to buy some jelly beans? Sure it ain't her mummy?"

"You have antique ideas. If I wanted to buy Mummy some jelly beans, I'd buy her some."

He waved and turned east, up Eighth Street, amused by Pete's notion. If he had wanted Josephine Willard, he would assuredly have taken her. . . . He had been back from France less than a week when on lower Fifth Avenue a gale blew a young woman into his arms and she turned out to be Josephine Caneday, of Custis. But not Josephine Caneday any longer. She had been just a scrawny gawker at true love years ago when her older sister had ravished Cy's adolescent heart, but now she was a woman with a husband, a daughter, a job, and, it developed presently, a lost career as well. He remembered that there used to be some idea that she would be a singer. She assured him that it had proved groundless: she had a good way with Sunday solos in third-rate churches, to eke out the family income, she said, and she could touch your heart with Stephen Foster. But New York had not needed long to uncover the remaining truths about her voice and she had met Sam Willard. End of story.

"We do *not* live in the Village," Josephine said at intervals, and they didn't, they had moved out of the Village, to West Twenty-Third Street in Chelsea, soon after Deborah was born. The Willards had the two-room third floor of a converted house and when Josephine got a war job had taken a room on the fourth floor for Deborah. Cy found Deborah playing on the sidewalk today, lazily watched by the colored girl who took care of her while Mummy and Daddy were at their respective offices. She flung herself into his arms, screaming, then danced on alternate feet waving her arms. She would be five this summer.

"Central Park! Central Park! Cy, you promised."

"But not with that face."

"Course not."

She tugged him up to the fourth floor, Anna, the colored girl, panting after, and scrubbed herself shiny. She got out an immaculate white dress and a yellow hair ribbon which she made Cy tie. It made her dark brown hair glossy but that hair was neither so lovely nor so dark as her mother's.

"Can we ride a bus?"

"Let's be rich and take a taxi."

"No, a bus! And on top!"

The prince's golden coach bore them up Fifth Avenue with the wind spoiling Anna's work on that hair, Deborah squirming in the circle of Cy's arm, and sun-drugged lovers laughing at her confidences about the zoo. Enchantment cost a bus fare and no more—Deborah flattened herself against cages, stood entranced while two elephants ate hay, squealed because a zebra was just like the picture in her book, and had to be hauled back from under the rail in front of the monkeys. Cy noticed the pulse in her neck pounding in the lion house—funny, no reason at all, she doesn't know she should be scared but she is scared. They went out and fed peanuts to the squirrels. Deborah loped across the yellow parody of spring grass and her patent leather shoes were caked with mud when he got her back. Then a climax beyond hope or fantasy for there was an inclosure with ponies in it. He lifted her to the saddle. She rode that shaggy, unpleasant-looking little beast round and round, her face consecrated, her legs tense, and heaven in her eyes He kept giving the attendant dimes for another round till he thought maybe the white dress was dirty enough.

"Come on down off your bronc," he said. "It's ice cream time." She fell off in his arms. "What's my bronc, Cy?"

"And you with a mother out of Custis!" he said, revolted. "You underprivileged brat from a degenerate metropolis. A bronc is a cayuse."

She was exhausted. Also magnificently soiled. He took her to a Fifth Avenue palace where a countess who directed waitresses eyed her grime without appreciation, and stuffed her with chocolate ice cream. The fats would build strength—if they stayed down. She was satiated but drooping when they went out into waning afternoon.

"You may take me home in a taxi if you wish," she said.

He did so but stopped it near Madison Square for a window had caught his eye. Deborah revived and was rapt and agonized, given a whole store to choose a toy from. She ended by making it a white teddy bear more than half her size and much cleaner. As they came out there was a sudden blare of music from down the Avenue and Deborah squealed, "Soldiers!"

Cy took her under one arm and the bear under the other and ran for Madison Square and its plaster arch. By now too many troops had marched through it for New York to get excited, but crowds formed, there was cheering, torn paper began to flutter down from offices. These boys had new uniforms and old flags, now uncased; they had clearly been drilled in close order ever since the Armistice, and they were trying to be bored and bleak above an ecstasy of homecoming. Unmistakably they were

26

veterans. They had been there. Cy Kinsman knew, for he had been there too.

A platoon marked time to dress its ranks and Cy was able to identify a collar ornament. This was the 178th Infantry! Cierges, Nantillois, la Ville aux Bois, Cunel, Brieulles-sur-Meuse—they were names on muddy, bloody tags tied to muddier, bloodier blouses when they reached Base 98. They stormed Cy's mind. Base 98 and Captain Kinsman and Colonel McAllister working, so the inviolable rules said, only twelve hours a day, twelve hours that frequently saw their second sunset and second midnight before any of the teams could be changed. He strained to identify faces, he wanted to shout names—but no face he could recognize would be here and no name he could shout would draw an answer from the marching ranks. He thought someone yelled "Hi, Doc!" and stared with unendurable intensity, but it was just a hallucination.

Only last October—those names were only five months old! He thought suddenly, you're older than you know, and scorned the thought as sentimental. Well, he was home now and the 178th were home—and just where were they? Not by so far as the eye could see where they had expected to be. The 178th kept coming through the meretricious plaster arch in double column of squads. The gimcrack splendor of that arch might nerve them for the more elaborate horror at the Public Library, where there had been built what was called The Court of the Heroic Dead— and thank God the dead could not see it.

The cheering in Madison Square was suddenly too long, the rhythm of arms and legs overpowering. Whatever you expect, you're wrong, he thought. Never believe the advance notices. It's too bad, or maybe it isn't. Let us not be simple of heart or simple of mind. He lowered Deborah from his shoulder and sought the quiet of a side street.

"You crying, Cy?" Deborah asked.

"I don't think so, honey. Sometimes you don't know whether it's crying or guffawing. You see, I used to be a soldier too."

"But you're a doctor."

"Promise to tell them that at Mercy."

When they got back to West Twenty-Third Street the business day was over. Josephine was back from Howe and Bergstein, where she was an office manager, and Sam Willard was back from Brett and Moran, where he was a sub-editor. Cy and Deborah walked into what was obviously a quarrel and was only interrupted by their entrance. Sam's round, boyish face was red with anger and his little mustache was bristling. Josephine's face was pale, framed by her dark hair, but her eyes had fire in them. At once they begot in Cy the attitude which he recognized as their principal interest for him: detachment. With the Willards he could be an impersonal observer of behavior, a scientist watching how response succeeded stimulus. At Mercy you could not quite watch the paramecia through a microscope.

"You get to look at pictures in your room, Debby," Josephine said. She led the child out, calling back, "This isn't over, it's just beginning." She was tall, taller than Sam, which was a clear violation of nature's plan, too slender, graceful in hip and shoulder and thigh.

Cy looked inquiringly at Sam Willard. In the three and a half months he had known Sam the detached observer had suspended judgment. The universal yardstick was a question: how good are you at your job? How good are you? The observing mind had no way of knowing about the literary calling. Perhaps juvenility was essential to it. Maybe behavior and ideas which would seem absurd on a ward floor were necessary for a proper functioning at Sam's job. Biological organization explained all behavior but there were adaptations and the detached mind would adopt no theory about literary adaptations.

"This is the How-Are-We-Going-To-Support-Our-Child number," Sam burst out. "What a town Custis must be! Custis, the queen city of Philistia."

"What's the trouble?"

"I quit my job. And now you'd think Gabriel had blown his horn and we were caught short." But indignant pride was yielding to grievance. Sam could not help looking as if teacher had slapped his face. "I let Brett and Moran look at the novel I've been writing. They turned it down. Naturally I quit working for them."

Sam's biological organization required him to be proud and hurt—and to rush home to Josephine to pout and sop up reassurance. But Josephine's biological organization required her to be terrified by the loss of income and then to get tearing mad at her little boy. It looked as if biological organization was too bad for the novelist.

"So what are you going to do now?"

"I'm going to quit playing it safe," Sam said, though his eyes were beginning to moisten. "Have I got the guts to be an artist or haven't I? I'm going to write the book over again."

Maybe it was going to be necessary to respect the literary organization. Sam was probably being cockeyed but he definitely had shown more decision and more guts than Cy had supposed he had. But Josephine came back, her shoes off for comfort, and pitched in. It was an absorbing scene for the observer of behavior. He could see the anxieties working out in her—she would have to demand more money from Howe and Bergstein, and probably wouldn't get it for it was an employer's labor market now. She would have to find churches that paid more. . . . Since behavior was implicit in biological organization it could be predicted and the scene went exactly as science had foreseen. But there was an expert touch when it came out that Sam had spent his separation pay from Brett and Moran for a new typewriter. Give the artist fit tools.

Cy had no doubt that the scene was already a cliché in the novels which friends of Sam whom he had met here were writing, and none that it would get inserted in Sam's—where it would prove that marriage poisons the creative impulse. Josephine was eloquent in derision and then at the right moment burst into repentant tears and began to cry with much enjoyment on the artist's vindicated shoulder.

"You should never have shown them a first draft," she said. And, "Brett and Moran are stupes—you just shocked them, darling, all their ideas are early nineteenth century. Anyone else will snap it up." Urgency grew on her. "Now you can really concentrate on it. There won't be anything to distract you or tire you out. Now you can really do your damnedest."

Cy was content with the findings of the detached mind. Stimulus had produced response as science had foreseen. Josephine turned toward him. "Go pick up something in a delicatessen and have dinner with us, Cy, you're rich and we're artists."

Sure. He would give her thirty seconds to get her dress off and say fifteen minutes to get it back on again. And most decidedly no. He had made enough observations for the time being. He went out into a wind that was bringing cold with it. Dissatisfaction had opened up again. He kept thinking of the 178th Infantry. He kept thinking of Base 98 and Mobile 48 which had preceded it. And of Lieutenant Kinsman of the British Expeditionary Force, with the Harvard unit for a year before we were in the war. And of Captain Kinsman, Medical Corps, United States Army. And of Custis.

And then he was thinking not of Josephine precisely but of her dress. He stepped into a drug store and found a phone. Rose Stine said, "I've been home three-quarters of an hour. I've been waiting for you to call."

The detached mind was quiet and the world was serene and seemly when he came down Eighth Street again, towards midnight. The bases of content—and discontent—were remarkably simple. As he came through the door into Mercy, Dorothy Sponberg hurried up. The repository of wisdom, the counselor and buttress of the young, was just perceptibly agitated.

"Cyrus," she said—and maybe there were a few women her age in Custis who would call him that, "they've been trying to get you. Get over to Private Wing. Dr. Feinman—something's gone wrong."

"Have you phoned Dr. McAllister?"

Dorothy Sponberg looked straight down the corridor. "He went to Albany with the Governor," she said without expression. She turned scarlet when Cy grinned at her, for she knew as well as he did that the chief of surgery does not leave town when he has a colleague as a patient. "You get there now, Cyrus," she commanded him.

He loped across the court for they had called for Kinsman in an emergency and the world ran on ball bearings. But he slowed down when he got there for it was an obligation to seem snooty to the young. They were at the floor desk on the fourth floor, Pete, Charlie Moss, Reynolds, and the head nurse of Private Wing. And it was heady stuff, the relief that showed in them when he came up.

"What's gone wrong at Millionaires' Rest?" he inquired. "Pete, did I or didn't I tell you to run Mercy right?"

"You got no call to be off pleasurin' yourself while the children get scared," Peter told him. "Here's somethin' the Trustees won't like at all. We been wonderin' can we be ships' doctors, maybe, or police surgeons after the Trustees speak their little piece."

They told him the simple story and took him to Dr. Feinman's room. Feinman's blood pressure had fallen and his pulse had started to climb and had kept on climbing. Now there was marked air hunger. A coherent picture formed. Cy read the chart, took pulse and respiration, asked the routine questions, and told Charlie Moss that it had been a serious mistake not to type the patient's blood and that was the first thing they'd get started upstairs.

Reynolds said, "Transfusions are getting to be another obsession, Cy."

"Maybe. And in five years we'll be typing everyone who comes in, no matter who or for what." He turned to Pete, "Why aren't you scrubbed up?"

"Me go in? While there's a chance of getting you? And what about those telephone numbers you didn't leave? I was going to phone the sheriff of New York."

"What's wrong with Feinman?"

"Profound shock."

"Sure. But why?"

"Could be the Old Man didn't take quite enough and she's pulled loose."

"Any time the Old Man didn't take enough we'd stop the press and put it on page one. I'd say he's bleeding along the suture line somewhere. Mac was going to Albany—there's probably one bleeder he got masterful with. Get scrubbed up, all three of you. I'm going in."

"He's my chief," Reynolds said. "Maybe we ought to send for a big shot?"

"Long ago but you didn't. Feinman's taking a bearing on the X Point this minute. I'm going in."

It was a messy job but Cy found the vessel that had been improperly ligated. The Old Man had probably tied it himself as a professional courtesy. "At a guess, I won't be told to write this case up," he remarked to his three assistants. Then he added, "The ethics of loyalty say we ought to decide faulty post-operative care was responsible. We won't." Charlie Moss gave him half of a grateful look. Cy closed the incision. He had the donor wheeled up to the table and gave the transfusion himself.

"Sit with him, Charlie. Ring me any time. Mercy's nose is now clean."

Pete and Reynolds rode downstairs with him and they headed toward Paupers' House. It would go down in no book that the house officers of Mercy had done what they were supposed to do.

"I thought I'd made it plain," Cy said, "that in Private Wing, and in fact with all paying patients, no carelessness is tolerated. Only with our clients the poor."

"Sure, Cy," Reynolds said, "you're a better man than McAllister. We get it. We got it long ago."

Reynolds turned off up a corridor. Cy grinned after him. Pete said, "You didn't act scared, Cy—weren't you? I mean, Feinman being on the staff?"

"That isn't the sort of thing that scares me."

"I could name you three M.D.'s that were just one jump from the privy."

They came into Paupers' House, damp air from before the

dawn following them and the scrape of someone's snoring resonant in the stair well. Pete had not been scared; he had faced up to the job. In a way that was all that anyone had a right to ask of a surgeon or of anyone else. In a way.

"Well, what does?" Pete asked.

"Does what?"

"Scare you?"

"I'll let you know. Get some sleep."

How solicitous they were for each other's sleep. The elegant and commodious quarters of Mercy's surgical resident vibrated with a question of discipleship. It depended on what job you had to face up to. Cy heard that imagined voice yelling "Hi, Doc!" at him as the troops went by, and shrugged away the irreconcilables with a brief remembrance of Rose Stine's breasts before he fell asleep.

... 
*iii*

AN ORGANIZATIONAL revolution sent him to the Willards' again a few nights later. Vincent Moriarty's lost night off had gone through Cy to the Superintendent and on to the trustees' monthly meeting. There it got involved with institutional pressures, cliques, and policies. In the end a new research was voted to the Medical staff, Mac was authorized to bring up another intern from the waiting list, and as an afterthought house officers were awarded more liberty. They would get from Saturday noon to Monday dawn once a month and, tentatively, could have two evenings a month as well. The sacred right of seniority procured the first evening to the surgical resident.

"How could I possibly have known?" Rose said. "I promised my family I'd spend the evening with them." She would not be moved. "You don't know what it means. You aren't Jewish and you haven't got a family." Mercy was luminous for a moment with the embrace of its acting pathologist and its surgical resident. "The stupidest rule at Mercy," she fumed, "is the one that makes you check in at midnight."

He had a family—a widowed sister ten years older than he, who had written him once while he was in the army, saying unnecessarily that she remained dedicated to the memory of her husband, a mad philosopher. Cy ate dinner at the Harvard Club where he could put it on the bill and faced an evening intoxicating with irresponsibility. It bored him intolerably. House officers talked about an evening off as though it were paradise; they didn't really want one.

34

But the sound of jubilation in Twenty-Third Street promised that the night would not be lost. The Willards had introduced him to a couple of these impromptu parties of emancipated young and they provided material for reflection that might last for days on end. You could collect idiocies that had the bouquet of vintage wines. Cy went up the stairs wondering whether this one would be emancipation, protest, or art—or with luck, all three.

The Willards' third-floor apartment was two big rooms, in one of them two studio couches, in the other Sam's typewriter with a length of brocade over it for loveliness and Josephine's well-tuned, ancient piano. The rooms were crowded, thick with smoke, noisy with talk that had been primed with the Dago red and other inexpensive alcohols that Prohibition would presently rule out. Josephine crossed to welcome Cy, her face lighting up. A pleasant girl, happily formed but too slender, tall, her dark hair piled high on her head, a green and gold tunic over a black skirt, scrolls of gold embroidery running down the sleeves that closely sheathed her arms. She was too glad to see him; she was too taut.

"What's the keynote?" Cy asked. "Beauty or the soul in protest?"

"Thank God they mostly brought their own drinks," Josephine said, the head of the family.

"Where's Sam?"

"Around." Her voice was level and Cy knew at once where Sam was. Behind a door with Cassie Morton. Josephine should contrive not to give herself away. She said quickly, "He got right to work. He's rewriting it from the beginning."

"How good a novel is it?"

The question struck unforeseen sparks from Josephine. She said angrily, "I know you despise him. You'd better not, Cy, if you want to keep coming here."

She went away under pressure, to a shadowy corner, and she had been quite wrong about Cy, who wanted to know how good a novel it was and no more. And he did not despise Sam Willard; he had no attitude toward Sam at all; if anything, he was beginning to respect him for backing himself and shooting the moon. Except that the fundamental question made a difference. If you were a Cam Steele artist—and the best bet was that you would be, in this congregation—the artist's dedication would just be silly.

He saw Frank Henriquez across the room and carried the question to him—an intelligent man who must consider a gathering like this about equivalent to amateur night at an athletic club, whose presence at it was beyond explanation. Frank had been a Village bookseller and was now a publisher, and ought to know.

"What I want to know is how good is Sam Willard," Cy said.

Frank had a sardonic smile and a sardonic voice. "You could tell me how good a sawbones is, couldn't you? You could grade him like a boar at a county fair. Sorry, Cy, it won't work with writers."

"Not even with . . ." Cy waved a hand at the room.

"As for that," Frank said, "just who the hell are you, Cy? Just a pair of hands. Your old man could afford to send you to Harvard. Or you'd be quartering beef for Armour."

Talent, Pete had said, for makin' folks mad. Josephine and now Frank. "Look, I get enough comeuppance at Mercy. I don't know anything about artists and I asked you a question. They look like feebs to me but they tell me they're artists. Maybe I don't like artists."

"You've never seen any. You just don't like bum artists."

"Now we're getting somewhere. I've seen Sam Willard."

"I tell you, there's no way of predicting. Publishers would have no risks if there were. Anyone you thought was a half-wit may turn out to be Henry James."

"With a lesion of the central nervous system?"

"Maybe all the better for it. Oh—" Frank waved his hand now, "these are just a bunch of young people who didn't play baseball well and took to reading books. Boys with a cowlick that roused something in an old maid English teacher's reveries. Girls that didn't get kissed at the junior prom. So Cranberry Corners couldn't understand the vision and they were off to daub linoleum with colors and write six-line poems of revolt. What's

36

wrong with that? They have a good time. They don't hurt anybody. They have no ideas, no talent, and they talk like all hell—does that make you the Holy Ghost? Must be an occasional phony in medicine too."

"What I asked was, how good is Sam?"

Frank smiled. "I'll be able to tell you. He'll certainly give me the chance of my lifetime with it. . . . Sam's been around—how long? Eight or nine years. He wrote a lot of poetry that was just Village ham. I printed some broadsides of it, every line a trick he'd picked up from a better man. But it doesn't mean anything that Brett and Moran turned his book down. They would turn down Henry Van Dyke as not quite in good taste. The chances are it's a diluted version of things he's read in the *Liberator,* or more likely as close to Sherwood Anderson as a man without mind can come. And it may be a damned fine job."

At that moment Sam was back with Cassie Morton from wherever they had been practicing emancipation. The male achievement of Sam Willard was printed in display type across his face, and Cassie was self-satisfaction in blond ringlets and eyes of worship. "A better question," Frank Henriquez said at Cy's shoulder, "is how many eternal mothers does he need to build him up? It isn't a matter of writing books—it's persuading yourself that you're a whole man. How long will Jo stand him?"

That was intensely gratifying, for Frank's presence here was now explained and he ought to learn how to practice detachment. "How long will she stand Cassie, you mean."

"A list of Sam's mothers would be a directory of bum she-artists south of Washington Square. The trouble with the small-town ego is that it's got a hole in it."

Someone asked Josephine to sing. She refused with more brusqueness than was called for and retreated into deeper shadow. Others would oblige and there began to be a lot of music as the liquor took hold harder. In a moment when it lapsed a voice came across the room, "And still I wish you'd pose for me, Jo."

It was an intense young man who made art with a camera. Josephine said, "No."

"You've no idea what the lens might do for you."

Sam called out, "Go ahead, darling. The only way any of us can last a century is to get into one of Tony's studies."

Josephine was looking at Tony with distaste. "You'd have too good a time," she said.

The varieties of behavior gratified the inquiring mind. They did not gratify Frank Henriquez, who supplied another specimen by saying, "He'd undress his wife in Macy's window if someone told him that the good life called for it."

Frank was a fool to come here, Cy decided: he certainly knew he didn't have a chance. A personage was looking at Cy and he crossed to speak to her. She called herself Rena, probably intending a Russian rather than a medical association, and a good bet would be that her name was Fern. What she was wearing was not gunny sacking, as one might have guessed across the room, but batik. Bracelets covered the famous scars on her wrists and she had taken poison too. She looked like a cadaver—substanceless cheeks not much like flesh, thin shapeless arms, attenuated ankles, a cyanosis that meant a decompensating heart.

Cy had liked her attitudes when he met her before and had an idea that Rena found him less dreadful than most of these faithful did. She said without antagonism, "I suppose all this represents the droll antics of your inferiors."

"I was admiring your—is dress the word? Do you wear it on principle, Rena?"

Sam and Cassie came up in time for Cassie to take that play. "You'll like it better if you think of it as a uniform, Cy," Cassie said. "You won't really feel safe till you've got all the artists in uniform."

That was a thousand carats blazing in the dark—and Frank Henriquez's loss for he hadn't heard it. Cy was deeply moved. "You mean you'll sew an A on your gabardines, Cassie? And the Village will be your ghetto?"

"Are you afraid of artists, Cy?" Sam asked.

"I think it's just the collector's instinct."

Rena said, "You're on our side, Cy. You're even one of us." Some tired, unhappy wisdom showed in her grievous eyes, very discomforting. "I think you may even be one of me."

If he had anything in common with Rena it was that they went to bed with the identical sex. But he was repudiating so strongly that he didn't like it. What did the cadaver mean?

"Cy an artist?" Sam asked. His crisp little mustache jiggled. "He's a home-town boy like me—Utica, Custis, it's all the same. But nobody would ever accuse him of an instinct for the beautiful —look at that tie."

"Ask Cy if I meant the beautiful."

"But of course!" Cassie fell on an idea squealing. "I should have seen it myself. It's the same psychic impulse, the instinct for workmanship. Cy wants to perform the perfect operation."

The evening could not rise that high again, and Cy was pleased to see laughter in Rena's eyes. "I want to write the great American gastrectomy," he told Cassie and turned away. The basic question was now answered and he knew all he needed to know about Sam Willard, for Sam could listen to Cassie unshaken.

He watched Josephine for a while. She listened to the patois and talked it expertly herself, for she too had intended to be an artist though she hadn't made the grade. Sitting on the floor, hugging her knees with gold embroidered arms, her face in shadow, she slipped easily into abstraction. As the uproar increased she had periods of complete immobility when she was probably not even thinking, was simply waiting. But she got as far away as possible when the need of a more general admiration came upon Sam. He had a reputation as a monologuist and Cy had wanted to catch the act. He had to admit that it was good. In the center of the cleared floor Sam became a Four Minute Speaker winning the war at a neighborhood vaudeville theater, President Wilson at Versailles, Vachel Lindsay building the Palace of Art at Springfield. There was caricature here, a mimicry more quick-witted than Sam should have been capable of, a truly skillful shading. Maybe Sam was an artist, Cy reluctantly conceded; if he got this quality into his book he might be good after all—and still need no mind. And Sam was happy. The mustache twitched, the boyish cheeks shone, people were admiring him. He began to be Isadora Duncan but this role required him to take unstable attitudes, he had had one drink too many, and he fell on his face.

The room shouted—and a high wail rose against the noise. It was Deborah, standing in the doorway, her nightgown twisted in her hands, her little butt bare. She was sleepy, she was scared by light and noise, and Cy reached her three full steps ahead of Josephine. He carried her up to her room, where it was dark and even quiet. She pressed her cheek against his shoulder and whimpered.

"Just pick up the dream again, honey," he whispered. "It's full of chocolate ice cream and ponies to ride and the tops of busses all the way." A knife got under the Kinsman guard and went right through him, anger because he was impotent to reassure a frightened child.

Josephine smoothed the bed, took Deborah from him, and knelt on the floor to hold her hand. Her dark hair showed against the sheet. After a while she stood up, leaned over to kiss Deborah's forehead, and whispered, "She's asleep."

At the turn of the stairs between floors Sam had nailed a length of blue silk to the wall and set up a small Winged Victory on a pedestal in front of it. Josephine smiled and sat down on the landing. The moments beside the bed had made her softer and warmer. She wasn't often soft or warm. She got little chance to be.

"You're tired," her physician diagnosed, sitting beside her. "I could run the artists out."

"Oh, Lord, Cy! As it is, every single one of them knows how coarse-souled a *Hausfrau* I am and no understanding of the beautiful at all. Besides, I'd only lie awake."

"Still an insomniac?"

"Sure. It's okay. I don't need sleep."

Her cheeks were soft in the dim light, her arms round and

soft in their embroidered sleeves when she leaned against him and yawned. She had to keep herself so hard and hold herself with such tension that you seldom noticed she was lovely, but she was. The detached mind wondered what it was that gave this doubtless only personable woman loveliness. Well, she wanted something and she wouldn't get it, had made her try and missed. Loveliness must equate with checked desire.

"What are you grinning at, Doctor?"

"I've decided you'd better cut your hair."

"I will not! I never will."

"It would only be logic, Jo. You new-issue wenches, you're nature's simplified design for wartime. You've flattened your breasts and tails—thinned out your legs—pared down your hips—cropped your hair. Strip you, and from behind which sex are you? It's nature being helpful—soldiers haven't got time for in-essentials."

"As the new-issue male, you're pretty filthy."

"Science isn't personal. You're merely tissue and metabolism. You must weigh twenty pounds less than Nancy did."

She laughed. "I see—it's my big sister. All your life that will be your ideal form, won't it? It certainly did curve a lot more than mine. Nancy was fat, lamb, and she has got fatter. What a revolting calf you were! . . . Would you like to go back to Custis?"

"God forbid."

"I suppose not. You've got to get your rope on the world and be a great man."

"Sure. I think I'll write a novel."

She shrugged resentfully and then slid off into a reverie which he could follow as easily as if she had been thinking out loud. Josephine would clearly like to go back to Custis, childhood's golden town, and she was seeing those vast peaks stand up straight from her dooryard. She could see them so clearly that Cy saw them too, rose pink with evening, purple in the gulches, the snow caps on fire. Presently she said, "No one should bring up a child on Twenty-Third Street. There aren't even bushes." That would be the Caneday children playing run-sheep-run through Custis vacant lots as summer twilight came on. A little later, "I'd better get some insurance." Several yawns later, "If I went to night school, could I learn something about business that would raise my pay?"

Cy said, "You don't have to be the head of the family."

"Oh, don't I?" She turned aside, disliking him. Presently, "I asked Howe and Bergstein for more money. They promoted me instead. Now I'm assistant-manager of mail order sales. I still get forty a week but I do twice as much work for it. You heroes have come home so fast that business gets to sweat us patriots. How can I run a family on forty a week?"

How, she meant, could she subsidize an artist? "Can't you get more singing?"

"Hardly, with my voice. Certainly not at odd hours after work."

"How much did you want to be a singer, Jo?" science wanted to know. "How good did you think you were?"

"Just that children will believe anything. I was simple-minded, Cy. All the Canedays could play the fiddle and the jew's-harp and practically anything. They were always singing. So when your fat girl, the honey and gold and brainless Nancy—when Nancy said I was going to be a great artist, well, didn't it follow I'd be singing leads at the Met in five years at the outside? You wouldn't understand—you're practically tone deaf."

He went on exploring the infected area. "So when you couldn't make great art on your own, maybe you could marry it."

She scowled. Sure, he thought, you're in love with him—and don't you wish it were that simple, don't you wish you could respect him too? Her face smoothed and she slid into Custis again.

"Actually, it's a dreadful town," he said. "If you went back, you'd find it duller than the Twenty-Third Street artists."

"Maybe. But there would be decent air for Deborah."

"City kids manage to grow up."

"I don't have to go back, I'm still there." She hunched a

42

shoulder. "The Twenty-Third Street cars run straight up Bannock Avenue."

Cy laughed. "I know. East is toward Mount Gallatin. That's how I find my way around New York."

Josephine laid a soft, smooth hand on his—she had liked that. He watched the sunset light on those snow fields fade into lavender. He could hear the wind on the slopes by night. Suddenly he and Josephine were very close—and in Custis, in the lost place and the half-forgotten time. A warm accord was flowing between them on the landing—so like the stair well at Paupers' House. Her eyes were gentle; brittleness had gone from her; her defensiveness had fallen away. Why, if she could be like this before the world! Not yet twenty-five years old, lovely with arrested desire, compelling, drawing you in. And she had a deep need of Cy Kinsman. She rested her cheek against his shoulder and there was a faint perfume in her hair. "We're just a pair of hicks," she said, "just small-town minds wishing we could go home."

"Stop wishing it. Stop longing for Custis and childhood or you'll burn your fingers."

"It was a good childhood. Why shouldn't I? I wish I could make one as good for Deborah. . . . You're swell with her, Cy. You're good for her. I think she's good for you."

"I like to watch the little blob of protoplasm expand."

Josephine curled a derisive lip. "You don't take me in. Protoplasm! That's supposed to make me think you're tougher than the rawhide hinges of hell's bottom trap door. You're a softie and I've always known it."

"See here, Jo. There were five Canedays. There's only one young Willard. Better get to work."

"Oh, my God!" Josephine sat up, suddenly all steel. "Cy! If chemistry should let me down!" She turned toward him, her profile in relief against that silly splash of blue silk on the wall. "Cy, promise me! Promise me if I get pregnant you'll take care of me."

"Is that why you can't sleep?"

"No, I never think of it. But it might happen. Cy, it mustn't."

43

Here was panic on the stairs. Science was able to relate it to Cassie Morton—and in six years how many of the predecessors Frank Henriquez had alluded to? Also to Sam Willard's splendid new typewriter that would have run his family for nearly a month, and the artist's courage in quitting the only job he had ever held for very long. Also to forty a week at Howe and Bergstein and a church on Sunday morning. The thought altered and Cy found himself resenting the possibility of this slender body's being fruitful again by Sam Willard.

At will he could produce a Western drawl that lengthened his syllables as much if not so sweetly as Pete Estey's Virginia; annoyed associates never quite knew if it was contrived or a natural disdain. He called on it when he quoted, " 'I will give no deadly drug to any, though it be asked of me, nor will I counsel such, and especially I will not aid a woman to procure abortion.' "

"Is that a poem?"

"No, it's an incantation. It's an obsolete superstition of my profession. Why sure, Jo, an abortion is a simple curettage. No fuss, hardly any pain, no anxiety at all, and naturally a great relief. I'll take care of you. Just phone Mercy and ask for Dr. Kinsman. Or shall I watch the calendar?"

Josephine nodded tranquilly. "There's a specimen of why so many people love Cy Kinsman so abominably that they long to throttle you. But you're entitled to that one, Cy. It isn't a pretty request, is it? Well, pretty or ugly, I'll hold you to your promise. Thanks. As you say, it's a great relief."

She stood up. "Let's go back to beauty and revolt."

She was silhouetted against the Victory of Samothrace. A tall woman, unfulfilled, with a half-sad loveliness that clutched at your heart. She had . . . well, what? Call it steadfastness. Gallantry. Guts. Yes—and what would it get her? Nothing at all. She had been stopped short. Permanently.

"On the other hand," she said, "nothing on earth can stop you, Cy."

"Clairvoyant, huh?"

"Enough. About one-fifth as clairvoyant as you."

They were looking at each other hard and they were both aware that each knew the other dangerously well. There was a strong potential of hostility between them; it had never flashed yet but it might at any moment. Cy was beginning to be bewildered by his capacity to arouse nearly anyone's antagonism. Pete Estey's line about his talent for making folks mad and Rose's more curious remark that the fight he was putting up was really with himself. Now this revelation that Josephine and he might easily come to combat. It ran right on to a knowledge that there was a deeper bond, and it was something darker. By God, he did not like ambiguities! "Get some sleep!" he said roughly. "Don't lie awake mourning the arias you'll never sing at the Met. Stop thinking Cassie Morton is a wound that cannot heal. I'll mail you some sleeping pills."

"That sounds so easy. Then again, we haven't said a word about you. Something has been giving you hell too, Cy. Sometimes I can hardly tell you from an artist in revolt. What is it?"

He snorted. "Nothing."

"Of course not. What could trouble Mercy's great man? Still, in three months I've seen you change. I think you're scared of something."

That was pretty funny and in a moment Josephine was laughing too. She softened again and took his arm, pressing it. "Well, come and watch the blob of protoplasm expand, my dear. And always remember to be tough. When you see a weakness in someone, stamp on it. If you don't, people might wonder if you're weak too and that would never do. Never let your guard down. You might get smacked on the jaw."

She started down the stairs, the light intensifying on her breast, her shoulders, her face, her hair. Cy followed, content. "You could study accounting at night school. Or business law. Or advertising. Pick any of them and go all out for fifty a week. You'll be able to raise both your children. And I'll show you how to wrap a bandage that will make you look as if you haven't any breasts at all."

45

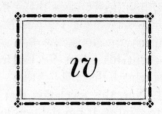

*iv*

SUDDENLY THE PLACE to find the resident was the records room. He was eating there, he was stopping off there on his way between jobs, he was burning Mercy's electricity there when he should have been storing up strength for the healing art tomorrow. Scratch pads on his desk blossomed with notes about the discrepancies between diagnosis and what the autopsy reports showed. The weekly staff meeting became too much Dr. Kinsman speaking out of turn and asking too narrowly, Why did he die? And he had to be shut up at the Central Pathological Conference which met once a month like a grand lodge with all the staff attending, where house officers were required never to speak.

"That's no way to endear yourself to men of solid worth," Rose Stine said, whose duty it was to present the findings of Pathology. And Little Mac said the same. "By God, you must like to get slapped down. I like 'em a little restive at the bit, Cy, but I can't keep my colleagues off your tail if you insist on spitting in their eyes. You're acting as if you'd just heard of clinical disagreement for the first time. What's on your mind?"

"Damned if I know, Colonel. Sometimes I get fed up with the guessing games we play."

"Then you're wasting your time. I'll find a lectureship in anatomy for you. Nobody ever learns anything till he has to teach it and you'd better learn anatomy. That's how a surgeon thinks."

That was whole-hearted, decent, generous, and according to the plan formed in a rainy garden back of the château at Toul.

But it set up in Cy a contrariness he was beginning to take for granted—and some sense of being led up to a high place and meretriciously shown the earth stretching away below. "With his fingers. With the infallible reflex. Sometimes, Colonel, I think maybe we should use the frontal lobe too."

"Cy," McAllister said with uncommon patience, "you work and you work and things happen to the way you're connected up. Good God, how many cysts, how many cancers, how many ulcers have I worked on? When you're an intern you learn to reduce fractures. By working on them. That's how I've learned about ovarian growths."

"Sure. The fingers that were born to work and get trained to think. Can't it be carried too far?"

"There is such a thing as skill. There is such a thing as judgment. If you're good enough at the job to have skill and judgment, you'd better trust them." Mac smiled and the smile became beaming approval, for that was a good line and would be useful the next time he addressed his peers.

"There's also such a thing as guessing. Put the sentient fingers on the place that's sore and still you don't know."

"Know? We speak of surgery as an art."

"Up to a certain point." Like Cassie Morton with Sam's hand on her knee. "Still, it comes down to this, when you line us up in the ward and punch the patient in the belly and say it's malign, you don't know it's malign. That's a guess."

"Guess! Well, by God!"

By-Godding could end the discussion but it could not answer the question. Mac said, "If you don't do what's expected of you at Mercy, you get fired. If you do do it, I don't see how you'll have any time left to think up a paper about Galen. By God, there is no after-hours for my resident."

He was boring the boys at six-thirty meeting too, and maybe if he did write a paper about Galen he could get the questions separated. There were too many of them and none clear. Charlie Moss protested the routine question. "After all, there are those statistics, Cy. You can't duck them. Somebody has to die."

"Too bad so many of them die of a bad guess."

"I'll bet it's all tangled up with the X Point."

That was Steele and he had wowed them again. After the laugh Woodard spoke up, a literal mind. Woodard protested unscientific language. There was no such thing as an X Point and to talk about it like this was unscientific.

"Sure there is," Steele said. "It's a spot before Cy's eyes."

"It wouldn't be like the X that marks the spot where the body was found in the *New York American,* Woody," Vince Moriarty explained.

"Woodard's half right," Cy said. "We can put a finger on Mc-Birney's Point. We ought to be able to locate the X Point just as certainly. It's there all right, Woodard, only we just aren't bright enough. Every man can take so much. Then he's reached it. Up to there he's had a round trip ticket. Get a millimeter past it and that ticket is just one way. Some day we'll know enough to calculate exactly where it is."

"You mean that, Cy?" Pete Estey drawled. "Some day we're goin' to have us a test or something so's you'll know when to not operate, or just when to stop carvin', or how to figure the victim's odds? You mean, just like a metabolism rate?"

Cy picked it up. "We'll work out a mil scale. Or invent a precipitin. Or a coagulate. Or whatever. If we don't, let's stop saying we're scientists."

Pete insisted. "You don't believe that for a little minute, Cy. You can't. You seen too many of 'em die when they had everything on their side. You've stood over too many of 'em who were on their way out regardless. You know damn well there's somethin' out there in the water—"

"Out there in the dark," Cy said.

"Anyways, there's something out there shovin' some of them past your precious X and be damned to you, or yankin' some of them back by the hair, no matter how wrong you've been. Science, hell! You seen too many of 'em, Cy—yes, and I bet in France too. Not science, Cy. What you want is a pinch of goofer dust, or maybe some holy water, or a thunder stone—anyways,

48

something that'll tell you is there a devil out there workin' and which side is he on, yours or the other?"

Cy laughed, charmed by Pete's drawl and exquisite illiteracy, and recognizing a kindred experience—they shared the helplessness of ignorance. Pete had been there. Pete had felt that impotence and rebellion. "All I mean, really, is: we murder more than we ought. No, there's more than that. Queer things happen out there in the dark, Pete. Us Westerners never have black mammies so I can't string along with your voodoo. If there's anything out there shoving them past or yanking them back, it's something we can get hold of. Some day we'll be able to get it stained, Pete, or centrifuged or filtered. Some day we'll be able to state it in figures."

"No you won't, nowise," Pete said. "You know what that is out there in the dark night and the roily water, Cy?"

"Damned if I do, Pete. What is it?"

"That's the Jesus factor."

The meeting roared and broke up. And it was a good line. The Jesus factor was no bad name for the unforeseeable or providential—for the unknown. So let science get to work on the Jesus factor. Let it stop murdering people, with whatever splendor of technique, through ignorance.

And Mercy caught him up and rolled him on and fought to roll over him. He had to be adjutant, confessor, wet nurse, assistant general manager. He conspired with Dorothy Sponberg to make harmony of the discordant parts. He lectured to nurses. He harried the juniors. He got odd moments in the files. Day by day with the sureness of a great man's understudy he performed the operations that roweled the juniors with bitter admiration. But there was no explaining why there grew upon him a restlessness without cause and a rebellion against nothing he could name.

It was Pete Estey's turn to leave the monastery for an evening. And it was true, they did look odd in clothes. Except that Pete's fine features and thinning hair enhanced any outfit. "This must mean marriage," Cy said. "You're shined up like a cowpoke coming in to Custis on Saturday night. You've never introduced me to your girl."

"No, nor I don't aim to," Pete said. "Not till she's sure that honest worth beats empty brilliance every time. She don't get off till six. Don't seem to be anything to do in the wicked city till six o'clock."

An ungovernable desire to fracture rules instantly rose up in Cy. "How would you like a drink?"

"I'm takin' all the drinks I can get before July one. Cy, you realize how valuable our specimen jars are goin' to be, come Prohibition?"

"I'll buy you one at the Harvard Club."

He scandalized Pete Estey to the core. Two crimes in one, both capital, both inconceivable: to leave Mercy while on duty and to take a drink while on duty. Until this moment they had been inconceivable to Cy. Call it the vagrancy of April, and he would be gone less than half an hour.

"They'll fire you sure."

"They won't fire me." Cy put on a raincoat over his whites. And it wasn't April: clearly, it was a defiance of the Old Man. He laughed. "I'm just an artist on Twenty-Third Street. I'm in revolt. Against the Old Man with a Beard."

There was something odd in that involuntary addition of the beard which Alexander McAllister did not have, whereas this rebellion was clearly directed at Alexander McAllister. It was odder still that in the lounge of the Harvard Club they saw a slight, stooped, fragile man with faded hair and a scrawny beard, and with the Yankee face that never grows older, being born as old as Yankee granite. Cy hurried forward and introduced Pete to Ezra Bartlett, speaking with a deference that would have caused talk at Mercy. The name of the professor of physiology at Harvard Medical School had gone round the world, for he had shared in the discovery of the mysterious vital potencies in food that were called vitamins. He stood talking to them in a querulous falsetto.

Cy mentioned a paper from Bartlett's laboratory. Bartlett didn't want to talk about it and pushed the topic away with both hands. "You're clear in your mind, Kinsman? You're going to settle down and open bellies for Sandy McAllister?"

There was an effect of hair rising and rebellion got abruptly switched away from Little Mac. "Yes, sir. And get appointed to all his boards, committees, and foundations."

A magisterial lip flared out and upward. A sniff raised the falsetto at least two notes. "Just what is it you admire, Kinsman? His circle of familiars, his chauffeur, or his bank account?"

Cy loomed twice as large as the physiologist. "His technique. He's a good workman. That's what I want to be."

"Workman—technique? Slitting intestines? Almighty God," the fifelike voice prayed in the Harvard Club, "forgive me my errors in calculation. There was a time when I thought you had enough brains for science." Professor Bartlett turned his back and strode toward the elevator.

Pete Estey was all reverence. "Ezra Bartlett! In the flesh. And he stood here talkin' to us just like folks!"

"I did his gastric analyses for a while when I began at Peter Bent Brigham. The hell with him! All right, I'm nothing but a pair of hands. They're good hands."

He was unquestionably in revolt, hurrying back to Mercy in a cab. Ezra Bartlett was a great man—and not as greatness was understood at Mercy Hospital. But Ezra Bartlett was by no means entitled to sneer at Cyrus Kinsman. Dr. Kinsman could be trusted to know what he was doing.

A few days later a pretty, redheaded nurse from Medical Wing consulted him and all the indications were that she had some kind of ovarian growth. "I'm afraid we'll have to go in and take a look," he told her, after exhaustive study. "Better let me put you on observation. I'll have Dr. McAllister take charge."

The girl whitened but was steady. "I wish you'd do it yourself, Dr. Kinsman."

He looked at her, speculating. Then he nodded. "If that's what you want. If Dr. McAllister says I can."

Dr. McAllister said, hell's bells, Cy had done enough cysts to

51

be trusted with a nurse, hadn't he? So before the week was out, Cy went in. He had assigned Moriarty and Steele but somebody, Sponberg doubtless, substituted Woodard for Steele. Pete Estey came in as they got started. "Who said you could take an hour off?" Cy asked.

"I thought Emergency could be the children's playground for a while."

Pete was a close observer, staring fixedly at the swathed figure on the table, the deep panting of her sheeted breast, the triangle of skin with Cy's incision in it. When he had exposed the growth Cy stopped and inquired sunnily of his assistants, "M'lignant or b'nign?"

Pete growled, "For God's sake, Cy, get on with it."

"Shut up. We've got to deliberate whether surgery is a science or an art."

Nevertheless he got on with it. Moriarty began to press and Cy said, "Get three of your hands out of the field." His voice sounded savage and it came to him that the room was more absorbed than usual. The nurse who was giving the anesthetic was watching more intently than was common even with anesthetists, the calmest, most disciplined people in surgery. Must be the sisterhood of menace; she was seeing her own womanhood as well as this fellow nurse's in peril. There was a tension here not Cy's.

Presently he had the growth excised and lifted out on a gauze sponge. "There it is," he said. "We've got it out. Do we take anything more? Do you know, Vince? Woody? You don't but the great surgeon would know. His fingers would be thinking for him. Mine don't tell me whether it's a cyst or a malignant growth. They don't know whether we're through or whether we go on to the ovaries. I propose to find out. Damn Rose Stine— she ought to be here."

He took a fragment from the tumor and sent it to Pathology. "Tell Rose to save two minutes and telephone us," he instructed the nurse. "Pete, have you got to go to the bathroom?"

"Sorry, Cy." But Pete went on jiggling.

The phone tinkled. A nurse reported, "Pathology says benign."

Cy said, "That's the trouble with a pedestrian thing like a lab report. It denies the great operator a chance to tear away everything in sight. This girl doesn't lose her ovaries." He gestured for Moriarty to use a sponge, and then roared, "Good God, who let a first-year medic into an operating room?" For Pete Estey had passed out cold on the floor, carefully backing away from Cy beforehand. "Let him lie there," Cy said.

Woodard looked up. "She happens to be Pete's girl."

Instantly Cy went cold and rotten with self-loathing. He worked with controlled haste and kept his mouth shut till everything was over and they were in the scrub room again, taking off their gowns. Then he said, "Everything the boys say about me is right. In fact, you all fall short." He put an arm round Pete's shoulders and, letting Mercy slide, went off with him to sit by the girl's bed till she was conscious and he could tell her, "It was just a cyst, my dear, nothing serious and it's all over. Take over, Pete."

The uprush of life in her eyes overwhelmed him with something that was close to shame. He went back to work raging at himself for arrogance and exhibitionism as bad as Little Mac's, and for failing beforehand to give this girl a human compassion that might have upheld her in the dark. He had failed her as badly as he had failed the scared Deborah, also in the dark. As badly as he had failed Pete Estey, standing behind his shoulder while he operated.

It was Pete who had procured the transfer of Cam Steele, the man with inexpert hands. Pete had ordered them to give Cy no hint of what they all knew. Pete had prepared the case.

He certainly had. There had been solemnity and fear when the girl began to tell Pete of her symptoms. He might have sent her to McAllister but he had sent her to Cy. He had known that Cy would refer her to McAllister and he had told her to hold out for Cy.

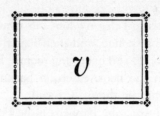

*v*

SOMETHING WAS ENDING, something was falling away. Josephine did not know whether it was marriage, or London Bridge, or what the artists called illusion. But as April warmed toward May in Chelsea it was splintering like glass.

Five o'clock woke her from stupor to life. She grabbed her hat, fled from Howe and Bergstein, and hurried uptown. There might be wind in Vesey Street, perhaps with the smell of the sea, as the smell of sage or pines or tule marsh had ridden the wind in Custis. Electric signs broke out across the sky—and to take Deborah through this fairyland of green and red! I give you the stars of New York, darling, I give you Colgate and Coca-Cola and Corticelli, I give you the city all of gold. She would rush into groceries, fruit stands, delicatessens, there would be the smell of sawdust and pigs' feet, never mind how often they had had sausage and toast and marmalade—for she was going home.

Deborah might be playing on the steps under Anna's remote gaze. She would run squealing and throw herself in Jo's arms. Bury your face in that young throat. "I'll take her up, Anna, you can go." Or Anna reading to her on the third floor and "She already took her bath, Miz Willard," and Deborah clamoring to have the reading continued. The same stories read to the Caneday children in Custis years ago.

Or enter with Deborah on one hip yelling, "Daddy's working!" And Sam yanking a sheet from the typewriter and getting up from the table where the poor devoted slave had worked all day. Both of them in his arms, Deborah screaming in your ears, Sam's mustache against your lip.

"A good day, darling?"

"Two thousand words. Maybe twenty-five hundred."

"Still a masterpiece?"

"Superb."

"I know it is."

"Do you honestly, Jo?" Anxiety clouded his eyes and the mustache began to twitch. "Suppose it isn't? Suppose it's cheese?"

"It's the best damn novel ever written."

"You don't really know."

"I know."

"How do you know?"

"It couldn't not be wonderful."

"It's got to be. You're swell, Jo. It's going to be a masterpiece."

Here was what she had been born for, and the muted sounds of Twenty-Third Street were an offstage obbligato to the overwhelming reality. She thrust Deborah at him. "You're a teller of tales—create some masterpieces for your daughter while your wife changes her clothes. You get a bath, Snooks, and barely in time at that."

She sat on one of the two blue-covered couches that were beds at night, unlaced her shoes, wiggled her toes, and was all glow. On Sam's knee, Deborah flung back her head, giggling. "Mustn't tickle her, I guess," Sam said regretfully. "It will make her stutter."

"That's an ignorant folk taboo from Utica. She loves it. Go ahead."

"I guess so. I've got a peasant mind."

Deborah said, "Sing, Daddy."

"You've got it twisted. It's Mummy who sings." But Sam broke crow-like into "Maxwelton's braes are bonnie."

Josephine snickered, went into the bathroom, sang "Where early fa's the dew," *bel canto,* and pulled her slip over her head. Damn! Where was that smock, and wouldn't it be nice to have an apartment that had closets, including one of your own. She put on worn slippers and went back to look for the smock.

Sam stopped singing. "Well!" he said.

She stopped instantly and glanced over her bare shoulder. "True," she said. Sam dropped Deborah, crossed in haste, and slipped a hand under her brassière. "You have such perfect responses," he said. She whispered, "Who cultivated them?"

She picked up Deborah and a picture book and ran out, Sam's laughter following her. "The neighbors will love that teddy—hurry, darling!" Plumped Deborah on her bed upstairs—"Read the Three Bears, Snooks, look at the Tinman of Oz, gaze out the window and think about modern love."

So the rumble of Twenty-Third Street could begin to sift slowly through curtains that the bridge lamp shone on. She could hear Sam's subsiding heart, voices on the sidewalk, the everlasting trolley cars—oh, orchestrate them in a splendid hymn! Touching his lips, standing up, and the woman who found the smock at last smiled in the mirror and saw that her mouth was tender and ran upstairs for Deborah. "You get to eat with the family tonight, Snooks, and no bath, no bath at all." It came to frying sausages. Sam put away the masterpiece and drew the brocade over the typewriter, setting out plates on what had been his work bench but now became the dinner table. Deborah read newspaper headlines in a confident, loud voice. It was not a voice that foretold a musical career but she was prettier than Josephine had ever been.

"I don't care," Josephine said from the pint-size gas stove in the half-gallon closet, "Annie Laurie can turn your heart to water."

Sure, there could be these orchestral climaxes. But sometimes Sam wasn't there when she got back from Howe and Bergstein. Then motherhood was a damned vexation. Deborah's gay abandon in the bathtub or an antic whim to eat supper sprawled on the floor might fall short of amusing. Josephine would yell at her or slap her fingers, then damn herself for a shrew and hug the child tight, kiss her, sit at the piano and sing "Oats, Pease, Beans and Barley Grows." And that was ghastly, it was unforgivable—to bully and then bribe the confused baby. Worse still, there was no use pretending that Deborah had anything to do with it. Splashed bath water or a picnic lunch on the floor would have been just childhood's happy hour if there hadn't been those ideas about Sam.

Ideas? "Kidding yourself is the worst poison," Cy had said and she was kidding herself when she said ideas. She looked at the pile of typescript on the table. It was neat, which meant that Sam had not written a word all day. She looked at the x-ed out lines of the top page. Sure, she was spying on her husband and that was low. She knew damned well where he had spent the afternoon! A pain that hit her in the stomach might have suggested appendicitis to Cy but to Josephine it meant that too much of Custis still clung to her. She could not rejoice in courageous emancipation. She was middle class and coarse-souled. She was jealous as hell and murderously mad.

Sam came in bearing a small, crumpled bouquet. She seized it thirstily. "Arbutus! Where did you get it?"

"Wops selling them in the Square." A speeding arrow said that in the Square he had been just two blocks from Cassie Morton's. But he broke the barb right off the arrow. "I wondered if they might be from the Catskills."

"Darling!" She turned to find a cup for them and hide her eyes. From the Catskills! Their friends had jeered for they were invoking bourgeois mummery on what was after all just a socio-economic fact and should merely have tacked their names to-gether on the door without fuss or display. But the rituals of Custis had prevailed and they had gone on a honeymoon in the Catskills.

"Take the masterpiece off the table."

There was a green salad and crackers and cheese. She owed at least one thing to the Village, that salad dressing. . . . Sam talked so insistently that she knew something was wrong. And Deborah had learned some new words from the newspaper and wanted to show them off, whereas he didn't want any part of it. "Damn it, Deborah, leave me alone!" he yelled. The child stood back and her face crumpled and she began to cry. "That's right, bawl! Stop it!" He picked her up and spanked her, then handed her to Josephine. "For God's sake, can't she be put to bed?"

Josephine took her upstairs. It's just the wholesome give and take of family emotions when I do it, she thought sheepishly, but it's vicious temper when Sam does it. She soothed Deborah for a while, then went back downstairs. Sam was feeling sheepish himself by now. "Sorry. But damn it, I've got a book on my mind."

A book and what else? Josephine waited for it to develop. Sam was in and out of his chair. He leafed through his typescript, his mustache sulking. Moment by moment he was growing into a younger boy.

Finally she said, "Yes, Sam, what?"

He looked up from the typescript. "It's good, Jo. It's hellish good."

"I know it is, Sam."

He flung it across the room, hundreds of typed pages snowing over the floor. "It stinks! I'm no good. I'm not a novelist. I'm not a writer. I'm going to burn it."

"Darling!" She started to pick up the sheets but his need was more urgent and she knelt by him, pressing his head to her breast.

He would not be comforted. "Either I'm worth believing in or I'm not!" He stood up, frantic. "I'm not! Frank Henriquez doesn't believe in me. He said how was he to know, maybe I had a novel in me but there was nothing to show I did. He said it was up to me. He said he wouldn't lay a nickel on the line I could write a novel."

"What's this all about, Sam?"

"Frank used to be one of the boys. He was on the right side. He believed in the right things. He's taken poison."

"I don't get it."

"I went to see him this afternoon. He said he wouldn't bet. He said all I'd ever done so far was be a basement-tearoom genius. He said maybe I was a novelist but maybe I was just a case of arrested puberty. He used to be my friend."

Tears ran down Sam's cheeks. She had never seen him cry. She cradled him in her arms. "Frank Henriquez can't hurt you, darling. He's—oh, somehow he lost out. He has to be cruel to keep going. He's nothing at all."

"The new draft was going swell! It's good, Jo. Nobody has ever done anything like it."

In the exaltation of being needed for just this, she nevertheless knew clearly enough that quite a number of people had done something like it. Sherwood Anderson, whom the faithful were admiring for a while, had done it several times, a lot more honestly. Sam was being a jauntier Sherwood Anderson in terms of Utica. Sherwood Anderson had pointed out the way. Yes, and Custis too. Many nights, lying in his arms, she had babbled on about her home town and her family and her girlhood friends, and it was all coming back to her now strained through Sam's mimicry.

"Darling, Frank doesn't matter. What matters is—oh, doing what you want to, doing it as well as you can, and living with your family."

"Nine years in New York, Jo. I've never done anything good. I'll never have any success. I'm just one of the little people."

No point in reminding him that he despised success. Success was the bitch goddess. It was the false god of maimed souls, of souls that could not take art as a sacrament. Her job was not to remind him of his ideas. Her job was to make him whole. She was dissolved in tenderness, holding the world away from him. So she healed the wounds and brought back his self-esteem, the job she had been born to do. His lips lost their pout and he could sit up, boyish, jaunty, unbeatable.

"The hell with Frank. Publishers will be fighting for it. It's his loss."

"Why did you go to him today?"

"I offered him the novel for a thousand dollars advance."

"A thousand dollars? A *thousand!*"

"I want . . ."

"What do you want?"

"Wouldn't you like a little more cash?"

Wouldn't she!—promptly she hardened with anxiety. Figure it any way, count on a couple of unexpected singing jobs which she probably would not get, and they might fall as much as fifty dollars short this month.

"I hate to have you always tired out," Sam said. "How you sweat, Jo—what a louse I am to let you. I sit here and write and let you work."

That pierced her with all the shameful thoughts she had had. "I'm doing what I want. It's the novel that counts, Sam. You write it. Then when it has lodged us in the Waldorf we'll weep with longing for the precious poverty of Twenty-Third Street."

"I'll beat that! I can't write the novel all the time. I'll get some reviewing to do. I'll do squibs for the *Smart Set*. I'll get some manuscripts to read. We'll have more money than ever. You can rent that other room upstairs. Make it a gorgeous Custis parlor. You can have a Rogers group."

He wouldn't. He was just thinking how dauntless he was. But the impulse was generous. And for tonight he was through being the world's victim.

She got a different slant on that incredible thousand dollars. There came a succession of days when he was obviously not getting anything done, when he wasn't even trying to. He was restless, depressed, touchy. And probably at Cassie's all afternoon, though Josephine dared not think it out in the open. Still less did she dare say anything, except indirectly and far away.

Sam would growl or pout. Or say that the novel was no good and he was going to start all over from the beginning. But one evening his mustache began to quiver and the grudge came out. "It's plain damn foolishness to give up everything so you can write a book unless you can write it in circumstances that will allow you to do your best work. You've got to do your best work or you're criminally wasting your chances. I can't work here. Who could?"

"Why not?"

Sam was ever so calm. "I'm afraid that's the exact hell of it, Jo. I don't think you can understand."

She repressed the spurt of anger. "Use simple words and I'll try."

"You can work anywhere. The kind of work you do can be done anywhere. But—Jo, you've got to remember there really is such a thing as sensitiveness. I look out of the window and what do I see? Twenty-Third Street! I go for a walk—push-carts, snotty-nosed slum kids, a hideous brutal town, millions of people tearing out their own guts for money. I sit here and try to work and what is it?—same old chairs, same old bookshelves, same old rugs."

"I think it's quite a nice place."

"It's all right—but I mean New York, all of it. It's not only the monotony, it's—hell, New York is the bargain basement of the world." Sam had been listening to someone. The ideas that came shooting out of his quick, thin mind were always those that had dropped into it at the last conversation. "How can any-one be an artist in this damn town? There's nothing for the creative talent to feed on. It's a hostile world."

"I'll bet it looked pretty good from Utica."

That burned him up but he turned patient. "You see, it's hap-pening to you already, Jo. You're surrendering, you're obsessed with tawdry things. What difference does it make whether we pay the rent on the first or the twentieth? Who gives a damn whether we eat hamburg or turnips? Some morning you'll come to and realize you're licked. New York will have killed your soul." He put an arm round her. "Jo, we've got to resist. We've got to hold by what counts."

At the moment there was no magic in his touch and she jerked away. "Just how do we keep the artist pure for the sacrament?"

She had finally bought a little insurance last week. The three-year-old dress she wore to sing in had to be replaced right away. It was almost time for Sam's hay-fever treatments.

"Don't you dare laugh at me, Jo!"

"It's certainly no laughing matter. So how do we go to Paris?"

"We've got six hundred dollars."

61

The savings from her war job. She had heaped it up while Sam was working and it might be shameful of an artist to save six hundred dollars but only that stood between her and terror. She thought, I felt I was stealing from Deborah when I spent fifty cents to stand up at *Boris Godounow* at the Met last week. She was impelled to say, "We haven't—I have."

That did it, and now there was a real quarrel on Twenty-Third Street. It had a prompt result for at the Schurz Street Presbyterian Church next Sunday her voice was wooden and her throat gritty. That had to be attended to at once or she would do no singing for three months—which would sink them all. Begging some time away from the office, she went to a singing coach and paid him ten dollars for fifteen minutes of relaxing exercises. Do that twice a day, Mrs. Willard, and see me three more times and you'll be all right. You have been worried about something—you must not worry, it is fatal to the voice. Better take a short vacation—a week in the country or why not Atlantic City? The damn thief! Forty dollars at a time like this, two Sundays' pay! Remember when a church actually paid you fifty dollars for Easter? Exactly once, Jo. . . . The worst was that this was sure to produce more brawling on Twenty-Third Street. These days they brawled like immigrants.

Sam was exuberant one afternoon when she came in but Anna had gone. "Where's Deborah?" Jo asked.

"By the grace of God I didn't have to be a parent at all this afternoon. Cy Kinsman came and took her off somewhere."

They came in presently. Deborah's face had chocolate on it and this time she was carrying a doll, a big one. Pleased by that doll as much as Deborah was, Josephine said, "You shouldn't, Cy. I know exactly how much you get—sixty a month."

"Hell," he said, "you can buy paradise for a kid for forty cents."

He had bought a large part of it today. They had been to the Staten Island ferry and the top of the Woolworth Building. They had ridden in a taxi and on the El. And Deborah wouldn't want any supper. "Red flannel hash, Cy. Stay and eat her share?"

"I've got a date."

"She adores that doll. It's probably reactionary, though, for a modern child, isn't it, Sam?"

"Stimulate all her impulses much too early."

When Cy had gone—on a date Josephine could stand to know more about—Josephine said, "Still, it's something or other when someone else has to give her her dolls."

"Excellent arrangement." Sam was being jaunty—the bearing of boyish self-approval that sometimes made you wish he would add to his repertoire an act showing the artist making up before a mirror. "Why shouldn't Cy serve the fine arts by taking over some of my routine? I can't wrestle with great thoughts if I've got to keep interrupting them to wipe a nose. No writer ought to have kids. A child is just an absent-minded moment, a biological accident. We shouldn't have to pay so high for our pleasures."

"That's not so funny. You mustn't say such things in front of her."

"Sorry, darling, I just can't feel paternal at the moment." Sam fluffed his tie and picked up his hat. "Where are you going?" she demanded. He was positively alight with self-satisfaction— "Out. I'm in no mood for a mood."

She had probably brought it on herself and she knew well enough where he was going, though she was too cowardly to say so. She rushed Deborah through a bath and supper and prepared to have a domestic evening mending Deborah's clothes, thinking about the rich fulfillment of married life, and remembering Custis where there was grass for children to play on.

But there could be worse things than solitude on Twenty-Third Street. Rena, the philosophical anarchist, chose this evening to clank in with bracelets and earrings and sprawl on Sam's couch and be a liberated mind. There was this difference between Rena and most of the liberated minds Josephine knew, that she really had written a book, she wasn't merely going to. It was advanced as hell, all about the free spirit that had to oppose the drift toward socialism, just the way Cy's brother-in-law had had to do the same thing thousands of pages at a time in

Custis long ago, though that would hardly count here. It had handmade paper and the magenta cover was stamped with objects which Cy had pronounced foetuses, and Josephine could not take it any better than she could take Rena. That was not all, for a hostility which she could never analyze always awoke in her the moment Rena appeared.

It should have been pity, for Rena was a damned soul clearly enough. There was no life in her eyes and the scrawny forearms which she put behind her head when she stretched out on the couch were hardly human. She had come to argue with Sam but was just as willing to discuss where Sam was, at Cassie's she supposed. Which led to Josephine's state of mind, and Rena supposed it must be unhealthy for she had wanted to be an artist, hadn't she, and office work must be frustrating. But the mind eventually got what it truly wanted and Josephine must have been mistaken about wanting to sing. So perhaps we must learn that the self-expression was more important as a fact than as a form, and perhaps the ledgers which Rena supposed Josephine worked with were expression after all. And Jake Offner and Emmy Carlson weren't living together any more. But they ought to agree on their stories for how could Jake have been seduced by Kitty Erb, as Emmy said, if as Jake said he was impotent.

Josephine took it like a little man. But the phone rang and the tenor who sang with her at Schurz Street Presbyterian was offering her a job. He was at a banquet in the Bronx and the soprano whom they engaged had phoned she was sick. There would be twenty-five dollars in it if Jo could get there before ten. Yes, they could use a contralto.

"You bet I can get there. What was she going to sing?"

" 'At Dawning' and 'Can't You Hear Me Calling Caroline' are on the program. But anything will do. Bring a couple of encores."

The fact of twenty-five dollars was more important than the form: Jo was a long way past the sensitive artist from Custis who could not have sung such tripe. "Thanks a lot, Bill. Evening dress, I suppose."

She phoned Anna to come at once. This was the third year for the black satin and she had remade it twice. Her clothes hung behind a gay curtain in the corner. The familiar longing for a closet hit her but this time it chilled her with a sudden, quite unbidden thought: you know, Sam, I really could get out of here. She shrugged, slid out of her smock, got out the heavy black glove-silk stockings and was subdued by the thought that they wouldn't last much longer, either.

"You're a beautifully made child, Jo," Rena said from the couch.

She went into the bathroom abashed and wanting to hold something in front of her, then giggled. Such a modest wench! Her body was sacred to her husband's eyes, by heck.

Panic struck her for Rena's arm came round her waist and Rena kissed her throat, murmuring thickly, "You are lovely, Jo."

After a paralyzed moment she broke away. "Don't be a damned fool!" she said. Rena took a step forward, looking drugged. Her lips quivered, then sneered, then were dammed again. "You are pretty, you know. Well, I'm sorry." Rena went out, the bracelets chiming.

Josephine was still shaking in the subway and she carried toward her professional appearance a fine reassurance, that Sam was in bed with Cassie and that she certainly was a beautifully made child in Rena's eyes. There wasn't any need for Cy to show her a bandage that would make her look as if she had no breasts. The point had been made. Too often.

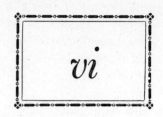

*vi*

CY WAS ORDERING transfusions for practically everyone, in so much that even Dorothy Sponberg wondered if she weren't being asked to sign too many blood slips. "Just the brilliance of our staff," he explained. "It's spellbinding how we get our reputation. We can do anything. We just go on and on."

Dorothy nodded. One way or the other, she had seen a lot of deaths in her time. She had seen a lot of hunches come to nothing too. "Blood helps," she said. "Sometimes. Sometimes it doesn't."

"I find the same is true of prayer. I'm only trying to push the cracking point a little farther to the right."

Mac barked like a wolf, scanning a blood bill for the wards. "By God, Cy, can't you give any of these people saline?"

That was pure McAllister. When it came to expending endowed funds on the poor one's duty to the trustees must be kept in mind as well as the weekly death report. No doubt the brilliant reputation of Mercy's surgical staff derived in part from Mac's taste for radical operations and so in equity some of the blood bill ought to be charged to him. But Cy was willing to accept saline as another hunch. He began ordering the wards to use it at the slightest indication and wondered if you could work out a differential between blood and saline that would cast a little light on the X Point.

One of Mercy's ambulances brought back one of Mercy's staff officers. It was Geist, the new intern whom Mac had been granted and who had been put on ambulance service under

Pete. There was a dock strike and the ambulance had been called when it exploded in a fight. Called to Emergency by Pete, Cy inspected Geist's battered head and sent at once for Mercy's brain man. It later turned out that he wasn't needed, that the head wasn't as damaged as it appeared to be. But there was something else about that head and Cy interviewed the ambulance driver. Yes, a cop had clubbed Geist. The driver did not know which cop. There was a riot squad under a police lieutenant and they had been swinging from the shoulder. It had happened too quick for the driver to get it all and he was too far away besides. Geist, who was kneeling beside an unconscious rioter, had apparently said something to one of the cops and the cop let him have it. Excited, the driver guessed.

Next morning Cy said, "Colonel, it was a night stick that worked out on Geist," and Mac turned into a tornado. He clanged down the street to the precinct station and Cy, who had seen him go through Base 98 at a similar pressure, would have traded his day off for a ringside seat. This was Colonel Alexander McAllister in action for Mercy Hospital, and every cop in the precinct was going to curse God.

Mac was yelling into a phone when Cy came into his office. "By God, we clean up after you. We mend the jobs your surgeons botch. We patch up the poor damn tramps your thugs work out on. We cover up for you. We take over the drunks and paupers you send us. We patrol Hell's Kitchen for you. We—by God, I want action. I want action now. By God, I won't stand for it. By God—"

His secretary whispered, "That's the mayor of New York he's talking to."

Presently it was the Police Commissioner, the chairman of a good government league, a Tammany big chief, the editor of the *Globe*. Cy watched his commanding officer tackle the general who had tried to give his outfit the short end. He should have warmed to the sight but did not. Too long ago.

"By God, they'll respect Mercy in this town," Mac told him the next day. "Got the lieutenants busted and the captain up for charges. I can't find out which cop did the clubbing—they're covering him. Damn wagon driver knows, I think. He's scared to tell me."

"He has to go on driving his wagon—you don't. What do you want of the cop?"

"By God, I'll send him up the river."

"What his pals will do to him will make Sing Sing seem like a promotion."

"You'll get his name sooner or later. Just let me know."

But Cy was able to take care of it himself. It was a couple of days later when the ambulance driver came looking for him, drew him into a linen closet, shut the door, and whispered, "We got a break, Doc. We just brought in Sturmer with a busted head—he's at Emergency. Sturmer is the cop that beat up Doc Geist. You mustn't know who told you."

Pete and his intern had the cop stripped to the waist and were appraising damages. The strikers had paid their debt. There were half a dozen superficial but copiously bleeding scalp wounds. The cop was bleating like a sheep and badly scared.

A nurse had laid out syringes and was making a novocain solution. "I don't think I'd give an anesthetic," Cy said.

"Well," Pete said, "it's your hospital, but why not?"

"An anesthetic is contra-indicated. I don't think the patient can stand one." Pete stared at him. "Haven't you noticed his alopecia?"

"You mean he's—"

"Alopecia," Cy said. The word meant baldness. "Take another look at those wounds, Pete. I want them well swabbed out. Very well swabbed out. There's been too much fear of causing the patient pain around here and God knows how much infection might develop. Go at them with a gouge if you have to. And I deplore this tendency to use mild antiseptics, too. You use something that gets its teeth in and holds on." He smiled. "The patient is from the riot squad. He filled a bed for us recently."

Pete smiled back. "I declare, it's too bad I haven't got a spare

68

bed left. He can get a good rest on the floor. Or he can go right back to his station."

"Want me to help you sew him up?"

"No, sir. I reckon I can be painstaking as all hell. At that, maybe I can find a bed. Some of the boys might like to give him some post-operative care."

A medical congress convened and for a couple of days Mercy's corridors, wards, laboratories, and operating rooms were crowded with delegates. Cy was a species of head usher, conducting committees who had managed to sandwich an hour of the Mercy system between the Carrel-Dakin solution show at the Rockefeller Institute and a demonstration of orthopedics at Mount Sinai. Mercy scheduled a number of performances by its stars, rising to climax with a gastroenterotomy and a gastrectomy by its chief of surgery. They were specialties with Mac's name on them and he did them from seven-thirty to noon in the amphitheater, where heads of services, professors of surgery, and presidents of societies from all over the Western Hemisphere watched him with a mixture of judgment and admiration that came down to the floor as tangible as sunlight.

Mac had neither bluster nor tyranny today. He was leading a team that would mean Mercy elsewhere: the staff anesthetist, Sponberg's best selection among the nurses, Pete Estey detached from Emergency to stand at Cy's shoulder. The audience saw skill at its utmost, the inexplicable mastery that is beyond challenge or explanation. Mac lectured as he worked, he worked at the summit of his technique, and the team was an extension of his will. Mercy meant just this to the world of medicine and here it was.

The audience scattered to other hospitals, and Mac had lunch and came back to private life. He had a simple gastric ulcer to round off the day and Charlie Moss was helping Cy. But when Mac got in it turned out not to be a simple gastric ulcer after all. It was a carcinoma that had metastasized to all the surrounding tissues. Cy could see three hard nodules on the liver and Mac's

69

exploring fingers reported them nearly everywhere else. Too bad. That did it.

But instead of preparing to close the incision Mac called for a different scalpel and began to attack the growth. "You're going ahead?" Cy asked, astounded.

"Certainly."

Protest leaped to Cy's tongue, and the vividest sense yet of the hostility that had been developing. But the discipline of the operating room was on him. There was nothing he could say. And after all, what difference did it make? The patient would die tomorrow, whereas he would have had a month or so of intensifying agony to endure if Mac had let it alone. Except that the foundations of surgery stood in between. Except that as Mac went on from stage to stage, doing a job quite as superb as the two he had done this morning, the master surgeon on the frontier of the future, he was really acknowledging the reverence of his peers in the amphitheater. Except that the thinking fingers were unable to forbear.

As Cy followed Mac out to the scrub room when he was finished, leaving Charlie Moss to give the transfusion and start the dismembered patient back to Private Wing, he wondered whether he might not have been mistaken when he told Dorothy Sponberg he could not feel tired. He and Mac got out of their gowns but Mac did not hurry up to his office to dictate notes on the operation. He stood there smoking, waiting for something. There had been no tantrum this morning but, though there was no point, it looked as though there was going to be one now.

But when Charlie came off the floor what Mac said was, "See here, you two, that case was not properly prepared."

There were three nurses in the scrub room, and no matter what rebuke a staff man might voice to a junior it was required to be in private. Moreover this one was grotesque to the point of idiocy. Charlie handed his gown to a nurse, looked at Mac, turned scarlet to the ears, and made for the washbowls.

Cy said, "Not a bit of that metastasis showed anywhere, Colonel."

"By God, you'll do them right or you'll stop doing them at Mercy."

"What do you want done that wasn't done?"

This was where Mac began to yell. "I don't know. It's not my job to know. I do know this was grossly mishandled. I can't run Mercy singlehanded. The men I pick have got to know their jobs. If they don't, out they go. I will not have carelessness." He built carelessness up till it became malpractice. Then, "By God, when a patient comes into Mercy he should have some chance for his life." At a sustained shout that was good for some time, till Mac felt eased and went away.

Charlie dropped on a steel bench. "By God, I love to be a house officer, by God, and what we do, by God, we face up to it like men, by God, and we say yes, sir, by God."

"And by God, you know who it was said a Mercy patient ought to have a chance for his life? That was the McAllister Wrecking and Excavating Company. Go on back to your pitch, Charlie."

Cy took the full case record to Mac's office. He had noticed that Charlie's hands were shaking and for the first time there was a tremor in his. Mac was at his desk. Cy put the record down in front of Mac, took a cigarette from the gold cigarette case that was open on the desk, and said, "All right, Colonel, make good."

"What in hell are you doing here?" Mac yelled. "You'll run your job, Cy, or you'll get the hell out of Mercy."

"There's the record. Take a look at it, Colonel. Right here is where you tell me what we did wrong or what we didn't do that we should have done. You told the great wide world we didn't prepare that case. By God, show me where."

"By God—"

"By God, you're the one that says by God." Cy picked up the record book and shoved it into Mac's hands. "Put your thinking fingertip on the spot."

Mac put down the book unopened. The tantrum had evaporated; he was speaking softly now. "I said in France I'd make a surgeon of you, Cy."

"And you can start right here. How wasn't that case prepared?"

"By God, if I have to teach you discipline, I can and I will." Mac, tiny at the desk, was looking at him with an aloof speculation. "You saw that gang this morning. Those are the boys that count."

"They certainly are. Come down to cases, Colonel. About that improper preparation."

Mac said, ever so gently. "You know, Cy, I can shut you out of the practice of surgery."

"I understand, Colonel. There's something you ought to understand too. Get it clearly in mind: you can't make me kiss your ass."

That did it with one line. Neither of them said anything more. But a flame of satisfaction almost unbearably powerful broke out in Cy. It was a liberation, an ecstasy of release that instantly had him drunk. The office was so quiet that the rumble of trucks from Tenth Avenue came through the walls. Just waiting. But it had been said. It was in the open.

"Oh, hell, Cy, forget it. If the chief of surgery hasn't got the privilege of blowing up his boys, what's the job worth? Haven't you ever felt sore when you lost a case?"

Case dismissed with a flagrant appeal to the happy time when they had worked their hearts out side by side. A long time ago, and a lot of water under the bridge since. It didn't work. "I certainly have, Colonel," Cy said. He picked up the record book, said, "Have you?" and went back to running Mercy Hospital.

A lot of water and a lot of bridges too. But it was in the open now.

An experiment reached an end. There was a shaded light on Rose Stine's bedside table, a small table in a small room in a small apartment, everything sparsely neat as befitted the healing art. A block back from Riverside Drive. On the Hudson some ship was signaling its tugs. Rose sat up from Cy's shoulder, where her head had been for some time. Her bare shoulders were exquisite, her short-bobbed hair was tumbled, her cheeks were winey. She swung out of bed and put on a russet robe, sat in a small cushioned chair, lit a cigarette. It was extremely pleasant to watch Rose move. She inhaled deeply. She crushed the cigarette out. Her shoulders shook under the silk. The eyes she turned on Cy were—abashed.

"Cy! I'm sorry. I'm not going to—see you again."

"What's wrong, Rose?"

"Too much."

"What's on your mind?"

"Let's say—oh, what's the use? Let's say we've had a fine time and now it's over." Cy sat up. "No!" she said. "Let's talk."

But she had some difficulty talking. She lit another cigarette. She shoved her feet into slippers, kicked them off. "Too much hell in the pot, too much blood on the moon—and we'd have to think a lot more of each other than we do. Or ever could. I'm a simple gal, Cy." She smiled. "Nobody has better reason than you to know just how simple. I know exactly what I want to do, where I want to go, how to get there. My soul is just as simple as me, too. I won't get out and fight wars. I like the safe and peaceful way."

"Whereas me?"

"That's right, whereas you. Cy, I simply have no intention of getting burned when the fire breaks out."

"What fire?"

"You're a complicated fool, Cy. I don't know why you have to charge head-down into the world at large. I just know you have to. Well, I don't. I don't charge into anything. I just want to run my lab. Let me go on finding out what I want to know and I'll get along with the whole wide world in person. You can't even get along with yourself. You're a man slugging himself on the jaw."

"Let's talk about knees. A girl with knees like those ought not to keep them across the room."

"Shut up." Her eyes shone with half-formed tears and she shook her head. "It scares me when I think how you're going to knock yourself out. Scares the pants off me and I can't get involved with what scares me, Cy. You're not going to be let off the least little bit of it. You're going to go on battling till

73

you find out what it's all about. If you ever do find out. I don't think you ever will. I suppose it may be interesting to watch from the sidelines. That's my cue—I'll watch, I won't get out in the ring."

"I'm no good at talking philosophy, Rose. And if you want to talk it, you ought to dress the part. That job you've got on doesn't turn a man's mind to thought—"

"I'm a simple soul. I'm so uncomplicated that you say things like that and I have to hold on to the arms to stay in this chair. Cy, you're all over the map. You were born to beat your brains out against any wall that got in your way. And if there happens to be no wall there, damn if you don't have to build one yourself."

"It's a good man," Cy said, "that can get a glimpse of his own motives for thirty seconds straight. It's a better man that can tell the truth about them."

"Maybe. I don't think I'm lying to myself. I'm exactly what I think I am. But you. I don't know what's opaque in you, Cy. I can't section it and no stain will seem to work. Maybe it's what they make great men out of. More likely it's what they make damned fools out of. It makes me sorry and I don't want to be. I don't want to see you any more except across a lab table."

"Except," he said, "that there's one motive I can't be fooled about. I wouldn't want to fool you, either, Rose. But it doesn't make sense at this distance."

"Oh, damn, Cy."

"Well, I could come after you."

Rose's sigh was half a groan. "I guess my new rule doesn't go into effect till midnight." She came out of the chair. "I wish we—oh, kiss me, you big fool."

A typical client of Mercy and of Pete Estey's ward was brought in one night, a truck driver mangled from a collision with a freight hoist. It was a case for Dr. Ewald, if for anyone besides the undertaker, but he could not be located by phone. Dr. Epstein, who was taking the service this month, also proved to be out of reach. Cy finally located McAllister at a banquet uptown, where he had to be called from the speakers' table beside his late

74

subordinate, the mayor. Cy described the case. "I can't find Dr. Ewald or Dr. Epstein. I think, sir," he was careful about that *sir*, "I think you'd better come."

"Lost your genius, Cy?" Mac inquired. "Or just your nerve?"

"It says in the rule book that when something like this comes in, I'm to notify the staff member on call. It says when I can't find him, I'm to notify you."

"Damn solicitous about the rules all of a sudden. You've notified me. Carry on."

Pete had called Vince Moriarty and Cam Steele as well. Cy joined them as soon as possible and got to work. Two hours later he turned the job over to Steele for a transfusion and he and Vince and Pete staggered out to the bare, nakedly lighted little scrub room just off Emergency's operating room. Exhausted nurses helped them pull off their gowns. Nobody said anything. There was nothing to say. Mercy's second team had done a job that was not only perfect but probably impossible. There should have been glory. There was just exhaustion.

Cy roused himself to say, "Go back and get some sleep, Vince." He watched Pete begin to get his ward back in its groove, then went out into the court heading for Paupers' House. Soft air and the glow of the city on the sky. There were vertical rows of lights in Mercy, the stair wells, the floor desks. Other lights here and there in Private Wing or Medical. He could read them all. Darkness in angles where walls came cornering into the court. Mercy quieted like the city falling asleep, and his finger on its pulse reading what the pulse said. There was remoteness, a man in dirty whites feeling too much alone.

He wavered on to the two little cubicles that were his home. A previously shapeless emotion began to have a shape. He thought, my old man could never have done this one. Never in his life. Old Doc Kinsman in his one-horse hospital in Custis. This one would have licked him. It would have had him yelling for mercy. He just didn't have enough stuff.

Cy sat down on his iron cot, took off one shoe, sat with his head in his hands. Sure, he thought, my old man could smell death. Sure. He could smell death and Alexander McAllister can think with his fingers. I can't. But they didn't do this job. I did.

Cy laughed aloud—and jumped, startled by the sound in complete silence. Me, I don't know how to guess pretty. I get in fast and I get out as fast as I can. I'm a bewildered soul—everybody says so. I don't like to do them wholesale. I can't guess, I can't smell death, I'm nothing but a pair of hands. But it was my hands that did this one. He took off the other shoe.

Pete Estey pushed through the door. Pete was haggard from the job he had helped to do. His morning beard was beginning to show black on his cheeks. He had a pint of bourbon.

Cy looked at it. "That violates the rules and the sacred trust of Mercy Hospital. By God, I'll have discipline here, by God."

"I reckon. Question is, have we earned a drink or haven't we?"

The bourbon opened little pockets of fatigue, then drained them. Not the bourbon, however, but something in Pete radiated warmth. Staunchness, friendship, courage taken for granted, or just call it warmth. Cy was suddenly aware that he had been cold. He was cold a lot these days.

Sour amusement in Pete's glance at the iron cot, the iron washstand, the blank walls, the prehistoric drop light without a shade. "All these comforts goin' to make us soft. So what you going to do when you get out of Mercy?"

"What are you, Pete?"

"I don't want anything but Richmond. I'll do appendixes, gall bladders, cysts, GI stuff. All us McAllister products are sound belly men. I'll have me a house with a big porch. I already got a shack up the river and my pa's got one in the Valley. When you come down from the big town we'll shoot us some birds."

That included the redheaded nurse, kids, the presidency of the State association. And of such, Cy thought, is the kingdom of heaven. I ought to want no more than that. His mind dropped down a deep chute, maybe it's that I ought to want as much as that. Nothing bothers Pete. He was never alone in the dark and never will be.

"But," Pete said, "I won't never do a job like you did tonight."

"Balls."

"No, nor Little Mac, he won't neither."

They passed the bottle ceremoniously—late at night, with the living prescience of a great hospital enveloping them. They had been the right and left hands of a single brain, perfectly doing an impossible job. Beyond that there was—it was not that Pete admired Dr. Kinsman but that he liked him. Bitter repudiation rose up in Cy—it was waste and folly, Pete should spend his warmth in a better cause.

"Something goin' wrong for you these days, Cy?"

"No."

"No?"

"Well, what's the word you poor-whites use? Fitten. Sometimes I get an idea I'm not fitten for the healing art."

Pete laughed. "Who's fittener than you are?"

"Somebody that wouldn't have to fight it all the way."

"Or could be, maybe, you're in love."

"No, son, you're thinking of Estey."

"That's right. You sure got her fooled, Cy. She thinks a good belly man did that job." They raised the bottle to the redhead.

It was no hour of day or night. It was time suspended. Mercy's obligations ebbed away. No call for sleep. Let them just sit here.

Pete said, very carefully, "Cy, I wouldn't like something to go wrong for you."

Cy's phone rang and Dorothy Sponberg said, "I can't find Dr. Estey. Is he with you?"

Cy laughed. "Sponberg never sleeps. There's something for Dr. Estey's idle hands." Pete stood up at once, Mercy instantly reassumed. "You probably mislaid a catheter inside somebody. Dorothy will smell your breath for sure."

"I'll tell her I got it from you. That clears it with Sponberg."

A fire died on the hearth when Pete went through the door and Cy was furiously wrenching at his memory to get a name. A friend of Wesley Wales Kinsman, who had innumerable friends. Huntoon! Gideon Huntoon, the mighty hunter and fisher, the mountaineer, the complete frontiersman. Gid Huntoon of Custis. It was the time the storm came down out of the mountains.

Cy was sixteen and in late November Gid Huntoon took him duck hunting. By buckboard, far out in the plain from Custis, with a river that had been swift in the mountains turning wide and sluggish here among tule marshes. Halfway through one short winter afternoon a column of slate-blue cloud stood straight up above a notch in the distant Ophir Mountains. Gid Huntoon did not even wait to strike their little tent.

They hitched the horses and drove into a gale that came screaming down out of the peaks. Sheepskin coats were paper against it and Gid made Cy get out and run behind the wagon, holding to the tailboard, then get in and spell him with the reins while he ran, turn and turn about. Ruts were stiff as iron and the outfit could make at most four or five miles an hour in emptiness that seemed never to diminish by as much as a yard. The clouds came down and spread darkness across the plain. Snow particles began to cut their cheeks and hands and the pitch of the wind rose. The terrified horses leaned into their harness. Then it was horizontal snow and no possibility of seeing anything at all. But Gid found the place he had started for at the first appearance of the cloud, a railroad embankment and beside it a box car with the wheels off that was used as an occasional section house. Found it through driving snow and complete darkness. Just beyond it the gale was whipping spray from the river.

Gid smashed in the door of a little tool shed and they got the horses unhitched and inside. They smashed the lock of the section house door—and found themselves in sanctuary. They lit lanterns and built a fire in the small potbellied stove. They made coffee, strong enough to hold up a horseshoe, its perfume mingling with the splendid scents of engine oil, thick grease, wet leather, last summer's dust. They made biscuits and a stew. They ate, then sat talking for an hour or two of storm, Gid Huntoon recalling the saga of his past. Gusts shook the shack, the river slapped waves against its banks, there was a sense of fury and infinite snow—but the place was warm, golden, secure. Deep shadows in the corners, the lanterns trembling to the gale. "Too bad Doc ain't here," Gid said sometimes. "Doc would like this." Doc's son liked it. Life was texture, life had grain, and the great storm overhead and all around but outside. So they spread blankets on the bunks and Gid blew out the lanterns, rolled up, and went to sleep. The cast-iron stove was red-hot from the base far up the pipe and Cy lay awake, feeling the walls shake, listening to the wind and the waters, wishing that the night did not have to end.

Dead or alive, wandering a real or a spectral gulch, where might Gid Huntoon be tonight? A damned odd man to dredge up out of nowhere, by night in Mercy Hospital, in another age.

There came a night when the poor chose to die. Cy gave a transfusion. He decided against another one. He reopened a peritoneum that had been all right yesterday and found that it was no use. He had a hand square over a heart when a wandering clot lodged in the valve.

"I never saw anything like it," Dorothy Sponberg said, joining him in a corridor, too simple of heart to need stronger words. "Go to bed, Cyrus. Dr. McAllister has a gall bladder at seven-thirty."

"You're supposed to sleep a little too, Dorothy."

Pete Estey fell into step with him. "They moved your X Point in close to shore tonight. Go to bed, Cy. If another one decides to leave us, I'll say the goodbys."

"Go down to Ward B and remind our apple-cheeked boy he's to send the lab pus from that septicemia every four hours. Suggest we don't mean maybe, we mean four hours by the clock in the hall. Then go to bed and wonder if you're too old to learn how to sell bonds."

At the desk of Ward C, set back in its dim semicircular alcove whence it looked down both corridors, he picked up the phone. "This is Kinsman. Dr. Estey is not to be called again tonight. If he's wanted, call me."

He went back to the dim corridors and walked down their

length, open doors showing dark rooms of varying size. He stood in one door. Mostly the poor had died with a decent or a proud reticence. But the one the intern was standing by had a choked, harsh screaming. It came hard. It roused the sleeping from thin to thicker pain.

Night after night. Here. And in France.

In France. In clearing stations by the Somme, in Mobile 48, in Base 98. Cy's mind filled with flickering snapshots of hundreds of nights. There was a function you never questioned and did not need to. We had something, I had something then that I have by no means got now. There was decency. There was— in God's name what was there?

The intern beckoned an orderly, who came on soft soles to place a screen round that bed, where the screaming sank to quiet as Cy watched. Intern and orderly went away. Cy made a gesture of impotent fury—damn their little souls to hell fire forever. He withdrew the oath for they had work to do for Mercy Hospital and the man had to die. He went to stand looking down at a face which now had no agony in it. You'll be all right in a minute, sergeant. But this was no sergeant. He stayed there and the man died quietly. He called an orderly.

Back at the window at the end of the corridor, he saw Dorothy Sponberg coming to join him. "You needn't have done that, Cyrus."

The cradle moved on rubber wheels and the sleeping poor did not hear it. "By Christ," Cy said, "there should be someone in New York who would wait while a man dies."

"By Christ, there was." At a guess Dorothy Sponberg had never before called on her God except in prayer. She went away. He hoped she was going to bed.

It was a big window crossed by angles of a fire escape, beyond it Eighth Street, and beyond that the blank wall of a warehouse sprayed with green from a corner street light. The night changed. Grayness blew along the empty asphalt and a warehouse wall stretched higher. But there came into the faint dawn not the warehouse roof but the creosote-reeking wards of

Base 98—and then, somehow horribly, the dingy frame hospital in Custis where Old Doc Kinsman had watched the poor die. Wes Kinsman, the hick doctor in the sagebrush, who could smell death.

Instantly Cy smelled a stench more horrible than death. He thought with complete clarity: Wes Kinsman had something I'll never have, I'm running a bluff, I'm phonier than Little Mac, and maybe I won't choose to keep it up.

He went down to the rotunda. Light came through the open door of Dorothy Sponberg's office. She had not gone to bed, she was sitting at the desk by the hooded green lamp, had taken off her cap, was holding a pen in her hand. She was wholly motionless, looking at nothing—worn face, gray hair, bowed shoulders, wrinkled neck, the disregarded staunchness of life. Cy went in to stand beside her.

At that moment the phone on her desk rang. She picked it up, said "Yes," and turned to him. "Emergency wants you to look at an accident case. I'm sorry, Cyrus."

He put an arm round those bony, bent shoulders. "I never was so glad for anything in my life," he said.

A nurse was bending over an unconscious man. Another nurse and two interns were working over a woman whose legs had been horribly crushed. They were just boys. As Cy said, "Get the operating room started," one of them looked up, very scared.

"The nurse thinks she's in labor, Cy."

The nurse nodded. "They must have been on their way to some hospital. Their taxi was crushed against the El."

"Where's the driver?"

"Dead."

The night's fog had vanished the moment Dorothy spoke to him. He took charge. "Get Reynolds here fast." She would have to lose the left leg above the knee, the right one lower. Maybe not the right one—maybe it could be saved. It could be if you were good enough, if you could pray for a miracle. Or rather it could have been saved. For clearly she was not going to live long enough for him to try. "Get the hemorrhage stopped," he commanded. "Stopped!" He laid a hand on the woman's abdomen and felt the spasm of a contraction. He waited, timing the next one.

"You'll do a Caesarean, won't you?" the boy asked.

"Of course. Reynolds will. I'll help him. Roll her in."

He turned toward the little scrub room but a scream swung him round again. The woman was conscious. He bent over her and her eyes came out of syncope.

Intolerably screaming, "I must not lose my baby!"

The intern who wasn't rattled picked up a syringe but Cy waved it away.

"Doctor! Save my baby."

"Your baby will be all right."

"Am I going to die?"

He nodded. Then . . . no. The tide that had been ebbing seaward in the sick dawn turned. "No. No, you're not going to die," Cy said.

He picked up the telephone. "I was wrong—call Dr. Estey to Emergency at once. Get Dr. Moriarty too." He faced the nurse. "Too damn many are dying."

Nurses were arriving. "Get oxygen," he ordered. He gestured at the interns. "Type her blood. Get some donors on the run. I'll have to transfuse her on the table. For the love of God, move your hands and feet."

The woman sank into unconsciousness but had heard his promise. Reynolds came in. "You'll do a Caesarean," Cy said. "Pete will do a fast guillotine on the left leg. I'm going to save her right leg." After one glance at the woman, Reynolds was looking at him with complete skepticism but Reynolds was wrong. There had been enough death. He was not going to let her die.

YET ON A WAYWARD Sunday afternoon the Willard family might stroll along deserted wholesale streets or to the Square or along the waterfront, quite as the Caneday family had strolled in the foothills on Custis Sundays. Young lovers in the Square or the wind making patterns on the Hudson, men in their undershirts reading newspapers on fire escapes, boys swarming on the docks—New York was anyone's home town. New York could be kindly and Sam could have warmth and kindness too, could hold Deborah's hand and compose nonsense for her, could find an agreeable nonsense for Josephine. When he wasn't wrung by doubt of his greatness or corroded by the fear that others might be greater, he had the charm that had melted her virginal heart six years ago. They really were a family. They could go on being one.

In the window of a secondhand furniture store, two hideous lithographs, "A Yard of Roses" and "A Yard of Puppies." Sam grinned. "Got to get them into the novel. They were on our sitting-room wall at Utica."

"Middle-class taste, the Willards," Josephine said. "The Canedays were artistic. We had Sir Galahad, the Coliseum, two cherubs kissing, and such terra cotta Indians as you'd never believe."

"You'd love to have them again—you're absolutely small town still. I bet you're eating your heart out right now for some mission chairs."

"Well, I am. Just show me a potted begonia and three geraniums. Just show me one embroidered guest towel."

"We never had guests—only relatives. Debby," he said, "you better grow up a sound specimen of Campfire Girl American womanhood, so your old lady will let you marry a Rotarian."

"Who would you want her to marry?"

"Hell, we believe by the time she grows up there won't be giving in marriage, oh, in Custis and Utica maybe. We believe she'd better have ideals."

Jo snickered. "Live the good life."

"Work for the great society."

"Love beauty."

"Find fulfillment in self-expression."

"Make life an art."

"Live for the age that is coming to birth." Sam was snickering now. "Make the revolution. Dream purely for the dream is to-morrow. Yield not to convention, for yielding is sin. Arise, ye daughters of emancipation." It was a corner of Ninth Avenue and damned if, out of a clear sky, she wasn't embraced and kissed right there on the corner. Oh, a little more of this would save Sam! Poor guy, he wanted so very much to be so very much.

Too bad that they had to sit up half of that very night quarreling—and she had to lie awake the rest of it paying for the quarrel. Quarreling, for God's sake, over five dollars' worth of vellum typewriting paper. Because when you're writing a novel you must have the best, because an artist must respect his instruments, because Sam's deepest instinct was for perfect things.

Sam growing instantly adolescent, his cheeks pale, his eyes hot, his mustache rising like quills—and all this simply because she had laughed at the five dollar typewriting paper. "You see, Jo, by instinct you're contemptuous of every artist. Damn it, if you're going to live with one it would be good sense to try to understand him."

"I can understand a fine talent as a stationer. There could be money in it."

"Sure I quit my job!" he yelled. "Sure I'm not the breadwinner. You're the breadwinner. You've got a drive to beat me down—break my resistance—paralyze my will. Just like a queen wasp.

What a triumph it would be for you if I gave up and sneaked back to a sound, manly, paying job."

Without having intended to, she took the dreadful plunge. "You won't, though. It builds up the ego more to just sneak back to Cassie."

Dreadfully cheap—but what was worse, it made him jaunty. When he was jaunty he was about fourteen. Then he turned expository. "We're individuals, aren't we? We always say we are —we said so when we got married. You never try to be any more —and you damn well refuse to let me be. You grow more possessive every day—more Victorian—more small town. My God, did I marry Christian Endeavor?"

If she had any guts she would make him face the question and admit it. She didn't have any guts—oh, what was the use? She said wearily, "Advanced is what we like to say. How advanced would you be if you found me in bed with . . ." Well, who? The trouble with that example was there were no offers.

"I'd apologize and go away," Sam announced, most correctly. "Look, I refuse to be just your stud horse. I refuse to let you be just my female. No two people can be absolutely everything to each other. If part of you needed something from someone else, if you fell in love, I'd wish you happiness."

"If I did I'd just have to scrape up some more money to support the gallant vision. My men live greatly. I pay the check."

That was the dirtiest thing she had ever said to Sam, and what of it? On and on. And this time there was no ecstasy of abasement and reconciliation in the dark, no nobility of forgiveness while your heart swelled and his arms reached for you. There was only a green glare from Twenty-Third Street seeping past the curtains while you lay awake and tried to work up some ingenuity that could be cashed for fifty dollars.

The most disturbing thing of all was that she was getting to feel grateful for the office because it could keep her from thinking about home. . . . She shoved her card into the time clock and went to the rest room. She made up her lips and combed her hair and stood staring at the mirror. Mirror-staring was getting to be her obsession. It could be sinister. What did she expect to see? Well, the business day ends. So go home and plunge into life's deepest realities and be an individual and all that tripe. Go home and raise hell with Deborah and brawl with Sam.

Well, get going, Jo. But in the lobby, there was Cy. "Coming to carry my books home from school, Doctor?" she said.

"How would you like to play first base in a revolt on the barricades?"

"Free verse, dress reform, or the single standard?"

"Dinner. I gave Pete Estey my last night off so I get his. I've got sixty-two dollars."

"You mean somebody can finish the month two dollars in the black?"

"I've been hankering for the feel of chiffon."

She glanced at her wrinkled linen suit. "My dear, I could never be anything but calico. What about my daughter?"

"I gave Anna two dollars. She'll stay till someone gets home. She can read the novel."

"I'm kind of scared how easy it is to pick me up."

He piled her in a taxi and asked what music she would like to hear. At Carnegie Hall a visiting orchestra was doing the Fountains of Rome. No busman's holiday—she didn't want any music. "Let's do what you want, Cy."

He stopped the cab and they got out. "Florist," he explained.

"Wait! Cy, you idiot! Find a subway station."

They found one and of course a man selling flowers. She pinned a bunch of violets to her jacket. Twenty-five cents. "As a rebel you're a flop," he said.

"They would have cost you a dollar. Do they look nice?"

"They look nice."

There was a gratifying appreciation in his face and, in a taxi again, she leaned against his shoulder. The contact was pleasant and Cy would understand.

"Sure I do," he said. "You like a little admiration that knows its place."

He put an arm round her and she settled into it. "I don't

know if I want my surgeons clairvoyant," she said. And she liked knowing that Cy would have no illusion whatever that his arm was round a manikin.

He took her to some queer upstairs café full of men playing chess and speaking Yiddish and ordered two Bronxes. That would have been very shocking behavior for a lady in Custis. "Relax the higher centers a little, and we won't be able to get them much longer," he said. Outside again, "Want to eat at the Brevoort?"

"Never. That's where the faithful go for a bust."

"Make it the Waldorf."

They walked toward it and night was coming up like a blue velvet backdrop and Fifth Avenue was growing quiet. Josephine was splendidly at peace in this arrogant, imperial city. A diamond necklace spat blue fire in someone's window. Teakwood and ivory, brocades, lacquers, ebony, gold, crystal. Shoes for the kind of women that were supposed to drug men's minds. A single pair of black stockings spread against white satin—they had lace ankles, drop-stitch, and embroidery. There were women in this town who could wear twenty dollar stockings, and Jo's legs felt rough and ugly. Farther up the Avenue there was an evening gown which only an empress should wear.

She stopped to worship. Apricot, deep-cut corsage, draped skirt falling in folds but narrowing, then parting to reveal gold slippers.

"Not on sixty-two dollars," Cy said.

She smiled. "Sure I had it on. Is that pretty silly?"

"I'd drop you cold if you didn't put it on at sight."

Odd that the skeptical Cy could approve her trivial rapture, whereas the faithful in Chelsea would have ridiculed it. . . . At the great hotel they swung away from the main dining room, where the captain clearly could not suffer anyone not in evening clothes, and found a more intimate place upstairs, softly lighted, an orchestra playing Brahms songs. Josephine had never been in such a room. She had tasted champagne just once before, half a glass permitted a young girl at some forgotten but probably majestic party in Custis. It softened the room's colors and blended them, enhanced Brahms, even brought out a touch of Abe Lincoln in Cy's massive face.

Suddenly she said, "You were intended to do it. You're the only one who has done it."

"Done what?"

"A lot of us were bright as bright could be. The world was absolutely sure to be our penny bank. But you did it."

She grew intent in the faint iridescence of the champagne. Cy looked—oh, unshakable forever. He must be six feet tall or more but wide shoulders and a chunky chest made him seem much shorter. People called him hard, arrogant, supercilious, cocky, and he probably was. All right, he was. Nevertheless he had gone straight toward his desire and taken it by assault. "You've written the big novel. You've sung Delilah at the Met. When you go to bed at night, it's not just a piddling little sixth-rater whimpering between the sheets because now he can't kid himself any longer. Because it turned out that he's just a home-town boy whose folks thought he had much too sensitive a soul to drive the butcher's wagon."

Cy laid his hand on hers. A strong hand whose square, long fingers were accustomed to work confidently a hairsbreadth from death. "Did you, Jo?"

Warmth and comradeship in his voice reinformed the champagne. "How do I know what an adolescent girl wants? Delilah? Sure, I'd memorized it before I was fifteen. You bet—and Amneris and Erda and Ortrud. There wasn't any contralto lead that wasn't me. Whenever I was going to sleep, that was me there with the roses coming through the curtain. Yes, and if you'd like to know I can tell you exactly how the young girl feels when she finds out the truth."

"Poor kid."

"Well, that's what I mean. You signed your name to it and the check turned out to be good."

Sudden darkness lowered in his face, something that fascinated and frightened her, an inexplicable repudiation. "Don't be a

88

damned fool! If you've got to get romantic about something, don't pick surgery. I'm the head errand boy of Mercy Hospital."

"You're the boy who took destiny by the tail and hung on."

"I'm a guy who carpenters damaged drunks. I'm a guy that thought it would be singing Delilah if I got to be a brilliant bastard. I'm a guy that loves the great surgeon for the phony popinjay he is."

She enjoyed having him dodge her so earnestly. And champagne was a serviceable and benevolent drink. For here they were, Cy and she, out of a little Rocky Mountain town, at a quiet table, and friends, old friends, an unpredictable friendship come actually to be. Accord flowed between them. How they knew each other! And how his strength could support her and somehow renew her. And all the past so short and sweet and lost. It drew them together with locked arms at twilight under the peaks and time gone crazy rushing on.

"You've changed, Cy. And just since winter. I don't know how or why. I wish you'd tell me."

Cy said, not quite willingly, with an effect of groping, "All I know is, nothing can be approached on your knees. If there's a sanctity it's false as hell." He abandoned that and said, "Jo, you've got a perceptive skin. Things go right through your skin without waiting for your mind. Well, that's the kind of skin I've got."

He looked square at her, into her eyes. So she had not hidden it from him. He knew about Sam, he understood all her mixed-up feelings. Shame should have engulfed her and somehow it didn't, she did not care. For the moment champagne or something else had made her invulnerable. She sat in this quietly beautiful room, with an orchestra playing, and she was raised to a high, grave serenity. Just that there truly was such a thing as being decent and it was not silly to believe in being staunch.

He said something that would have been brutal if it had not come out of that complete accord. "If you did go back to Custis, you couldn't hide there any better—you just can't hide." But an association set him off at a queer tangent, as if an unexpected meaning had opened up. "My old man tried to keep a notebook.

89

I found a stack of them when he died—almost fifty of them, maybe. Not much medicine in them, though that was the idea. He listed every trout he caught and every sagehen he shot—and God how he loved to fish and hunt. Or he'd write, 'Aggie Stiles is a dead beat—owes me for thirteen years of telling her she don't have cancer, then gets the idea she'd better go to a pay doctor to find out.' But maybe once a month he would really make a note and some of them are the damnedest. 'Only prospector I ever knew that didn't get sick in the winter time was Appanoose Bob. Appanoose carried a bag of pine nuts and always ate some every day. Said they kept off his rheumatiz. Didn't keep off his rheumatiz. Did take the curse off sowbelly and beans.' That was my old man, Old Doc Kinsman talking. He was just an up-country sawbones in the sagebrush. But thirty years ago Old Doc Kinsman had his hand for a minute square on what Ezra Bartlett is finding out."

"Who is Ezra Bartlett?"

"Harvard's great man, an old man with a beard," Cy said explosively. Then, "He's a great man, a physiologist. He's a man who really knows what he knows, and that's not surgery, dear."

That seemed to release a catch. For though Cy absolutely never talked about the hospital, now he began to tell her stories of the wards, sardonic tragedies, sharp ironies, crises in the operating room, death at dawn, laboratory experiments that came to nothing, a wish that more could be known than was known. He moved on back to the Base Hospital in France—how someone had worked a miracle, how someone had gone on operating while the Base was bombed and the cordite fumes stank in the operating room, how a ribbon of steel had curled in a broken bowel and somebody's horrible cursing, Cy's no doubt, trying to get it out.

Josephine was hardly breathing, for nobody had ever talked to her like this. Fascination grew to awe. How much he had known. How this razor-edged reality cut through the pretenses of Chelsea's beauty-floggers. Then that awareness yielded to another one. Why, they were side by side, they were an island of friendship in New York, and Cy—it was clearly impossible

90

that he should need reassurance but he was reassuring himself. He was humble and she was his friend. He was holding out his hands to warm them at her. Then thank God, then it must be true, she had warmth. And Cy needed it.

He broke off. "How I talk! You'd think I was an absolutely fearless critic of Imagism. Let's find a supper club and dance."

Josephine stood up—and had been deeply healed. "No. Take me back to Twenty-Third Street." But if Sam were there, they would find that supper club.

"Look, Jo. I've got all this money. I want this to be a big night."

"Save your money. It is."

In the taxi she declined to believe that it was due to the champagne. The truth was she had ceased to be just the girl whose sister had agonized Cy Kinsman in the home town, in the vanished time. She had identity for Cy now. He knew her and he knew they were friends. She did not want him to feel anything more than that but it was good to know that he found her pleasing and was aware of her in this dark car, that he knew her thigh touching his was soft, that he believed she was sweet and true.

For the first time in her life she was glad that Sam was not home. This oneness, so fragile and so fleeting, could be unimpaired and their secret a little longer. There could be a few minutes more of feeling that she had dignity. Anna said good night. Cy sat on the blue-covered couch in the living room that was Sam's bed at night and Josephine sprawled on the blue-covered couch that was hers. Chin in her hands, she scrutinized him, massive face, heavy-set shoulders, a grin that meant he would never be able to see rainbows round her.

"I used to think you were homely as Job's turkey, Doctor. All evening I've been finding a slight resemblance to Abraham Lincoln."

"You look pretty good. Must resemble some nurse at Mercy."

"I don't know whether that's a grin or a leer. You can make me feel as if you were looking right through my clothes. Swell, if you're the graduate sensualist people say you are. But I have an uneasy idea you're just an anatomist."

"Let's call it hyperesthesia."

She grappled with the word, then laughed. "Fine, only who's hyper, you or me?"

"An anatomist is always interested in atypical formations, and yours are. Science learns a lot from the abnormal."

"What about me is abnormal?"

"Well, take the ischial tuberosities. Yours aren't at all textbook. The gluteus maximus is so small it could almost be called vestigial. The extensors are not what we're taught to expect. I'd go so far as to say that your gastrocnemius is actually deformed. By what the texts say."

"Coming out of the clinic, put that into English."

"Just that you've got a small fanny and your thighs are flat, which may not be what anatomy calls for and so much the worse for anatomy. And calves like yours, well, Jo, they catch the eye. They manage to hold it too."

She hooted. "Remember on the stairs, a few weeks ago? You were sure that I was the new-issue woman making it ever so easy for the war-shattered male."

"You're a damned pretty woman, Jo."

She peered over her shoulder at what were her ischial tuberosities if she understood him. "God knows you give it all the icy fervor of science but thanks, Cy. It's nice to catch your eye. If you had any poetry in you, you'd call me callipygian."

Grin or leer, it was favorable to her, it was personal, it was aware. So now she found herself thinking of his long discipline. Harvard Medical School, Peter Bent Brigham Hospital, then the British Army and a clearing station on the Somme, then the American Army and the Mobile Unit and the Base Hospital, and now Mercy. For years Cy had been subdued to a job of which every moment, every detail, was from outside himself and would never take his wish into account. No private feeling of his could count for anything at all—he was disciplined to the iron reality, the thing that was. A husband's sleeping with ringleted blond tarts could not matter if there was so much as one dressing to be changed. Heartbreak, the good life, the great novel, the great society, the goddess beauty—mere dust if one degree of fever could not be explained. The necessity of self-expression, materialism stifling us, middle-class America breaking its artists—nothing of it was left, not even a gas, when you thought of that curling piece of steel in the exposed bowel and a team of exhausted men quiet at their work and a line of soldiers in agony but silent on the floor, waiting to be next. In Chelsea an hour of adding little words and an hour of describing how you had added them quite wore the artist out, so that his very soul needed to be refreshed. At Mercy Cy rose at six and till midnight went confidently where, besides him, only death dared to go, and before dawn was waked twice to go there again.

"The hell with heartbreak!" Josephine said. She had a sudden overwhelming desire to know who his women had been and what they had meant to him. That moment when there comes into a man's eyes that look of desperation and necessity, of abjectness and pleading—what kind of women had transfixed Cy and served to kindle in him a need deeper than she could reach? Abruptly Josephine veered away from that, with "Cy, what are you going to do after Mercy?"

"I'll tell you when I know."

"Don't you know?"

Curiously, he said, "If for five minutes we could have five cents' worth of honesty. I don't know that I'd ask for more."

She said, "I don't understand, Cy. I don't know what you're talking about."

"Damned if I do, either. And damned if my boss does." His hands made a curt thrusting away. "I'm a brilliant bastard, I guess I could call hogs. If I don't find out what I'm talking about, hog calling could be attractive. There are worse jobs."

His words were quiet and without color but they weighed more than the world. For a moment a gulf of black fear opened at her feet. "I wish I understood," she said.

"The closest I can come is this. There's something you've got to have or the hell with you. I know Little Mac hasn't got it. Either I have or I haven't, and if I haven't, the hell with me."

"What is it, Cy?"

"I can't tell you. It's just the integrity of the job."

No one had talked to her so truly and she was sure that Cy had talked to no one else so truly. And almost at once he said something that she could not hear and live through. The words were only, "I know what cuts you up—I'm on your side," but now that somebody outside herself had said it, she would never be able to deny it to herself again. Probably that was what Cy had intended. She was stricken, pierced through, and somehow strengthened.

"Fidelity matters less than you think, Jo," he said. "If it isn't there, then it just isn't worth having. What matters is having integrity and you've got yours and nobody can take it away from you. Nobody ever had more and it is never going to be violated. You've got it for good, come hell or the wrath of God."

Her eyes stung with tears. In this room there had strangely come to be security. She had been made whole. Now she could never be wholly without self-respect and Dr. Kinsman had truly been a physician tonight.

"That's a good chin, Jo."

"You don't need to say anything, Cy." It was as if they had clasped hands across the room.

Now he glanced at his watch and Josephine could see the resident come alert. Friendship, intimacy, this living comradeship, a damned pretty woman—they could not in the least prevail against the wards, the staff, the sick, the dying poor. And that, Jo, that is discipline and it's ever so different from what you're accustomed to in Chelsea.

She sat up. "Don't go for a minute. We've had a good time."

He came to sit beside her. She pulled his arm around her, rubbed her cheek across his, laid her head on his shoulder, murmuring, "A little admiration that knows its place." If you had a taste for ironies, here was one: that these walls had inclosed a living warmth between two people tonight, this room had had the human worth, the human truth, it was supposed to have, and it was not Sam who had given it that dignity, not Sam but Cy.

They sat so for a while. She was glad that he had not had his guard up tonight. She was glad that her atypical formations pleased him. She was damned glad that Chelsea could produce a friendship after all. An ineffable sadness shook her, that the two of them were so alone and their armistice must be so brief. It ended in a subdued sweetness, that they should be here at all.

She took Cy's face in her hands and kissed him. She had intended a casual kiss—friendship recognized, her restoration acknowledged. But it turned out that Cy was not a man whom you kissed that way and she was clinging to him hard and her very blood was answering him. So much the better, she thought, and stood up triumphant and a little weak. Their shoulders touched, their hands clasped.

"Good night, Jo."

"Good night, Doctor. . . . Wait a minute, Cy. Well, just this. You aren't hard as hell's trap door. You aren't half hard enough."

*viii*

THE WOMAN with the crushed legs did not die. The juniors at Mercy came to wish fervently that she had died. For she loosed their resident on a hunt for the Jesus factor. Cy could not even phrase what he was looking for, but whereas the habitual question had been *Why did the patient die?*, now it was *Why didn't she die?*, and whereas he had been troubled by a conviction that the patient had a right to live, now it was that the patient had had no right to live.

The woman had had crushing wounds, the kind that produce shock most quickly. She had lost much more blood than was permissible. On top of that two major operations had been performed on her simultaneously. It made a neatly packaged problem and in clear light. On any calculation she had passed Painted Post. But she had come back.

Cy concluded that there must be an unobserved element, and one of the juniors mourned, "Oh, God, now we got something else to look for. I liked it better when it was just the X Point."

Cy grinned. "Further definition of the X Point: the point where shock becomes an irreversible reaction."

Was there a clue in pregnancy? Cy plunged into a search of Mercy's obstetrical records so thorough that Mac protested. "Any time you want to practice surgery by statistics, better take a librarian's job." He came out with a finding: that over the decades a number of women had not died in childbirth who ought to have died. Accident victims mostly but women with grave infections too, and women who had had emergency Caesareans in horrifying circumstances, and women who had attempted suicide by poison. He brought them together, women who had no right to live but had lived nevertheless, grouped them as he could and made a summary. "What do you make of this?" he asked McAllister.

Mac read the report with close attention but was not impressed. "This is what the boys do who can't operate. Theoretical reading matter for the second rate. It comes off the press by the bale—I don't mind, good thing to build up *esprit de corps*. But Cy, hell's bells, you can go through a hospital's records and find anything you want to look for. With thousands of cases to pick from, you can prove that a saint's femur cured them or that they died because a hex slipped in the door. It's the good old game of library medicine. You hide whatever rabbit you like in the hat. Then you go looking for it with all the instruments of science. So you bellow with surprised delight when, lo, you've found it. I prefer the clinic."

"Still, Colonel, granted that knowledge may be a serious handicap to the surgeon, you don't think it's insuperable, do you?"

"Tell you what you do, Cy. Set up the experiment sometime and we'll see. But in your time off."

One obstetrical case kept nagging him, a woman with a burn that covered two-thirds of the body area. Her child had been stillborn but she herself had not died until the ninth day. She ought to have died within twelve hours—and hadn't. There was something wrong and it might be that some element present had gone unobserved. There might be an unobserved element in all these paradoxical cases. It might be the same element. Suddenly he realized that what was troubling him was a note he had read in Wes Kinsman's record of game birds shot and bills unpaid.

"Saved Clara Mackay's baby," Old Doc Kinsman had written. "Clothes caught fire at the stove. Burned to hell and gone. Started labor. I done a Caesarean. Clara ought to of died on the table. Took her a week to die. Just like Jake Cool's wife in '99 that got kicked by a steer in her eighth month. Her baby died but she didn't. Like Helga Halvorson that run a manure fork in her thigh and got blood poisoning. I saved her and the baby both. Shouldn't be. Sure as God's anger, her note was due, she didn't have no right to live."

Which was word for word what Cy Kinsman had concluded about the woman with crushed legs in 1919. But Wes Kinsman had gone on to say, "Maybe there's something in the placenta."

Maybe there's something in the placenta! That might be more than a hick doctor's superstition, out of medicine's dark ages. Some strange things had been found in the placenta since Wes Kinsman's time and more might be there waiting to be found. Conceivably there was something in the placenta that acted as —well, as what? An antibody? Cy broached the idea at six-thirty meeting but nobody would buy. "Don't seem to make 'em immune to pyemia, Cy," Pete pointed out. He carried it to Mac, with a suggestion that Mercy forthwith commission a research on the placenta, to investigate chemical or metabolical or bacteriological processes that might increase immunity or fortify against shock.

"Out of your field, aren't you?" Mac said. "That's a Medical job." He laughed. "Cost ten men and fifty thousand dollars. I'm sure the trustees will be glad to vote it if you'll find somebody with a loose fifty thousand. Get it if you can. But I won't assign you. Probably the answer to what to do with Cameron Steele."

Cy humbled himself to write a long letter to Ezra Bartlett at Harvard. Was there any indication that pregnancy increased either immunity or resistance? Was pregnancy known to increase resistance to shock? Had Harvard immunologists made any observations relevant to such questions? Had Dr. Bartlett any clues? It was a careful letter, with the details of his case and from the records stated accurately and no suggestion made beyond the element of mystery. Two days later he got an answer.

My DEAR KINSMAN:

That is not one question but many. I do not know. No one knows. Why do you not investigate?

Yours most cordially,
EZRA BARTLETT

The curtness and resolute refusal to answer suggested that Cy had no right to ask questions of science—and the hell with Bartlett, the high priest of science. Or did they? Bartlett knew what he knew—he also knew what he did not know. And he was right, for if Cy wanted his questions answered, he knew how to make a start toward seeing if they could be. He wouldn't. Inquiry closed: retire the possible immunities of pregnancy to the inactive file.

The next morning McAllister, after spending an hour taking out an ovary, spent another twenty minutes taking out the appendix and then remarked that he was going to take a look at the gall bladder. The patient had had the most scrupulous and exhaustive study beforehand and it was true that there had been positive gall bladder indications. But another operation would get into the wholesale class.

"Wouldn't it be a good idea to take the afternoon off, Colonel?" Cy asked. "We could leave our tools here and come back later."

"Suppose she dies of it in the meantime?"

"Sure, but is it likely?"

Mac thrust in his hand and felt for the gall bladder. "Infected," he reported. "Full of stones."

"Still, a couple of weeks—"

"Shut up, Cy. Close the incision. I'll have to go in higher up."

Mac left the table and phoned to the room where the woman's husband was waiting. He explained that he had found the gall bladder involved and asked permission to take it out. That was most punctilious—and just what could a husband say? You're in charge, Dr. McAllister, it's your case.

Mac made his new incision and, working with a dexterity that no man in America—saving a tentative exception?—could excel, took out the gall bladder. He had minute care. He was adaptable and inventive. He worked with absolute sureness. The job he did had beauty as pure as logic or music.

And it was beauty in a dimension of its own. Beauty that was empty of content. It was—unconcerned. In the shadowless light of the operating room, with the team working, the nurses intent and efficient, Cy found the words at last. Mac's skill has integrity, Mac hasn't got a bit.

In the scrub room Charlie Moss dropped his gown on the floor and looked ready to jump on it. "Three and a half hours. Are you sweating too?"

"Think of your privilege. You had a grandstand seat and it didn't cost a dime."

The woman died that night, with Cy, Pete, and Charlie trying everything in the book to bring her out of shock. In the morning nobody could doubt the genuineness of Mac's regret. He spoke soberly of the dead woman, of her charitable activities, her earnestness and usefulness, her husband. He shook his head. A difficult case. Every indication had been favorable. It hurt when the indications turned out wrong.

"There's never any way of knowing. You saw scores of them get well in France after they had had a lot more done to them than we did to her. Yes, and after they'd been lying round for three or four days at that. Remember that Frog with a hundred and eleven intestinal perforations? We worked on him the better part of a day—and he'd been rained on for two full days. He's begetting peasants this minute. Every case is different. You never know."

What was different in Cy was that he recognized a smouldering anger in himself. It had been burning for months but he had not identified it as what it was. "Sure," he said. "We kid about it at six-thirty meeting. We call it the X Point. You know what I think, Colonel? I think it's a cagey idea to stop before we get to X. I think it may even be our job to stop."

"No doubt, Cy. And just how do we determine where X is?"

It was oddest of all that he could not remember ever feeling anger at any time in his life till a few months ago. "The Trustees put a clock in every operating room," he said. "There's no bylaw that forbids us to glance at it."

"Look here, Cy," Little Mac said quietly, "it is not your job to criticize my work. In my judgment it was best to take that gall bladder when I did. I may have been wrong but I don't think so.

My judgment still is that it was best. Possibly she would have died from shock from what I had done already if I had sewed her up and left the gall bladder alone—we don't know. Possibly it would have burst and killed her if I had waited—we don't know. I used the procedure indicated. That's what a surgeon does—he uses the procedure indicated. It's all he can do. She died. I'm sorry she did but a percentage of them do."

"Do you play them on the percentage basis?"

Mac bellowed, verging toward a tantrum, but the fuse never reached the powder—he ended by guffawing. "I like 'em fresh, by God I do!" He stood up. "You may be satisfied that you're doing your job perfectly, Cy, but I'm not. Young Woodard was late for an operation Tuesday—that's your responsibility. A nurse ruined an autoclave on Monday—you're supposed to teach them how they work. On Wednesday the police had to call twice for a wagon—that may have been Estey's fault but it's your responsibility and I won't tolerate it. Dorothy Sponberg says that only a miracle prevented an oxygen explosion in B—who is supposed to keep track of those machines? Do your job and keep your nose clean. Furthermore, I want my ovariotomies written up."

"Yes, Colonel," Cy said. "Shall I include this one?"

The case had brought him to something like a showdown, though perhaps only a showdown with himself. It was not merely that he had recovered from an admiration and not merely that resentment of futility and dread of ignorance had rushed into the gap. It was not merely that the rituals and hierarchies of the profession had come to disgust him, or that he could not respect a perfection of skill that lacked responsibility. A detached mind could take all that. There was something more instant and urgent, deeper by far, something that had to be faced at once but could not quite be understood. Medicine had to be otherwise than he had found it or else the foundations of the world were broken up.

There came a job on the pancreas. Cy summed it up at six-thirty meeting, which had been largely devoted to the bewilderment of Moriarty and an intern in the presence of one of yesterday's admissions. Nobody could make much of it.

Cy summarized. "She comes in here with a bag full of candy bars. She tells you that she keeps syrup by her bed and has to swallow some several times a night. Every few hours during the day she gets weak, dizzy, and scared. She tells Newton"—the intern—"that she feels as if the devil was chasing her and she had to run, she doesn't know why. Pete would translate that as a feeling of impending disaster, if they had scholars in Virginia. So she goes into a drug store and eats a candy bar or drinks a malted milk. So she's okay for the next few hours—no weakness, no giddiness, no devil. Vince and Newton get Medical on the job and run all the tests. They don't indicate much of anything— except one. That one knocks your eye out. We get a blood sugar of thirty-five milligrams per cent."

About a dozen M.D.'s were now listening attentively. Dr. Kinsman could lecture when there was no call to be snooty. "We stick to the tests—that's what they're for. Thirty-five milligrams per cent! About nineteen cents on the dollar. Well?"

Nobody said anything. Cy grew impatient. "We're supposed to have learned about diabetic coma before we come on to Mercy. It was what scared the pants off you when you went gonging out with your first wagon. This appears to be the exact opposite of diabetic coma. I won't say that anyone knows a hell of a lot about the pancreas. Furthermore, I can't think with my fingers. But we got that blood sugar by test and I say we'll find a tumor on the tail of the pancreas. Everything is accounted for if you say that the islands of Langerhans are running wild."

The silence stretched out. It was ended by Steele, heavily incredulous. "Did you say 'we'll find,' Cy?"

"Certainly. I'm going to take out most of the pancreas, a big hunk anyway. How does it differ from what we'd do with a toxic goiter?"

"You and who else?"

"Pete, I think, and Vince."

"Excuse me, but have you looked at a pancreas lately?"

"Lately enough so that I can recognize one."

"Know how to sew one up?"

"Give me twenty-four hours more to run the tests again. Then drop in day after tomorrow and I'll show you how. Now I want you to stay with her tonight, Newton, and tomorrow night. Pump a lot of glucose into her. Peg Mason will spell you, if you ask her prettily. But that doesn't license you to get a hand on Peg's tail—"

"That's right, Cy," Pete said, "endear yourself to the boy."

He wanted that extra day not so much to repeat the tests as to get McAllister's permission. He laid the test reports and chart on Mac's desk before ward rounds and said, "Here's one I'd like to tackle, Colonel."

Mac looked through the papers, shot a glance at Cy, and grunted. "Why did you suppose you had to ask?"

Several of the boys contrived to be on hand the following morning and he found that Dorothy Sponberg had assigned the case to Room 4, except for the amphitheater the largest operating room at Mercy, with a steep bank of seats up one wall. Mac operated here on Saturdays so that he could lecture to his students. And Pete said, "Somebody must have sent out cards."

Looking up, Cy saw that a dozen or so of the seats were occupied, half of them by surgical eminences. Then, gowned and masked, McAllister came in, earlier than he had ever arrived before. He nodded and took up a position just back of Cy.

Steele learned how you sew a deeply buried, soft, and spongy organ that threatens not to be sewn. And Cy was raised to a high serenity, for this was a perfect job, at the extremity of skill and no less of intelligence. It was suddenly, without plan or forethought, his vindication before a jury of his peers. Then he assisted Mac through a cyst and an ulcer and gathered his platoon for the tour of the wards. Mac practically galloped today; if any of the poor needed judicious thought it was just too bad. Then he bore Cy away to his office.

"About that pancreas, Cy."

"I thought it was fairly obvious."

"The diagnosis? Oh, unmistakable. Did you know the operation had never been done in New York?"

"I gathered as much when I looked through the literature yesterday."

"I only know of three cases," Mac said thoughtfully.

"I found five."

This seemed to be Mac's day for pensiveness. Eyes meditative, hands at his chin—and was that gesture the reason why sometimes he had seemed to be stroking a beard? But such a figure of the eminent surgeon, a thousand dollars' worth of clothes, hot summer sunlight on his close-cut gray hair, a small Napoleon back of a big desk in a room with exquisite leather and prints of New York harbor. And a print of John Hunter. And a print of Ambroise Paré. Paré!—*"Je le pansay; Dieu le guarit."* I dressed him, God cured him.

"What do you intend to do when your year is up?"

Mac shot him the wholly unexpected question. And yet it was immediately seen to be the inevitable question. Why, if they mean to have a war, let it begin here. I dressed him, Colonel. Cy met his gaze. "Why, if you put it that way—I expect to go on doing the job. To go on being resident at Mercy."

"Suppose the Trustees don't renew your appointment?"

"I'd say promote Pete. No need to go outside. The Trustees couldn't find a better man anywhere."

The chief of surgery smoked his cigarette with delicate grace, reflectively, as if immersed in reminiscent satisfaction. "I've been president of the College of Surgeons. I'll be president of the AMA three years from now. I've served on more damned committees, written more damned reports, conducted more damned inquiries. There's no big city in the United States where the key men aren't friends of mine. There's hardly a Class A hospital. A lot of them are my men."

"It's a sound product, the McAllister man."

"I've turned out God's plenty," Mac agreed. "I don't know that I ever turned one out who would have done that pancreas on his own. Who would have done it without seeing any reason why he shouldn't. I staff the hospitals, I fill the chairs—"

"Colonel, I know you're a gee-whiz."

"There are big hospital appointments. Lots of medical school chairs are damned desirable. It's a good life. Fine people, public distinction, chance to make as much money as you want. Probably got it coming to you, Kinsman. Or almost. I like your hands, Cy."

Here the Old Man stood up from the desk, erect, six inches short of Cy. He said, "I don't like anything else about you, not a damned thing. I don't like your tongue or your insubordination or your defiance. I don't like your ego or the way you act. I don't like your hallucination that you're too damn brilliant for this world. Get back to your job. And do your job. Write up that pancreas. And bear in mind you may not be reappointed. You're on probation at Mercy. I doubt if you'll make the grade."

About four o'clock that afternoon Cy realized that no one could talk to him that way. And certainly Alexander McAllister could not. The realization hit him as a gust of rage that blew him quite out of control. With no reason he began to bawl out a nurse and an intern, standing at a ward desk and fairly beating them over the head with abuse. Pete came hurrying up. Dorothy Sponberg materialized out of the air. And Cy was overwhelmed with shame. "You'll have to forgive me," he managed to say. "You did nothing wrong, either of you. I'm a fool. I'm suffering from a delusion that I'm Sandy McAllister."

He swung downstairs and out across the court. Pete was hurrying after him, only to be half-paralyzed by the discovery that Cy was crying. He fell into step but could say nothing all the way to Cy's rooms. By the time they got there Cy was not crying.

"You never know what the machine will give when you drop the nickel in," he said. "Damn me if I've bawled since I got knocked out of the box in the ninth inning at Custis High School."

He saw Pete stare at the wall with sudden horror, then avert his gaze. Someone had taken down Captain Kinsman's picture from the row of former residents and had substituted a large framed photograph of the rear end of a truck horse.

"That would be Steele," Cy said. "In fact, it would be anybody at Mercy except you. It would even be Little Mac. And how right." Pete grabbed for it but Cy stopped him. "Let's just let it ride."

"Cy, will you for the love of God tell me what the almighty hell has got into you?"

An overwhelming disgust, a knowledge that when he thought he was Little Mac it was not a delusion. "I think maybe," he said, "we shouldn't let me roam Mercy without a keeper."

"Look here, is it anything—I mean, would a little—oh, hell, Cy, my old man's rotten with money, if you need money—"

"With Mercy paying me its princely wage?"

"What's gone wrong, then?"

"Nothing."

They sat miserably silent till Cy said, "Mercy doesn't allow for time out. Let's go back and run our side show. Well, I'll tell you, Pete. It's come to look as if the healing art and I weren't meant to live together in holy wedlock. I don't know why. A lot of people tell me why but they don't seem to know any more about it than I do. If I ever find out, I'll write it up for you."

Veil after veil of illusion was getting torn down the center but there were always further ones behind. He had slowly grown resentful of the regimen that kept him from Twenty-Third Street. His infrequent evenings off were far from enough and he had worked hard to invent an occasional legitimate errand for Mac that would give him a half-hour at Josephine's—best of all if it was the half-hour before supper. Sam was seldom home at that time, Deborah was relaxed after a bath, and Josephine came closest to being whole.

She had grown thinner and her personal physician thumped her and made a blood smear. "I guess you'll live, one way or another," he reported next time. "Just under five million, which is all the license calls for. Hemoglobin close to ninety. See here, you aren't abnormally thirsty these days, are you?"

"Not for anything to drink. It's just that I never sleep any more. It's just that nobody can live in New York."

She sat with the little white-nightshirted figure on her knee, the damp ringlets against her cheek. Deborah was such superb biology—sweetly plump but hard, vibrant with health, a child who laughed easily, a child who liked Cy Kinsman.

But you came to ignore Deborah for Josephine. She was a neurotic madonna, tense, skinny, somehow emptied, surely unfulfilled. A reek of slum streets came on a hot wind through the open window. Cy knew that Josephine's thoughts had retreated to Custis, where summer smells were clean. Her brown eyes were dark with distance and remembrance. They were tired; there was regret in them. Her skin had a curious luminous quality. The flowered blouse had short sleeves and its open collar made a shadow above the division of her breasts.

The moment stopped short like a picture arrested on a screen and Cy's mind was thundering with a question. How long had he been wanting to touch her? There were few women he had wanted to touch from whom he had withheld his hand. But without acknowledging the desire he had been wanting to, his hands had been wanting the ecstasy of making themselves free with her body, and all along some fundamental, dark wisdom had made him forbear. He suddenly remembered telling Pete, no, taking care not to tell him, that if he should want to take Josephine he would take her. That flippant conceit was sharp with irony, for deep as the desire was the wisdom to forbear was deeper still. When had he first wanted to touch her? More than that. He wanted to hear her contralto voice speaking to him out of the darkness, speaking in the night, richness and sadness in a room that held them both. How long had he been wanting to hear her voice by night?

His nerves jangled, Cy took Deborah on his knees and gave her a tawdry little picture book he had bought at the corner newsstand and watched Josephine narrowly. The clairvoyance between them was fortunately cut off for the moment; she had no sense of the turbulence that was rioting in him. She was relaxed against the pillows on one of those blue-covered couches, looking through the windows at something twenty-five hundred miles away, her dark hair making a shadow on her forehead, her long, subtle legs swung up beside her. After a while she took Deborah again and began to sing old nursery songs. "The Farmer in the Dell." "Oats, Pease, Beans." They were songs the Caneday children had sung in Custis and therefore a magical incantation now; they were to bring Josephine healing and wholeness and safety. That voice had beauty, it had disturbance and desire. He must have known so all along.

After Deborah had eaten supper, Josephine took her upstairs. When she came down she was still humming absently, "Where oats, pease, beans, and barley grows, 'Tis you nor I nor nobody knows." Yes, an incantation. From the vanished time, from the sweet safety when Jo was Deborah's age. She had carried her daughter upstairs, singing. But it was the child Josephine being carried upstairs and sung to, in an old house on a leafy street in Custis, of an evening in early summer under the peaks. And time was without movement in those evenings, time held still and was no menace, there was no growing up, there would be no doubt and no loss, no need to know the iron and the cold stone of the world. Custis and childhood were in Josephine's eyes and forlornness had made her altogether beautiful.

"Krazy Kat," Cy said.

"What about him?"

"That place he talks about, the Enchanted Mesa. There really is a place named that. It's near Acoma—I've been there. But the name is just a name, Jo. It isn't enchanted."

"Damn you, Cy!" she said, furiously rebellious. "Let me think so, can't you? At least there would be a place for Deborah to play. And a place for me to . . ."

"To what?"

"Let it go."

Music was on her still, she was still reaching for enchantment. She sat at the piano and began to sing. A song he had never heard before—"Everybody got to walk this lonesome valley, you got to walk it all alone." It laid a hand on his throat. He wasn't taking this very well.

"What is that song?"

"Spiritual. Probably white spiritual first." Her voice grew

rounder. "Poor sinner got to walk that lonesome valley, he's got to walk it all alone. . . ."

She stopped singing and swung round on the bench. "What about hay fever?"

"Protein sensitivity. And that's about all the boys know. They talk and talk but mostly they just treat the symptoms."

"Sam's treatments have started. Last year they cost sixty dollars. I just haven't got sixty dollars."

"A chap named Kunkel runs a clinic at Mount Sinai. Experimental, too—a good man. It wouldn't cost him a dime there."

She smiled. "You don't understand. Certainly it is society's duty to take care of its artists. Yes indeed, and in purple and silk at that. But a clinic—why, Cy, that would be charity and you know that charity kills the soul."

"If I had to pay sixty dollars he would go to a clinic or his precious mucous membranes could swell *quantum libet*."

He had not supposed there was any dynamite in that. But it brought her to her feet in a pale fury. "I've told you before, you'll stop despising him or you'll stop coming here. Make up your mind and I don't care which."

Eenie-meenie, he thought, they all do it to me, I do it to them all. But scientific detachment had been cracked across forever and he could be furious too, quite as furious as Jo. "Take a tumble to yourself! If he needs sixty dollars he can damn well get out and earn sixty dollars. You pay his rent, you not only cook his dinners but pay for them too, you pay for the splendid vellum his soul has to have to write on. Why don't you make your boy grow up a little?"

"I'm not doing anything I'm not proud to do."

"You're kidding yourself. You're skinny as a rail. You can't sleep. You're stretched tight with worry. You spend half your time in a daydream of running hell-bent home to the Rocky Mountains. Why? I'll tell you why. Because if you did, maybe it would be all right to wear a skirt. Maybe for a while you could be a woman. Maybe that would be better than being a half-woman keeping half a man."

"There's Deborah, isn't there?"

"Does Sam know there's Deborah?"

"You can't say such things to me!"

"Tell the truth, is your fancy man worth what he costs you?"

They stared at each other, shocked by the violence revealed though evidence of its latent possibility had always been there. Shame darkened Cy's mind, and a secondary anger because she had no right to make him feel ashamed. . . . Josephine made a gesture of abasement, her knees buckled, and she sprawled on a couch. "Things aren't going so hot with us, are they?" she said. "Know anyone they go right with?"

The reverie she fell into clearly had no comfort in it. She looked fragile. Her shoulders drooped and her slender calves seemed forlorn. Subtle calves, compelling, yet less compelling than her hair. He had to keep looking at her hair—not brown, not quite black, very dark and yet almost with a light of its own. He should have had the decency to forbear that cheap jeer, telling her to cut it in order to acquire masculinity. He tried to force his eyes away from it but could not. And an impalpable response led her to jerk out the comb and let the dark waves fall over her shoulders. Poor child! she was invoking the resources of her womanhood.

Cy thought with the most lucid clarity: the warmth in Jo is still trying to break free but it won't try much longer.

He was being too lucid. His eyes were feeding on her in the full knowledge that his hands wanted to be as free with that slender body as his eyes, that there was the need to hear her disturbing voice speaking in the dark. And he had been evading another truth as earnestly as he evaded truths at Mercy Hospital, that all year he had wanted to sleep with her. It's more than that, a lot more—I want to live with her. It might make the difference, it might be logic in my life at last. And too late, by all the doubts he had finally had to face at Mercy. Out of the question.

So far out of the question that there was nothing left to do, not even laugh.

She buried her face in a pillow and he thought she had begun to cry. That was not to be borne. Josephine was not allowed to cry, it was the prerogative of the surgical resident. He crossed to the couch and turned her face up. She was not crying, she was only scowling. But touching her had gratified a desire so strong that it woke one which was irresistible and he took her in his arms. She came into his embrace so eagerly, her breast was so soft and her cheek and throat so warm, she was so yielding and surrendered, that overwhelming sweetness enveloped him. He had taken life itself in his arms and it was as if for the first time he had come to understand tenderness. With a deep sigh she drew him closer and clung and pressed, her lips opened to his, her breasts hardened. He kissed her again. She struggled away from him and moved quickly across the room.

"So now," she said angrily, though it was by no means anger that had stained her cheeks, "is there some idea I want to be one of your women?"

"Don't be a damned fool."

Scarlet began to fade to pink in her cheeks and her eyes were all conflict for a long moment of indecision. Finally she said, "Well, I won't be. . . . This just isn't our day. . . . I won't be. Still, I didn't like any part of that, Cy. Remember, I didn't like it. Don't do it again."

The trouble was that while he made his way back to Mercy it happened repeatedly. On every block she was in his arms and no reality could get her out of them. A damned good thing she didn't like it, or that they must agree she didn't. A damned good thing it was not possible to live with her. For though let us grant that his were superb hands, they worked in an anarchy that was empty of meaning and conviction.

Three hours later he startled Dorothy Sponberg with a roar of laughter. "Nothing," he told Dorothy, but there was something. He had caught himself intent on another movie reel of Josephine, a more detailed movie whose simple theme was living with her all his life. And another thought had phrased itself with that same admirable lucidity: he was just like the artists, he could make up engaging fantasies, but he wasn't like the artists for he could not write the masterpiece.

In his office Little Mac introduced Cy as his assistant to a young woman. Her name was Claire Pollock and the great surgeon's deference merely underlined the obvious, that she was rich and well born. She was about twenty, pretty, charged with vitality—thousands of volts.

"Miss Pollock will come to Private Wing for a few days for observation, Cy," Mac said. "I've examined her most carefully. I want you to do the same."

Claire Pollock's eager sensitiveness won Cy's concern quite as much as her anxiety. He identified her. Her frank face had smiled at him from Sunday rotogravures. He had seen her pictured in evening gowns and riding habits, in opera boxes, at horse shows, behind the wheels of automobiles. She was young, fashionable, rich, enchanted. And terror had come upon her.

She had been completely studied, with every resource of medicine expended on her, when finally Mac asked him what he thought.

"There is certainly a growth on the ovaries," Cy said. "I'd say it's a big one."

"It is. M'lignant too."

"How do you know?"

"I don't know. Won't know till I can see and feel it. But it is wholly a malignant picture. For one thing, look at the sudden severity of the symptoms."

"On the other hand, look how far back they go. Some for nearly two years, some for nearly three—that's against malignancy. Probably unregarded ones for longer still."

"Know that, do you?" Mac inquired.

"No. I don't even propose it. She certainly ought to have consulted you long ago." But of course there had been Aiken and Newport, there had been balls, hunting, all the fascinating world for which the girl had so exquisite a talent. She had not had time to be afraid till fear was forced on her.

"Probably did ask some Park Avenue fraud. He probably told her to take hot foot baths when she menstruated and billed her father for five hundred dollars." The great surgeon repeated what he did not know and was quite sure about. "It's the malignant picture. I've done a thousand. My God, Cy, by now I can tell 'em blindfold."

"She's only twenty. All the statistics are against cancer."

"You saw me take one out of a girl of fourteen. Hell, I took one out of a girl of five."

Unhappily, that was quite true. You can't practice surgery with statistics. Cy kept arguing the symptoms one by one, but you can't practice surgery with symptoms either, not when you can tell 'em blindfold. Mac was no longer able to question what the picture told him.

There was a controlled terror in her eyes when Cy stopped at her room. "Can't you tell, Dr. Kinsman?"

"I'm sorry, nobody can be sure. Don't be afraid, Miss Pollock. You're in the best hands."

She whispered, "I'm going to be married," and roweled him for she was unfulfilled, who deserved to be fulfilled.

He prepared her for the operation with the full resources of what he had learned, and harried Charlie Moss who did not need the spur. Step by step he talked out every detail with the Old Man.

"I hope to God you'll be able to leave one ovary. Or even part of one."

"Damn sight more likely I'll have to do the whole job."

Certainly; he had anticipated that. The Old Man was what God made him. Or don't blame God; he was what he had come to be. "Hysterectomy?"

"You know what you're likely to find when you get in there. You know how it usually works out."

"You know, Colonel," Cy said, "for a girl like that, there's a lot in life it would be a pity to lose. So much that it seems wrong to make her a woman of fifty in two hours."

"Better be fifty than die of cancer."

Cy's mind flashed the unpardonable heresy that had become familiar: he was not so sure.

He spent odd moments in Claire Pollock's room, giving her

a focus for her courage, letting her use the strength she felt in him. He went there to make sure she was asleep, the night before the operation, and found that she was not. In the murk of a nightlight she reached out to grasp his hand.

"I'm ashamed of myself, Dr. Kinsman, I'm sorry—but I'm . . . I'm scared."

"Don't be. Trust McAllister. He's the best man in the country. You'll be all right."

"I know I'll . . . live. But . . . cancer!"

"It isn't cancer. It's just—look, you've probably had a little wen on your shin or your shoulder. That's all this is, except it's inside you. There's no reason to be afraid of a cyst."

"You don't know what it is." Her hand was a steel clamp. "You don't know. Do you know?"

"No," Cy said, "we don't know. Either of us."

"There. And . . ." her voice sank in the shadow, "I'm terrified."

"Everything is terrifying," Cy said, to whom many had confessed fear. And who needed no confession in order to know what it was. "Look, Miss Pollock. You're young. You're strong. You're tough, you'll bounce back fast. You've got all of life on your side." There was no healing in anything he could say. It was indecent to say anything. "Do what you can, my dear. Don't feel ashamed if you can't do much. But nothing is as bad as being afraid. Except being ashamed."

"You're kind."

Cy went back to tell Charlie Moss to give her a hypnotic, shaken because no one before Claire Pollock had ever called him kind, more shaken by something else. There was no resemblance whatever and yet something in her face under that dim light, something in her fear-racked body, had made her seem like Josephine. As if Josephine were at Mercy and in danger. Some threat to Josephine.

He went out into the court. Summer night, still and hot. "You don't know," she had said, and all surgery was inclosed in that despair. Why, he had pointed out to Mac a half-dozen possibilities that might make it non-cancerous. There might be some anatomical aberration. When Claire Pollock was born or when puberty came upon her. Some congenital defect—that and a mere cyst might explain everything. You don't know. It would be good to know. You ought to know.

A steamship whistle somewhere down the bay. Someone was laughing. Lights in Private Wing were going out. A column of red lights marking the kitchens of every floor of Medical Wing. A laboratory was lighted. A rank perfume from some shrubbery in flower. Ringed round by walls, the court shut off from New York, the city a glow and a subdued sound. The world within a world. Once his nickel's worth.

Cy crossed to the basement of Surgical. There was a clatter of dishwashing machines. Steam from autoclaves. A vast dark space that was Outpatient Department—a quarrel over changing its system was due to come up. He went down a corridor of X-ray rooms. A belated charwoman was sweeping out.

Joe Geist came up to him and asked whether he should give so-and-so morphine. Cy said, "That's your jurisdiction, Joe—do what you think best." Oh, the hell with it. "Is there any counter-indication? Then give it to him." Joe's hair had not yet covered the scars on his scalp where the cop had worked out with him. He nodded and went away. . . . It was an institution, people working together as they best could, with more frailty and stupidity and pettiness than was right, yet better than most, to a good end. Mercy came up to you and was alive.

Cy toured the wards, whispering with interns and nurses. In a storeroom across from the desk of Ward B Woodard was sitting at a metal sink, half a sandwich beside him, writing up his endless notes. Dorothy Sponberg came up and mentioned a shipment of contaminated antiseptics discovered just in time but not yet explained. She asked him about a septicemia case, about a delirium, about the growing instability of a nurse, about the discharge of a lung case who didn't want to go home. A nurse came out of B, crossed to the storeroom, and came back with Woodard, who was stuffing his notes into a hip pocket. Mercy was rolling.

Without friction. And as places go, a good place. Adieu, kind friends, adieu, I can no longer . . .

At the Ward A desk Pete was answering the phone. "All right. It's been known to happen. He won't die. I'm coming." He grinned at Cy. "Emergency has got a compound fracture."

Cy went back across the court to Paupers' House. An open door sent a shaft of light angling toward him. A voice, elegant and superior, scornful, "What you ignore is the fact that the gland has a cortex." Reynolds. How long without interruption had medical arguments resounded down this stair well? Eighty-odd years. Time for a hell of a lot of Claire Pollacks, a hell of a lot of Cy Kinsmans.

An over-ripe bass, certainly Vincent Moriarty's, roared, "I'm a rambling rake of poverty, the son of a gambolier." Who was off tonight? Steele.

Cy shut his door. "You don't know." And yet a good place. It lived as the work of men and women in common. It inclosed you. All his stuff would go in a single suitcase.

Presently he got out a sheet of paper and unscrewed the cap of his fountain pen. "Dear Doctor Bartlett." he wrote. "Is there a place in your laboratory I could have? Is there anything I could do there? Sincerely yours, Cyrus Kinsman." He stood up and watched the ink dry. That did it. He held the sheet up to the light. The hell with it. You don't know. He tore up the letter.

He telephoned Rose Stine's apartment. "Rose, I'm asking you to do something for me. The Old Man is operating in Room 2 tomorrow. Seven-thirty. Ovarian cyst or guess what. Rose, I want you there. Let it be your own idea. Or things happened that way. Or now you're going to be there on all suspected growths. I don't give a damn why you're there, only I didn't say a word." For if it were suspected that he had said a word there would be no chance at all. There was no chance anyway.

There were no spectators. Just Cy and Charlie Moss, the anesthetist, three nurses. And it was as always. Working with concentrated intensity, Cy had time to pay tribute to the supremacy and integrity of Mac's skill. He was a great surgeon.

Gowned, masked and capped, Rose Stine came in and busied herself at a table in the corner, as if preparing something for a later operation. The Old Man got everything exposed. Not a chance. Not a chance in the world. It was a large tumor, curiously shaped, not quite like anything Cy had ever seen. The problem had instantly phrased itself in his mind. The right ovary would have to go. Dissect well along that side. But . . . but by God! It might be done, it was possible. The way it lay, if you were a master surgeon, if you played for the life the way you sometimes played for the achievement, then you could safely leave almost all the left ovary. Or all of it, even? Play for the life. We take the long chance for death with the unparalleled courage for which Mercy stands. Why not the long chance for life? Play for the life. You could save almost all the left ovary. So you could save everything.

Mac glanced at Charlie, who was holding a retractor, and at Cy, who was using a sponge. He stepped back. "M'lignant or b'nign?"

Charlie grunted. Cy said, "You don't know."

"It's malignant as hell. Probably spread all through here." Mac sketched lines in the air with his scalpel, beyond that slowly welling line of blood, while Cy, working automatically, used another sponge and handed it to a nurse, who counted it aloud before she hung it on the rack. "In through here. See how it divides. See how that prong dips down and around." Mac handed the scalpel to the nurse. With two gloved fingers he touched the growth, pressing it gently. He followed it up, down, across, around the perimeter—thinking with his fingers. "I'll have to do a hysterectomy."

"Only take a minute to send a specimen to Pathology," Cy said.

"Plenty of time later. No time now. And no damn need. Look at it. Feel it. Look where it goes. Remember the picture. You've seen plenty by this time—I've seen a thousand."

"There's a chance it's benign."

"No chance whatever. . . . Nurse!" He held out his hand for the scalpel.

Cy looked around and discovered Rose Stine. "Look, the pathologist is here."

Alexander McAllister drew himself up straight. He was five feet six. "We're losing time. Have you got anything to say?"

In all surgery, in the practice of the mystery of medicine, in the organization of the world, Cy could have nothing to say. And he could do nothing. He could not stay Mac nor throttle him. He could not walk off the floor. He could only, for another hour and a half, take his appointed part in the operation which removed womanhood from Claire Pollock. It was a perfect job like all Mac's jobs, a demonstration of the mastery of an art, as well the apprentice's part in it as the master's.

Claire Pollock was still out cold when Cy looked through her door after rounds. Charlie Moss, at his side, looked too and said nothing. Cy went straight to the pathology lab.

"What was that tumor?"

Rose handed him the little light-blue card on which that specimen of tissue was numbered, described, and reported noncancerous.

"Just a cyst," Cy said.

"H'm."

"A damned big one too. Well, that's the healing art. Make out a duplicate of this, will you?"

"What for?"

"I want one."

"There's no regulation says I'm allowed to." Her lips formed a sarcastic smile, then a tired smile. "So that's the way it works out. See what I meant, Cy? You don't have to be little Sir Lancelot. I suppose you do—oh, hell, it's your funeral." She wrote the data on another blank, scored a heavy line under her signature, wrote "Duplicate" across the top, and handed it to him. Her eyes saddened, warmed, went hard—pity, admiration, affection, distaste. She laid a soft hand on his cheek for half a second. "I don't want any part of it. I just report on what's sent to me."

The medical art would regard it as a commonplace incident in any surgeon's practice. The medical art would be quite right.

He determined to stand on his two feet and tell Claire Pollock exactly what had happened to her. To be some five per cent of a man. Canceled. It would not be safe to tell her anything at all for many weeks. He was going to last just three days.

He was a military pace to the left and one to the rear of Alexander McAllister the next day when he paused at the floor desk and studied the clipboard that held the charts and records of Claire Pollock. Mac scowled, said "Benign, hell!," took a fountain pen from his pocket, drew two neat lines through the word, and wrote "Malignant" above it.

As the chief of surgery hung up the clipboard again, Cy met his eyes and allowed himself to grin. They both knew that Pete Estey was now surgical resident of Mercy.

He lived with Mercy the next day as a man spending a last day with a mistress. The following day was the monthly meeting of trustees. He had routed matters so that he had only one operation and finished that one by nine o'clock. He handed his gown to a nurse. He looked at Moriarty and Woodard, who had been his team. His last team. He nodded. Say nothing. At ten he walked into the board room and at ten-twenty-four he walked out again. As he had foreseen, the castration of Claire Pollock was an ordinary incident in surgery. All the obligations of the healing art had been fulfilled. The discretion and judgment of the surgeon were absolute: there was no issue. He had no quarrel with that. But he had read the little light-blue slip to the trustees. He had said what he wanted to say.

He was free now. He had the sense of freedom. As free as he had been the night his father died. Old Doc Kinsman. He might easily perish of freedom.

He phoned Josephine at Howe and Bergstein. "I'm leaving," he told her.

"Leaving what?"

"I'm going home."

"I didn't know you had a home."

"I'm going to Custis."

"That's a good one."

"I'm not joking. I'm making the Enchanted Mesa before you do. My train leaves in an hour and five minutes."

Jagged alarm came into her voice. It turned him cold. But if Jo had been fool enough to develop any need of him, then she was a fool indeed. "Cy! What for? What has happened? You can't go."

"By the way, I've given up medicine."

"Cy, have you gone crazy?"

"Some say so. Pete will take a look at Deborah now and then. Call him when you want somebody. . . . Look, Jo, there are a lot of things I wish I'd got around to saying—"

"What am I going to do?" Her voice was shaking.

"I've been bothered by that, my dear. Whatever it turns out to be, it will be better than if it depended on me."

"I've got to see you."

"No chance. Some other time. So long, Jo. I meant to tell you —oh, hell, you're a sweet child. Don't let anything get you down."

He hung up. A man is good for only one fight and he had made his at ten. Maybe a man could be good for one decency too. Call this one his.

Months later he learned that she went straight from the phone to Mercy but he had left it straight from the phone. He carried his bags down the main corridor, a suitcase half-full of clothes and a not large bag of instruments. He had expressed a box of medical texts.

Last night Moriarty, Woodard, Geist, Moss, and Reynolds had come to his room and been awkward and concerned. Reynolds was most surprising. No more. Pete fell into step with him and took the suitcase. As they passed the main desk, with a knot of people—concerned people, people frightened because their families were sick—Dorothy Sponberg came running up. She put her arms round him and sobbed. So there were tears—and they hurt. He smoothed her cheek. She said "Cyrus!," kissed him—so he had been kissed—and went away.

As the door closed behind them Cy got a whiff of the complex smell that would mean Mercy all his life and would stir an uneasy pain sometimes when he dreamed. Half a block away an ambulance came noisily out of the alley. It would bring back one more broken hulk from the streets. That was no affair of his. He looked at the Pregnant Auk. If it were ever delivered, its progeny would be stone.

"Hell of a way to begin your residency, Pete—leaving the joint on duty."

"I reckon. If anybody don't like it, I'm willing to tell them what they can do." Pete thrust out both hands and muttered obscenities, for to him too had come the experience of helplessness. Later, in a cab, "Somethin' will happen, Cy. The old bastard will loosen up. He'll have to. You're the best man he ever had. You'll get a first-rate appointment somewhere—"

"He won't. I don't want one."

"But—oh, God!" What Pete was saying was, the world cannot be like this. "Cy, at least let me buy you a berth."

"I don't want one. The good book says it's time I started feeding on husks."

He did not tell Pete that his total wealth would carry him a little beyond Omaha and from there on he figured to travel in box cars.

They stood at the gate in the Grand Central. Pete Estey, a kind man and a loyal man, his friend, exactly half his friends. Cy thrust out his hand. "So long, Pete. I'll be seeing you."

"You sure will, Cy."

He turned down into the gloom of the tunnel. Jets of air spat as an engine was coupled on. . . . He would like to be sure that this too was not illusion, self-deception. He would like to be sure that there was not something deeper than what he believed, deeper than Mac, deeper than the practice of surgery. Something that killed but perhaps could be explained.

At least he was sure he had played this one wrong. Somewhere far back, a long time ago.

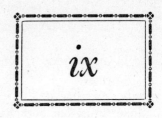

*ix*

JOSEPHINE COULD not tell how good the master-piece was. She was too loyal to it and hated it too intensely. It was probably nearer the center of her life than of Sam's. Long ago she had accepted the fact that she could not respect his mind; in the meaning Cy gave the word, he had no intelligence at all. Moreover, all his life he would acquire not only his ideas but his heartfelt beliefs from whoever happened to be at hand, and would discard them for others the moment some other conversationalist impressed him. He would always see life, understand it, and portray it—in fact he would live it—at the instigation of stronger personalities. Yet there was a ferment of talent in him. His lack of individuality made him sensitive to other people, his mind was so unencumbered that he could manipulate it rapidly, and he absorbed impressions, hints, ideas, fantasies like blotting paper.

He was calling the rewritten version "Moon of My Desire" but an incautious word from Josephine killed that title. "What does it mean?" she asked.

"It's from the *Rubaiyat*."

"I thought you looked down your nose at the *Rubaiyat*. One of those cheap admirations of the bourgeois mind. Like the *Idylls of the King*."

"It's not the Fitzgerald version." He was beginning to pout; his mustache showed that she had made him doubt himself again. "I want 'Moon' in the title."

"Why?"

He couldn't explain: it was a feeling. Say a symbol of unregarded beauty. The serene loveliness of the moon drenched the earth but only the sensitive and lost ever perceived it. You had to have awareness of the sensitive and lost.

"Hooey!" she said unthinkingly. "Weren't you ever out with a girl when you were sixteen? Hasn't everybody been? Every hayseed and his sweetie?"

You could not say "hooey" to Sam. Any kind of criticism proved at once that you had no faith in him and that he was no good. As the manuscript thickened she had to flatter him so desperately that she was glad Cy had never overheard her. Now she had ruined his title, which proved that she thought the book was lousy.

He thought of himself as a satirist; he was wrong. He had a gift for mimicry and caricature that made the characters stand out of the page in relief. You knew them; in fact you recognized them. Some of them came to Twenty-Third Street and had recorded themselves for a fraction of posterity. More were from Utica and some were from Custis. He had a fine time with Professor Asa Caneday, his drooping mustache, his sun-faded eyes and desert-tanned face, his groping speech. He came out a small-town professor with a nature so cramped and astigmatic that you cringed. Asa's daughter had served art.

Sam served it with a diligence that compelled her respect. He kept hard at work all through that summer of 1919 and the pile of typescript on the refectory table grew thicker every week. But words like "hooey" and further dullness of soul eventually cost her her knowledge of it. She no longer had it read to her and was in no doubt who did hear it. The great unmentioned was now the mutually assumed. Sam had got well beyond the timid liberation of merely pawing she-artists in dark corners. He was flinging roses riotously and in fact a rumor rose that he was flinging them miscellaneously and Cassie Morton had discovered that there might be something in old-fashioned fidelity after all.

The world had grown degrading, as when contrition or a canny thought that he ought to be discreet led Sam to make love to her, and her need to be vindicated drove her to respond, which ended in bitterness and disgust. It had grown cowardly; she ought to confront him with an ultimatum and make him behave decently or else get out, and she didn't have the nerve, she could only feed on humiliation and hope. And she learned that it could grow defiling when a manager at Howe and Bergstein made a mild pass at her and she was absolutely unable to keep from responding a little. Then it took her weeks to convince him that there was nothing in it. And there you were: she had sunk so low that she had actually found reassurance in a lecherous hand mauling her legs. Cy had said he would like a job he could do with self-respect. Josephine would have closed for a good deal less than that.

Cy's departure had given her a brief alarm about him and a permanent alarm about herself. As she lay awake at night reviewing her endless movie film of the office, Deborah's future, and the lost time when she and Sam had been lovers, there would come glimpses of Cy in the mountains. Why had he gone? What dreadful thing had happened to him? What was he doing? Why couldn't he write a letter? His grin, his affection for Deborah, his satisfaction in Josephine—she had been able to build them into a buttress whose strength was proved the moment it was broken. In this filthy city he had been Custis and the memory of childhood, in a city that was no treasury of friends he had been friendship, and now she would please be so good as to get along without him. Lying awake and alone at night she could be restless with the memory that toward the end it had been something more than friendship. And that might be the most degrading thought of all as the summer wore on, that she had come to reassuring herself by realizing that she had roused desire in Cy.

A migration was getting under way. The artists were calling on families, agents, dealers, and publishers to subsidize a richer life. The artists were hell-bent for Europe where it was known that freedom and decency could still be served, on whose gracious soil was no avarice or ugliness or vulgarity but a culture that would make amends for the sterility here. Sam dropped Paris and began to long for Auvergne. All he knew about Auvergne was what he had heard from well-traveled artists, for he was never a man to read the books of others. But it developed that he had longed to go there since early boyhood in Utica. It had a peasantry and the strength of the soil, which he needed and which were unavailable here. Josephine grew so alarmed that she took action.

Sam came in fuming. "Have you moved our six hundred dollars to another bank? Why didn't you tell me?"

"I just put it in another account. In my name."

"Why?"

Because it was evidence that if she had paid a price she had got something for it. Because it was a windbreak. Because it was hers.

"Because I want a second thought to come between you and steamship tickets."

At once she saw, though she truly hadn't before, that this was really an insult and a drastic one. She had been so intent on safeguarding a safeguard that she had ignored the implications. Well, call it another milestone on the way to disintegration.

She could not blame him for being mad or for going into the poor-Jo-how-small-souled monologue. But she refused to blame herself for being fed up with that act. "What did you want money for anyway?"

"I wanted some. Do I have to ask you if I can spend a dime?"

You had to be just; he had a point. If the artist's wife rejoiced in backing the artist's dedication to his book, and if marriage was sharing things—there was all that line. The trouble was that what the artist had wanted money for was to take one of his girls out so that his soul could get understood some more. Cy's question rose in her mind: how do you like keeping a man? It was always the kept woman who two-timed her proprietor.

She handed the grievance right back to him. "I never know

how much you make. Here's this clever skit in this month's *Smart Set*. They must have paid you fifteen or twenty dollars. I never heard about it."

"Last week I got my shoes shined too."

He was right: she was a shrew. "Oh, Sam, it's only that I've got a house to run and a kid to raise."

"Do you want them to cost you your soul?"

She lacked time to consider her soul.

Early August brought Deborah's birthday. Josephine baked a cake the night before, glad that her wholesome sister Nancy who had broken Cy's heart, had made a sound cook of her. It was superb with white icing, candy drops of a dozen colors, and five green candles in pink rosebuds. As if Deborah were a bourgeois child, as if Josephine believed she ought to be. There had been a million kids in Custis and they all came to the Caneday birthdays. Going to Jerusalem, London Bridge, All Around the Mulberry Bush. Professor Geist playing his fiddle, or Frances Sargent or Nancy at the piano. Ice cream frozen by the Caneday boys on the back porch, cakes like this one only four times as big, kids shouting across the lawn in the shade of box elders. Air that was electricity in your lungs, coolness, the shadows of clouds moving across fifty miles of mountainsides.

She got the next afternoon off, put a clean white dress and a red hair ribbon on Deborah, and took her uptown. A ride on the Sixth Avenue El seemed to delight the child as much as a walk in the foothills above Custis could possibly have done. A heat wave had subsided, New York had its high windswept sky, and there was a fine breeze. Deborah went from cage to cage at the Central Park zoo too blissful for speech. Better still was a monkey in pants and coat on a curving walk, a hurdy-gurdy, a proprietor of both who bowed and swept off his hat just like the monkey. There was ice cream from a cart and probably it was made of Paris green, but so much the better for a girl who was on a bust. Then the grass drew her and that small white figure galloped through crumpled newspapers and candy-bar wrappings. Josephine's eyes stung, for this scrofulous, gritty substance was not a lawn, there was no smell of earth, there were no peaks to look at, no bushes to burst through or weeds to hide among. But Deborah said, "This is the most beautiful day of the world," and there was no answer to that. Except that she also said, "Cy should celebrate with us" and damn Cy. Why didn't he write? If Josephine could not get his attention, how did he dare forget Deborah?

Satiated with pleasures at last, they started back. "Cy takes me home in a taxi," Deborah observed.

"I'll bet he does. You see, Cy's rich. Oh, heck, on birthdays so are we."

So they taxied to Twenty-Third Street, where it proved that Cy had not forgotten. He had sent Deborah a score of those finger-length Pueblo dolls—kachinas. Josephine suspected that in the Pueblo witchcraft their meaning was something short of chaste but Deborah adored them. She bathed sedately—five-year-old girls do not splash—and arranged Cy's dolls and Josephine's books in a semicircle on the table. Josephine crowned the day by putting a drop of perfume on the fresh nightgown. They ate supper and the expression on Deborah's face when she saw the lighted candles—it was a supreme day, once in her life, just once, never a second time. She blew them out with a single puff, then sawed and crumpled the cake into three pieces, but Daddy wasn't there.

He came in after she was asleep and turned contrite at a sarcastic word from Josephine. "Honestly, I meant to get back. I *am* sorry. Poor kid! I was going to bring a present. I will, tomorrow."

"You see, Sam, forgetting a child's birthday present is something that a parent simply cannot do."

"One day or another day—what's the difference?"

"I'm sorry, sweet. A child has got just its father and mother. You kissed her this morning, sure, but a father brings a present. You let her down. She'll remember that."

"Bet she didn't even notice I wasn't here."

Five years ago this morning he had been shot to pieces, pacing a corridor at St. Francis Hospital and the sidewalk outside through long hours when no one brought him any word and maybe Josephine was dying. The difference was that they had been in love then. You held on to what you could. There was no reason why she should not, five years later, hold on to the first hour when they could talk, there were tears on Sam's cheek, and the Willards were now a family of three.

"Cy remembered. He sent her some Indian dolls."

"Admirable fellow. He has the orderly mind."

Josephine pounded the arm of her chair. "He isn't even in the family! A father must give a little girl a birthday present."

She had given him a chance to be explanatory. "You see, Jo, you want the little things for her. I want the big things."

"For instance."

"I want her to be a person. A whole person. A woman who will be able to master life. Hell, you want to cripple her with the superstitions of a tawdry, fake morality. You want her to cramp and clutter her soul with silly things like birthday presents— tribal folkways meant to make her conform to the safe and mediocre. In the first place, that's unhealthy as hell. For your true motive is to buy her affection, make her love you willy-nilly, whether you deserve it or not, whether she naturally loves you or not. In the second place, it's a step in hardening her into a pat-tern—you're trying to turn her into one more conventional woman—"

"Whereas you want to liberate her from all the crippling weakness of one happy afternoon—"

"Childhood's happy hour—nuts! I want her to grow in her own way into her own strength. So she'll be free."

"You do pick up the damnedest things over the checked table-cloths. Do the forthright thinkers believe it's wrong for a baby to know that the family loves her?"

"It depends. I suppose you'd be horribly shocked if I told you that parental love can maim a child's soul—"

"Look, with the sixty-cent dinner we don't get to maiming souls till the tapioca pudding comes on—"

"Jo," he said, "I seriously believe that there is no hope of building the great society, no hope at all, until we are willing to take infants from their parents and put them in nurseries where experts who know their job can bring them up free of the sickness of parental envy, the poison of parental jealousy and rage—"

Josephine made a vulger sound, loudly. "Tridon—Shaw—the Fabians—the *Masses*. Sam, honestly, a moderately bright mind is supposed to work its way past that particular idiocy not later than the middle of its seventeenth year. It's quite all right to pick up ideas anywhere you please. But why don't you turn them over and inspect them after you've picked them up?"

Kickoff for another brawl.

Another heat wave made Chelsea intolerable, especially to the nose. On Saturday evening there was to be one of those impromptu parties in a basement restaurant after hours—another artist breaking his shackles and heading for a restaurant that would be on the sidewalk. Late in the afternoon she and Sam sat on the steps, watching Deborah, on the sidewalk, try to handle a big blue ball. Her muscles were unco-ordinated but she was willing and stubborn. . . . Hell, there was only one answer, that's all there ever would be. She was in love with her husband. He was not in love with her. He couldn't be in love with anyone, really or for very long. He was just a fragment trying to be whole. Just like her but trying in other ways. He had to be built up all the time and always by fresh hands. That was that. Nothing could be done about it.

The big blue ball bounced away at an angle. Deborah rushed, missed, and before Josephine could stand up, stepped off the curb. Josephine screamed as the little body crumpled away from the truck. But she was crying—she couldn't be dead.

As she carried the child back Sam was standing with a hand to his mouth. "Get Cy!" he croaked.

"Cy is two thousand miles away!" she flung over her shoulder, running upstairs. "Get Pete Estey—oh, let me!" She seized the telephone from his fumbling hands. "Get her clothes off. But be careful."

It took forever but at last Pete was on the wire. "I can't—I've just been called to a consultation. We can't leave. Wait—I'll send Moriarty."

It couldn't be fatal! There was blood on her face but Josephine washed that off and maybe it was just from her nose. She was crying so loud she couldn't be dying—maybe she was mostly scared. Get the clothes off. Sam could only shake and swear.

No one could get here from Mercy so fast but the big Irishman came surging up the stairs, and at sight of Deborah his face cleared instantly. He began to search her bones with gentle, instructed fingers. Restoration flowed along Jo's nerves, and how deft doctors were with children! Dr. Moriarty had actually got Deborah to smiling, though she whimpered whenever he came back to her right shoulder and her ribs.

"Pretty lucky," he said finally. "I don't think the truck hit her. She ran into it and bounced back on her nose. Her guardian angel had her by the hand. Her shoulder will be sore tomorrow, plenty. You'll find bruises here and there. But that's all. Deborah, you play ball on the sidewalk. Next time it rolls in the street, call the cop. You see, you didn't and so you got an accident. Now I can't take you for a ride in my wagon."

"Heavens, did you bring an ambulance?" Josephine said.

"Couldn't leave Mercy if I didn't." He said that Deborah had better go without supper, gave her half a tablet from his kit and a lemon drop from his pocket. "Put her to sleep," he explained. He looked at Sam. "If you've got any whiskey laid away, better take a slug. Take two slugs."

Relief had turned Josephine so weak that when she thanked him she had to lean against the door. He looked at her professionally, seemed about to make a suggestion, looked politely away. "Pete will phone you, I guess. I'm glad there's nothing to report." His candid eyes turned mournful. "Too bad Cy isn't here. Too damn bad. I wouldn't have thought I could miss anyone the way I miss him."

They carried Deborah to her room, heaped her crib with toys, and stood beside it till the drug put her to sleep. Impalpable wings still fanned Josephine softly—death had been near but had passed by. Downstairs, it was suppertime but who wanted to eat? Sam set out some plates, then sat beside Josephine and stroked her cheek. Remember! Remember what it means. Whatever we have never been able to get and won't ever have, nevertheless marriage is living together. Marriage is life against death. Three of us who are one another and at any moment may be destroyed.

Sweet conciliation enveloped her. You can't have the earth. People are what they are. If Sam isn't so much, you're not so much either, and Deborah is safe.

It lasted till Sam remembered the party. Anna had been told to come at nine. It was out of the question! Dancing in a cellar—when of course to dance at the Odeon in Custis would have been provincial. Getting a little tight, talking so superbly, fighting off someone who wanted to take you up to the roof and maul you among the chimneys. She was going to stay home and be grateful about Deborah.

"We're not going," she said.

That set them off. Sam said that she wasn't really sunk by Deborah's accident, she was rationalizing. She said she needed sleep. He declared that she would get more sleep if she were willing to check her righteousness sometimes—he was willing to admit that she sweated self-sacrifice but it would be healthier if she would occasionally purge herself of self-admiration. She wanted to know how this family would get along without self-love—he had made a career of it. . . . And five minutes ago they had been united against death.

"We're going to stay home and take care of our kid."

She picked up the phone but Sam took it away from her. "I'm going to the party. Deborah will sleep straight through it. You can go with me or you can stay here. Do you want to call Anna or don't you?"

That was cracking the whip. The threat was so naked that she could not face it. She said, "Oh, I'll go," and took a bleak satisfaction in being coerced.

They made abashed apologies for the scene. "You've got to

have some fun, darling. Relax. Take a little time off from being grim."

"I know. I was born a virago."

"You're a good-looking virago. Be the belle of Custis tonight."

She put on a long tunic blouse she used to like, remembering that Cy had approved the gold girdle and the long embroidered sleeves. Sure. Remember when Sam could not keep his eyes off you, or his hands, while you were dressing or undressing?

But it proved to be no use—she was spent. Dancing with Sam extinguished what was left of her resentment. Slight tunes like "Pretty Baby" and "Jada" touched her for a moment. But nothing could soften the cavernous, breathless cellar and she was tired out. By eleven o'clock she sought out Sam. He was dancing with Rena. There! If you wanted a symbol of these parties, of this way of living, there was one. The incomplete and the inverted. Still, Cassie was not here, or anyone else to get concerned about.

"I'm out on my feet, Sam. I'm going home. You stay and be joyful."

"All right. Poor kid! I'll be quiet when I come in."

She told Anna she could go, stood in the dark to make sure that Deborah was breathing, undressed, and fell asleep. Then she was awake, thinking apathetically, well, here we go again, here it is, it will pass, I'll be asleep by five o'clock. She pulled the nightgown off her hot body and turned and twisted in breathless dark. The scream of trolley car wheels tore her nerves apart and the waking nightmare closed in. It wasn't a nightmare and it wasn't quite dementia. It was the hour when you met yourself face to face and God gave you no room to turn away.

First you lay there and felt the swollen sac burst. In mercury-vapor light that made their cheeks corpse-like, workmen moved across green windows. Ash-scows moved down the bay to dump char and dead rats and today's abortions. Oil scum and rotted oranges heaved among pilings and a corpse floated in the garbage. People lay awake in this soul's sewage. They slept unrestfully in thousands of apartment houses; then they woke and were unable to escape knowing what truly is. The smell of urinals, rainbows in the oil scum, manic arm rising and falling like part of a machine. People went crazy this way. So much the better. You wouldn't hurt after you got past that point Cy called X and merely went to pieces.

A switch threw her into a more obsessive path. The books were right and the Sunday Schools were right. A betrayed wife was just exactly that and she could stand it no longer. All she had to do in order to be all right—no, not that, but all she had to do in order to be held together in one piece—was to pick up Deborah and walk out. Not Josephine in his hungry arms, not Josephine's body ravished by delight. The image poisoned every ganglion of her mind.

It was get out of here or die. She could get out. She would. She would bully Howe and Bergstein to forty-five a week. The Schurz Street Presbyterian paid her fifteen. But never in the Village. She would need only one room and a closet for a gas plate. Say forty-five a month. But oh, God, for your own sake to do that to a child. Corridors fetid with grease, Deborah growing up among hall toilets, the smell of stale gas. The lurking perverts. She would have to find somebody more intelligent than Anna to stay with Deborah.

Plum blossoms blinding white in Custis vacant lots. Thick cream on cereal. A porch with rambler roses, motes in sunlight in the barn, the sweet clean smell of running water. She had six hundred dollars in the bank. It began to shrink. If I paid everything I owe, I'd be failing to swing this place by nearly fifty a month. There must be a church that will pay me twenty-five.

Hot as the night was, she began to chill. Deborah might have died. She got off the bed and groped upstairs and stood beside the crib to watch the little breast slowly rising and falling in the dark. This flesh and breath and expectation had been formed in her, had taken life from her—to grow up in such a world. Downstairs again, she turned on a light and tried to eat a slice of bread on the theory it would put her to sleep. She could not swallow and went to stand at a window looking down into an areaway so mercifully dark that she could not see the rubbish.

"I told you," she said aloud. "I told you you didn't have the guts to face it."

Back on the bed, she brought her knees up toward her breast. The slimy tide began to ebb. It hurts like hell, doesn't it? Sure it does. Nothing could stop it hurting, ever, except cowardly, dishonorable things.

Dishonor! Her mind hooted. Honor, oh, my God!

Yes, honor. Bring the word back and have the guts to face it square.

So parts of Sam had been left out? Well, was she whole or had she ever been? Something of a tyrant, something of a hag, something of a scold, altogether a shrew. But much worse than this was her unclean will to make him into what she wanted, to make him what she thought he ought to be.

The steel-trap fact was that she could impute no blame or guilt to Sam. Was it his fault if he had to restore himself in his own sight by petty triumphs over women who were softer, kinder, more malleable, more . . . yes, more truly women than she was? Yes, it was his fault, it was wrong as hell. And that was a lie; it wasn't. It was her fault. Why had she not been given softness? She shuddered, remembering that scabrous prescience of Cy's: cut your hair, Jo, and I'll show you how to wrap a bandage that will make you look as if you had no breasts. The Amazons had to cut off a breast in order to be warriors. But not Josephine. There was no need of surgery.

There is only one fault and it's mine. If this marriage has become a filthy cursing, I'm responsible. Be a mature woman, be grown up. Forget the filthy dream of the impossible. Desiring the impossible is what makes failures and fools. Take the marriage in your hands and make of it what is possible. Don't try to shape Sam into something he cannot possibly be. Don't try to shape him.

He wants to be a great man—is that a shameful or a ridiculous desire? He never can be, not possibly—is that his fault? Why don't you help him cherish the pitiful lost, forbidden image of himself?

134

Whatever has happened, however we have hurt each other, we have grown together beyond unraveling. There is no cure for love. We must be humbler than we've been. I must be.

There is no cure for love.

Try to be tender. Try to be kind and gentle. It's his life, it isn't mine. I've tried to tell him what to do with it, and who am I? Stop this idiotic demand for the impossible. Learn, Jo, for the love of God learn.

Peace flowed over her, a gentleness like mother's milk. There is still a chance for us. I'll be decent. I'll be humble. I'll be what I intended to be but haven't ever been. . . . She lay exultant in a no longer hostile night. Love was real and so was hope.

The back of a chair stood out. Dawn had come. She heard a muffled shuffling on the stairs. She called out, "It's all right, Sam, I'm awake. Come up like a conquering elephant, if that's the way you want to come."

"You poor child! Can't you sleep?"

His voice had a tenderness that was like an echo of her own renewal. When he turned on the light, the room was not dreadful at all. He was quiet and compassionate. She sat up hugging her knees. He picked up a blanket from the floor. "It's turned cool," he said. The blanket lay on her shoulders like a caress.

"I wish you could get more sleep. You work too hard, Jo. Isn't there some kind of pill you could take?"

"Sure, but it would be silly. This won't last, Sam. I've got an idea I'm going to get over it completely. And right about now."

"You need a rest." Why, it was true, he really was deeply concerned about her. "Can't you take a week off somewhere?"

"I don't want to."

"Let's all go away somewhere, you and the kid and me. Let's just lie on our backs somewhere in the shade. We'll all get cool and rested."

To have just the three of them alone somewhere, miles from anyone or anything, would drain the last dot of weariness and fear from the last cell of her body. It was impossible for if she stopped working, income would stop. But Sam had proposed it!

"It would be swell—but silly." She smiled. "That's us, swell but silly."

"I worry like hell about you."

"Darling!"

"You're such a good egg, Jo."

"How H. G. Wells, darling."

"Well, it's the right word. I'm not up to you. I never was."

"Stop! Sam, we're a terribly queer pair."

"Half an inch more and we'd be in the booby hatch."

"I read somewhere marriage is godawfully solemn."

"That must have been in the *Times*."

"Sam, marriage has been—well, I've made it pretty harrowing for you."

"You have not. I'm just no good, I'm lowdown. God knows how you've stood me."

"What about you? You honestly thought the Caneday girl would be sweet and pleasant to live with. She turned out to be a hellion."

He laughed. "Give me credit, I never slug you in public."

"You ought to. You ought to slap me down. Honest to God, Sam, you ought to wring my neck."

"Are you trying to make me bawl?"

"Listen, Sam." Here she was and there he was. They were the thing that was real. The only thing. Oh, it would never be complete, there was anguish ahead still, there would be rebellion, straining back and away, and anger and frustration and failure—but with their own hands they could build the future firm. Josephine was soaring up and up toward a light. "Listen, Sam, we're awful fools. Both of us. But I'm the worst fool. And I'm not going to be any longer! It's my fault this marriage has lost a wheel. I ride you. I try to dominate you. I try to make you feel ashamed. Oh, hell, I've spent years trying to give you a guilty feeling that you've let the king's daughter down. And just who am I?"

The shine of tears showed in his eyes. "Why, Jo—"

"No, let me say it. Well, I'm not the king's daughter. I'm just

136

somebody who ought to get slapped down. But I think you're grand."

"You're a darling."

"I'm not. But I'm going to try to be."

He looked unbelieving, frightened, wistful. He said, "Darling!" and took her in his arms, as he ought to have had the wit to do long since. "Jo, you mustn't get ideas about me. They scare me. I'm not up to—"

Ecstatic in capitulation, she wound her arms round his neck, whispering against his cheek. "Darling, when a girl starts to sprinkle ashes on her head, whoop it up. Dive for a potsherd and tell her to start scraping. No, look, Sam, I've come to my senses at last. A lot is ended. For good. You've got to remember I'm dumb, it takes me a long while, but I get there in the end. We've meant a lot to each other—"

"What do you mean, meant? We still do. We mean everything to each other."

"That's what I'm trying to say. Sam, we're young, we've got a swell kid, all our life is ahead of us."

His arms tightened. "Stick by me, Jo. Somebody has to help me through and you're the only one who can. Don't run out on me, no matter how I stink."

"Stupid! Look, don't let me raise hell with you—it raises worse hell with me. Kick me in the pants. Kick the pants right off me."

"I'm crazy about you, Jo."

She could hardly breathe. "Whatever you want to do, that's what I want. I'm just the girl who does what she can to help you out. I don't count except as you count. You're what matters— what you are, what you want to be, what you need. . . ."

So here in the room, with dawn coming on, there was peace. She had broken through her own barrier at last, into peace. Sunday morning. In a few hours she would be singing "O, Lord Most Holy" at Schurz Street Presbyterian. O, Lord Most Holy! With her cheek against Sam's the troubled years were ended and fallen away. I've done you great injury, my dearest, but now we both know it can be healed. The hellish nights were ended. And

137

for this firm foundation those nights and all that tide of pus and death were a small price after all.

Peace. And bedrock. Cheek to cheek and in his arms, and time had come to a full stop while she realized what certainty was like. Then time leaped on again and with it necessity. Her body woke. She shrugged the blanket off her shoulders. She pressed against him and her breasts rose—well, Sam, well, my dearest, and her lips searched his.

He whispered, "You need sleep, Jo."

"I can sleep any time."

"Aren't you singing in the morning?" He moved a little, hesitantly, while her lips burned. An abashed shame, a rueful apology showed in his face. Then he moved away from her, saying desperately, "You're tired out, dear."

The arrow did not reach her heart.

Of course. This sweet contrition of his, this tranquil gentleness, this exquisite concern and humility—why naturally, the poor lamb, he felt that way, all soothed. All night long he had been in bed with Cassie Morton or someone indistinguishable from her, while Josephine lay here and love and anguish wrought their noble reconciliation with fate.

She began to laugh. It was a clean laughter, rising deep down, iron-hard and final. There was no knowing what else it might mean but it had taken from Sam forever all power of hurting her.

"Go to bed, dear," she said when she could manage to speak. "You need sleep. You're tired out."

It took less than six weeks more. Habit ran on and the accustomed jobs and the fear of the unknown. There was some notion that she had better make plans. Careful, detailed plans that would work out. It proved that she could not make plans—and what was the use? The mere passage of days did not matter. Since he could not hurt her, she was under no urge to strike at him. She went about her business. Sam raged, he posed, he suffered, he declaimed, he pleaded. He cursed and wept, he made passes at her, sometimes he tried a tentative kind of rape but lacked character and only made her laugh. She hardly noticed any of it, hardly heard what he was saying, never slept with him again, and didn't give a damn.

The approach of October first made clear that, though she had not decided anything, something was decided and she was going home. Maybe the idea was that at Custis she could sort everything out and foot up the bill, which would take plenty of thinking and plenty of time. She would have to find out what six years of marriage and art and love and motherhood and all that had done to her. And how much she was going to have to pay for it. A safe bet that it would come high.

As it turned out, he beat her into the king row. She told Howe and Bergstein that she was leaving, told the agent she was not renewing the lease, bought tickets to Custis. Maybe that made clear what the six hundred dollars had been meant for all along. She had two days to finish up. She intended to tell Sam the morning of the day her train left. If he happened to be in. If he wasn't, so much the better, one final scene avoided.

The first was Wednesday. On Monday night Sam came in, very firm, very dignified, very important and bucked up. He began to make a speech. He was moving back to the Village, he said. Tonight. Their marriage had been a mistake; he granted it had been one for her too. He might be able to repair that mistake with a freer union, a union based on love and freedom, on the artist's understanding of the artist, on confidence and shared belief. He and Cassie Morton were going to try.

"Why not wait till Wednesday and move Cassie in here?" Josephine said. "Deborah and I are moving out on Wednesday."

He scowled. But that was because an effect he had carefully prepared had been damaged, not because of anything else. So Josephine added, "Or can't Cassie afford this much rent?"

As the train slid through autumn twilight along the Hudson, with naked rock giving a promise of the peaks above Custis, the excited and terribly bewildered Deborah said, "Will there be playgrounds?"

"Sweetie-pie, I don't know what else there will be, but there will be playgrounds. Better ones than you ever saw."

"Mummy, what is it like?"

She did not know, she was afraid to guess. It was never what you thought and Cy had forbidden her to believe in the Enchanted Mesa. But at least it was something else.

"Are we going to see Cy now?"

"We certainly are."

Josephine had done a lot of worrying about Cy, where he fitted in all this, what influence he had had on it, what pattern the months ahead might weave. Now as the train moved smoothly into the twilight and you could see channel lights winking in the river, she found that for Cy also she did not care in the least. She ought to feel something, one way or the other. She ought to have some feeling about Cy, or about Sam, or about Deborah, or about Custis, or about the future, or about the failure of a long effort to live honestly. But she didn't.

# 2

## Custis 1920

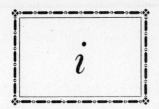

*i*

ONE MORNING in April Cy Kinsman scrubbed as much garage grease as he could from his hands, put on his only respectable jacket, and drove his Ford to the county court house. Josephine's lawyer, who had been in Cy's class at Custis High School, was waiting on the steps. Presently Josephine and her father came and they all went into the District Court. The judge came in and nodded to Asa˙Caneday. The bailiff declared the court in session and called the case of Willard *v.* Willard.

This was the last act, the decree, and it did not take long. The honorable court declared the contract of matrimony existing between Josephine Caneday Willard and Samuel Frederick Willard dissolved and terminated. There was nothing else on the calendar and the judge came off the bench to shake Josephine's hand and chat with his friend Ase. Josephine looked at her lawyer and asked "Is that all?"

She was dressed in clothes which Cy remembered from New York—pleated blue silk skirt, silk jersey jacket, straw hat almost as dark as her hair, dark brown oxfords and stockings. She was fantastically neat and that was still a touch pathological—but she was on the mend.

Ase Caneday and Jo and Cy went out to the worn sandstone steps, to mountain sunlight. They stood looking out down the big bowl-like valley which the Ophir Mountains ringed on three sides. Josephine shook and leaned against her father. Ase patted her shoulder. "It's going to be all right, Josephine. You'll feel a lot better now."

She linked one arm with Ase and the other with Cy. "You've probably missed a class, Dad. We'll drive you to the U."

Asa Caneday no longer wore the sandy handle-bar mustache that Cy remembered. Though the head of the department of geology was gray now, he was still lanky and weathered and tanned. But he was old: the elders had grown old.

They got into the Ford—it was third-hand and five years old— and Cy drove south and east out of Custis, through three miles of foothills to the University. Snow had withdrawn far up the peaks but the bottoms of high gulches would still be glazed with ice. The sun was languorous, precocious spring had brought the box elders to flower, plowed ground smelled rankly fecund.

The U had five times as many students now as when Cy had lived here and three times as many buildings. The medical school which Old Doc Kinsman had bullied out of Cyrus Hockett, the friend for whom he had named his son, now gave a full course instead of the first two years it used to offer. Another multimillionaire was commemorated in a new mining school where, somewhat ill at ease in luxury, Asa Caneday had his office.

Ase got out. "Don't you fret even a little bit, Jo," he said. He looked at Cy, wanted to say something, didn't say it, scowled, and gazed at the peaks. "Snow's all gone from Wildcat ledge— rivers be flooding next week." He slouched away with his hands in his pockets and his shoulders bent. Nobody could miss what he had meant to say: "Guess we'll be hearing about a wedding now." Or perhaps more likely: "Guess we'd better be hearing about a wedding now."

Intense sun beat on the Ford, on the college lawns which it had turned light green, on bright dresses of passing coeds. Cy reached for Josephine's hand, which gripped his hard. "I don't think I'll bawl," she said.

"Want to drive somewhere?"

"Don't you have to repair cars?"

"I work when I want to. I've got some money."

"Bootlegging?"

"Technically, rum-running. No, I haven't needed to drive a load lately."

She wasn't curious, merely idle. "How much does it pay you?"

"Twenty-five dollars a trip."

"Save your money." She slumped lower in the seat, squinting against the sun. "All right, let's ride. I'll have to change."

He drove to the drab old house on Orchard Street. Deborah came racing across the front yard and climbed into the car. She was tanned, tough, and electric. Josephine put out a hand to ward her off: Cy marked the gesture. It had become habitual and Jo supposed he had never noticed it.

"You're going to build a sun porch on my doll's house," Deborah said. She sat on his knees and wrapped her arms round him. She was a demonstrative child.

"I'm going to take you up in the mountains and show you a grizzly. You know what grizzlies do?"

"You can't scare me!"

He set the child on his shoulders and Hattie Caneday came tumbling out of the house to fold Josephine in her plump arms. Hattie too was frayed and gray.

"It's all right, Mother. This isn't the end of the world."

"Of course not. It's a better beginning for you."

Josephine wrinkled her nose at a Christmas card sentiment and went in the house. The steps and porch railing had been bare of paint for years. Inside the house nothing had changed or ever would, except that the walls were a little shabby, the remembered carpets a little threadbare, the pictures silly. The house, like the Canedays, had grown old.

Hattie was studying him, bewildered concern in her face. She was a gentle soul; so was Ase; astonishing how they grew gentle as they grew old. They were puzzled by the complexities of young people, especially their children, who lived in a world they found incomprehensible. They had long since stopped asking Cy why he was not going to practice medicine and be a second Dr. Kinsman in Custis. They no longer asked him much of anything: he was inexplicable.

"Cyrus," Hattie said, "you be good to her."

That exhortation was as near as she would come to the urgency in her mind. Like Ase she could not say, Of course you'll marry her now. Of course you'll make her what restitution you can.

It was easier not to say, "I'll do right by your daughter, Hattie, if I can find out what the right thing is." So he said nothing but only sat on the top step ruffling Deborah's hair and gazing passively into April's golden haze above the foothills.

There was no doubt how, after disbelief and grief, Ase and Hattie had sized up the situation and reconciled themselves to it. When Jo's nerves collapsed it was: She's lucky to have Cy to take care of her. Then, They're in love. Then, That was what went wrong with her marriage—she and Cy fell in love. They've grown up after all, the groping decision would be, and young people's morals are different from those we were taught—we must try not to blame them—we must not hurry them. And always, Everything will be all right when Jo gets her divorce.

They made a fundamental error. There was no affair. Josephine was virgin of him. There would be no marriage. It was just—and Ase and Hattie lacked experience to understand—it was just that two weaknesses had been lucky enough to find support in each other. So much support that it was almost a strength. Almost.

Josephine came back in a khaki shirt, old heavy shoes, a tan blouse. "Are we taking Deborah? Then I'll drive."

"We're taking Deborah. Stop somewhere and I'll buy food." He got cheese and bread and sardines for sandwiches and pop for Deborah. The Ford could be forced up to above thirty miles an hour; at that maximum it shook and heaved and bounced. Cy held Deborah on his knees, sunny air blowing through his mind, and pointed out ducks and magpies and blackbirds with great gold medals on their breasts.

"Mummy, what kind of clothes can I have for school?"

"Good heavens, that's September and this is April. You'll be dressed."

"What kind do you want?" Cy asked. "Pink silk dress with lace on it and a starched petticoat and long silk stockings and patent leather shoes and a veil?"

"Silly! But, oh, gosh, Cy, I want a dress like Susy Blake's."

"We'll fix it so you'll look like Susy Blake. Only no freckles."

Deborah laughed and wound her arms round him and played with his open collar. Josephine said, "It's revolting. She practically tries to seduce you."

"Maybe you don't remember how much school meant to you."

Josephine drove up Custis Canyon, where spring was only beginning. Ophir River was coming into flood. Where Jo stopped, in a meadow fifteen miles up the canyon, it poured in rushing brown swells almost to the rim of its banks. They found a dry patch between cottonwoods and the river, and stretched out in the sun.

"How do you spell seduce?" Deborah asked.

"Never mind."

"S-e-d-u-c-e," Cy said. "It means to make a fuss over people. . . . You've got an educated daughter—don't underestimate her intelligence."

"Are there rattlesnakes here?"

"Of course not."

"Then go pick violets, Debby. Or talk to chipmunks."

"You don't know very much. Cy says no chipmunks till next month."

Josephine murmured, "Pedantic, too," as Deborah obediently trotted off.

Cy watched the child. She was growing up and she was health itself. A bewildered child and she needed Cy Kinsman and her Uncle Andy for obvious reasons but the Enchanted Mesa had worked its miracle on her body. He was keeping a minute record of her development. He turned his gaze to Josephine. "You all right, Jo?"

"I'm all right, Cy."

She thought she wasn't but she was—better than she knew. She was mending rapidly, she had put on a good five pounds in the last month, but it had been a bad time. She had gone to work in November, keeping books in the State Treasurer's office. But within a couple of weeks she had crashed in little bits. Panics swirled up in her without warning and for no cause; a half-dozen phobias clamped icy hands on her; she was agonized and terrified. It was a good old-fashioned nervous crisis, anxiety attack in the patois, and Josephine had never been remotely aware that such things happened. She was most secure with Cy. He had walked her hundreds of miles, mainly at night. Cold weather had made it hard till he thought of snowshoes. It was in order to buy some that he had accepted Art Ricco's offer and driven his first load of liquor from Wyoming. By simply being with her he had pulled her through. Or walking had pulled her through. January was the worst month but soon afterward he knew she had made the turn which she could not believe she ever would make. By now she had no symptoms left except an occasional hour of blind panic, always at night. Cy believed she would lose that one too if she would admit the truth and face it. The truth he was not supposed to know.

They ate lunch and he took Deborah down to the river to toss sticks in it. Then they sat on a boulder above the water and talked about the dolls' house he was always building for her—it was an apartment house by now. Then she yawned and he said, "You get to sleep," and covered her with his jacket in the rear seat of the Ford.

An arm over her eyes, Josephine seemed asleep too, completely inert, her breast a slow rhythm. Black cotton stockings were an indignity to her fine legs and his memory reproduced the intent look on her face at a Fifth Avenue window in blue dusk with a pair of twenty-dollar stockings displayed inside.

Long legs, narrow waist, wide but sloping shoulders. The poets of Twenty-Third Street had talked of a fundamental triangle of beauty, shoulders to pelvis, and of lesser triangles of thighs and breasts and face. They had been reducing beauty to an abstraction. Cy realized that that was what he was doing now. An abstraction is not a woman, an abstracted beauty causes no fear. Well, coming back to the concrete, that added five pounds was a clear gain. Ten more would be ten times as good.

She sat up. "So this is how a marriage ends. I don't feel anything at all."

"You'll be all right."

"So you keep saying. But I never am. On the day of your divorce you ought to feel something. Overjoyed or heartbroken or hopeful or gay or sunk. I don't feel anything."

"You will. In fact you do—you just won't face it. I'll discharge you from the clinic when you realize just how you feel."

She scowled with the ready anger that was now almost exclusively directed at him. She was grateful to him, she could not do without him, and it was clear that she usually resented and frequently hated him. "That will be on doomsday," she said. "Unless we're way past doomsday now."

She took off her blouse and gave her shoulders to the sun. An absurd, wide, constricting brassière, exactly like the ferris waists she put on Deborah. The strong light evoked a luminous tawniness from her skin. How round her arms were.

"Those bones will rise again," he said. "You've got just one more river to cross."

She believed him quite simply. She trusted his judgment altogether. He was the gospel train. "What river is that?"

"If I tell you, you won't cross it."

"When can I get a job?"

"I'll let you know."

Her head went back on her knees and the sun made modulations in the just less than black tones of her hair. After a while, she said accusingly, "But you are practicing medicine."

"No. I'm practicing the clairvoyance we talk about. I've come to know you pretty well."

Jaggedly, "Oh, good God! Stripped naked before you a hundred times and nothing to hide behind—me and my mind and my nastiness and my craziness. You ought to!"

He let that go, watching the shadow of a cottonwood branch moving across a handsbreadth of brown earth to touch her. It was touching her when she said, "Cy, it could be you that pulled the trap under me."

He had faced that one too—was there anything he hadn't faced? He did not believe it. But if it were so, then God help them both for there could be no other help. . . . She stretched out prone, arms at full length ahead of her, to bake them and her shoulders in sun. There was the subdued rushing of the river, the clatter of kingfishers, the smell of the warming earth. Wisdom to take the moment that followed the moment and ask no more.

After a long silence, she said, "Is it true that there's a Mount Caneday?"

"Down in the Snowy Mountains—the Blue Mountains of the Mist of the Throne of God. About a hundred miles from here. The Geological Survey named it for Ase when he was a boy working for their pack train."

"Is it beautiful?"

"The Snowy Mountains are beyond belief. Beautiful as heaven. They're the northern boundary of a forest your brother-in-law saved for the good people."

"I'd like to see it."

Cy smiled. Somewhere else, beyond the farther mountains rimmed with snow, somewhere far off, not Custis, not the Enchanted Mesa, but somewhere it must come true and there must be heartsease. Poor child. But he said, "There's a road there—of a sort. I'll take you sometime."

"On a bootlegger's pay."

"Sure."

Deborah woke up, waved to them, went down to the river and busied herself among the stones. She would get superbly dirty. Her slight figure was black between Cy's eyes and the sun.

Josephine said, "Forty thousand people in Custis. Well, forty thousand people, less maybe as many as four, are dead sure I'm living with you in what is locally called sin."

"The evidence indicates as much. Don't blame people for following the evidence. What bothers you, your reputation?"

"What reputation would that be?"

"That's the answer. We can go on letting our precious souls

150

salve their wounds at any hour of the night the whim comes. We can keep up this—this alliance of the exquisitely dismayed. But the evidence has got to fall where it may."

"My father and mother hate the evidence."

"They'll live through it."

Interesting that her first direct reference had come on the day of her divorce. He got up and went down to the river. He told Deborah that the yellow flecks in some of her lapful of stones were pure gold and she was scornful, informing him that they were pyrites. That would be grandpa. "Well, Butch," he said, "if you've got fourteen stones and I heave eight of them in the water, how many have you got?"

"Twelve."

"Don't be an ignoramus. I thought you wanted to go to school."

"I'm good at reading. Numbers—oh, Cy, are numbers hard?"

"Nothing is hard at school. Work it out, Butch. Count out fourteen stones."

She scowled intently, putting them in a row. "Six!"

"See. It's easy."

The brown flood sliding among great boulders was hypnotic with speed and power. He stood looking at it, a tremendous force barely contained within banks. Could it be swum? He stripped to his shorts and plunged in. A vast brown and tumbling roar fell at him from every direction, hurled him on and up and sideward and down, spun him, buried him—twisting, fighting, thrashing his arms and legs. He pulled himself out by an overhanging willow branch, his lungs frantic. Must be nearly two hundred yards downstream from where he went in. He went twice as far upstream before diving in again. His mind was a single roar except that he was weak. A boulder rushed at him. He got round it with a spasm, was hurled against it, blacked out, reached the bank, lay panting.

Josephine stood over him. "Very bright, Cy. Brilliant. Bandage your leg."

There was blood on it. The hell with it. Lucky not to have cracked some ribs. "Don't think I could do it again."

Deborah was dancing up and down. "Oh, try it, Cy!"

"Just make a theory about it. Get dressed—and out of Deborah's sight, please. What was the idea?"

"Just could I swim it?"

She laughed. "I thought I had a corner on craziness."

He came up to her, reflectively buttoning his shirt. "Must be a critical point with fatigue. Coming back was hard out of all proportion." Deborah had climbed up a lovely gravel slide; she would be all sand, especially her hair. He whistled and she came charging down, well out of control, hurtling into his arms. Josephine gazed at her, lower lip caught between her teeth, expression untranslatable. Cy waited. She did not offer to take the child in her lap. After a while he said, "You drive," and picked up Deborah.

Josephine's face was quiet when they drew up at her house. She said, "It was a good afternoon. Come on, Debby."

"Will I see you tonight?"

"I don't think so. I feel fine."

Eyes untroubled, no tension in her face. She walked toward the house, erect, her hips flat, taking long, lazy steps. If he could hold her to that.

He went home to the barn and worked there for an hour. Wes Kinsman had bequeathed his house to his daughter, and a few years ago, a widow, she had moved back to it to work her life out on the thousands of papers of the genius she had been married to—genius was her word, eccentric fool was Cy's. Polly Kinsman Zeeland was ten years older than Cy and a predestinate old maid in spite of marriage, though it was Cy's unshakable conviction that the marriage had never been consummated. He and Polly had always disliked each other. He had lived in the house for a month when he got back but, like everyone else in Custis, Polly had wanted to run his life and had deplored him grievously. So he had moved to the barn.

Scalpel or mason's trowel, he could use any tool. He had made three rooms downstairs, dividing the big space with wall board.

He had dug a sewer connection and put in sink and shower and toilet, gas range and water heater, from a junk dealer's. He had wired the place and installed a telephone. He brought down some of Doc Kinsman's office furniture and old medical books from the loft where they had gathered dust with old magazines, clothes, lumber. He counted on remodeling that loft too some day.

Meanwhile, his downstairs apartment was a lot better than Paupers' House. He lived there with the sparse, stripped neatness of a man who had been both a soldier and a surgeon. He had an army cot with QM blankets precisely folded on it, and Old Doc's sagging leather sofa. Old chairs spaced in exact order. A desk made out of the grain bin, with various notes and records he made for amusement. A small kitchen with a few pots and dishes, kept immaculate. A few books. In a faint, agreeable smell of horses long dead, he lived where he had so often harnessed them for his father in the morning and unharnessed them late at night when the old man came in from emergency calls. It was a good place. He would never need anything better.

He went downtown and ate at Timmy's Diner. Myrtle Hill, the hard and wholesome girl whose tyranny over cooks gave Timmy's the best food in Custis, was on the morning shift this week, but he talked amiably with her alternate, who was just as hard and much less wholesome. He crossed the street to Lloyd Tanser's Ford Agency and Garage, where he worked for such money as he needed, and talked for a while with the night man. He looked in at various of the town's pool halls and back-street soda fountains that were becoming blind pigs.

A serial penny ante game was going at one of them and he sat in on it for an hour. They called him Cy and Professor and were his friends. He had an amused realization that he was just like Sam Willard's gang, he had seceded from middle-class respectability. These people at Tanser's, at the pool halls, at the blind pigs, extended to him a fellowship that had no reproach in it. Nobody supposed that he had betrayed any ideals. Nobody wanted to shame or evangelize him. Nobody cared a damn. He met plenty of good men whom he had gone to high school with and plenty of strangers who were willing to be friends, to talk, to swap yarns, to make pungent comments on the world and experience. These were the best people. They did not kid themselves. They did not soften life or romanticize it or lie about it. They lived it offhand and to the full. They knew what men and women were, what jobs were, what the world was.

He cashed thirty cents' worth of winnings and offered to buy a drink. "Sure, if you mean it," a railroad brakeman said. "Trouble with you, Cy, you think a drink is just one."

"I'll get drunk with you sometime."

"Do you a hell of a lot of good."

"Let's not do good. Let's just get stewed."

He went back to the barn. He got out a pad and made abstruse mathematical calculations, problems in dependent variables. Granted a car a stated distance behind his, accelerating at a stated ratio to his speed, and granted a stated series of dependent interruptions at stated rates, at what point . . . He had re-discovered mathematics some months ago. It was the perfect art, the perfect skill. He was filling a bookshelf with ever more abstruse texts and treatises.

At eleven-thirty Cy turned in between his army blankets and fell asleep at once. A tapping on the window above his head had him on his feet, completely awake. Josephine was hoarsely whispering, "Cy, Cy! We've got to take a ride."

Once more: another panic. She had lain awake, pondering her manifold impossibilities, and suddenly terror had come swirling up from below the lowest depth where she could probe for it. So as always she had fled to Cy. He dressed, wrapped a blanket round her in the Ford, and drove westward from Custis down the valley. Farmland in deep darkness flowed past them on both sides. Josephine sat rigid and taut, holding fear away from her at arm's length. She didn't have to talk; he had nothing to say. For they had talked all this out so often that there was nothing to be said. There was nothing he could give her except motion, darkness, and his presence and that was just enough and no more. It was not medicine but it was the only treatment possible.

Once she said, "What's that big word about me in bed in the dark?"

"Nyctophobia."

"Fear of the dark. But I don't understand. Cy, we love the dark too, both of us."

"Nyctophilia, then."

"We do. We take the night in our arms and hold it to us. I don't understand. How can you be in love with what you're afraid of? How can you be afraid of what you love?"

Just names. They designate, they don't explain.

Sometime after three o'clock she sagged against his shoulder, asleep, dead to the world. Snap, like a spring broken, then unconscious. He drove back to Custis. He lifted her out of the Ford, carried her up to her room, laid her on her bed without waking her. A white blur at the head of the stairs, a contained but terrible apprehension in the dark.

"She's all right, Mrs. Caneday," he whispered. "She gets scared, then she goes to sleep. She'll be all right."

He went back to the barn and went to sleep.

*ii*

THE CITY of Custis divided in judgment of Cy Kinsman according to what it remembered about him from before 1906, a long time to remember anything. The pillars of society thought of him as the son of Wesley Wales Kinsman and therefore damned him for betraying his father by failing to practice medicine. The greater electorate remembered that he had pitched for Custis High School for three years and had twice helped to bring the state championship home, and therefore thought of him as a servant of the people and granted him full citizenship.

He did not remember Myrtle Hill of Timmy's Diner—she must be seven or eight years younger than he. But Myrtle remembered him as a star athlete, and moreover, seemed to think that he might resume stardom at any moment and sign on with the Custis team of the Intermountain League. That possibility justified and vindicated him in part, but Myrt was disdainful of his labors at Tanser's Garage.

"Here comes Harvard," she might exclaim with cheerful contempt, if it was eight-thirty when he got to breakfast. "Two straight up, Giumetti! Cy, you'd ought to phone me. I'd a-brought you breakfast in bed."

"As you were. I'm on my way to work."

"You mean you're goin' to be kind enough to spend an hour or so at Tanser's, giving the boys the pleasure of your comp'ny."

"I mean I'm a good mechanic, whatever time it is. Ask your boy friend Art."

"Art ain't my boy friend, he's Emmy's." Myrt, efficient, pretty, case-hardened, leaned against the counter and smiled at him skeptically. She was a crusader against dirt and the insect world, the conscience of Timmy's cooks, an expert dissuader of the amorous, and a realist about Cy Kinsman. "You're just an amachure mechanic, and amachures—they don't count. You can't kid me. No and I don't think you're fool enough to try to kid yourself."

Myrt and he had identical philosophies, that the worst thing was to kid yourself. But Cy said that his Greenwich Village friends would call her an economic puritan. Myrt thrust out an excellently formed, supercilious shoulder and hip and asked what that meant at Harvard. "You think God said we must labor and the man who doesn't is committing sin. That's screwy. Work for what you need."

"Sure. See if you can cheat the time clock."

She was wrong. None of Tanser's regular mechanics was any better than he, not Tomcat Jones or Art Ricco or Joe Bates, who was the head one. They might call him Wonder Boy or Professor but that was only a democratic scrupulousness to scale down Harvard. They liked him but what was more important, they respected his work. No mechanic's tool could throw him; wrenches and dies were as docile in his hands as a scalpel. Perhaps he lacked something as a diagnostician of motor ills but his operating technique was faultless.

But Tomcat Jones cautioned him, "Might as well save your time, Cy. You can't get to first base with Myrt. We've all tried. No soap."

Cy explained that he wasn't trying and presently had to explain as much to Myrt. He came into Timmy's one midnight when she was on the night shift and found the place deserted except for her and a drunken printer from the *Sentinel* who had her backed in a corner with the most explicit intention. As Cy entered the printer was pinioning her right arm, which was futilely swinging an ice pick. There was a moment of action, Cy grabbing him by the collar and putting a gratifying slug on his jaw, but the printer was drunk after all and went away fast.

Myrt was already calling through the hatch, "All right, Pazareskis, you can come out. He won't bark at you. . . . That damn Greek! Are all cooks yellow?"

"Why didn't you yell for a cop?"

"I hate cops!" she said with inexplicable fierceness. "Yeah, and I'd ought to have sense enough not to get caught in a corner when the place is empty. If I'm dumb enough to, it's up to me to fight it out. Coffee, Cy?"

He sat drinking it till her relief came in, then offered to drive her home. She lived near the river with her parents and her younger sister Emmy, whom Art Ricco was diligently trying either to make or to marry and Cy could not tell which. On the way they passed Dreamland, a dance hall. "Couple of dances before they close?" he suggested.

"Not tonight."

"Well, shall we tomorrow?"

"Sure," she said. Then, "It won't do you any good, Cy, if that's what's on your mind."

"Nothing's on my mind except I know you like to dance. So do I."

"Okay. But I've seen you there. With chippies. I know a chippie when I see one."

"It doesn't follow any farther than that. But you take it for granted I'm a bum, don't you?"

"It ain't any of my business. You're a good guy."

"Still, I'm not worth hellroom."

"It ain't my business, Cy."

"What do you think I ought to be doing?"

"I wouldn't say you're a bum," Myrt said with admirable detachment. "Same time, if I was Lloyd or Tomcat, I might take a poke at you some day. They got a job to do. You just drop in on a job. I don't like chippies, they're amachure. I don't have to like any amachure. So long. Tomorrow night if you say so."

Myrt got out of the Ford, leaving a faint fragrance of soap. He decided that she ought to belong to the Home Culture Club of Custis which had identical ideas, especially about Cy Kinsman.

She did not make him mad. The astonishing thing was that, whereas everybody used to make him mad, now nobody could except Josephine. He spent an hour at Dreamland with Myrt the next night after she got off. They danced well, with unexpected satisfaction. She was a good girl; she made her way without favors; nothing dismayed her, nothing got her down. Adequate for whatever she might be called on to meet.

But he would damned well do as he saw fit.

Sandy McAllister's writ did not run in Custis. Late last summer a letter reached the hospital which Wes Kinsman had founded, saying that though Dr. Alexander McAllister wished to stand in no man's way, he was obliged to report that Cyrus Kinsman had had to be discharged from Mercy. Old Frank Bramwell, once a protégé of Wes and now the head of that hospital, replied formally. He replied that Dr. Kinsman could join his staff whenever he might want to.

It had taken them all fall to believe that he was not going to, that there would not be a second Dr. Kinsman in Custis. Dr. Bramwell kept urging him to submit to a mere formality and take a State license. He patiently repeated his invitation to join the staff. He sometimes asked Cy to consult with him. Cy refused as courteously as might be. Just as courteously he refused people he had known fourteen years ago who wanted to become his patients—wanted to consult a Dr. Kinsman again at last. Then there was Josephine's brother-in-law, Nancy's husband, the Congressman. In Custis for Christmas, he undertook to straighten out Cy's difficulties. The State Board of Health, the Public Health Service, the new Veterans' Bureau, various other government departments needed trained medical men. He was even more tiresome than Nancy, who proved to be as fat as Jo had said, and was a Washington bridge player out of Custis with no mind at all, and so sweet you nearly died of it. Cy ended by being rude to the Congressman, as he didn't have to be with anyone else, and the Congressman decided that he was a fool.

Most did. Old Doc Kinsman seemed to fill Custis and the world. His friends would not let Cy alone, bewildered by him or reasoning with him or swearing at him, till it was easier not to accept their invitations to dinner and to avoid their public haunts in favor of the blind pigs. When it dawned on them that he wasn't going to practice, one of them offered him a job at a department store and old Metz of the white mustache creaked up two hundred miles from the range country to make him a cattleman. Bewilderment turned to resentment and little tales about Cy's eccentricity began to circulate. Shortly after Josephine returned they began to be tinged with scandal. They would go all the way if anyone learned about the rum-running.

That was simple and infrequent. There appeared to be a distillery in Wyoming that had not been closed, was operating under protection, or had not heard it was illegal. Its product was probably bound eventually for Denver or Salt Lake City or Butte. Cy didn't know; neither did Art Ricco, who had dealt him in. Half a dozen times Cy had gone there by train, reported to a garage outside of town a little after dark, and driven a medium-sized truck all night to Custis, leaving it at a warehouse whence presumably it was taken elsewhere the next night. Twenty-five dollars, a simple enough night's work, and no bother. Josephine, who had wormed it out of him, talked as if it happened every day.

He found one supporter in the old Custis, however. Gideon Huntoon appeared in Custis—heavier, his hair graying, but still powerful, still Gid Huntoon. Gid had always operated mysteriously, a smart man, a man so smart that his activities were a little suspect, and he was some kind of contractor doing something very profitable at a big Nevada dam. His room at the shiny new hotel was filled with excellent liquor—and here was one man who was glad to see Cy Kinsman. They ate dinner to an accompaniment of ducks and grouse and quail shot long ago, and the evening moved on to the larger fauna, Gid Huntoon's innumerable elk, bighorn, pumas, bears. He had a head of iron: Cy, drinking freely for the first time in Custis, presently had to abandon hope of keeping up with him. Old Doc Kinsman was in and out of the talk but with a difference; Gid was not beating Cy over the head with him, he was just Gid's great man and that was all.

Finally, Gid rumbled, "What's all this hell about you, Cy?"

"What hell, Gid?"

"You know damn well. Town's prophesyin' against you. You run off with the payroll. You pack too long a rope. Your cows seem to run to twins."

"I didn't know I was mavericking. I thought I was just a maverick." The wary readiness that he needed among these people rose up through his drinks.

But he didn't need it after all. Gid said, "You want a job, Cy?"

"No thanks, Gid. I'm satisfied."

Gid downed three ounces of rye, said "Whuff!" courteously, sweated a little at the forehead, and added, "Well, if you do, I got plenty. I got any job you want. Just let me know."

"I will, Gid."

"You ain't going to set up in the doctoring business?"

"No."

Gid nodded, and after a while Cy understood that that was that. It was all right with Gid; he was not shocked or protesting or pitying. Presently he said, "Old Doc's son, he can have anything I got. But Old Doc, he hung up his saddle a long time ago. You play 'em the way you see 'em, Cy."

Gid Huntoon had voted and there came into the pleasant alcoholic haze a kind of gratitude. Soon their voices joined in song and then Cy was remembering their blizzard. It was hard to untangle from Gid's infinite reminiscences but he eventually arrived at it. He'd thought they were headin' for the big jump, he said. Been a little uneasy, havin' a kid with him. Come out all right.

"You want to shoot some ducks this fall, Cy? Or I got a ranch down in the Snowy Peaks country. Let's go somewhere and shoot anything. My God, Cy, I never get a chance to enjoy myself no more. I'm a God-damn businessman. All I can do to stay out of the legislature."

There had never been a time when Gid didn't have a good

hunk of the legislature in his pocket. "I'll go hunting with you, Gid."

"Damn it, when?"

"Sometime. I've got something to do first."

"What's that, Cy?"

"Damn if I know."

"Trouble with you," Gid complained. "You're a moderate man. I must of never taught you how to drink."

"I'll get drunk with you too, sometime."

If he did, he thought hazily, it would be a good one. But this was a good evening. There had come into it something of the ease of that little shack beside the stormy water and the potbellied stove red to the damper in the pipe. He left late, Gid still sweating at the forehead but otherwise untouched, shaking his hand and soliciting him to go hunting.

But then Gid Huntoon had always been something of a dissenter in Custis; as he would have said, he liked to swing his own loop, and the final judgment was passed by Hayes Sargent. All his children had been Cy's friends, as he himself had been Wes Kinsman's; he had been the governor of the state and he would be nominated for the United States Senate this summer. More patiently than anyone else he kept asking Cy to dinner, to Sunday breakfast, to evenings at the Custis Club. He was studying a phenomenon and refusing to make up his mind. But about the time of Josephine's divorce he came to the barn one night to have it out.

"Look here, Cy, some of us are entitled to get an answer from you. As Wes Kinsman's son, you're not just anybody. A lot of Custis money went into your education."

There was this change from Mercy: there he had assumed that nobody had the privilege of rebuking him. Well, a further difference, that when someone did it had once made him mad. Now it just made him obstinate. "It was the old man's money, Mr. Sargent."

"He earned it—oh, yes, Lord! Fifty times more than he was ever paid. But it came from Custis."

162

Cy said carefully, "I spent four years at Harvard Medical School. A year as an intern and part of a year as senior intern at Peter Bent Brigham. Nearly a year in the British Army, a year and a half in the AEF, nine months at Mercy Hospital. I did that, Mr. Sargent. It was me—that was my time, it was me that got tired, nobody else had that grind. Nobody ever said I skimped or dodged any of it. Nobody ever said I did it badly. Okay. That was what I chose to do. Now I choose to do something else. I can't see it's anybody's business but mine."

"Well over nine years," Hayes Sargent counted up. "Nine years ought to be enough to produce quite a useful instrument, I'd think. So! You did the work, it was your father's money that paid for it, and now if you want to throw the instrument away, we can keep our mouths shut. Is that it?"

Cy nodded. "That's about it."

"He was a good-sized man, Doc was. He brought my kids into the world, kept them alive, saved my wife's life, saw my parents out of the world. All over the state there are hundreds of people that he did the same for—and a lot more. Wes liked a good cigar, a good shot of whiskey, a mug of cool beer. He liked to hunt, fish, fork a good horse. Liked to sit around Mahoney's saloon and swap lies with his friends."

"Well?" Cy said, when the pause lengthened out.

"Well, he was quite a chunk of man. Life burned pretty high in him. Life never got too strong for him and he was never too fine for it. Well—" Hayes Sargent repeated, "I don't know what turned soft in you, Cy. Too much sulphur in the iron. Brittle, maybe, maybe just yellow—I can't pretend to know. But as a friend of Wes Kinsman I say he'd boot you out. But not till he'd beaten your ears off. I'm glad he's dead."

"Sorry. I don't know how to speak the language, Mr. Sargent."

It was the language of the poltergeist of Mercy Hospital, the old man with a beard, and it no longer disturbed Cy. His final defiance of Sandy McAllister had paid off some ancient and uncomprehended grudge. It had freed him: he was free. He was under no obligation to probe deeper than that. He had a sunny and peaceful mind.

A single strand still bound him to medicine, Rulon Williams. Williams had been with Cy at Custis High, the class of Naughty-Six they called themselves in that innocent morning. He had taken the Cyrus Hockett Medical School's two years and finished his course at Nebraska. Now he had the growing practice which Josephine and her parents and the whole town thought Cy ought to have. Glistening office equipment practically paid for by now, studious habits, expectation of growing old honorably. Cy's training impressed him and Cy would sometimes sit talking with him. He was free to talk medicine with Williams as he was with no one else. He read Williams's journals and used his equipment for his aimless records of Deborah Willard. After a while Williams stopped asking him about his cases and inviting him to consultations. He got the idea: Cy would talk, he would do no more. He didn't understand but fortunately he didn't feel called on to understand.

In spring twilight Deborah came to the barn—with bare feet in sneakers and a coat over her nightgown. "Look, Cy," she said too eagerly, "I made you a dish towel."

She had—out of a piece of green cloth, hemmed unevenly with gigantic stitches. Cy received it gratefully, and she beamed, then her face clouded because he said, "Look, Butch, you're supposed to be in bed, aren't you?"

"No!"

"Yes?"

"Mummy should have let me come! Cy, don't be mad!"

He phoned Josephine. "If you haven't missed your daughter, she's here. I'll bring her home." He drove to Orchard Street, one arm round Deborah. "Anyway, it was bright to put on that coat. Next time get dressed. We can't run round town in a nightshirt."

"Cy, when are we going to see Daddy?"

That was it: the gnawing fear. "Debby," he said, "it's just that way. You've just got to take it. You'll see Daddy sometimes. I don't know when. But we all had to start over. Daddy and

Mummy and you. It's tough but lots of things are tough. I promise you, you'll see him sometimes."

She wound both arms tight round his and rubbed her cheek on his sleeve. Probably crying, and no help for it. Josephine came out of the kitchen where she had been helping Hattie with the dinner dishes. "All right," she said quietly. "I said no. So the dolls' house gets locked up all day tomorrow."

Deborah whimpered. Cy said, "Don't bawl, Butch. You asked for it. You weren't supposed to come tonight and you did. So you get punished."

"Put me to bed, Cy!"

Josephine scowled but he put her to bed, sat beside her, told her another chapter of a serial story. He told stories badly but that was what she wanted and who was he not to try? He came downstairs and Josephine had finished the dishes.

"Aren't you sorry you didn't bear her?" she asked sullenly. "Then you'd have a monopoly. Did she give you that idiotic dish towel? She spent all afternoon making it."

"Well, who made my curtains?" Josephine reddened, for she had made them—they were part of that submerged situation, part of the bad time. "She's worried about Sam. She can't make sense of it."

"So she runs to you." Cy grinned at her and this time she blushed fierily. Then she said, "What I mean to you is that I'm her mother. Exactly that and not a damned thing more."

That was one to carry away from the Caneday house, to an evening of quiet pleasure in the Custis underworld. And it was in the pattern. Whatever conflicts had been solved, the central conflict went on intensifying.

At the garage he prepared to install a new set of bands in a Ford. Art Ricco turned from the bench where he was dissecting a carburetor and thought it was time to needle him a little. "You ain't going to use a wrench on that, Cy. Not a Harvard mechanic. I'd of thought you'd just feel them in with one hand."

Cy laughed. "You mean a mechanic thinks with his fingers. Well, what would you call good time for a band job?"

"Oh?" softly. Art calculated in silence. Then, seductively, "Would you say you can do it in twelve minutes?"

"Left-handed. Make it ten minutes."

"For five dollars?"

"Ten minutes by your watch."

Art fished in his pocket for a greasy, creased bill, and called, "Gang! I got a sucker." He put back the floor boards Cy had taken out. "From scratch, Harvard."

"That's right, never give the sucker an even break."

But Lloyd Tanser was in the office door. "Cy! Telephone."

It was Josephine, much agitated. "Cy, the little Blake girl next door that plays with Debby. She's having a convulsion."

"Easy. Walk down to the corner, count fifty, and come back."

"You get here as fast as you can."

"Call Rulon Williams if you want. He'll be careful not to hurry. That's standard practice. If the doctor doesn't hurry the convulsion is over when he gets there."

"I want you. I want you right away."

"Sure, it looks scary but it isn't. It's just something the kid ate. If you've got to take action to be happy, run a tub full of warm water and put her in it."

"You mean you won't come?"

"Call a doctor."

He hung up and went back to the floor. Art Ricco said, "You wouldn't run out on a bet, Professor?" He explained the terms to Lloyd and Tomcat Jones and Joe Bates.

"Ten minutes? Can't be done," Joe said.

Lloyd Tanser asked, "Can you do it, Cy?"

"Certainly."

"Okay, I'll fade anyone." Two more five dollar bills were tossed on Art's bench. "Now you're working for me twice." Lloyd took out his watch.

It was simply a question of digital deftness. If you let a nut fall off while coaxing the bands over the drum, it would run to three hours. You had to work fast but you had to be sure. There was no question. In two seconds more than nine minutes Cy picked up the bills, gave two of them to Lloyd, and thrust the others in his pocket. "The pancreas can be sewn if you know how."

"Yeah?" Lloyd admonished his crew. "Don't let the union know I got a mechanic—maybe I can begin to show a profit. Let Lonny run the pumps. I'll buy coffee."

The five of them filed across the street. "My God, the working man," Myrt Hill said and ostentatiously bolted the gate that led behind the counter. "If you can't keep 'em busy, Lloyd, lend me a couple to clean up the kitchen. You boys made a dime or what?"

"I got a dollar, Myrt," Tomcat said.

"Your wife holding out on you?"

They roared and Lloyd said, "Somebody thought it would be a nice idea to learn Cy how to fix a car. He win."

Myrt drew five coffees and spread them out on the counter. "Cy?" She tossed her head. "Oh, him."

She thrust a disdainful hip at Cy. He reached over and pinched it. At once she slapped his face amiably and so hard that his ears rang. "Good God, Myrt, what do you weigh in at?"

The delegation roared and Tomcat said, "Myrt means, not in business hours."

Myrt leaned on the counter, smiling disdainfully. "I sure like to have you comics come in. Seems to me ever since I was thirteen and comin' home from Mass there you been smokin' cigarettes behind a billboard just like a man and rushin' out to whistle at girls. Honest to God, ain't none of you had any luck with a girl yet?"

"No hits, no runs, one error," Art Ricco said.

**iii**

LET THE heart's desire remain just that, for if you get it you will be lost. Josephine could come that close to understanding what had happened in Custis when she fled there from Twenty-Third Street toward the desperately desired. And no closer.

If there had been a chance that after seven years of absence she could resume her place among her old friends, the phobias that erupted when she fell ill destroyed it. The girls she had played with as a child and giggled with as an adolescent and walked arm and arm with at Custis High School were the young wives now. She had lost intimacy; she was an outsider. She was trying to master their houses and living room sets and husbands and children and gossip and contract bridge when the hurricane struck. At once they became hostiles. They were arrayed against her and at any cost she must keep them from seeing through the surface to the welter of madness inside her.

"I run out of names," Cy said when she repeatedly demanded an explanation. "They're nice, pretty names—take your choice. Agoraphobia—you don't want to get away from home. Xenophobia—you'll be damned if you like strangers. What does it matter? It's very mild. It's the last day of a head cold."

He was wrong on every point. It was that she could not stand their pity and would not stand their curiosity. Her sole treasure now was to be left alone. And they became leprous when they began to work Cy into their picture. What friendship needed to be perfect was a touch of the salacious, and what a time they must have exciting one another with this flagrant liaison. They must support a normal number of surreptitious adulteries themselves but here was one that advertised. And what gave the protagonist's anger its final edge was her knowledge of the facts.

At least Cy was right about her not wanting to get away from home. If she had a fortress it must be on Orchard Street—and that in the face of innumerable irritations. Her family did not understand what had happened to her any better than her friends did, any better than she did. She bewildered them, shocked them, frightened them, defeated them—but they accepted her.

Betty had died six years ago. Nancy, when she came home at Christmas, proved to be slow poison sweetened with saccharine. She pried and plumbed with inexhaustible curiosity, wanted to make Josephine's life over, had a mind like a kewpie, and had been elected to heaven with a unanimous vote because she had married a man and borne children. It was Josephine's sacred duty for the vindication of human personality to find strength enough to quarrel with her—at a time when she had no strength for anything.

"Stop being a warmhearted, understanding little woman!" Josephine banged down one of the teacups from a Washington shop whose name nothing could have restrained Nancy from telling you. "I don't want to be understood. If there's one thing I can stand less than a little woman it's a woman who thinks she's a little woman."

Nothing could penetrate Nancy's iron sweetness. She had run woman's race and carried off the palm. She understood life and men. She understood women and Washington and the great world and diets for children. "You didn't used to be difficult, Jo."

"I was always difficult. We call it self-defense."

"You can't expect to see yourself clearly when you're discouraged and unhappy and unwell, can you, really? But we have to make something of life even when we've been hurt." And a Congressman's wife meets people from all over the world. People so interesting, people who do things.

"I bet you got that from a good book." Josephine went home

to rage at Hattie, "Have I got to let Nancy win her U regretting that I'm not married any more but look, Jo, tomorrow's sun will surely rise?"

Hattie said, "Well, Nancy married Phil Corse," straight-faced, and made Jo look at her, then giggle. Hattie was wholesome and unworldly and uncomplicated, but after all she had raised a family that included Nancy.

"God help the United States. How can we trust it to a man who didn't strangle her within six months?"

Her older brother Chuck had stayed in the army as a major of engineers. Her younger brother Andy, a junior at the U, lived at home and voted Jo's way. He was so college boy that he amounted to a cartoon, with his fraternity affairs, his corduroy trousers, his flip and invincible absurdities. But Deborah delighted him and he liked Josephine, even in a way seemed proud of her. She must seem as old as a great-aunt but he kidded her like an equal, professed to find her an attractive wench, took her to movies when she could muster the courage to go, even took her to a fraternity dance. She made a dress for the dance, from a remnant in Hattie's attic, and whether or not Andy was driving them with a whip the brothers were attentive. It was an evening with fear withdrawn, which was all she asked of any evening now, and even a faint satisfaction in lively tunes and healthy adolescents.

"You laid them out—Beta is yours," Andy reported. "Must be the sophistication of the big city. That or the legs."

"The trouble with the young is, you can see it coming from so far away."

"Want to tackle the faculty? Maybe you could get me a mark in my French."

She had grown wholly beyond the understanding of Ase and Hattie. Her illness frightened them and her divorce shocked them very deeply. They had no way of comprehending the ambiguities that tortured her. And none of this mattered at all for she was in trouble and they loved her. Their most admirable restraint was in regard to Cy. They hated the situation altogether and yet if that was what Josephine needed, then that was what they wanted her to have. They could not quite manage an equal restraint about her marriage and divorce. They had never seen Sam, never seen Twenty-Third Street, knew nothing about the way of life, could not begin to picture it to themselves. And she had no words that could explain it.

"I had one child, I couldn't manage two." But that explained nothing for Hattie knew that men were weak and wives were to uphold them, men were children and wives were to take them by their little hands. Furiously, "It was forcing me to be something I couldn't possibly be—I had to get out of it." But that also was just words, and the obvious comment was that the fears and discontents and frustrations she had fallen into at home made no better bed to lie on than the marriage bed she had forsaken. She always ended with "He was sleeping with everyone and I decided not to take it any more," and that came close to being an acceptable explanation. Except that you could see it wake in both Ase and Hattie the question they still charitably repressed: what was she doing now?

But Hattie was overjoyed to have another child to raise and Josephine gratefully relinquished Deborah to her. At least that much of the dream on Twenty-Third Street had come true: Custis was right for Deborah and there was no stay to Hattie's love.

"If you don't mind spoiling her it's all right with me," Josephine said. "Of course you'll give her the idea she's a princess. She isn't."

Hattie's gentle smile. "When I remember how I used to beat you."

"Oh God, and look what came of it."

"Don't you think the baby needs to have a fuss made over her? She hasn't got any father."

"Who said she hasn't?" Jo flared. "She's a foster child. You're her mother and Cy's her father."

"Cyrus is awful nice to her. . . . You don't have to lock her door at night, Josephine. She won't go to his place any more unless you say she can. What if she woke up and found she was locked in?"

Ghastly cold struck inward: Hattie was not supposed to know that! No one was supposed to know. "I don't know why I did. I couldn't have been thinking."

Hattie sighed, holding her peace. No go! Hattie knew that she locked that door every night when she went to bed and unlocked it as soon as she got up. Oh, shameful!—and she was truly ashamed. But she was more afraid.

But with the world terrible and strange home was a kind of tent within which she had worked out something neither precarious nor, quite, trivial. She took most of the work off Hattie's shoulders and made the shabby old house glisten. (Cy had a long word that meant fear of dirt and said that her dusting and scouring and polishing were part of the picture—but she noticed that he kept his barn spotless and that he brought his tools to Orchard Street and made the repairs she demanded.) She cooked Ase the roasts and hot breads and pastries he could not get enough of and won him to salads, which were hardly in the Western cuisine. She knew Ase for a man of strong will and strong ideas but he kept them off her; he was proud of her and kind. And she had always the sight of Deborah—the big yard, the trees, the swing Cy had made for her, the multitudes of neighbors' children, cleanness and quiet and health. Josephine's own childhood certainties repeated for her daughter. Josephine was as far as ever from understanding what had happened to her but there came to be periods of quiet that seemed almost or quite real. Evenings with Ase smoking and reading one of his innumerable reports or studying his innumerable maps, Hattie sewing and supplying amiable arpeggios of talk, Josephine content with the simple absence of pressure or fear. Or late afternoons when the scent of mulberries came through the window and she sat at Nancy's old piano and played and sang for no reason except that she wanted to.

"Sure," she remarked to Cy, "but it's slack, it's a kind of drift. I suppose I should be glad to just drift. But it's dangerous."

"Why?"

"I've got to get a job! Look, the sugar company would hire me to run a comptometer. There are a dozen things I could do at the capitol."

"Not yet."

"Well, when?"

"I'll let you know. Why do you want a job?"

"The family is entitled not to have two people dumped on them," she said. "Ase is only two or three years short of retiring. He's old, Cy, he's tired—and God knows a professor at a Rocky Mountain college can't afford Deborah and me. He's entitled to be left alone!"

"Been complaining, has he?"

"What chance has he got? A family has to take you in. Crippled or drunk or worthless, you're the folks."

"You'll get a job. You'll look any man in the eye—or whatever that urge is. But of course you're lying. That isn't why you want a job."

"Well, Svengali, why do I want a job?" Cy merely grinned. She didn't, or wouldn't, know what he meant. Half the time she didn't understand what he meant—and all the time, of course, she didn't understand the one important thing about him. She said heavily, "I could stand it if you knew less about me."

But he knew all about her. And when you told the truth it was Cy, not her home, that was the fortress—except that the fortress was also the dungeon and the peril. Know her? Through those worst weeks she had poured out all the cowardice, all the cravenness, all the nastiness and idiocy and pettiness, all the fear. Those hundreds of miles at night, those hours in his barn, the whirl and falling away. When had she needed him that he hadn't been at hand, and what if he had not been? Half of her was gratitude absolute and illimitable—and yet somehow dark, on the edge of evil as if gratitude itself were shameful. Probably he had saved her life and certainly he had saved her sanity—and therefore rejoice! Except that he had earned not only her gratitude but her enmity too and it went quite as deep. They were the rock in the darkness, they were friends to the foundation of the world—and they had been made into adversaries.

But most of the crazy fears and drives were gone. All of them

173

. . . all of them except . . . but gone. She could laugh at the trivial vestiges. It was true that she would catch herself scrubbing a floor or a window with an ardor that was absurd. Or washing her clothes. Or herself. And could stand back and smile—sure, Jo, you really are immaculate, you aren't soiled at all, how pure! And she kept coming abruptly to and finding that she had been staring in a mirror—and that one had begun long before, in New York. Eager to make sure you're all there? Well, with justified satisfaction, fresh from a bath in which she had scrubbed herself quite probably clean, standing in front of a mirror with a studious scrutiny, she was all there. And come right down to it, was the scrutiny silly or the view distasteful? Few would be depressed and had not a lot of Chelsea artists asked her to pose? But assure yourself you're womanhood's fully opened flower, your thin-flanked sinuosity drives men mad, you're Deirdre Caneday, Faustine Willard, "curled lips long since half-kissed away, still sweet and keen" and let's not bring the crude facts in for that would require you to put on some more weight, wouldn't it? and get a somewhat better record than the book shows.

In soft spring evening Andy's voice floated in from his window at the far end of the ell. "A nice eyeful, sis. But get thrifty. You should sell tickets."

She slipped into a wrapper and sat at her own window. "Look, Casanova, I've given you baths in a wash basin. Nudity just isn't news in the Caneday house. Besides, lambie, you won't have to be a Peeping Tom much longer. You're growing up, you're bound to find out all about the female figure."

"Why, Toots, I was lost in admiration. I just wondered why the long stare in the mirror." He intended to be a hundred per cent imp but was shooting too close to the truth. "Lost your self-confidence, Jo? Can't you bring in your man?"

Andy's variation on the family assumption was more realistic. Damn it, I haven't tried. I don't intend to. You're right, I couldn't. She was furious—being furious was her metier. She repressed it. "Grown-ups never tick the way adolescents get all hot thinking they do."

174

"Honest? College girls hold their men, anyway. What about the Railroad Avenue floosies I see in your half of Cy's Ford?"

He was too young and too innocent and too irresponsible an idiot to guess that would double her up from two directions at once. Sam and Cy, Cy and Sam, this is the way we grind our meal so early in the morning. She didn't own any part of Cy's Ford. Nor had she ever supposed, simply because Cy treated her with a considerate impersonality that raised Plato to an all-time high, that garage mechanics led ascetic lives. That was just one thing, out of ten million things, that she smouldered with, waking late at night and thinking across Custis and the years and the great gulf and wondering what Cy was doing.

"Don't bring your juicy stories to me!" she said, in flames. "Trade them with the other boys back of the barn."

Andy whistled. "Did that get a rise!" He went youthfully solemn. "Jo, say the word and I'll beat his brains out with a base-ball bat." Then, recovering, "Get out your forty-four and go root-a-toot."

Andy was simplifying the contradictions, which was a bad mistake. She owed Cy everything. And part of what she owed him was a fee for destroying her basic beliefs about life and what people were supposed to make of it.

One evening he brought his scuffed bag of instruments, as he did every so often, and went over her again, very minutely. And made her mad again, as when didn't he sooner or later? She had the fascination of a cadaver for him. Well, Jo, don't you keep wanting him to practice medicine? Remember, the Doctor is not making a pass, he's taking a reflex.

He put away his stethoscope, blood-pressure gadget, ophthalmoscope, the whole outfit—slowly, thinking over the data. She noticed for the first time that the months since Mercy had done some sculpturing on his face. It was less massive. It was refined a little, more in drawing.

"Look up an agreeable convalescent home," he said. "I gave your blood the works at Williams's office—it would do credit to a prize beef. You've put on twelve pounds since the first of

January. Your interior sounds like a tone poem. Your reflexes are as good as Deborah's. Drop you off a cliff and you wouldn't dent."

"You mean you're not going to work out on me with hammers any more? God is good. So now I can go to work."

"How about your night terror?"

Oh, God, he hadn't made it plural—and must know. "See?" he said. "The doctor will tell you when."

"All right, there's this, then." She prepared to be masterful. "Mother is badly scared. Yesterday she found a lump in her breast and it hurts."

He overbid her by making no fuss at all. "Only yesterday? Let's take a look at it."

The demonstration of how everybody had stopped thinking of Cy as a doctor was that Hattie was abashed, reluctant to be examined. "Don't be silly, Mother," Josephine said. "He's got to look at it, hasn't he?"

And at once she was too angry to be worried about her mother for Dr. Kinsman was here from Mercy Hospital. The rightness existed before her eyes, the old sense of harmony, the admiration that flowed from the well of life, and in five minutes he would be lying about it.

Cy said, "You must not take my word for it, Mrs. Caneday. Go see Rulon Williams or Dr. Bramwell. But this is one of the easiest diagnoses in medicine. There's nothing whatever to be afraid of. You've got cystic mastitis and it's absolutely harmless."

Hattie was pale and shaking. She cried a little. As if hope were coming back. How many had felt so at Cy's word? "What is that, Cyrus?"

"Exactly what your bright girl told me it was, a lump in the breast. Not cancer. Not possibly cancer. That's what you were afraid of."

"You're sure, Cy?" Josephine asked, and at last she could forget about being mad at him and share some measure of her mother's anxiety and relief.

"We get fourth-year medics so they're sure."

"But I thought—at mother's age—why so suddenly, just in one day?"

"Any age. Any day—there has to be a first time you feel it. Any moment there may be one in your breast. Or both breasts. You don't even have to have nursed a baby."

"You're pretty positive."

Cy exploded in a rough, uncalled-for laugh. "This is one you really can think out with your fingers. The minute you touch it you know it isn't any of the things to be afraid of. It just happens in a breast and the brightest thinkers don't know why."

Hattie got her corset cover and shirtwaist back on. She lay back in a chair and closed her eyes and cried some more. She stood up and put an arm around Cy and kissed his cheek. "Thank you, Cyrus."

"Go see a doctor," he said. "There isn't any doubt but go see one so you'll know. Of course if you're superstitious about it, he'll take it out. It's a minor operation. Lay you up for a week or a little more."

Josephine went out with him. He tossed his bag of instruments in his Ford. It was walking tonight, then, not driving—and wouldn't it be interesting to know what made the choice, for certainly neither she nor Cy did, something just determined it. They did not even determine they were going to spend an evening together. They just automatically did so. They were a kind of automatism. Press the button and the bell rings. A plus B equals C. The inventions of the Lord were crazy altogether.

The box elders were in heavy leaf, early syringa was perfuming the air, the high tide of spring was past, summer was coming in. There was an elation in Josephine that was half a taunt—or more than half. She loosed it.

"What do you call practicing medicine?"

She got a thousand volts. "Get it through your thick head," Cy half-shouted, "that was not practicing medicine."

She came in, the expert fighter with a fist cocked. They would be failing each other badly if either of them missed a chance to draw blood, well, be honest, if she missed one. "It was pretty hard to tell from the real thing. As a matter of fact, if you told my lawyer you weren't practicing medicine on me a few minutes earlier, he'd advise me to swear out a complaint."

"If I told Ase to bake his stiff shoulder would that be orthopedics? If I took a sliver from Deborah's finger would that be pediatrics? Or surgery?"

"Stop yelling or I'll start screaming! All I want to know is what the rules are. I'm willing to play it your way only I've got to know where out of bounds is."

"I'm not licensed to practice medicine."

"When are you going to be?"

But Cy was calling it off with one round tonight. "Look, Jo, we're just out for a walk."

"You walk my shoes to shreds."

"Any time you want to ride, we've got a Ford."

He could make her furious with immovability and disarm her with gentleness. Trout season had opened yesterday and he said he had put some trout in the icebox—he and Lloyd Tanser had driven up Custis Canyon after work and caught a few. So she had to think that out. It was inconceivable that Cy could be content to catch fish, to be serious and absorbed, as if that were the summit of ambition. But the inconceivable was their daily fare.

The foothills were within easy reach, the eastern streets ran right up to them. Houses moved farther apart and then you were alone in the darkness, above the city, remote from everything. They sat under a scrubby willow on the top of a small domed hill, and Cy scraped up a handful of twigs and held a match to them. He liked fires; they were part of the inexplicable love of the darkness which he shared with her, as assuredly he did not share her fear of it. Light enough to see dust on her shoes and stockings, to fall to studying Cy's face. He looked untroubled, serene. Could it be true that he was content with what had happened to him? That would be most horrible of all.

Then her discontents lapsed and she too surrendered to the soft night. It was the sense of remoteness and aloneness, the withdrawal of tension, the quiet. The wholly unjustified optimism she had sometimes felt of late was suddenly running free. Then she was singing. And Cy liked to hear her sing. Something deepened in his face while he listened. Her voice broke with an involuntary giggle, for though he was not the Met he had turned out to be her audience. Cy was the last phase of the Schurz Street Presbyterian.

She felt her voice full and rich, surprisingly so. "I'm just a poor, wayfaring stranger," she sang,

> While traveling through this world of woe.
> But there's no sickness, toil nor danger
> In that bright land to which I go.

Her very bones turned weak for she saw dampness shining in Cy's eyes. He said, "Those are your best songs."

"I like them best."

"I wonder why."

"They're simple. And they're real. People really meant them."

He shook his head, not satisfied. Must be more than that— she could read the thought. The trouble was they could read each other's thoughts much too easily. He put no more twigs on the little fire; he said no more. Josephine lay back, hands behind her head, and looked through the fleecy willow at the stars. Her mind was quiet. That was what terror taught you, to rejoice in the simple absence of terror. If you weren't afraid, then you were —almost—to ask no more of life. That was as simple and real as any song. It was ignominious. Why, that was the word, she and Cy had established a concord of the ignominious.

Cy said, out of his silence, "Yes, I like to go fishing with Tanser. Want me to sit and mourn?" Then presently, after some more silence, "My mind hasn't exactly died this year, you know. I've been using it."

"Oh, good! Where does it come out?"

"Nowhere much. Put it this way: you've only been sick."

Only! The word knifed through her. Or was he trying to be funny? He went on, "You're going to get well."

"So you say but it doesn't happen. Unless humbly thanking God because I'm not scared blue is getting well. How do you know?"

"I was apprenticed to the trade. Health is what nature intended. Health is right. Mother Eddy said it all—disease is just an error."

Josephine sat up, resentful again after being at peace. "I see, somebody just made a mistake. I crossed the wrong t or I didn't count my change right."

"You were off down the field but somebody came up and cut you down from behind. Too bad—no first down. But you'll run with the ball some more."

"Let's go home," she said dispiritedly. "I don't know why all my men have to be poets. Is that supposed to mean something, Cy?"

In step down a dusty road that would presently be a street, and Custis coming up to meet them with corner lights and the resumption of the familiar. This automatic, this almost manic accommodation of steps. If she took his arm their feet fell precisely on the beat. If she dropped it, just the same. Their arms swung together, their hips were the same rhythm, probably their breathing was synchronized. And between them a dark, dangerous fog, ominous and foreboding, dreadful with something still to be fought through, and Cy certainly knew it as well as she or better. You never knew what the worst was; you only knew that it was still ahead.

Cy was saying casually, even indifferently, "Mother Eddy, or life, or the concept of health is on your side. We used to be learned about it at Mercy. Nobody knows what's out there but something is. Anybody who gets to the marker is either going to go right on past or else come back. Nobody knows the odds. Some of them are sure to come back only they just don't. Or some of them haven't got a chance but something gives you the horselaugh and yanks them back and throws them in your face. It's nature or it's life or it's chemistry or it's a complex variable. I liked Pete's name—he called it the Jesus factor."

"And you called it the X Point. You certainly were deep. My brother Andy would be awed."

"Okay," Cy said, just as indifferently, "I'm talking nonsense. What are you talking?"

About whether she was ever going to be glad to be alive again. Ever going to do a job. Ever going to find a function. So she thought it over for blocks, under the gently swaying box elders, late at night in a sleeping town.

The house was dark. And Ase and Hattie with their periodic stress when she was out with Cy. And why not? She could do nothing about the thoughts they must fall asleep on; no one had ever been able to do anything about hers. She stopped at the hedge, the unkempt hedge that was now as tall as she was and had been half her size when she was a little girl.

"But about you, where does this bring you out?" she asked.

"I'll tell you when I find out."

"I bet you will! We're the people that couldn't possibly not tell each other."

He said mildly, "I think the difference is I'm on the deathward side of X."

Words. Probably they would have appalled her once—or to-night, in any other mood. She had certainly got into the wrong mood. She sniffed. *"Il y a des gens qui croient comprendre cela."*

"I made a mistake when I taught you that line. So long, Jo."

Don't for God's sake kiss me good night—I might misunderstand. She went in and got a glass of milk and sat in the kitchen sipping it and disliking Cy Kinsman with a poignancy that grew toward rage. Suddenly she laughed, for while she sat here and swore at him she was docilely obeying him: get fats into you, put on weight. That realization dissolved her anger and, soothed, she went upstairs.

But as she passed Deborah's door she was instantly sick and weak. Her heart was pounding, her throat constricted, her palms moist, her legs shaking. By what amounted to superhuman strength she got the key, locked Deborah's door, got downstairs and put the key on the dining-room table, and wavered upstairs

181

again, past Deborah's door draggingly, into her own room. Made it! She got undressed and lay quaking. This was one she was not going to carry to Cy—not after tonight's anger. This was one she was going to sweat out alone—she would have to eventually, why not start? She sweat it out moment by successive moment of un-intermitted fear until a moment came when she was asleep.

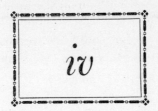

*iv*

RULON WILLIAMS drove into the rear lot of Tanser's Garage, where Cy and Art Ricco were testing the clutch they had just finished putting into a big truck. Rulon thought he smoked too much and always gazed at a cigarette for some time before giving in and lighting it. He gave off a scent of antiseptics, anesthetics, and soap; coming up, Cy had a glimpse of a Mercy corridor. Traffic of nurses at the desk, intern unlocking the drug cabinet, hum of an elevator. But Sponberg and Pete—there was the hole.

"Change the oil, Doctor?" he inquired. "Better leave it and have us wash it. Now, my Aunt Susy—she gets these hot flashes, how about it, Doc?"

Rulon decided that one more wouldn't matter and lit it. "What do you know about the common duct?"

"You had a gall bladder this morning."

Rulon nodded. "Like I never saw." His face lighted with something between puzzlement and the holy enjoyment of the connoisseur. "I'll show you." He took a prescription pad from his pocket and began to sketch. Left and right lobes of liver. Left and right hepatic ducts. Gall bladder. Cystic duct. Duodenum. Common duct.

"Let me guess," Cy said. He took the pad and pencil and began to reproduce the sketch on a fresh blank. "Maybe this?" He drew the cystic duct higher, above the gall bladder.

"Oh, you've seen it?"

"Or thereabouts. Where was the gall bladder?"

Rulon took the pad and drew it leading off the right hepatic duct. "Right there."

Cy nodded. "Shows up once in a while. I hope you took a tumble in time."

"I had a margin of about, well, ten seconds," Rulon said, very solemn. "There I was ready to clamp off the gall bladder only I'd have put that clamp on the hepatic duct. I got the idea something didn't look quite right. And it wasn't. Why don't they tell you about those things?"

"They tell you nature is pretty ingenious and you're supposed to go from there."

"I'd have killed him, wouldn't I?"

"Probably. He probably wouldn't have lived to die of the liver —he'd have gone out in shock. We had one of these lightning express boys at Peter Bent Brigham. He was for the minimum of everything—minimum incision, minimum exploration, minimum dissection, get out fast. An idea that will never get you jailed too but let's not get fanatical about it. I'd been there about a month when he ran into one of these."

"What happened?"

"He couldn't take time to whistle for the crossings. Just as you say, he was taking out the gall bladder. Only pretty soon we found he'd cut the hepatic duct. The moral I drew was, let's dissect out the field."

"Yet you're always talking about getting in and out fast, yourself."

"Sure," Cy said cheerfully. "You can't win. But let's anyway wait and take a look. Nature just loves to cross you up."

"We learn that gall bladders come off the common duct. When you find one coming off the hepatic duct . . ."

"I know, you want to protest to the umpire. Nature won't play by the rule book."

"Just an aberration, huh?"

"Just an aberration. What did you want, Rulon? Gas?"

Rulon returned the prescription pad to a vest pocket. He put the pencil in the breast pocket of his coat beside the thermometer. Must carry his ophthalmoscope in his bag. Custis High, Class of Naughty-Six, and an unconscious dignity had come into his pleasant, nondescript face. "No, I don't want any gas." He kicked the starter. "What a damn fool you are, Cy."

Dr. Williams's coupé went out of the lot. The whistle at the P. & F. W. shops blew five o'clock. Promptly Joe Bates shut off the electric motors. Everybody made for the sink. Cy was still scrubbing his hands with waste and mechanics' paste when Lloyd Tanser yelled from the office door, "Fall down or something, Cy? Must be slow off your marks."

"The boys get out fast, all right."

"Like a scared cat. Give me two dollars. We're throwing Joe a party tomorrow. He'll be married ten years."

Cy produced a greasy bill. "A good record at that."

"Better'n I could do. Want to eat?"

"Not tonight, Lloyd."

Cy drove off, wondering about Lloyd's marriage; you never heard anything except when he cursed the alimony. It was the metropolitan hour in Custis. The office buildings had emptied on the sidewalks, the population of the state capitol was coming down the hill in a procession, the wide streets were filled with cars, all blowing their horns. Late May, late afternoon, barbaric red light on bricks, windshields throwing it in your eyes. The vast amphitheater of the peaks brimmed with copper and scarlet and vermilion, the upper snowfields incandescent, violet and purple beginning to well out of the gulches and seep along the edges of cliffs, with shadows beginning to cross the land. A small flat cloud hung poised just above the tip of Mount Gallatin, its upper edges red, its base black, the sky beneath it clear green.

Cy drove to the barn, took a shower, dressed in clean, faded shirt and trousers. And maybe Jo would like to go to dinner. But there was a package at his alley door and when he opened it he found a copy of *Endymion at the Finger Lakes* by Samuel Frederick Willard. Frank Henriquez had sent it to him and a note dropped out of it: "I told you we can't calculate artists with a slide rule. I guessed wrong. F. H."

That changed the program. Cy made an omelet at his gas range, ate it with appreciation, methodically cleaned up his kitchen. Better police the living room too. He got out brushes and dust cloths and prepared for Saturday inspection of quarters. Then, satisfied, he sat down to read Sam Willard.

It was midnight when he finished. And you couldn't predict anything at all. He had no way of knowing how good it was, except that Frank Henriquez appeared to regret having turned it down, but it was done, it was finished, and it was done in its own terms. It required you to respect Sam Willard, the man who had no mind at all, the boy who wouldn't grow up, the Chelsea Casanova and Peter Pan, the artist with the quilled mustache and the boundless capacity to give you back in good faith anything he had picked up. Many times Cy found himself nodding approval—a mixture of identifying the invariable Sam and at the same time recognizing an unexpected sureness of touch. This was Sam fairly wriggling his tail with pleasure while Chelsea applauded his ever so droll mimicry, and yet it was a man who knew how to accomplish what he wanted to accomplish.

Cy had been wrong about Sam. Was there anyone he hadn't been wrong about? Or had he been wrong? With so little mind, could this be anything but a trick? Was Sam the pair of hands working in a void? Better not conclude so, better not raise up an illusion to hide behind. You never knew. You never could tell. The infinitesimal Sam, the echo of everyone, the unbuttoned and practically undiapered—Sam had done what he had set out to do. And the resident of Mercy Hospital sat in his snug bachelor quarters, finding relaxation in Chelsea's art after a day at the garage.

He would have to take it to Josephine in the morning. So predict that one! Cy gazed at the book on his desk. It was not that she also had contributed glimpses and vistas and notions and people in tableaus and people in moments of emotion—Sam swept up clean wherever he happened to be, and a man who couldn't think had to get his thoughts as needs must. It was that so much of Jo's hope and expectation had been wrought into this book, that it impalpably embodied so much of her clean and quite impossible desire. And was so thoroughly her failure. Here were years of Jo's life—negotiated and disregarded. Coming to nothing. Josephine too an author of the book, an unsuccessful author.

It was damned queer. There was no theory that would account for permutations. In Cy Kinsman's clothes closet, which had been the harness closet of Wes Kinsman's horses, hung various of her garments, a heavy skirt and sweater she had worn snowshoeing, a hat left here he could not remember when, a scarf she had made from a length of bright silk. Heavy shoes on the closet floor. In a drawer a basket of sewing things, dating from an evening when she was exasperated to find him sewing a button on a shirt with surgical gut. He had made the windows but Josephine had made the red-checked curtains. She had given him the photograph of Mount Gallatin with sunlight on its snow—it had meant something obscure to her, some reference to their hours on its slope and she holding on to herself solely by means of him. The permutations refused to work out right for Josephine Caneday and Cy could not like the darkness that the realization brought to his heart.

She was at the gap at the hedge the next morning when he drove up, waving goodby to Ase, who shambled off down the sidewalk in the direction of the streetcar line, lanky, loose-jointed, long-armed, growing old. Barelegged in oxfords, wearing an old blue smock, her hair in a long braid wound round her forehead.

"He's going to teach summer school this year. It's the first time in his life he hasn't spent the summer in the field."

Deborah came flying down the sidewalk and climbed into Cy's arms, and a good thing he was not a white-collar worker for she had been at the garden hose and was already grimy. "Ase is getting pretty old for field trips," Cy said.

"Not while he lives! No, it's just I've got to get a job—Cy, I've got to."

"Here's this," he said.

"Oh." Did she pale a little? No—excited. "I'll—thanks. And he got the moon into the title after all. I'll read it tonight. Come to dinner?"

"I've got a party. I'll take you to dinner tomorrow."

He would offer odds she would sweep no floors this morning till she had read *Endymion at the Finger Lakes*. He put Deborah firmly down, waved to them, drove away.

At quitting time he and Tomcat Jones and Art Ricco took a truck and called for a battered old piano which he had bought for thirty-five dollars from a downtown joint that had been closed. They put it in the barn and Tomcat asked, "Can you play her, Cy?"

"Not yet. I will."

"Oh, like that?"

"Sure."

Art Ricco could play her. For fifteen minutes barn and alley resounded with ragtime, waltzes, and the sextette from *Lucia*—which Art was even willing to sing part by part. A good man. He and Tomcat drove off to get ready for Joe's party.

It was a good party, a little stiff at first, with the sexes tending to separate, but fried chicken and more especially rye—the occupational contribution of Art Ricco and Cy Kinsman—dissolved the starch. And testimony here to change in Custis, for in Cy's adolescence, to which his whole knowledge of the town was referred, there had not been coeducational drinking. Joe's children had been sent elsewhere to do their sleeping and Joe's bungalow had been brought to a high polish. Golden oak furniture, an enormous bouquet of red roses for Joe's wife, whose cheeks were almost as red, a table piled with anniversary presents accompanied by verses which had to be read when they were opened, laughter growing heartier and more frequent, singing at a piano much like Cy's.

Pride of ownership grew on Joe Bates and he conducted Cy about his domain: furnace and work bench and lathe in a basement as clean as any operating room, garage door that ran up along the ceiling at a touch, garden with sweet peas well up in their trench and many flowers coming into bud. Outside, it was pleasant to look at light slanting through the windows, hear the hum of people having a good time, and look off to the peaks with the line of dim light where their black bulk met the sky.

Cy was remembering a similar remote noise of enjoyment. Twenty-Third Street, the artists celebrating Sam Willard's emancipation. The identical sound, the identical emotions—and, identically, some inability of Cy Kinsman to enter in. He was detached from these people as he had been from Sam's pals. Except that then he had been superior to the emotions, as assuredly he was not now. So his mind fell away into a reverie of Josephine sitting beside him on the stairs, her profile in silhouette against the Victory of Samothrace. That night there had at least begun for him a knowledge that Jo had to lose her fight, and maybe there had been other beginnings. Well, she had lost it.

She was thrust upon him now. Art Ricco had brought Myrtle Hill's younger sister Emmy, and to Cy's surprise Myrt had come too. Pleasantly made girls, the Hill sisters, Emmy the blonder and more seductive, Myrt much the more self-contained. Myrt in a white dress, drinking a single highball, always with an air of alert but confident wariness.

She came up to Cy in the garden and said, "Where's your girl, Cy?"

"I didn't think to ask her."

"Would she of come?"

"I don't think so." Myrt shrugged and Cy said, "You're wrong. Josephine—well, she's had her troubles. She doesn't easily face a lot of unfamiliar people yet. She'd be, well, dismayed."

Myrt appeared to understand or at least accept the explanation. "She was a year ahead of me at High. She's okay. Why'n't you do something about it?"

Cy's turn to shrug. The municipal illusion, the universal illusion, and quite impossible to translate into words what he had done about it. Myrt said, "She's a good girl. Too good for you." And too bad, for he would have liked Myrt's respect.

Several drinks drew a slight veil across the evening and no

more. There was more frequent singing, there was dancing, a slight but decorous amorousness permitted you to put an arm round a woman without offense. After a while Art and Emmy simply faded. Cy was on the front porch when they went out to Art's car and drove away. And Myrt came out and stood on the steps with the light shining on her and said, "Damn!"

Cy went to stand by her. She was hard with indignation—very much like Josephine in her commonest emotion about Cy. Myrt said, "I'd like to cut his throat."

"He's a good guy."

"He's a bootlegger."

"Well, it's a new service trade. He probably handled that drink you took."

Quite unexpectedly, Myrt took his arm; more unexpectedly still, she was appealing to him. "Cy, he don't have to bootleg. Look, he likes you. Can't you talk him out of it?"

"You mean, I might have some use?"

"He's got a good trade. He won't never need to worry. I can't have Emmy marrying a jailbird. Talk sense to him, Cy."

"It's his business, Myrt."

He simply made her angrier: that was his predestinate mission, to anger women. Myrt turned her back on him but Lloyd Tanser had come out on the porch and her emotions boiled straight at him. "Do you have to hire tramps, Lloyd?"

Lloyd belched gently; Lloyd was pleasantly tight. "I got no tramps, babe. I got a crew of lazy bums, sure, but they're the best damn mechanics in the state."

Cy explained, "Myrt's sore at Art. She thinks nobody should run liquor, just drink it."

"It ain't my business," Lloyd said, and drew a withering glance from Myrt. It passed on to Cy too. Lloyd added, "He don't sell none on my premises."

"You could fire him, couldn't you?"

Myrt was erect, a little belligerent, altogether disdainful. She was giving Lloyd a curiously straight look, which Lloyd gave back to her untroubled. "No, babe," he said gently, "I couldn't."

So Myrt leaned against the porch rail and retreated into sullenness, and women were curiously alike. Lloyd said to Cy, "Tomcat and me and a couple of others think maybe there ought to be some serious drinking. We're going over to my place. I guess you wouldn't come along?"

"What makes you guess that?" Myrt demanded.

"Cy don't go in for it. We've tried."

"Just an amachure drinker, too, huh?"

Cy took her resistant arm. "Some day I'll show you both what a real drunk is. Time you were going home, Myrt. I'll drive you."

"I'll say it is—I got to be at work at six o'clock. Yes, and a stinking bad evening, if you ask me."

It hadn't been; it had been a good evening. But Myrt had her problem in the mathematics of a complex variable to solve and couldn't solve it. The night wind of the mountains was murmurous overhead when he stopped the Ford in front of her house, and a bit of floss drifted against his cheek—the cottonwood buds were ready to open. Myrt sat beside him, still sullen.

Cy laid a hand on hers. "You can't bring it out even, Myrt. Might as well not try. People just won't be the way we want them to be. Try having a little charity."

Myrt said, "Nobody ever wasted none on me." She faced him, said "Good night, Cy," and turned up her face. They kissed with the greatest chasteness and Myrt got out of the Ford and went into her house. She had kissed him according to the folkways of Custis—and it was not a stinking evening at all for whatever she might think of him, she had accepted him.

There was a Waldorf in Custis too. Its food was by no means as good as that of Timmy's Diner but it was a place of fashion. Derision showed in Josephine's eyes when he took her there the next night. "It could be the Village. If I see a bottle of red ink I'll expect someone to come over and say have we seen the new *Poetry* and isn't Vachel Lindsay losing his grip?"

"Well, is he?"

She would not say much about *Endymion*. He could see that it had agitated her, stirred up emotions she was not ready to talk about. She would be! They talked and talked. They were a species of self-winding dialogue. They were a life in words. . . . But she said Ase was reading it tonight, was curious to see what kind of son-in-law he had had, would be hurt by the portrait of the professor. She said it had changed a lot since she heard it in manuscript.

"He was right all along," she said. "I was wrong. He did it. I didn't think he could."

There was that. It would clang in two minds, differently, with weary implications. Josephine said, "You know what the next one will be? It will be me. And how dead right." But also, how her function would go on in spite of divorce. Damned odd.

Darkness was brimming in the great bowl whose sides stood up above the town when they came out from dinner, and the last color died as they watched. "You wore that suit the night we were helling at the Waldorf in New York," he said. "The blouse is new." The suit was beige linen, the blouse a splash of terra cotta silk.

"I made it today—Hattie has kept every remnant she ever had. This is the fourth year for the suit and I've shortened it three times—do you realize, we're on the way to showing our calves?—it's eight inches off the floor. But imagine, you remember some clothes of mine!"

"You stopped at every window on Fifth Avenue. There was one dress that made you practically curse God. It would have been fun to buy you all the clothes on the Avenue. It still would be."

He had depressed her somehow. "So what do we do now?" she said. "I mean till tonight's fight starts."

"Let's go up to the barn. I've got some things to show you."

Damned queer. The words had become a nauseating iteration. But it was damned queer and he thought with a full heart that the queerest of all was her lease and habitation of Old Doc Kinsman's barn. It had been her fortress, it came close to being her home. In terms of Joe Bates, her bungalow.

But she was delighted with the piano. She rippled through

some cadenzas and banged some heroic chords. There was an echo from the sloping ceiling where there had once been a grain chute and so they tugged the instrument to various positions till they found one that satisfied her.

"But just what is the idea?" she asked, swinging round on the stool, under a drop light that made her hair glisten.

"Well, there's a contralto visits me sometimes. And maybe I'll take up music."

She laughed; in fact she hooted. "And with your ear?"

"If I want to play the piano, why shouldn't I?"

"No reason. Except heaven be merciful to whoever teaches you."

"Then pray hard, for you're going to."

She laughed again and turned to the keyboard. She sang a couple of operatic songs, gently burlesquing them. She sang several in German which he could recognize and several which he couldn't. And as always she moved on to the songs that were her best, old ballads, hymns, jubilees, river songs. . . . Her bare arms with complex shadows on them moved in fluid patterns and the lights that moved on her hair seemed to give it sentience. She was absorbed; she had no awareness beyond the songs. He recognized that the year had added something to her voice, a purity it had not had before, some subtlety between sadness and joy. She had reached her Wayfaring Stranger again—and the moment was of eternity. Her voice had created in this foolish room the things that never changed and never could be changed.

"I may have a bad ear," Cy said abruptly, "but you're more a musician than you ever were before. Divorce or breakdown or whatever—it's made you a singer."

She glanced at him swiftly, then away, a desperate forlornness showing for a half-second in her eyes. "Tanktown Schumann-Heink," she said. She struck another set of chords and sang, "My father got to walk this lonesome valley." She went through the whole thing, my mother got to walk, my brother got to walk, my sister got to walk, poor sinner got to walk this lonesome valley.

Clear enough. The voice he had wanted to hear in the dark

was the voice of a wife and lover. "Nobody else can walk it for us, We got to walk it by ourself," she finished and, cheeks flushed, eyes rapt, sat looking at the keys for a moment while the melody repeated itself in Cy's mind and he acknowledged the prohibition that was as strong as death. She left the piano and sat in the chair across the room, where the light fell off. She crossed her knees. She picked up the evening paper, then threw it aside. There could be no doubt that she knew exactly what her singing had done to him; she was intolerant and defiant.

She crossed to sit at his grain-bin desk. She had any wife's privilege of going through what she found there. She picked up a yellow pad covered with calculations. "What's this?"

"Eclipses."

"Are we going to have some?"

"Not those, anyway. Those are Jupiter's moons."

"You mean you sit here and figure out when there's going to be an eclipse on Jupiter?" He nodded. "Whatever for?"

"Purely in the amateur spirit." He waved at his Nautical Almanac and his lengthening shelf of mathematics texts. "My art. I'll calculate anything you like. Want a viscosity formula for dishwashing soap? Formula of four variables for mayonnaise?"

"Not profoundly." She studied him for a while, shrugged, and picked up a notebook. " 'Deborah Willard, from December 1, 1919,' " she read. "What about Deborah?"

It was an exhaustive record of measurements and correlatives, and she would make nothing of it. "Does this lead anywhere?" she asked.

"Not unless you want to check one week against another. If you do, there it is." She picked up another notebook but he rose and took it away from her. "No, that's Deborah's mother. Psychiatric ward."

A flush rose to her cheeks and faded. "I suppose I'm not on Jupiter," she said after a while. "All the rest of this is?"

"Why, yes," he said, without emotion. "If you mean, is there any end in view? No."

Josephine went back to her chair on the edge of the shadow,

big leather chair from Wes Kinsman's office, scuffed by years of patients. She lay back in it, feet stretched out ahead of her at full length, arms lax. "Were you on the track team at Custis High?"

"No, lady, I pitched on the ball team."

"You might have been a good man in the sprints. Or the distance run."

But the moons of Jupiter were so far away that no feeling carried over. They had reached the inevitable moment: a perfect equilibrium of hostilities. There was no need to calculate a formula for that complex of constants, but if he had to, he could.

Yet as always the resentments dissolved into quiet accord and presently she called him back from reverie with, "You said things to show me. Anything else?"

"Why, yes." He got a package from his desk and gave it to her. "Maybe I do buy you Fifth Avenue. A little at a time."

It was a dozen pairs of black glove-silk stockings. Quick delight showed in her face and she let a pair slide through her fingers, feeling their smoothness. "Heavens, Cy, I've never had more than three pairs at a time."

He said, "There were darns on those you had on the other night."

And he had reawakened the hostilities. "I see. I shame you in public. My clothes don't live up to those blue shirts you wear. With the grease on them."

"I won't have you wearing darned stockings."

"As a bootlegger, you'll have your wench well turned out."

"Sure," he said wearily. "I drove a load ten days ago."

"Never mind, business is bound to pick up." Hostile, then disdainful, then indifferent. "Well, thanks, Cy, whatever paid for them. They're nice." She slipped off her oxfords and put on a pair of the stockings, rolling them below the knees. Two gestures of supreme disturbance and supreme delight: a woman, Jo, putting on her stockings, and a woman, Jo, arranging her hair.

He said, "You're . . . damned pretty, Jo."

"Why, thanks. And thanks for the very best grade of ladies' hosiery."

She raised her face and he kissed her. Precisely like Myrt, the amenities of Custis. Her lips formed a smile that was momentarily tender and became satirical. But that disturbance too ebbed and after an hour of easy talk he drove her home under the silver arch of western sky. The thick bulk of peaks black and all Custis asleep. She made no move to get out when he drew up at her house. A box elder rustled over their heads. On Mount Gallatin a party of climbers had built a fire that made a garnet and fluctuating speck in vastness.

Jo said, "God knows what forbearance it takes for Ase and Hattie to keep their mouths shut. Why must we hurt people so?"

"Maybe it's worth it?"

"Anyway, it's what we've got. Good night, Cy."

She went silently up the walk and he drove back to the barn. He realized that he was whistling something. "Nobody else can walk it for you." Right. That was what they had, what they had won through to. If either of them was disposed to resent its incompleteness, it was more than either of them had been justly entitled to expect.

THE LIVING ROOM was suddenly beautiful with summer afternoon. Josephine had come into it from the kitchen, where she had just finished putting half an inch of icing on a chocolate cake. She came through the door taking off her apron —and the room was gold-filled and brimming with a peace so profound that it held you in its hand. Her eyes stung with tears that had no cause. Except that she was rejoicing.

Hattie had taken Deborah downtown, which might account for a little of the peace. But her delight went on intensifying. She was humming. She was experiencing a sharp pleasure from rubbing a hand across her cheek. She found that she was standing in front of the bookcase without having looked at it, and on impulse she picked up a shabby volume. It proved to be an anthology she had used at Custis High and she grew absorbed in a fifteen-year-old Josephine who had filled it with scrawls and drawings. There were heads of Gibson Girls; they all looked like Nancy. There were phrases of music that didn't say anything—probably that was the Young Composer. There were cryptic notes about school dances, and no doubt excitement or heartbreak was in them if she could remember. The text was crisscrossed and decorated and had flip comments in the margins. Why, Cy was at least a little wrong—there had been the Enchanted Mesa if there wasn't now. Spring came on forever at Custis High.

"Memorize!!!!!" a direction read, with some stanzas framed, and curving arrows pointing to them, and a series of grace notes at the beginning and end. It was from "In Memoriam" and she had not obeyed the command to memorize it for it was new to her. Tennyson! The bearded old fossil had never lived to learn enlightenment. The artists would despair, for he actually used rhyme and capital letters, the *jusqu'auboutist*. You could intone it, you could practically sing it, which was a great vulgarity, and she read aloud as at Custis High:—

> and in my breast
> Spring wakens too, and my regret
> Becomes an April violet,
> And buds and blossoms like the rest.

She put down the book, transfixed, for the old fossil had re- vealed to her that it had happened. The violets were gone long since but in her breast had at last budded an ability to feel cleanly. To feel pain without fear, to feel regret for what was lost and still not corrode it with anxiety or rebellion. Cy had said life was on her side. He and the fossil—Alfred, Lord Kinsman.

Not for long, of course, but it had happened. Deborah blew it far out to sea by turning into a problem child overnight. What- ever else she had been, she had always been biddable, easily led, compliant, amiable to obey. Now you got her to do anything by indirection, if at all, and any compulsion would produce a tantrum. Hattie's large patience had room to contain the most annoying behavior, but Josephine could stand very little of it. She was screaming at the child a good part of the time and slapped her more often than would have seemed possible—her own guilt and uneasiness redoubling every time. What was in- tolerable, however, was that Cy stepped in. After he had brought Deborah home from the barn twice, after what were in Deborah's mind final leavetakings from home, he took to calling for her in the morning and disappearing with her for the day.

It worked. Mother or daughter, he seemed to have the needed touch—and exasperated Josephine equally with both. In the quieter and more obedient Deborah there was a smugness, a pos- sessiveness as if she were aware that she had some power over Cy, and Josephine had moments of detecting in her a condescending kindness toward her mother. That increased anger and uneasiness in equal measure, but there was something still more suspect in Cy, though she could not find its name.

He brought her home in early evening and had charmed her by giving her supper at what she reported was a dining car. She experienced a rush of affection for Josephine and climbed into her lap and wound dirty arms round her. Josephine tolerated it, under some stress, then put her aside. "Go take a bath," she said.

Deborah looked at Cy—appealing to the judge. "Go take a bath, Butch. That's what you're told to do."

She had every appearance of thinking it over from all points of view, then deciding. She graciously agreed: it was a favor extended to Josephine, a kindness or reward. "Then you may put me to bed, Cy."

"Mummy will put you to bed."

"Thanks," Jo said, "I won't impose on you."

"I'll put you to bed, then. Yell when you're clean."

They sat in June twilight under the big mulberry. Annoyed and careless of showing that she was, Josephine asked, "What do you find to do all day?"

"We find a river and play in it. Or we climb a foothill. Or we read books. Or we sweep out the barn."

Just like you and me. "What I don't get," Josephine said, "is whether she understudies me or I'm her stand-in. Then again, you have no job to do?"

"None that I have to."

"That's it, isn't it? There's nothing you have to do. It may be a cold cave but it's all yours." Cy didn't answer. He was being imperturbable, or was he just being? Did it mean anything at all to him? The invulnerable garage mechanic in neatly laundered, very old clothes. He was the self-respecting poor. He was the Chelsea poet. He was, in a word, abominable. She said, "Deborah is simply one more thick stone wall that you get to hide behind. She must mean a lot to you."

"Well," Cy said, "one wall or another. Somebody has to convince her she's important."

Just like tennis: you drove one and your opponent drove it back. She was going to be madder than usual tonight. But Deborah called with piercing shrillness and cloying sweetness, "All right, Cy." Cy got up and went in the house. Josephine sat under the mulberry turning her resentments and irritations and frustrations and miscellaneous grievances over and over. The light in Deborah's room went out presently but Cy did not come back. No doubt he had joined the family circle and was chatting with Ase and Hattie. It didn't matter to him that he had undermined them. He was the boy who had apprenticed himself to an anarchist and made good: nothing mattered.

He came across the lawn at last and there rose in Josephine an intense loathing for the fixed, compulsive routine they had ever so carefully built up. They would now ride in the Ford or they would now take a walk. To no destination, for no reason at all. Or they would go back to her *pied-à-terre*, the Kinsman barn, and instead of being an itinerant, a peripatetic mania they would be a conversational, sedentary mania.

Even as she spoke she was standing up in complete acceptance of the compulsion. But she hit as hard as she knew how: "You even have your children by proxy, don't you?"

Cy said, "My children don't terrify me."

He won that one. She felt it as a jar that traveled down her spine and paralyzed her. But as they strolled aimlessly eastward, picking up the shuttle where they had dropped it last time, weaving one more figure just like the last one, she quickly forgot that she was paralyzed. A few blocks were enough to bring that irrational, inexplicable well-being flooding back.

She said, "I suppose I ought to tell you you're right. Sometimes I stop feeling that Judgment Day is here."

He put an arm through hers, saying nothing. As they got above the town, here was the night again, that odd symbol, that queer security, that deep love. Part of its power was that it peeled away antagonism. Another climbing party had got to the top of Mount Gallatin and built a campfire.

"Let's climb Gallatin sometime," she said.

"Okay. It's rough going in places. Better take a reef in a pair of Andy's trousers."

"I will not wear pants!" she said with altogether astonishing vehemence.

"You don't have to look chic on a trail."

"Why should I wear pants? You mean I might look immodest? All right, I'll put on a union suit. Or tights. Anything you say. I won't wear pants."

Cy said, "All right, don't bawl. You don't have to."

She relaxed just as abruptly. "Cy, how we act! What an idiotic thing to say. Of course I'll wear pants. What would you call that one? Pantophobia?"

"We've got that one in the book, too. It means fear of everything."

She laughed, released. "Let it ride."

So the darkness won and accord settled on them. Except that when accord came, it invariably ended in the questions no one would answer. As they neared the hill with the willow on it, where the iron hand of habit would make them stop and stretch out on the grass while Cy built a little ritualistic fire of twigs, she said, "Cy, pretend you aren't cryptic and inscrutable. Pretend I'm bright enough to know that I'm not the only one who got cut down from behind. I want to know: do you want to practice medicine again?"

This time it didn't ring down the asbestos curtain. Cy said, "I can't answer that one—I don't know. I can tell you I'm never going to."

"Cy, why?"

"Because I can't."

"Why not?"

They reached the little hill, as predicted, and as predicted they sat down under the willow. Presently Cy said, "I haven't operated for ten months. Don't you realize a man can lose his skill forever in ten months?"

"I don't believe you."

As predicted, Cy was rummaging for twigs. He stopped.

"You're right, of course. I'm lying. A week in the dog lab and I'd have all I ever had."

"Then stop lying and tell me."

He got his three fingers of fire going. Like a boy scout: you're disgraced if you use more than one match. Maybe a match was disgraceful, maybe he had already lost his rating—she was unable to repress the anger that she was willing to admit was anger not at him but at his betraying her illusions about him. Which was atrociously unjust. For in his damned firelight she could see that he was trying to give her what she wanted. One thing could be said about the change that had been wrought in his face: arrogance, superiority, snootiness had gone from him, that part of Cy had disappeared in the storm. Why did she keep forgetting there had been a storm?

Cy said, "It's just that I can't. If I find out why I can't, don't fret, I'll tell you. If there's ever anything I don't tell you, that will be news."

Like the rock in the dark. But at least she had struck rock, not fog. There was something austere. She was heavy with what was not so much grief as fellowship. It was pretty easy to forget that she had had one overmastering need and Cy had supplied it. Strip things to the essentials and what mattered was that you didn't die.

She lay back and stared through the willow leaves. The June grass that had been green and soft a couple of weeks ago was dry and prickly now. Her stockings and the bottom of her skirt were full of its little barbs. Time had been running on. And would. The handful of years that had been a marriage for a while and then weren't. She had the high-school girl's town now and it looked from within just as different as she might have had the sense to expect. She had what she was to make the rest of a life of, if one was to be made.

"What about Mount Caneday?" she asked suddenly. "Weren't you going to take me there?"

"It's just a mountain."

"I know. Your little patient must not think it's any different

202

on the other side of the hill. How we repeat ourselves. Or," she said willfully, "are you worried about the amenities?"

"Sometime I'll take you to a ridge when there's a late moon and let you see daybreak and moonlight at the same time."

"Have you seen it?"

"I had my Kit Carson period."

As a matter of fact she remembered it. Her brother Chuck had also been a mighty outdoorsman. She was suddenly invigorated and sat up. It was natural to sing—and astonishing how much pleasure in singing had lately been vouchsafed her. And Cy was right. Her voice had a fullness and a roundness it had never had before. When a thing is really sung, you know it. It was incredibly absurd to be sitting here on dry grass, under a willow tree, singing at night for no reason. Absurd and absolutely gorgeous.

It seemed to be Josephine Caneday as a recital artist tonight. She had more timbre than you would believe.

> Du bist die Ruh, du bist der Frieden,
> Du bist vom Himmel mir beschieden.
> Dass du mich liebst macht mich mir werth—

"I'm sorry," Cy said, "that stinks. Stick to your stuff. Nothing is worse than a Kraut feeling sorry for himself."

"Sure," she said, fully aware that he wasn't thinking of Krauts. "Germans are always weeping into their souls. They're always telling some overweight Gretchen that she's their quiet, she's all the heaven they can get. That's Schumann and very fine, my dear, and there's a Schubert about thou art the quiet that's much better—and just who are you after all? Music is not what it says, sweetie-pie, music is what it does. Music is realizing that you never will have what you want like hell but here's this that makes it not matter for a minute."

"August, 1906," he said and cut short a soliloquy on music that ought to have developed into something illuminating.

"I was crowding twelve. That was the year Nancy got married. Only in December. Oh, I see, that must have been your heartbreak."

"Do you remember my father?"

"Certainly. He was enormous, and a thick brown beard, and always laughing in it. Or swearing. I loved him. A horse threw me and he sewed up my knee. There's a little scar still. I remember when Andy was born. Old Doc Kinsman brought all the Canedays into the world."

Cy laughed. "He must have been midwife to a whole state." Something in Cy's face! There was just enough light from his handful of embers to show it and nowhere near enough to prove what it was. But it set Josephine's skin to prickling. "My old man knew about my hands."

He looked a little owlish in that dim red glow, bothered and professorial. "My damn hands," he said, "gold in them hills—very comical at Mercy Hospital. The old man loved to fish—and he saw that I could tie a good fly. He never threw a baseball in his life but he knew I was good at throwing one and it interested him. He got pretty much interested. I had better co-ordination and control than most people. Some neuromuscular quirk. A kind of variant, maybe. The old man got interested in the damnedest things. But he was always trying to make up some kind of test for my hands." Cy sniffed, edging the words with a weary satire. "Jo, you must remember. It was the year the whole state dried up. The big drought. Ase made a flurry somewhere with some observations!"

"The water table," she said. She was breathing unevenly for somehow this mattered, and though he was talking from a great distance as if it didn't matter in the least, he must go on. Must!

"That day in August. I don't know what I'd done but we can guess I'd raised hell for him some way. It couldn't have been a lot of fun being my old man and Polly's, and our mother dead long before. Anyway, he didn't raise hell right back. He took me over to Paul Schmidt's."

"He was a jeweler," Josephine whispered.

"He tested eyes too. There was no ophthalmologist in Custis then, maybe not in the state—if you had an oculist he was just some G.P. that had got fed up with making night calls. Paul

Schmidt was a friend of the old man's. Who wasn't? He took me over and had my eyes tested. I guess he was looking for some clue; I didn't know; I was just glad he hadn't scalped me. But then he had me put some little wheels in some watches on Paul's workbench. I could do it better than he could and as easily as Paul Schmidt. Then he said, don't use the instruments. So I put the wheels in right with just my fingers. Paul Schmidt couldn't."

Cy had slipped back into that August. He had forgotten she was here. "You must remember—the peaks were burned brown where they weren't black. There we were outside Schmidt's, on Bannock Avenue. The old man leaned against a telephone pole and started to talk. I can still hear him. Rubbing his shoulders on that pole and talking there in that hellish sun. Pretty soon he didn't even know I was there."

No, I'm not here, Cy. Something in his voice or his distance had faintly sickened her, given her an actual nausea. He seemed to be finished. Desert August sun on Bannock Avenue, long ago. She waited. He must go on. "What did he say, Cy?" she said.

"A lot of things. I didn't make much of it, I didn't give a damn. He said looked as if I could be a good watchmaker, which meant I could be a good machinist, or a good surgeon. I was bored. I knew he wanted me to go into medicine and that was all right with me. I was agreeable. Didn't I always take it for granted I could do anything? If the old man wanted me to be a sawbones, okay. . . . Did I tell you I wrote to Ezra Bartlett just before I left Mercy and asked him to let me work in his laboratory?"

"No. Why didn't he?"

"One reason, I tore up the letter. . . . But hell, all the old man wanted was for me to be good at my job. 'Man that ain't good at his job ain't worth hellroom.'" Cy had produced a voice deeper than his own and it really was Old Doc Kinsman talking out of his beard. Josephine had ceased to feel sick; she felt uneasy and sad. Cy went on, urgently now. "He stood there and said that medicine was on the threshold of its best age. Just like the West had been when he'd come out here and wasn't now—the good time, the great days. I'd heard all that—I didn't care. He said they took him out of a medical school when he was nineteen and made a surgeon out of him. Sure enough they had—he'd been a divisional surgeon in Hancock's army in the Civil War, smack out of a year or so at Jefferson Medical. There he stood scratching his back on a telephone pole and talking to nobody. He said sometimes in '64 he went to sleep on a pile of legs he'd cut off, just like a stack of cordwood. That was the Wilderness. They'd let him carve those legs off, medicine had—but we should have saved those legs, we'd save a lot of them right now, he'd learned that much, and we'd save a lot more tomorrow. In the great age."

He had always seemed as if he had no nervous system at all—as if he were either unmoved or unmovable. Except when something got through. When it did nobody had better reason than Josephine to know how he could be like a man without skin, feeling directly into your own feelings, knowing exactly what you were thinking and feeling. He could not possibly be as unmoved as he looked now, and no emotion whatever in his voice. There was plenty of emotion in her—her heart was laboring. Put his damn machine on her and find out how much that counted up to!

"But we were going to learn a lot now. He was sorry he was old, he'd like to stick around and see what they found out. He was sorry he'd had too good a time to look into any of the things he'd thought about. Probably couldn't anyway—he snickered and said he liked to think he was a wise old coon but he wasn't. But we'd find out now and, by God, it was time. Ought to have found out long ago. I can hear him. 'Ain't no pain nor shame nor mortification in the world like seein' a man or a child die because you don't know enough, because nobody don't know enough but you always take the blame.' I know what he was talking about," Cy said, and now there was emotion in his voice—a hard bitterness. "I've been there—I know that shame. I've lost enough of them because I didn't know enough, because nobody knew enough, but I took the blame."

Josephine reached out and took his hand. Was this the darkness that had overspread him? But then—why, then he must want with every atom of his soul to be back there, it was true—why, of course, he wanted the endless thing, she had always been right about him. His big square hand clasping hers was hard as metal.

"He was right as hell!" Cy said explosively. "In the last fifteen years medicine has learned more than it did in fifty years before. All you need do is think of old man Bartlett and you know that in the next twenty years it will learn ten times as much. And sure enough, I learned it too. Next time there was a war there was Old Doc Kinsman's boy doing the job in his stride and saving all those legs General Hancock's surgeon had cut off so needlessly. There I was, the blue ribbon product, the brilliant bastard all wrapped up in tissue paper and tied with tinsel. I dressed them and the progress of medicine saved those legs."

His hand gripped hers so brutally that she almost screamed. And had the sense not to. And his voice leaped up. "The Mercy operating rooms were full of gadgets that Old Doc Kinsman would have wanted to cry over—a damn sight better than anything he ever operated with in some farmer's kitchen. And I was the best of them. When the old man's brilliant watchmaker came into one of those operating rooms, well, there was more medicine trained into my fingertips, more I took for granted as mastered long ago, than he ever heard about in his life. Too bad he didn't live to learn it. Too bad he couldn't be born again and learn it. He might have saved a leg or two more, or a life or two. He might have been spared a little of that shame of watching a child die because he didn't know enough, because nobody didn't know enough."

He dropped her hand, thrust his own hands straight out from his chest as if shoving something away, stood up in the shadow under the willow. "In his lowest moments he was a better man than I ever could be! I could operate rings round him. I could look at a batter and throw a curve for a third strike—and just like that I could do offhand things that were altogether impossible to Wes Kinsman. There wasn't anything I couldn't do—and be damned to him. But he had the bowels of life in him and he was inside the art of medicine. I wasn't, I was outside turning flips on the flying rings. I was a pair of hands, I was a damned vaudeville act, I was the village show-off." Standing above her in the dark, Cy said horribly, "What right did he have? I hate his guts."

What Cy was saying reeked of evil; it was evil itself. He was talking blasphemy, something out of the black mass. A furious wrath leaped up in her, for what he was saying was not evil at all, it was simply a lie. It was wrong hideously but the point was only that it was wrong.

She was on her feet too, the willow branch drooping toward her head. Hot and headlong, "But you wouldn't get in there and help with a little of the next twenty years! Never, no soul as pure as you could, not possibly. Not this absurd little up-country hospital and this bush league medical school and these tank town doctors. Not with a lot of inferiors. Not Cy Kinsman, never in the world."

"I would not. And that's the infection I've told you to stay clear of."

"I know all about you," she plunged on. "All my marriage was spent among you. You're one of those great artists, you've got a noble soul—nobody could ever know how noble. The vindictive world wounded you and how pitiful you are! You're one of those hurt souls. So to hell with learning or saving lives."

"The hell with medicine," he agreed. "The hell with Wes Kinsman and Sandy McAllister and Ezra Bartlett. And the hell with you, sweetheart."

Josephine leaned against the rough, scarred willow, loathing Cy with a sick detestation. Then she didn't and was only breasting the familiar weariness and bafflement. Who was she to condemn Cy? And he had talked straight. He had tried to explain something—and if she didn't know what it was, maybe he didn't either. He had been as honest as he could be, had tried to be honest.

"I'm sorry, Cy."

"Hell, we're both sorry. We'll say worse and get no farther. It's just part of this—this imperfectly mated *Gemütlichkeit*."

He had a phrase for it. She would have used a different one. They always went home slowly, as if exhausted but at peace. And maybe she had better not follow that thought any farther. Quiet at night, under the peaks, and at the hedge Cy said, with a long glance backward, "Actually, I didn't have any quarrel with Mc-Allister. Why should I? I was a better man than he was. I don't know what happened, but it wasn't Mac. Damned queer."

He got in the Ford which he had left there when he brought Deborah home. She stood at a downstairs window watching it drive away, its loose whine dissolving into the dark. She knew a lot about Cy Kinsman and there was a lot she did not know. It seemed too bad and she was a patient wench with stubbornness in her soul but at any rate when they could talk like that to one another! And quite beyond the odds it had been an evening with peace in it. Of a kind.

She faithfully drank her glass of milk. And so to bed. As she passed Deborah's room fear rose in her like the shrieking of a fire siren. She was all prayer, please not tonight! She hadn't put Deborah to bed, Cy had, the door was not locked. She got to her own room, took the key from her dresser, locked the door, put the key on top of the jamb of the bathroom door. She managed to get back to her room and undressed and to bed.

Sleep came on her heavily, in a rush, with a confused image of Deborah and Cy dying in her mind. Then she was awake and it had come to protest. This was the worst, this time it had happened. Nothing could have stopped her. She got the key and had the door unlocked and was at the bed. She managed to stop there, the footboard digging into her frantic hands. Counting. Counting the slow rise of Deborah's breast in the dark. She must have lost consciousness for she wasn't counting, but the child was still breathing, still asleep. She managed to force one foot back, then the other. Out of the room, into her own. Groping. She found a pair of shoes and fled downstairs, got a coat in the hall and got it on, stood poised, forced herself out the door. It was over a mile to Cy's and every step of it might be the step she would fail to make.

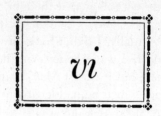

*vi*

THE SOUND of her hand groping for the switch woke Cy and brought him to his feet fully awake and ready to report to whichever ward of Mercy Hospital had called him. When the light went on he saw the dilation of her eyes first. Automatically he noted: something over two months, this was the first since the day of her divorce. Shallow, rapid breathing. Blood pressure would be up thirty or forty points. Palms moist. All the signs of a minor disturbance of the sympathetic nervous system. Physical manifestations trivial out of all proportion to the way she felt. She had on a pair of shoes, a nightgown, a long coat. Just like Deborah.

And blank terror like falling down a dark gulf, like a hurricane blowing. It made those dilated eyes blank. It narrowed her consciousness to a mere dot. It carried her almost out of personality. She was a body that was an automatism and she was fear. She was driftwood on the flood, a leaf that the gale blew, a burrower in the ground out of the light, a crawler in the mud under the water. In the hands of an angry God. Red in tooth and claw. Aberration in nature's plan. She was torment, torture, the preyed-upon. She was the possessed.

Well, the ward had summoned him. He said, "What's the trouble, Jo?"

She collapsed against his shoulder. "Cy, it's no use. We can't pretend any longer. I can't handle it. I won't get better. You've got to put me away."

"What's happened?"

"Cy, I tried to kill Debby."

"No you didn't," he said. He knelt and looked at the shoes, took one off and looked at her foot. "You haven't got any stockings here—you ought to have waited long enough to put some on. You should have waited long enough to get dressed. That's your mother's coat."

"Don't work your sickroom manner on me!" she said furiously, eyes turning fiery, voice shrill. "I stood there by her bed. I do every night. It's all I can do to force myself away. Night after night."

"As a matter of fact you don't, do you? You lock the door so you won't be able to get in on the first rush. You never do go in. Tonight you went in?"

"I meant to kill her. I don't know how I didn't. Unless you put me away, sometime I will. I'm not sane. I'm crazy."

He was wearing a pair of track shorts. Cool night. From his closet he got an old skirt and sweater which she had worn snowshoeing. "Put 'em on." Most decently, he took his clothes into the bathroom and got dressed. He picked up a QM blanket from his cot. "Back to our cradle. Back to our nursery on wheels," he said. He wrapped the blanket round her in the Ford and drove off.

A moment later she began to shake violently. "That's your autonomic nervous system discharging. You'd call it nerves," he said. "Pretty soon it will just be shivering from the cold and quite normal. You're a good deal of a damn fool—why didn't you get dressed? You've done it often enough to know you'll be cold."

"Cy, I was going to kill her! Understand, kill her! I wanted to. I couldn't help it. For months I've been terrified I would. Tonight I almost did."

"I used to murder McAllister every night. Damn good job. Not bad fun, either."

"I had to go right to her bed. I couldn't stop myself. I simply couldn't. I stood there and—" She was panting and couldn't finish.

"You stood there. Pretty soon you came to the barn."

"I counted her breathing. When it was ten, I'd have to. Then

I could hold out till twenty. My hands weren't six inches from her throat." Those hands were opening and closing on the blanket.

Cy drove the Ford. Its best speed, under thirty, as smooth as it would run, the idiotically weak lights probing ahead. After some time he said, "Strangling your favorite method? Or are there variations?"

That loosed a spate of wretched, hysterical confessions and accusations. No sequence, almost without meaning, just the raw stuff of fear rising up into the night air. When she could find no more to heap up against herself, he said, "As you say, I'm only a parent by proxy. Still, I don't think it ever gets beyond slapping their little tails."

So she began to ask the old frantically despairing questions. Why am I this way? What happened to me? Why can't I master myself? Why isn't there any fairness? Where did I go wrong? What does it mean? He drove on southward through farming country and let her worry it for a long while.

Finally he said, "But people are so logical you have to admire them. You're logical. You wanted to be a singer but you had a kid instead. You wanted to be Sam's untarnished and how sensuous houri—but Deborah turned you into an anxious housewife. You wanted a perfect love and a perfect marriage—but the crack in both of them was a little girl that simply stopped you making up dreams about them—"

Josephine broke in on him. "From the moment we got out here it's always been Deborah you thought of first, never me. I never get through to you because she's in between."

Cy slowed the Ford to stare at her dim face in the dark. She could not possibly be aware of having said that: it went too deep. "You in competition with your daughter?" he asked. She heard him, he supposed, but it meant nothing at all to her. "Well, the point is, you set yourself a lot of things. None of them crashed through. Deborah's fault. She was to blame. Logically, why not kill her?"

"That's crazy. I've wanted her to have everything I was never able to get—"

"Sure. And she kept you from getting everything you wanted—"

"But oh, God, Cy! I love her—"

"Some book you read say we can't play hell with people we love?"

She was abruptly finished with Deborah and turned to denouncing him. He wasn't honest—he lied to her. He treated her like a child and fed her pap. He would not realize she was grown up and wanted the truth. He kept promising her she was going to get well and he knew she wasn't. He made up fairy stories—they were silly beyond words. He kept saying that she was going to come out of this triumphantly, she had life on her side, some day she was going to soar up over disease like . . . like, she hurried on, the great ascending octaves at the end of a symphony.

"Hold it," Cy said sharply. He stopped the Ford, the motor running. "Now we're getting there. Look at that one—look it square in the face. Like the great ascending chords at the end of a symphony. Very pitiful words, Jo. God, how you suffer! Look it over." He cupped a match in his hands, lit a cigarette, let her look it over. Presently, "I'll say it's pitiful. A few minutes ago you had the fear of the Lord on you. Terrified. You were going to commit murder. How long—half an hour maybe? Now you're so little scared you can think it all out and find splendid words, perfectly swell words. Just like any beauty-buster in Chelsea. I ask you, are you a potential murderer? Or are you just kidding yourself? Damn fine time either way. Which is it, Jo? And how important is it?"

He had shocked her silent. He drove on again in open, dark country. After a while he added, "That's the one you've been holding out on me. Sure, tell Cy everything except that. Just why? Was I so appalled by the rest of it that it would be shameful if I knew you've been hating her?"

"But I don't!"

213

"Certainly you do—sometimes. Stop kidding yourself. It isn't blasphemy."

"But I love her. I love her more than—"

"I didn't say you don't. Can't you hate her too? Who stopped you singing at the Met? Never you, never a voice that wasn't good enough. And a pure soul would enrapture Sam too except a little girl with a runny nose isn't the great dream. Don't tell me —I've been there."

He drove a mile or two more in silence. Josephine wasn't saying anything. She wasn't in a panic, either. Blown out to sea in the dark. Yeah. And coming back from Painted Post. Let her have it. "That's the last river. I told you you had to cross one more and damned if you haven't. You had to stop being afraid to face your feelings. When you can tell me, you're in."

"I don't know what you're talking about."

"I can pick up my tools and go home. This is the end of it. I'll write you out a discharge."

"After the first few times you said that it was funny. For a while. It isn't funny now."

"You see, I haven't said it before. This is the first time. You're cured."

She was staring at him and God knew what she was feeling. He drove the Ford off the road. A dirt road out somewhere on the edge of hills. He thought one was falling away at one side but couldn't see for darkness and oakbrush.

"Okay, Jo. Start bawling."

Obediently, she did just that. She sobbed quietly at first and then with great racking sobs. He let her cry for a while, then took her in his arms and tucked the blanket round her knees, feet, and shoulders. He laid a hand on her cheek. Tears and her soft hair. She cried heavily, then aimlessly, then just reminiscently. She stopped crying. She had gone to sleep.

She had had to stop denying it and running from it. She had had to admit it and face it. You stood above a ward bed in the dark and wondered what was happening in that mysterious body worked on by the inscrutable forces. Sometimes though there had been no change you turned away knowing that everything would be all right now, life was flooding back. Josephine had regained her wholeness. This was the end of that chapter.

The stars swung westward and, holding her in one arm, Cy grew cramped and very cold. Grayness began to tremble back of the eastern ridge. He could see that they were on the rim of a valley brimming with night. A thin edge of light slanted up from behind the peaks and touched the zenith to a glow. The whole east turned pink in a single instant; dark was running out of the great gulches like water. It was as if the earth were rising from the sea. We love the night, she had said, we hold it to our breasts.

As the pinkness turned golden and gold ran in reflections from gulch to cliff Josephine stirred and murmured, "It's beautiful and I'm all ice."

He relinquished her at once. "You sleep at half a ton." He got out of the Ford and began to swing his arms. "Never mind the milk and cream. You've fatted up. We can really use a fire now."

He gathered sticks in a near-by clump of oakbrush. Josephine came out of the Ford to sit by the fire, wrapped in his blanket. Her face suddenly went hard with anger. "Look at your hair!" she burst out. "Look at that hideous stubble on your chin. Look at those disgusting clothes. Do you absolutely have to look like a hobo who's been thrown off a freight train?" She closed her eyes and shuddered. "Well, there it is, that's me, Cy, that's the way I am. You see me through the most terrible night of my life. So I light into you."

"Just the way you used to light into Sam." Sourly, "For the moment I am Sam. Well, I do look like a hobo. On the other hand, you look—"

She smiled. "Straight from the hands of my maid, but of course I'd never think of that. We seem to be wearing skirts over nightgowns now—and what a skirt! I'm glad I can't see my face."

There were tear stains on it but her cheeks were delicately rosy. Her shins had brown dust on them—that would be from her panicky flight to the barn. Her hair had fallen halfway down her neck. She took out some pins and let it all down, then started to put it up. Hands behind her head in that loveliest and most shattering of gestures.

"What, Cy?"

"Never cut it! Never dream of cutting it." He turned away. "I've got a can of coffee in the Ford. If I can locate some water—"

"No. Is there a chance you can get me home without a policeman seeing me?"

He was surprised to find that they had come less than twenty miles. In the early daylight the sagebrush was fragrant. They saw a badger taking the early sun on a rock. Farms came awake as they passed. . . . Hattie was in the kitchen and troubled, quickly pale at sight of them. "Don't be alarmed," Cy said. "You have an antic daughter. This is just her antic whim to go walking in the dew."

"Josephine! That—that get-up! What on earth—"

"You mean Lord-a-mercy, Hattie. Maybe you mean Lawks." Cy put an arm round her plump waist. "Hattie, tell your idiot child about the time when you used to make Nancy put her to bed because something crazy had happened and you were afraid you were going to strangle her. . . . For that's true, isn't it?"

Insupportable pain came into Hattie's face. "Not Josephine— it was Betty. I didn't seem to get well after she was born." She faltered. "Every time I had to pick up a butcher knife . . . Now she's dead." She flung her apron over her face.

"God simply won't let you be unique," he told Josephine. "Go take a bath."

She did and Cy stayed on in the kitchen, frying eggs for Hattie. "You can stop worrying about her," he said. "She'll be all right now. I suppose you must have known how she locked Deborah's room." Hattie nodded. "Well, you got to the point where you could use a butcher knife without shaking."

"Cyrus," Hattie said, "I just don't know what to make of you."

"I think I must be the parish priest."

Ase came downstairs, was surprised to find him here, but

216

only grunted and lost himself in the morning *Sentinel*. Andy, driving an ice wagon this summer, had gone long ago. Then Josephine came down. She had put on the skirt of the beige linen suit and the terra cotta blouse. Color was running in her cheeks, her eyes were brilliant and her lips made up. She had Deborah by one hand and had put a shining white dress on her and a blue sash and blue hair ribbon.

"Going to a party before breakfast, Butch?" he said.

She certainly did make flagrant love to him. She stood on tiptoe and tried to wind her arms round his waist. She pulled his hand down over her shoulder and slanted her eyes at him. "Today let's go to the barn and scrub your floor."

"Not in that dress."

After breakfast he and Josephine sat on the steps in full morning. The sun of late June reduced everything to flat planes and raw primary colors that seemed to glow of themselves in the shade.

"Butch!" he called to Deborah. "For the love of Pete! That's a clean dress." She was throwing herself headlong into a pile of cut grass.

"Leave her alone," Josephine said. "It can be washed."

Cy kept his lips straight. Presently she said, "What filth I've made you look at. It isn't decent—there should be some pride. I suppose you don't mind. You've looked at lots of broken bodies and suppurating wounds. A craven soul pouring out its repulsiveness doesn't appall you. But I'm sorry, Cy. I really am."

"When I can't stand you is when you're being a complete fool."

She swung her legs under her and leaned against a post, content, altogether graceful. There was no sign that she had been shattered and pulverized with fear a few hours ago, and no doubt she had forgotten it entirely. A shadow from her hair made a curving line across her forehead. Her clear brown eyes were intent on some inner movie show of which he could make out nothing and needed to know nothing. But there was no distress in it. Her throat was full in the V of her blouse and her breasts high. Cy turned his gaze to desert sun.

"Mr. Foster at the sugar company," she said. "He offered me

a job. A hundred and twenty-five a month. That's a lot for Custis and maybe more later. I'm going to take it. I'm going to go down today and take it."

It truly was desert sun, a fire of gold, light realized and interpenetrating, life-giving, life-obliterating. "Go ahead," Cy said. He could close that file and put away his notes. "Yes, Jo, get your job. You've been washed in the blood of the Lamb."

She stood up, lithe, supple, a faint scent of soap and lavender coming from her cheeks. Her cheeks and her bare arms were in that full sun and her blouse was fire. Her vitality was all but overpowering and the sardonic edge of his words had brought a shadow of derision to her eyes, as if she were suffused with laughter, as if she had found knowledge during the night and had found it charged with mirth.

"So long, Cy. And thanks."

"Don't be a fool."

This was the woman who had waked him after midnight, in terror. The thought moved from his mind to hers, as so often. But on the way it got refracted. She put one foot on the running board of the Ford. She held back Deborah, who had come clamoring, and put an arm round her, and her lips were gently satirical. "What a night to spend together. One more night of our—well, what is the word, Cy? Our androgynous honeymoon."

He drove off through the living luminescence. How prompt of Jo, being told she was cured. Well, when something ended, something else must begin.

THE FORMER SENIOR intern of Peter Bent Brigham, the graduate of Harvard College and Harvard Medical School, was answering Pete Estey's questions. "Their manners will be the hardest thing to get used to," he wrote. "Bostonians make good medical men and, making all allowances for the Johns Hopkins, Harvard trains them as well as anything you've seen. They will amaze you by deploring the late radicalism of William McKinley but a medical idea has a little more chance among them than anywhere else. A little more integrity and a little more freedom, and most of all at Benjamin Waterhouse—you'll be at the freest place in America, I'd say. The trouble is that practically all of them are not only Bostonians but Harvard men who were church-school boys, and in all their lives nobody ever taught them how to behave. It will take you time to realize that it isn't rudeness, it's only gaucheness. They're awkward as farm hands and uncouth as cowpokes and they've never seen any manners, they don't know what manners are. The best of them at their best will have about the civility you'd expect from a poor white with a hangover after a night in jail. As a Virginian who was brought up to treat people civilly you'll mistake for boorishness what is only a gross ignorance of urbanity. Stay with it. In moments of maximum stress you can always reply in kind. If you treat a Coolidge the way you'd treat a share cropper you'd caught shooting your horses you convince him you're an aristocrat and probably a Coolidge once removed."

Cy put down his pen. Pete did not want instruction in Boston folk habits. He wanted certification from Cy Kinsman. He wanted assurance that he was up to the appointment that had unimaginably been offered him at the Benjamin Waterhouse Hospital. The cluster of brick gothic from the age of U. S. Grant that housed a great research foundation was about to be superseded by a glistening new plant, and among its new appurtenances was to be the surgical resident of Mercy. Pete Estey's year was ending and McAllister wanted him to stay on and his father wanted him to come home to Richmond, but the Waterhouse had looked him over and offered him one of the three new research posts in surgery it was creating. And Madge, the red-headed nurse whom Pete would marry the day he left Mercy, would not say a word either way. "Who said I'm bright enough to do research in surgery?" Pete had written. "Who said I know enough? I never did. I ought to go on opening the abdominal cavity on the lines laid down—it's you ought to be out there where they lay them down. I ought to tell them this is a job for Cy Kinsman, he'd reflect some credit on your fine new building and its daguerreotype of Dr. Warren by Dr. Holmes. It's your job, Cy."

It had been a fruitful year for Pete or the Waterhouse would have passed him by. He was the faithful husbandman. Day by day he had laid down a little more on top of what he had. Pete was honest, careful, critical. He knew what he knew; he knew what he didn't know. He was a first-rate worker and a first-rate mind. A year ago Cy would have said that Pete lacked the spark, the leading, whatever that final entity might be called. But now let us not believe there are sparks or leadings. There is no final entity. The Jesus factor is a name for the difference between sterility and fruitfulness. Between potency and impotence. It is a generalized concept of the difference between life and death.

Cy wrote, "You are certainly not a genius and after two years of watching one you are cured of wanting to be. You work clean, you don't show off, you are subdued to the job. Leave the rest to the Waterhouse, which does not make mistakes about its staff. They'll let you feel around till you find out what you really want to do. When you've found it, they'll put the resources of medicine at your disposal. It's a simple and ordinary thing and nobody buys an orchestra seat to watch it, but it means you'll have a function and respect yourself and enjoy the job. You are not fool enough to want more and you may be lucky enough to get more. You may find out some of the things we used to gas about. If you don't, anyway you'll have your try. You're an honest man. The job is no bigger than you are, no job is, except in the implications. Accept the truth about it, don't kid yourself, hold to what you know, inquire into what you don't know. What you are clumsily working toward and may by accident find is knowledge. Treat it with respect but it must not frighten you. I say, don't kid yourself. But don't let medicine kid you, either. Distrust everything till you can prove it, then trust it. But when you have to go ahead without knowing all you ought, go ahead on the basis of what you know. Disbelief has got to be your faith and you've got to dissect away illusion like old scar tissue, but if science is just skepticism working with care, it is also humility working in the awareness that the mystery is greater than the disbelief and if the unknowable stops you or even frightens you, then you'd better leave science alone. You work in the knowledge that you can't do much and the confidence that what you can do is worth doing. You'll be in on some good things. Guts and obstinacy will enable you to do some of them. Good luck will add a little more. Do you want any better odds? Get in there and pitch and don't kid yourself."

Writing a testament, Kinsman? Then in the spirit of the purest amateur, for it did not come near him. Pete thought of himself as Cy's heir. He wasn't Cy's heir, he was his vicar. Other men married Cy's wives, other men begot his daughters, and another man would now have his career. He was writing a testament to a man who had potency and fruitfulness, as he did not, and writing it from the far side of Painted Post.

He added, "I would not venture to kiss my late patient for myself—be so good as to kiss her for me. And why not tell me what has happened to all the boys?" The stupidity of Cam

Steele's hands would have landed him somewhere else by now and just where, and did Moriarty's syrupy bass still resound in the stair well of Paupers' House, and had Reynolds taken his intelligence of ice out into a world he was sure to master, and did the patient mind of Joe Geist still grind its meal exceeding small in Mercy's wards? In whose arms the ardors of Rose Stine? But Pete would not know about Rose, a woman of warmth and kindness who understood one lover much too well. "Yours," he wrote, "and some day may we have a drink together, Cy." Peter Estey was walking beside him in a post-midnight corridor off which doors opened on their common job. The moment when he was free to be tired and in that cubicle at Paupers' House Pete sprawled in his chair and friendship flowed between them like a current jumping a gap. And Pete working with him, the other half of his brain, the dependable partnership. In a time when mastery was named Kinsman.

Dissect away illusion like old scar tissue. Well, if you could. When you peeled the skins of the ultimate onion you arrived at—Tanser's Garage.

He wrote to Gid Huntoon who had all the West in his pocket, bidding him find the most trustworthy Indian trader in New Mexico and order him to send to Dr. Estey at Mercy Hospital the two best Navaho rugs in his stock. Might the redheaded Madge like them, for all Pete would need to know was that they came from Cy. They would take quite a bit of paying for. But the resources of Cy's little world were elastic: there was always a truck to drive for Art Ricco. He had solved the problems of his world by contraction. Reduce the radius of need or desire to what was possible. Do that and you would be content. Cy was content. He had the quiet mind. He was St. Francis of the Ophir Mountains, vowed to poverty and the annihilation of pride.

Josephine had phoned him that she was a member of the working class again and her voice had a repulsive unction, and for a week he had not seen her. He worked full time at Tanser's. Lloyd had conceived that a Harvard education should enable him to sell Fords to farmers and offered him the job, but he stuck with the black gang, metal, and the fellowship of his peers. Hot afternoons were cool in the garage, and the texture of reality was the talk of men who were on top of their jobs. At Timmy's Diner, his professional club, Myrtle Hill had less irony for him and seemed ready to believe he was qualifying for a merit badge. He and Lloyd Tanser talked of a camping trip on fabulous trout streams and might even make it. Advancing summer brought the desert to Custis, especially at brick red, vacant evening when the earth could be felt breathing after the sun went down. Cy walked it like a garden, not a glorious garden but one you could be at peace in, if the radius were short enough.

"The name is Josephine Willard," she said on the phone. "You may remember me as Jo Caneday. Have I got to come looking for you? Where have you been?"

"I supposed you'd gone on a drunk of virtuous labor."

"Does that go for Deborah too?"

"I thought she'd like to make your acquaintance."

"You can't play fast and loose with her affections. It has given her ideas."

"What ideas?"

Josephine laughed. "Malnutrition, I think. Her heart is breaking because you have no one to cook for you. Obviously she sees herself in your kitchen. She thinks she and I ought to have a party for you."

"Well, why don't you?"

"I haven't got a chance not to. Sunday afternoon. At your place—Deborah wants no one outside the family circle. Get a steak. Get lettuce and olive oil and vinegar and mushrooms. I'll bake Deborah's love into bread and pastries for you."

He swept the barn to a facsimile of officers' quarters. He dusted everything till an inspector's gloved finger would have shown no stain. He aligned his books and spaced his furniture as with ruler and dividers. It was a dwelling for the peaceful mind, he decided, it was satisfaction by simplification, and he drove off to call for his hostesses.

Deborah was eager—and enchanting in a new yellow dress

and yellow bow pinned to her silken hair. But Josephine! Cy stood back and laughed. "The job's got a good credit rating."

It was a dress of thin silk, silvery green, bits of straw-colored embroidery, a gray frill falling from the deep V of the neck across her breasts, which it was not intended to depreciate. Big oblong buckles of shiny steel on new shoes with high, curved heels. A small hat of straw with a band of that silvery green round it. And the substance of Josephine riotous with health and pleasure—she had leaped up like those ascending octaves she talked about.

"It's the first dress I've bought in two years. Do you like it?"

"It's gorgeous. A little flagrant maybe—or do I mean seductive?"

"Surely we don't say seductive in relation to you," she said sweetly. "I promise you I bought some other clothes too. I'm solvent with society now and there are going to be some amenities. Get yourself some clothes."

"Do I feel just a trace of whiplash?"

"Maybe. The point is, Ase and Hattie want you to come to dinner Friday. You can darn well dress for it. Get some clothes and do me credit."

Sunday afternoon in Custis—but with the Fourth of July tomorrow and an occasional premature giant cracker in the neighborhood. Coolness and subdued light in the barn, his curtain drawn. Deborah began to set the table, grieving because he had so few dishes but staunch to make the best appearance with what he had. He showed Josephine a new batch of clippings about *Endymion at the Finger Lakes* which with perhaps ambiguous thoughtfulness Frank Henriquez had sent him. They had little news for her; at the Carnegie library she had watched the critics take the book with almost unanimous satisfaction and seen it grow into something that would be a best seller soon—as Frank's penciled note said, "re-orders tell the story."

"I wonder if it will make a conflict in his soul," she said. "It's so dreadfully inartistic to make money."

"It's a conflict he'll be able to resolve."

"Now what?" she wondered. "Paris, I guess. And thinking

what dreadful oafs the people are who bought the books that paid the passage. . . . You know, I thought Ase would be furious. He isn't. He knows that professor is just Sam making a soulless Philistine out of what I'd said about my Pop but he thinks it's a fine book. He thinks Sam is a first-rate man. Ase is dead sure now I was a fool to clear out."

"What about Hattie?"

Amusement glinted in Josephine's face but she didn't answer. She went to stand by the piano. "Liszt? Who's been playing this old battle piece for you?"

" 'Rhapsodie hongroise, No. 2.' I have."

"What?"

He sat down and began to play. With an axe in each hand. Striking fully two out of five notes right if perhaps not at the right time. He heard Josephine shriek, and it gratified him for he would have felt that way if he had seen Cam Steele lance his first boil. A series of rapid notes threw him. He went back and started over. Back again. Again. She came over and leaned against the piano, in tears. "When you get round to it," she said, "in the middle of that run the figure eight with the dots means an octave higher than you're missing."

"Can't think of everything."

He tackled it again. Josephine wept and moaned some more. She fell into a chair and he could hear her heels drumming on the floor while he fought some chords. "The two $p$'s mean softly," she gasped. "That means don't hit it with a club. Give me the stool." She sat down. "This is how we do the run." She ran through it several times. "Now the chords. . . . Now you do it."

"Give me time," Cy said. "I will."

In the big leather chair again she lay back and closed her eyes and shook. "How long did it take you to master those four pages?"

"About a week. You give the critique now."

"Well, a few points. Usually we like to have both hands play their notes at the same time. The reason some of the notes are black and some aren't and some of them have those little tails and bars at the bottom is that we think some should last longer than others and some should be faster and some slower. Liszt liked it that way. Measures are supposed to be the same length and you're to do what Liszt asks—he won't meet your convenience. Some of us believe there should be rhythm and accent too. You see, Liszt had ideas about what it should sound like."

"What you've heard," Cy explained, "is the first approximation. I'm proceeding by successive approximations. See me in a month or two. Or a year or two."

"You simply walked up to the 'Second Hungarian Rhapsody' and said, let's go? You started from scratch? You figured it out and went ahead?"

"I bought a musical dictionary."

"No Czerny. No scales. No finger exercises. You wouldn't begin with, say 'Swanee River,' or 'Fair Harvard.' You'll show Josef Hofmann where to get off."

"I don't see any reason for signal practice. Get in and try for a touchdown—nobody can lose. I wouldn't hang up my hat at Harvard Medical School and walk in and operate on the brain straight off. But I can't kill anyone trying, here."

"Liszt maybe, or the neighbors." But, still radiating mirth, she was less amused. "You know, Cy, just for that I wouldn't be surprised if you pull it off."

"Of course I will." Deborah came and climbed on his knees and remarked that she hadn't known Cy played the piano. "It's time I did, Butch. It's time both of us did. What about getting her some lessons, Jo? Is she too young? I'll pay for them."

"I might as well have two pupils."

His women put on their aprons and got to work. Deborah concentrated on her jobs, her forehead creased and her eyes solemn. An arm round her, Josephine helped her through a French dressing for the lettuce, then covertly threw it away and made another one. At dinner she was regretful that Cy had no candles and it was too light anyway, but otherwise at a peak of dignity and pride. She was at least twenty years old.

"It was a fine party," Cy told her. He kissed her forehead and rubbed his cheek across her hair. "You're a fine housewife, Deborah, and a first-rate cook, and the best hostess in the world. And I owe you a party."

They washed the dishes and restored the living room to its geometrical neatness. Deborah read the Custis *Sentinel's* comic section while her parents talked and then they put the Caneday equipment into the Ford. An evening breeze was coming from the canyons to cool the town and Cy drove out to the University on its southeastern foothills before turning home. Violet dark came on and from somewhere in the town a rocket swam up the sky and burst in a spray of stars.

"What was that?" Deborah said.

He realized it was the first she had ever seen. "It's jumping the gun but I'll show you." He found a stand selling fireworks and bought an armful of pinwheels and flower pots and Roman candles. At the Caneday house he began to set them off, across the big vacant corner lot next door, and Deborah sat on her mother's lap, transported to fairyland. He should have remembered fireworks! He should think faster and farther ahead, he should remember how cheaply you can buy happiness for a child.

Ase came down from the porch and took over the display, using his stogy as a match. "Here, Debby," and he helped her hold a Roman candle. Then he slapped his thigh and laughed. "Your pa bought a crate of those one Fourth, Cy. He lined up about a dozen of us on two sides and we had a war. Charged each other with Roman candles. Wonder we didn't all lose an eye."

Josephine said "Bedtime," and carried Deborah away, her good night floating back in the dark. That equation was solved— at least for the time being—and Cy went to sit on the front steps and listen to the creaking of Hattie's rocker and an occasional remark from Ase. Josephine came back and sat beside him. Too dark to get the effect of that dress but there were many radiations, health, peace, satisfaction, confidence.

"We ought to give her a real Fourth tomorrow."

"You're doing all right, Cy."

The four of them sat there in the mild night, the rosebushes and box elders swaying and a clean smell overcoming the desert dust. Till Josephine remarked that the working classes must watch the clock and he thanked her for a good day, said good night to Ase and Hattie, and went home.

In a cheap new suit and new shirt and tie he intended to speak pointedly to her on Friday, but when he got to her house it was clearly an occasion. Her brother Andy was in white flannel trousers and blue coat. Josephine, in and out of kitchen and dining room, had an apron over another new dress, white and tight and short-skirted and, to the anatomist's eye, an acknowledgment of July in that there must be very little underneath it. Deborah had been put to bed and required a visit. He came downstairs again and Albert Warren and his wife had arrived. The President of the University, elderly, pompous, but able to evoke respectful manners from Andy.

It was a dinner in the Custis culture, with chicken and a gelatine salad and hot biscuits by Hattie and icebox cake by Josephine, and Josephine rising to change plates. When it was over the three women went to the kitchen to wash the dishes and Cy remembered the shock of a Harvard professor who had lectured at a college in the Middle West. "Why," the adventurous pioneer had remarked to Cy, "the professors' wives do their own cooking!"

It was clear that this had been contrived but just why had not yet appeared. Puzzled, Cy went out to the front porch with Ase and President Warren and acknowledged the solemnity of the situation by accepting a cigar. They sat behind the softly fluttering Virginia creeper. The academics talked about their institution. The summer term had begun on Tuesday and there was a heavy registration. A new regulation from the State Department of Education was requiring most schoolmarms to get summer credits. Mr. Warren had no confidence in the requirement but supposed that some of the younger ones might acquire husbands too. Ase regretted the passing of the summer school that had been just the students you'd flunked during the year and some high school principals finishing an M.A.

The President got round to administrative problems and presently reached a vacancy he had been unable to fill for the summer and had to fill before fall. It paid sixteen hundred dollars, which was high for an instructorship, in fact the highest paid. He needed a man to teach Physiology A at the college and repeat the course in more detail for first-year students at Hockett Medical School.

Cy had not foreseen the knight's move. Mr. Warren made it, said, "Dean Sorenson and I have been wondering whether we couldn't get you, Dr. Kinsman."

No one had used the title for months. But it was not the title, it was the offer that begot in Cy the first degradation he had ever felt. Any other emotion would be more tolerable but he said quietly enough, "That's kind of you, Mr. Warren. But I don't know any physiology."

"You must know enough for this job."

"Only what I had at Medical School. My training was surgery, not physiology."

"Sorenson and I have looked up your training. We're sure it's adequate."

"I wouldn't teach what I don't know." Rage had come alight in him. He fought it back. "It's kind of you to think of me, Mr. Warren. . . . I'm sorry. I'm—the truth is, well, I've got to say no. But thanks."

Ase Caneday threw back his head in an angry movement but said nothing, merely looked at Cy, took the cigar from his mouth, put it back, went on staring and smoking. The President said, "Maybe this state should never have had a Medical School. Certainly it ought not to be in Custis. It ought to be in Windsor—more hospitals, better medical men—most of the faculty commute from Windsor. I realize our facilities and our standards are way below the training you've had. I thought maybe you'd help us improve them."

"You mean you thought you'd hold out a helping hand to Wes Kinsman's boy!" Something interfered with his fury and he struggled to identify it. Vision of Sam Willard. The artist cannot accept charity. But they had no right to make him feel ashamed.

"Lay off, Al," Ase Caneday said. "If Cy's too good for the job, he's too good for it."

Degradation, ignominy—they were new sensations and he had supposed there was nothing new for him to feel. This particular contempt was one he had prepared no safeguard against. He had made a logic for his life and this violated it. Cy stood up and could not even speak. But Josephine came out of the house and they went down to the Ford together and got in.

"You turned it down, of course," she said.

"And you put Ase up to it. Are you trying to bring me to Jesus?"

"I don't even want you to come to Jesus. It was Ase's idea. People have this idiotic idea of trying to help out."

"Physiology! What do I know about physiology?"

"Nothing, of course. And it's just a hick college. After Mercy Hospital. After Harvard." She hummed a phrase, then sang it without words.

"What's that?"

"Haydn. 'He hath cast down the mighty from their seats.'"

"As a matter of fact," Cy said, "that was Ase getting down his shotgun."

She looked at him unruffled. "Well, put yourself in his place. Your daughter has messed up her life. Nobody in your family ever got a divorce before. And she has taken up with a tumbleweed. She lost her virtue to him long ago. You do what you can, don't you? You see, he doesn't know about our naked sword. He wouldn't believe for a minute how chaste we are. Who would? I hardly do myself."

Cy let it pass. He started the Ford and drove off down Orchard Street. By habit he headed down the valley. Josephine said, "I'm fed up with driving nowhere."

"Want to walk?"

"Have we got to spend our lives driving or walking?"

They had been of some service to her, now the hell with them. Did she want to dance at Dreamland? Did she want to play slot-machines at a spa? Did she want to go to a movie?

"We could go to the barn and have a music lesson," she said, probing for a nerve, and just for that he drove to the barn.

She arranged herself in Wes Kinsman's office chair and was looking for some kind of showdown. Theirs was a versatile relationship, they had a surprising repertoire of emotions for each other, but the one constant was hostility. Start down any path, let any emotion run long enough, and in the end they were facing each other with weapons. A fundamental and inescapable battle. And it was only partly obscured by a dilemma, by her ability to storm him with her loveliness. As now, on the edge of light and shadow, the beauty of her hair, one cheek highlighted, the sweet meeting of her neck and shoulder, the resilience of her thighs under that simple white skirt. The long curve of thigh and calf, and stockings by Cy Kinsman, and how much of the lithe pose she had fallen into was a weapon for the battle?

She said with ready clairvoyance, "Of course not. What you should have told me was to cut half my hair. And at that, Cy, I'm half alive at least. I think that gives me the edge."

"That's what I told you long ago," he said, evenly.

"What you're going to tell me now is why you won't take that job. And I've had all the lies from you I can stand."

Cy supposed there could be no greater dishonesty than for her to exercise her unquestioned right to demand and receive honesty from him. However, she had the right, just as she had a dower right in this barn and all its implications. He said, "If it's the garage part, that's easy. It's a job I can do in its own terms. It's a good job and I do it and the results are there. Maybe you remember a faint longing back long ago—wanting to live at peace with yourself."

"So that's the grease monkey. What about the bootlegger?"

"It doesn't bother me. There's no pretense about it. I'd call it decent."

"Is it decent to waste a fine talent? How decent is it to throw away nine years of training and everything you were meant to do?"

231

"That's harder. I thought it was a brawl with McAllister. That's what it looked like but it wasn't."

"What was it?"

She was outdriving him: she was making him mad, which wouldn't do. "How many ways can I put it? All the little poets that used to gather in your Twenty-Third Street purgatory—they talked about anarchy. The drivel they thought was thought! But I was the thing itself. I was a pair of educated hands—nine years of it. I was hands for their own sake—skill without function—skill in a vacuum."

Josephine nodded. "You're getting to be a fine little poet yourself. I've seen it coming on. You talk beautifully."

He crossed to the big chair and gripped her soft shoulders with both hands. "Remember, I don't have to explain myself to you!"

She sat quiet and said quietly, "Yes, I think you do."

"All I know is, there are two things a man has got to respect. He's got to respect himself and his job. If he can't find an integrity within the job and toward the job, there's still an integrity left to him. He can stop pretending and get out. That's what I did. I quit."

Whether that explained anything to Josephine, he was sure it was as near as he would ever get to explaining it to himself. If you lose, you cut the loss. If you've been wrong, you concede the error. If you can't have what you want, you reinterpret the universe and learn to live on the diminished margin. All of which, now that she had found her own terms, would mean precisely nothing to Josephine Willard, née Caneday, a handsome wench, harmoniously formed, who lit desire in you like any movie romance and was fool enough to think that if they just loved each other there would be no failure or despair.

"I suppose we all have to seem noble. Cheap enough at that," she said. Cy Kinsman had taught her that the foundation of knowledge was absolute disbelief, or as odd a relationship as the permutations could produce had instructed her that you disbelieved Cy altogether at the moment when he was doing his utmost to tell the truth.

The light fell off still more toward the wall where his cot was. She stretched out on it prone, chin in her hands, the remembered posture out of Chelsea when all this was going into the solution. Neither of them had any more to say. Josephine stared at the tapestry of her discontents, or his, and he stared at Josephine, all warmth and softness, forbidden. After a while she saw something on his desk and went to look at it—a four-inch kitchen cabinet he had made for Deborah's dolls' house, a job of fine joinery, ready to be varnished.

Josephine picked it up and held it to the light, put it down and looked at him. "Me, yes—my daughter, I think not," she said slowly. "I owe you something—Deborah doesn't. I think it's a kind of disease to use a child for shelter, Cy. You want even parenthood for nothing, don't you?"

Suddenly, appalled, she put both hands to her cheeks. "I'm talking just the way I talked to Sam!"

"You often do. For the same reason."

She had produced the effect herself but he was grateful for it; hostilities were over for one night. Restlessness carried her on to the piano. She stood looking at his "Hungarian Rhapsody" and wanted to say something about it but didn't. She sat down and began to play, then to sing softly and aimlessly. "Oh, once I wore my apron low!" Effortlessly produced, that deep contralto with its power of disturbance. She went on from song to song and as Cy felt the room growing electric he knew that she did too—this so odd room with its faint smells of horses and leather and grain, its spectres from a simpler time, its ambiguities of this year. She had probably not intended it as a weapon when she began to sing, but within a few notes she had remembered what a weapon it was, and by now she knew what it was doing. Her anger had almost got through, now her voice got entirely through. Till there was no escape from it, till it was triumphant, and she finished and swung round on the stool looking at him, her cheeks flaming, her breast high with a caught breath.

She looked away. She crossed to the big chair again, un-

steadily, as if under a drug. Simply sat there, not looking at him
Waiting.

"Jo! Take down your hair."

She gave him part of an oblique glance. Her fingers were
slow, clumsy; she took out a half-dozen pins. She could not
speak above a whisper. "This is . . . it's lewd." Her hair fell
over her face and shoulders.

"Never cut it!"

"You . . . you're making me cut it."

He stood above her chair. His fingers were as awkward as
hers, touching her hair. She sat quite still, her lips set in something less than a smile. With slow effort, she said, "Then after
all I'm not . . . then you're not . . ."

Whose will had his arms reaching for her there was no
knowing but she stood up inside them and fled against him.
They could not get enough of each other's lips and need and
necessity, desire and fate, were fused. He was again holding
life itself in his arms and they strained together, but even as
his hand went to her breast he stood away from her and managed to mutter, "That's what you wanted. And be damned to
you."

She slumped to the arm of the chair. "Not altogether," she
whispered. She rejected the chair, crossed to the cot, stretched
out on it as before. "Only in small part." Her breathing was
still as rapid as his own and no doubt her arrest as painful but
she looked altogether tired. "Still, we seem almost daring to
face it. Or are we?"

"You want to be paid in full, don't you?" Savagery which he
knew to be checked desire went into the question without in
the least relieving him. "All right, here goes." He drew a long
breath, felt it quiver, let it go with a long sigh. He began again.
"Sixteen months now. You were just any pretty girl that didn't
like her life too well and then I had to live with you all my
life. Sixteen months. I close my eyes and there you are. I come
to suddenly in the street, or at the garage, or here—and I've
been listening to your voice, I've been sleeping with you, I've

234

been living with you all my life. I take you to bed every night. There's no escape from you."

"Quite accomplished poets have said those things to me, Cy. It's very beautiful language. I wonder why you don't do something about it."

"I'm not going to."

"Oh?" She made the syllable mildly inquiring, then repeated it with simple disregard. "Oh."

She was looking at the harness closet of horses dead long ago. Wherever she looked, she could see it plain—now. This must correspond to something. To facing the truth about that panic beside Deborah's bed. It was in the open. She had forced it there.

After a while she sat up and said, "Aren't there more words that go with that?"

"You've got to have the full fee. All right. I could sing it like a song—okay, Jo, I love you, I have for sixteen months. It's something new, there's never been any other woman I absolutely had to have, or—"

"Or couldn't? Sure, Cy, no one doubts you."

"That's the word you want, isn't it? You want me to come down under a pink spot and say it. I love you. Do you want a comment from the gallery? There's nothing to do about it except laugh."

"One trouble with that speech is, it's a filthy lie. You don't love anyone except Cy Kinsman."

He shrugged, "Then just say I was tipping you your dime." Then his rage leaped up again. "Love?—God almighty, Jo! Love? It's a pale word—all right, you like people to talk like a poet on a drunk. Last fall, this winter and spring—good God, can a man and a woman go through that together—what is there that can be deeper?"

She nodded. "Anyway, there's one thing you've said that's true. Only, it seems to mean different things to us."

"Love? My God, Jo, we won't be free of each other till we die."

"That's true. I still say, it doesn't seem to mean the same to both of us."

235

He had nothing more to say. Presently she began to put her hair up. It had been her barren surrender. No sign of emotion was left in her but her hands working at her hair stabbed him with desire.

"You know, Cy, I'm not proud of my mind. But the things you've just said—if there's any center of the world, they're it. Well, in my book you don't just say them and feel pleased you've said them nicely. If they're true, they're what anyone's life means and it's indecent to just say them. To just say them. It's kind of dirty—a little obscene—it seems, oh, I said androgynous once. You don't just say them, you act on them."

Cy said quietly, "I'm not only in love with you, Jo, I seem to be in love with death too."

Also quietly, "Or could we put it this way? It's safe to make love to Deborah."

"I don't know what the name of the infection is or how I caught it. The point is, I won't pass it on to you."

"For your sake, I hope that means something. I don't think it does. It's just some pretty words. You know some good ones."

She picked up her hat, then put it down again and faced him. "I suppose I always did mean to try. I tried hard too but one of us didn't have quite enough. Do your words explain what shame is? Am I shamed or are you? Of course it isn't as if you were, well, forgive me, Cy, it isn't as if you were . . . impaired."

She smiled at him. She came up and locked her arms back of his neck, pressing against him, her breasts soft, her waist firm, her thighs slender, warmth and tenderness and promise. He felt her breath catch. She stood back and smiled again.

"We talk so much about being decent—there are so many ways not to be, aren't there? And it's been the hell with so many things lately. But we must remember that I do disturb you a little, in my way. So the way to take care of everything is to hurry out now and find one of your little tarts, isn't it?"

Shelf of books. Shelf too of Old Doc Kinsman's medical notebooks. Stack of Cy Kinsman's notebooks. Clipboard of mathematical computations, including many eclipses on Jupiter. "Second Hungarian Rhapsody" in its seventh page. Miscellaneous properties: furniture, a rug, old surgical instruments, a knife for carving gifts to Deborah, photograph of snow and sun on Mount Gallatin.

To Jo the victory. She had stormed the position and made it untenable. Retire in good order and prepare another position farther to the rear. A retreat could be conducted indefinitely, forever. Or it couldn't.

Cy went to his desk and picked up a half-finished problem in integrations and began to set up equations. For a minute or two. He got up and went out. It was eleven o'clock and should have been sometime next week. The night wind from the peaks threshing in the trees. A light came through the open window of Polly Zeeland's living room and he stopped in the driveway to look at his sister at her desk, bending over her job. What would she do when she had made order of the mad philosopher's hundreds of thousands of pages? What will any of us do when the illusion runs out?

July, the parched month, month of the desert, of desiccation and blowing away. She had done a good job of work tonight. She had forced it out from under the brush and rubble that had been heaped on it. It was in the open.

Late at night in summer Custis was a dreary town, with the movies emptying, mechanical pianos pouring their music through the open doors of spas, a traffic at false-fronts known to be speakeasies. A strain of orchestral music came on the wind from Dreamland, the dance hall several blocks away. Cy walked faster. Certainly. That was what he had come out for.

An automobile horn spoke a syllable from the curb. Emmy Hill and Art Ricco in his parked roadster. Sight of a friend was the shadow of the tall rock and Cy went gratefully to stand with a foot on the running board.

"Goin' somewhere, Cy?" Art asked.

"I'll buy you a drink."

"We had a drink," Emmy said.

"What else have you been doing?"

237

"We've been driving. We've been dancing. What else is there to do?"

"Well," Art said, "we been fighting too."

A wirelike tension between them and that was too bad for these were people who lived in the light, who did not fumble. They were foursquare, they subdued circumstance to their will. Emmy with carmine lips and eyes of eagerness, at the crest of youth, fresh and full-blown—but strained and unhappy. And Art mutinous. It should not be.

"Better let me get you the drink."

"I don't want a drink!"

And Art, "By God, I do!"

"Go get it," Emmy said. "You brought it in. You can drink it."

Cy looked at that pretty, stricken face, then at Art. "I think you ought to marry her."

"What's it your idea we brawl about?"

"I won't—" Emmy said but Art cut in. "Babe, it's up to me to say what I do."

Cy swung away without even raising a hand. A one-step from Dreamland sweetened the night and he headed toward it. The wisdom of the aloes seemed to indicate that it had to be shown to someone unspecified that someone else was male and if the late resident had a succession of vicars, so also might Josephine.

JOSEPHINE MADE an appointment for the lunch hour and went to see the superintendent of schools. He had been principal of the high school in her day and he called her "Josie," the nickname of her classmates. She asked if he had a job for someone who knew music.

"Why," in answer to his question, "I've never liked office work. It's always been just something that paid a salary. For the long pull I'd rather have music."

He questioned her about her training but that was just a formality, she knew. After all she was a Caneday, she was a member of the office-holding caste, the Custis oligarchy. A daughter of Asa Caneday was entitled to claim her perquisites. It proved so. The music teacher at Custis High had resigned and got married and the vacancy had not yet been filled. The schools would open on September 7, the day after Labor Day. The principal was on his vacation now but when he came back Josie could find out what would be expected of her and could work out the details. The superintendent was happy to have her and was sure that she would do a fine job for Custis High.

"You aren't thinking of getting married?" he asked.

Her cheeks heating, Josephine looked at him narrowly. But apparently she did not have to pay that particular tax here, the question was in good faith. "I'm not thinking of it. I'm twenty-six, Mr. Petty, and after a divorce you don't marry too eagerly."

She went back to the big-windowed offices of the sugar company on the tenth and top floor of the one Custis skyscraper. This must be a landmark or a meridian. The Met's contralto had made the circle from Custis High to Custis High. And a good thing too. Delilah and Amneris leveled out as choruses, the glee club, the spring cantata, and something showy for commencement day. Artiste was the word; the Caneday family's artiste had had her talents appraised exactly at last. She thought, I always said I'd live by my voice and that's right, I'm going to.

But how swift and brief, a few hours and the speed of light. She had gone to New York to be a singer and there had been failure and love and marriage. And motherhood and hard work and failure. And coming home and divorce and love and failure. In the course of no more than a forenoon.

The iceman who would be a senior at the U next fall was superior. "It's an old maid's job. The big boys on the football team loaf in the music room and the teacher gets girlish."

"Miss Peterson must have been pretty. Did the big boys cut you out?"

"I ran the orchestra for her. So what are you going to do about the orchestra? You have to teach them all the instruments. Can you play a tuba?"

"In this family we play anything."

"My sax, maybe?"

"Want to bet?"

He got it and in a few minutes she could play it recognizably. Andy at the piano lacked something, so Hattie obliged. Hattie's repertoire, which had sweetened the evenings of all her children, had shrunk to hymns and "Songs of the Hearth." Which was convenient, for Josephine would not have cared to begin with the "Second Hungarian Rhapsody." She could play the saxophone, all right, or would be able to, for the orchestra of Custis High would probably not get far beyond "Hearts and Flowers." But Andy's "You're not bad, you know, maybe you'll draw some girls too," was not a premium reward, since there was a touch of Cy in the performance.

She had pleased Hattie and Ase. Somehow teaching would be more ladylike than office work—or was it higher in the social

240

hierarchy? And it proved to them not only that she was well but that she had the character to start over. They saw her as picking up the pieces and putting them together again. However else they might see her was still veiled by their affection. Or their fear.

She would not reproach herself for converting so much of her sugar company salary into clothes. They were a satisfaction denied her for too long, and was not so feminine an interest proof that she had regained a healthy normality, and would not Custis High want its music teacher neatly dressed? So there were pleated flannel skirts and a couple of crepe de chine dresses and some georgette blouses now and they justified pride before that mirror. It was one of them in light blue belted round with taffeta flowers and a strong hint that this was a good figure that renewed the iceman's admiration. Andy took her off to a summer-school lawn party at the U, with a big moon and Japanese lanterns, a string quartette, dancing here and there, and a pleasant show of other pretty dresses. It was disproportionately exhilarating, so pleasant a time could hardly be composed of such simple ingredients. And it was doubly emancipating, for not only was she enjoying herself without any overtone from last winter, she was enjoying herself quite out of relation to Cy. Moreover, it led straight to Mr. James Gilson.

He proved to be an English instructor, two or three years out of the University of Chicago, and a most knowing and assured young man, with the manner of easy omniscience and expert knowledge of women that was the ideal Andy seemed to have set himself. He must be the new model of young man. Josephine had known no young men of the period and was absorbed in the experience. Mr. Gilson produced a good effect of making a mild play for a pretty woman which was most welcome. Then he tumbled to something that sharpened the relationship.

"Why, you must be Mrs. Endymion," he said.

"Not since April. A court stepped in."

She mightily impressed James Gilson. And was impressed in turn, for the remainder of the lawn party was sitting in a cove of shrubbery and answering questions about the creation of literature and the gestation of a best seller. Mr. Gilson's trade was literature and this was the closest he had yet come to its living sources. And respected names in type on deckle-edged magazines cherished on his bookshelves were artists whom she had called Bill, whom she had fed spaghetti, whom she had listened to by the hour. The listening paid dividends too; the chatter of Twenty-Third Street was heady wine at State U. The mountain breeze shook the Japanese lanterns and whipped leaves across her knees and it was as odd as possible to be talking here about Sam Willard, that distinguished novelist.

James Gilson's Ford was much younger than Cy's but Josephine found herself appreciating it on the simple ground that it was a different one. When he drove her home—Andy had acquired a double armful of blondes long since—he contracted for dinner the next day. Also for another dress, which proved able to compete with Spoon River and Winesburg and the Finger Lakes for his attention. He took her to the little country club west of town which marked the extreme of fashionable life in Custis. She had never been there before: it was beyond Cy's means as it doubtless was beyond James Gilson's and no matter, or beyond Cy's interest, or perhaps fraught with some threat to Cy since you would meet the high *bourgeoisie* there. But it was cool in desert sunset and a smell of damp grass came from the fairways, and there were summer fashions for women here.

The young man of the period had a large leather-covered flask which he told the steward to use in the construction of manhattans and then return. Josephine had a qualm. "I suppose that's all right for the business-machine operator who can aspire this high. But I'm going to be a schoolmarm in September. Mr. Petty warned me against even smoking."

He admitted things were little better at the U. "We have to lock the door and pull down the shades. But superintendents and deans don't move in this circle. After dinner we can get out of their reach."

She liked that cocktail. Then she was laughing. "Just," she answered his glance, "just that I know the bootlegger."

She found some justification for the trade too, for a little liquor made the evening most companionable. An antic willfulness came upon her and she tossed at this student of contemporary letters all the epigrams she could remember from Twenty-Third Street. A lot of anecdotes too and it was surprising how glamorous life had been in Chelsea. She was a formula of importance for him: an attractive woman, a literary past, and a knowledge of Bohemia from within.

She was a sophisticate too. When he drove the Ford toward the rim of northern foothills, she wondered if there were no other pattern of Custis pleasure, if only the integers changed. He drove off the road and down some ruts behind a clump of willows where a little creek ran. Well, variations on the theme. Collapsible square cups from the bottom of his flask were the first new note, and she could sip rye in a realization that if there was something cheap in being necked where a campus Don Juan probably brought the unattached women among his colleagues, as she was going to be, a drink or two would obscure the tawdriness. The young man of the period had to be a sophisticate because she was and he had heard of the advanced liberality of Bohemia. And she found it not at all bad to be in the arms of a man who seemed to want you there, to be kissed with attentiveness, to have demonstrated that she could produce effects. She put a stop to it when it began to be fervent and James Gilson would think he recognized that as acceptance of the gambit— far enough tonight but tomorrow is another day and no need to rush things. Falling asleep she could face with dry distaste the fact of cheapness, a vulgar little necking party willingly and even gratefully accepted, as if at the first chance, as if any man would do. And perhaps that also could be charged against Cy.

Yet nothing had been settled about Cy, regardless of the shattering scene at the barn which ought certainly to have been final. She was restless, she was embittered, she might even be called obsessed. It had to go on, it had to be fought out. It was a darker battle than at her darkest she had thought but there was no escape. While they still had weapons those weapons would have to be used, no matter to what destruction. He had said that they would never be free of each other till they died. It looked as if that stated the terms of the ultimate battle: maybe what she had to do was to fight to be free of him. She had lost the great issue only to make that loss a greater issue.

Then Hattie brought another issue cutting in. She came home one evening from visiting Mary Heath, whom all the Caneday children had always called Aunt Mary. She had been a friend of Hattie's and Ase's forever, a friend of everyone in the receding Custis of the past, a friend of Old Doc Kinsman and his wife, Cy's mother. And Aunt Mary, Hattie said, was in bad health and looked shocking. And had a lump in her breast.

Josephine's nerves flashed the alarm. "If you mean Cy, Mother, he won't."

"By God, he'd better." And this was Ase, the mild man, who would sometimes flame with the terrible anger of the gentle. "Why won't he?"

"I wish I knew. How I wish I knew! He thinks he can't. Maybe he's right."

"There's been enough nonsense. He'll look at Mary or I'll know why."

"Then you'll ask him to," Josephine said, sick and sad. "I won't."

Ase went to the telephone, got Cy, and simply directed him to come here. That battle had been shifted to other hands but it was all-out. Ase's face was scarlet and she was surprised to see that Cy's was pale. He did not practice medicine, he said, he was not licensed to practice it, this was a case for a practicing physician and surgeon, and the circumstances made it an urgent case.

"You examined Hattie, didn't you?"

"Mr. Caneday, I know it doesn't make sense. It does to me. I can only say, that was different."

Wills clashed head on. Ase was saying things that he would certainly regret, things that made Josephine shudder with concern for Cy for if she could not make him out at all, she knew

244

by now, as Ase could not, that the prohibition was real. He was condemning Cy forever but in the end he had to give up before a granite finality. Cy won; he won all battles, except that neither of them could ever win the one that underlay them all.

It was no friend of the Canedays who left the house. Josephine could not have helped walking to the hedge with him. She could not cope with a crazy world; she simply gave up to a distant sadness, that it had worked out this way, that nothing could be done.

"Cy," she said, "it wasn't my doing. I told them not to try."

"She should see Rulon Williams. Tell her to have him in tomorrow. She must not wait."

"Cancer?"

"That's what you must always suspect."

Sadness grew bitter. In Cy's mind at this moment was running all the knowledge that had made so fair a promise. His hands were the ones that had meant mastery. And stopped short. Powerless. Josephine knew it at last, and knew that she and Aunt Mary Heath were under the same interdict.

He said, "I know. They think I may have brought something from Mercy that Rulon Williams or old Bramwell hasn't got. I didn't. There aren't any gadgets. They think I can help them know. I can't. But I'm sorry to hurt them."

"It's just that Ase wants to do everything if there's a chance a friend doesn't have to die."

"People are friends. I'm sorry."

They could go on saying they were sorry forever. Was there anything they weren't sorry for? Cy left without a further word and Josephine went back to lie awake being sorry for Cy, sorry for the universal craziness, sorry for all the little fictions everyone made up so that he could go on living.

It got crazier. Just before noon she was called to an outer office and was instantly weak before a gust of violent emotion which she could not analyze. For here was Sam.

"Sam!" Her breath as taut as in one of those night panics. "What are you doing here?"

"Come to lunch with me and I'll tell you."

245

In her confused excitement it didn't make much sense. He was on his way to Denver, the guest of his publisher on some outing or celebration or errand that she did not get clear. Except that to go to Denver by way of Custis was hundreds of miles out of his way. He had got in half an hour ago, taken a room at the Gallatin House, would take the midnight train to Denver, wanted to see Deborah, was glad to see Josephine. And as surprise ebbed and took an unacknowledged fear with it, she was glad to see him. Honestly glad without apparent overtones, and intensely curious.

It was Sam who was ill at ease. He was abashed—he was bursting with pride and unsure of it. He had to impress her and knew quite well that he had something to impress her with—and was afraid that he couldn't. It must be the same old inability to make the role good with her. She was in command again.

He laughed sheepishly when she commented on his mohair suit, the thin gold watch chain at the lapel, the obvious expensiveness of everything he wore. "Sure, money—I'm making lots of it."

"You're making time for me in Custis. Even the ex-wife of a best seller!"

"Did you like it, Jo?"

"Of course I did. How could I help?" Except that loss and fierceness swirled in her. "How do I know, Sam? I don't know how I felt about it. I've hated you quite a bit. I'd read for a while and I'd laugh or I'd think how swell this is, and then I'd hate it for making me feel that way. I couldn't tell whether it was you or the book I was hating. It didn't have any right! It had meant so much to me once—it wasn't right to mean anything to me now."

He nodded. "We were a pair of fools." And looked apprehensive.

"My father liked it—he thinks it's great stuff. The truth is, I don't know anybody that doesn't. And heavens, what a splash it's made."

That was better—and if it was the old, simple, direct route to

246

his self-esteem, still it was dignified now. She telephoned the office and was granted the afternoon off and they taxied to his hotel for lavish gifts he had brought Deborah and on to Orchard Street.

"Sometimes you'll have to let me have her," Sam said.

That roused the dilemmas, protectiveness, and jealousy of hundreds of hours. And then they lapsed, for of course she would have to let him sometimes. "The court says no," she said, "but of course you must. Where are you going to be that you can have her?" Yes, and with whom?

Sam didn't know. "I want to go to Paris for a year or so. When I get back. Or over there. If I stay." He flushed, then blurted. "Cassie—well, it didn't work out."

Josephine thought she perceived something of the pattern now. It hadn't worked out—of course it hadn't, it never could, and neither would any subsequent arrangement—and there was an oblique accusation of her, she should have been on hand to bind up the wounds.

Deborah was either the perfect child or else a diabolical one and it was hard to say which. Sam was inconceivably awkward with her, and in spite of all the tears and tantrums she had exhausted on him Deborah insisted on treating him as a stranger. A welcome stranger, a generous stranger who had brought her desirable things, a stranger who must be put at ease and entertained. Josephine grimly understood that this would be paid for with tempests later, and it annoyed her on Sam's behalf but was wildly amusing. And it pivoted on Cy. Deborah conducted him to the swing which Cy had built for her, displayed the dolls' house and furniture Cy had made, sweetly proved the skill at reading Cy endowed her with, quoted him, referred to him, dragged him in by the heels.

"What's Kinsman doing?" he asked.

"He isn't practicing."

"I've been expecting to hear that you were—married."

"Never. Never in the world."

"I always thought you two had something. I was sure you'd fallen for him. Toward the end I wondered if maybe you weren't sleeping with him."

"You knew I wasn't."

"It would have explained a lot."

"We'd have to be in love." It was strangest of all that Sam could rouse no emotion in her with that theme, neither anger nor disturbance nor regret.

Before the afternoon ended, however, Deborah had melted to affection and Sam lost his fear of her and they were having a good time. Josephine watched them with a slow wonder—that there should be no pain or regret in it, that she felt little or nothing. How thoroughly she had been cured of heartbreak, and yet here was what had meant sleeplessness and agony and failure on Twenty-Third Street, and now come to nothing much. Had it been so trivial as it seemed now? Or had the wound healed well?

"Where can I take you to dinner?" Sam demanded.

"There isn't any place you could splurge."

Sam reddened but laughed. "Damn it, I do love it all. I used to think it was shameful to make money. I love it."

"There's a Waldorf here but you wouldn't believe it. There's a country club but you have to belong. There isn't any place, really—Custis does its dining at home. Have dinner with us."

So once more she was cooking for Sam, if only helping Hattie. She was inclosed in a cool, crystalline irony. The same numbers only they made a different sum, the same cards only they had been dealt differently. But Sam set out to be entertaining and he was. He clearly charmed Ase. And why not?—his deft mimicry was now supported by the experience of achievement, the confidence that he had always needed so much. He really was a personality now, something of a success, something of a celebrity. His face was pink, his eyes bright and amused, his mustache eloquent, and she knew all this process by heart. She watched and listened, the scene playing itself against a reverie of six years that was tranquil and sharp, poignant and harmless.

After dinner Ase got out his hoarded bourbon and Sam could

not know that that was an affirmative vote, an accolade. But in the kitchen, scraping plates, Hattie said, "Jo, you did right," and made Josephine smile for a salty intuition that went right through to the reality.

He watched her put Deborah to bed, which also had its vibrations deep as the bass pipes of an organ and yet were without disturbance. Then he said, "Where's Broadway? What do you do for fun in the wild West?"

"Go to the movies. Dance—outdoors in summertime. Or play bridge. Take a ride in the family Ford. Take a walk."

"Just like Utica—just like 'Endymion.' These whistle stops —you wonder if the human spirit can survive. Shall we walk?"

No. Walking in the foothills was dedicated to a particular kind of folly and frustration. So they ended by just sitting in deck chairs on the baked lawn and looking at the dim bulk of the peaks and talking.

Or rather, Sam talking. For Josephine sank into her reverie again and his voice ran lightly across its surface, heard, followed, and yet so thin and distant that it was unreal. Reverie of an ex-wife. The past shook down to a handful of dry waste and a nerve twitched with a slight pain that was mostly regret, regret not that it had ended but that it had ended in so little. So little that it cast doubt upon the best of it. It had been the best! Granted what she was, she had been clean and decent—she had been in love with Sam, she had lived love and marriage and motherhood to the full. To come to so little in so brief a time! It simply could not be that agony and the shattering of hope and all the fierce despair surging from the most secret parts of her could sink to a handful of dust and she be free of him and of the past, here under the box elder and the remote peaks. And it was not only that pain was ended; he had waked her body and her spirit to the only ecstasy she had ever known. Not the greatest skill maybe but he had played on her with such skill as he had and it had been compact of tenderness and hope and anger and despair, now all equally come to nothing at all. Love, hope, despair—a handful of dust in this diminished hour.

He had been talking about the novel he would start—in Paris or wherever. So a divorced wife must help him think well of himself for even this trivial moment, and again why not? She had told Cy long ago what that book would be and now Sam told her, growing grave and hushed. It would be how love crumbles because of human fallibility and misunderstanding, and wisdom comes too late. That meant Josephine and Cassie Morton in counterpoint, and it would be a sin to laugh at Sam growing more austere, more regretful, a more comic figure as the words were more splendid. In fact she had no impulse to laugh, only to smile.

Wiser, you grew, but wearier too. He was austerely sad and Josephine's mind, ranging its usual distance ahead of his, foretold that he would soon be poetically sad, and he soon was. Then there would be strained pauses in his talk, and there were. She knew now how Sam was picturing himself and the role he had created for his hero, as she always had known.

After a truly difficult pause he reached for her. She stiffened and felt a hot surge of anger—he was not so much burlesquing the reality that was her dry regret as he was cheapening it. But anger fell away and for a moment she slipped into his arms readily enough. Why, it had taken only Jim Gilson to show how much earth there was in her and to suggest that maybe the discontent which seemed so exalted meant merely that she had slept alone too long. But too cheap! It might be quite true that any man would do but there was the edged amusement of an ex-wife's knowledge of how he made love, and the memory that she had once lain in his arms with belief rose up to denounce her cheapness and Sam's absurdity. She was out of his arms again, angry at herself and the solid satisfaction she had taken in being kissed and disliking him intensely—for the moment.

She had checked him into a rhapsody of love and sacrifice. Surely Josephine had by now learned forbearance, charity—surely, since the loss of her had taught Sam how to love her. Loss and wisdom—they brought you to realize the best of yourself and surely marriage could be built of them at last. Out of

250

loss, riches; out of folly, the heart's desire. She aloofly listened and watched under the night sky. What was there about her that inspired men to literary heights? Cy had been no more eloquent about death than Sam was about love.

She stood up. "You honestly believe that, don't you, Sam? It's so convincing that it must be true, a minute or two. Get it down on paper." She touched cool fingers to his hot cheeks. "You're sweet, Sam, you really are."

She launched him into passionate pleading and would have none of it, so it faded off in frustration and restlessness. That was the old pattern! She had broken the image of himself he had set up so eagerly. She always broke his images. She always diminished him. She always reduced him to a boy, and now the successful novelist with money in his pocket and a knowledge of public admiration was as hurt as he had ever been on Twenty-Third Street.

"I've got some Scotch at the hotel."

All right but he would get no help from liquor. On the way there she thought suddenly, why, he has to make images of himself and what Cy can't tolerate is an image. Sam's shiny, pretentious fictions were his life; Cy would destroy fictions if in the process he destroyed himself.

"This is my home town," she said at the Gallatin House, "you'll have to keep your door open."

He counted on not keeping it open very long and was buoyant again, a plotter. But she enjoyed the Scotch and it soon drew a mild mist round that unfortunate thought about Cy and round Sam's absurdity and his attentiveness and his purposive plot.

"I tried hard to think well of you," she said. She seemed to be the talkative one now and she was beginning to get a lot of instruction from the evening. She held out her glass and Sam positively leaped to fill it—just wait, Jo! "I tried hard to think well of Cy. I tried hardest of all to think well of myself." She waved the glass. "Got ditched somewhere."

She seemed to be thinking that over with great care. "It doesn't seem so much to ask, to think well of yourself. It's more than I can get. Seems to be more than I can let you have." That was owlish and it was either owlish or conspiratorial of Sam to agree. An owlish hour, in fact, for she was saying, "I'm not an admirable character. Nobody seems to know how simple women are. How simple I am. You don't. Cy doesn't."

"There's too much talk of Cy!" He reached for her and she was grateful to the Scotch for letting her not mind being cheap —I simply am not an admirable character and this is what we call earthy realism, you just don't care so long as you're kissed. But not enough. No, she could not think well of herself. "You do passion more convincingly in fiction," she said and pushed him away. "Never a trace of awkwardness in paper passion."

The Scotch did not withhold her from realizing what a dreadful thing that was to say, more dreadful than Sam realized, but she had had enough to go on and admit that, alas, it was quite true. She had failed to make an imposing figure out of Sam, though she could have his help now, if she said the word. The way he had written it, she was supposed to want it. She just didn't. Too bad. "Or Cy," she said aloud. "God knows I tried to make him seem heroic. My men simply will not live up to my innocence about men."

Why, you're a little tight!

"Will you stop talking about Cy!" Sam was going to impose his will on her and vindicate himself forever in his eyes and hers. "You haven't suffered half enough in ink," she said and deflated passion with what amounted to about an amused glance. "It's getting on to train time." She put on her hat and, yes, the mirror was a little blurry from the Scotch. No manners but some mirth. "If I knew just how far you came out of your way to get to Custis, I could work out passion and the wisdom that builds tomorrow. I'd know exactly what the insufficient wife will be in 'Endymion in Chelsea.'"

She willfully drank what was left of two highballs and on the way to the station Sam made clear, at least for purposes of eloquence or heartbreak or literature, that it was the wisdom of sorrow and not just a publisher's ranch party that had brought

252

him to Custis. Denver was the excuse, love coming to knowledge through loss was the reason.

"There's no such thing as divorce!" he said. "A marriage can't be broken up by a law. All those years—Jo, you've got them forever in your heart."

Not as you think. He would go on always letting his books write his life for him. They might be pretty good books too, even if the life would just be fiction. He would go on picking up his books from such ideas and emotions and experiences of bigger men as managed to strike root in the thin soil of his own. She could not honestly say that that was not as good a life as any other. It would make him think as well of himself as anyone could, and if someone would be forever breaking the very fragile image, there would always be someone else to glue it together again just long enough. But no such thing as divorce? There was divorce so absolute that she could not even care, now, that the reality that had been the best of her seemed just as inconsiderable as the broken image did.

The station smelled of gas and coal smoke and hot oil—the romantic odor that had meant distant places in childhood. How droll that it could mean Paris if she said so, now that he had convinced himself for a chapter or two that he was on fire for her.

"How right I was to come! Maybe you won't admit it yet, but we've cleaned things up. It will come out right, now. I'll come back. Or you'll come on."

In terms of Twenty-Third Street, she had won. She could always win over Sam. "Then what?" she said.

"You know what! Look at your cheeks! Look at your eyes! Oh, God," Sam said wildly, "let's get out of here."

He hurried her out to the platform and down beyond the glare, his hand tight and trembling on her arm. Why, with Cy she looked at the stars above the peaks and made what she could of them, whereas now a scene of passion meant looking at the green and red dots of switch lights across the yards, and she need not make anything of them at all.

Sam was masterful and agitated. He all but groaned. "You're

lovely! You're beautiful." There was a deep shadow at the corner of the freight house and he took her in his arms with what made a good facsimile of hunger—and might be hunger according to his powers. The Scotch was honest: she knew exactly how she felt and took no pride in it and still she would not refrain.

"You do!" He grew omnipotent. "Darling! Jo! You really do." His arms tightened. "Come on to Denver with me! I'll get a stateroom! Oh, Jo!"

Long ago, far away, and just a handful of waste. Yet she acknowledged a thought that rose clear above the Scotch and stayed there for the tenth part of an ignominious moment: it would not be much but it would be a little, it wouldn't be a honeymoon the way there might have been once, or even the way there was one once, but it would not be an androgynous honeymoon, either. And that brought the double chill of disgust and of Cy, and the earthiest of all realisms always proved in the end to be self-contempt. And worse still, Sam was pleading. "Jo! Come with me! Please, Jo! Jo—oh, you must!" She wanted never to be pleaded with again.

"No gain," she said and broke the grip of his frantic arms. She pointed down the yards where a beam of light had swung round a curve and was beginning to grow along the track. "That's the Denver Limited. It's your train."

Sam was neither a dominant male nor a beseeching lover; he became just a man who had to catch a train. At the steps of his car a ghost kissed her again and was spectrally masterful. "I'll be back. I'll make you marry me." Light slanted across his rapt face and his shoulders, he stood in the vestibule and kissed his hand, and with its freight of slight, induced emotions the train slid away in a nostalgic reek of coal smoke out of childhood and a trivial distaste or disgrace out of marriage.

No, you won't. You won't make me do anything at all. Wonder what would happen if someone simply told her to shut her mouth, grabbed her, and threw her on a train. Probably work, nearly anyone, for with this streak of the earth in her and these quite simple needs, with the way she took a running broad jump into any arms that opened, probably Jim Gilson or the traffic cop could make good, and no, for he would have to be one point more than half a man and all my men are half-men, and that's exactly right and just, dear, that old chestnut about the donkey between two bales of hay dying of starvation and indecision, it's that way, it isn't that you have morals for you clearly haven't, it's just that half is the same as half and cancels out, a full stop, work as hard as you can and you can't beat nature's figures, you simply have not got enough, Jo, you come out exactly fifty per cent.

Slight tendency of the mind to skip an inch or two off the ground. But at any rate it was New York Scotch, not something the local bootlegger had brought in. Post-midnight Custis was so quiet you could not hide your thoughts from yourself and her heels punched the sidewalk as if she had some personal animus against it, shoes that were supposed to make her insteps elegant and again a man was supposed to fix his eyes on her insteps and burst into flame. So quiet, so empty that you could not hide anything at all. Sam would always be unstable and charming and vain and weak and delightful, and for Josephine Caneday-Willard-Kinsman-Caneday always dusted and varnished with the preposterous. Yes, and Willard again if she said the word and there was this, that never again could he break her heart. She would always be more of a person than he was, brighter, ahead of him—is the word you are earnestly dodging "dominant"? She would always be dominant. Stronger. Oh, God, I get so tired of being the strongest.

And that word came back when she was in bed, alone in bed she reminded herself with conscientious recognition of the earthy streak, and her skin a little hot, a little gritty with the end of July and the desert summer and the day's contradictions. Not stronger than Cy. Drawn battle. Exact equivalence of strengths. Fought out to the end but to no outcome, simply rest and wait for a while and then get up and fight it out all over again. But that was what had happened to Sam, that was why when he came into this desert town it was just something vagrant, of no moment, a wraith of old emotion long ago, and he left it as empty, as wide-spaced and sparse as the furnishings of an apartment in a barn, and left it forever. That was what had happened to Sam: Cy had happened to him. Well, the darkest battle did have an outcome after all, it had made everything else trivial. Josephine buried her face in the pillow, if she had to bawl let it be one drink too many, let it be Scotch, let it not be love.

*ix*

THIRTEEN and a half months after the first one, Cy had written a second letter to Ezra Bartlett. He addressed the envelope to the Department of Physiology, Harvard Medical School, Boston. He read through the brief half-sheet of penmanship. Then as before he tore it up.

The answer would be a question: why should I make a place for you, Kinsman? And the question would have to be answered: there is no reason. Ezra Bartlett had said in the Harvard Club of New York, of a late afternoon with Pete Estey, that he had once supposed Cy had brains enough for science. Ezra Bartlett, Fellow of the National Academy of Science; Fellow of the Royal Society; Foreign Member of the *Académie des Sciences;* member of the *Deutsche Akademie der Naturforscher;* student of Claude Bernard and Karl Ludwig; student of Asa Gray and Jeffries Wyman and Oliver Wendell Holmes and Edward Pickering; student and friend of William James, of Henry Bowditch, of Charles Sanders Peirce. It was enough to certify that Ezra Bartlett was a scientist and a scientist would be willing to entertain the hypothesis again: it might be that Cyrus Kinsman, senior intern of Peter Bent Brigham; Lieutenant Royal Army Medical Corps; Captain, Medical Corps, U. S. A., surgical resident of Mercy Hospital, repairman, Tanser's garage—that Cy Kinsman might still have brains enough for science. But a scientist would ask to see the data and there were none. If you want to join this laboratory, Kinsman, provide me with some evidence of things done.

Why, he had done a satisfactory job repairing Fords. And he had spent over a year looking for the answers to a few questions, which would seem to be a scientific effort though he had not found them. The frailty of the intelligence is that it will accept subterfuges. The letter to Bartlett was one more subterfuge, whereas the illusion of pride had been that he was done with subterfuges. Throw it away. Till the first step is taken, no step can be right. There was no way out except straight ahead on the path he had started down.

The slight, stooped figure of Ezra Bartlett, the face of weathered granite, the nondescript beard fading to no color, the mild eyes lingered in Cy's mind. And why did he assail Bartlett, who had done him no injury, who had touched his life not at all, with an accusation that was fully half hatred? He picked up a scratch pad and wrote on it, "To stop seeing things as persons. To stop seeing words as things." He crossed out the line. "To know what you're doing." He crossed that out too. "One more than one is not enough." Amusement broke out in him as he canceled that too for he was envying the gift of Sam Willard and his kind to put thought into words. No. His pen suspended. That was exactly the difference. Their whole point was to put words into words; his was the harder job, to put things into words still knowing they were things. "To know that things are things," he wrote and then drew two lines through it. If it happens over and over, if you encounter it again and again, it is a thing and the name you give it doesn't matter and you must not be content with giving it a name.

"A man who talked about genes or germs or endocrine secretions or a virus in 1800 would have been talking about things but he would have seemed a mystic or a madman." He knew now that he was writing to Josephine. "Polly said that our mother was religious. Maybe you had the right hunch: maybe I have to be born again." No, that was a subterfuge. He crossed out all three sentences. "If something is prohibited, there is someone who prohibits." No. "It must be ascertained what is forbidden and who forbids. If I threw away nine years and another year. If I threw away whatever we consider you to be. It is not willed but forbidden. We had better find out what is forbidden and who forbids. So far, result negative."

Hell, it was still another subterfuge and he tore it up. There was no way out except straight ahead. He sat down at the piano and began the first measure of the "Second Hungarian Rhapsody." Give the notes the value called for. He counted aloud.

He made a deal with Tomcat Jones and reported to Lloyd Tanser, "I'm on Saturday afternoon but I'd like to trade it with Tomcat and take the afternoon off."

"You don't need to ask me, Cy. Just tell me."

Past five o'clock, the garage silent, the bookkeeper in Lloyd's office powdering her nose and ready to go home. Well, if you don't know when you cross it, presently you know you have. Cy leaned against the edge of a desk and said, "You'd say I earn my pay?"

"I got no kicks. I never paid you a dime you didn't earn."

"You'd go on to say that the work is up to par?"

"You're good enough mechanic for me. Why, you thinking of quitting, Cy?" Cy nodded and Lloyd nodded in return. "There never was anything in it for you."

"There was a good deal." There had been so much that Cy felt impelled to construe. "You people know what you're doing and how to do it. You do it till you've got it right. And you run Mercy Hospital right. You've got an institution. It's a half dozen more than one." It's not only that I'm one of them; also, for a dime's pay I do a dime's job.

"When do you want to quit?"

"I'll stay the month out."

"Then what?"

"I don't know," Cy said. "Whatever water I wade into is bound to be a damn sight colder."

"If a man's on his toes, if he knows the business, sellin' Fords and repairing them is a good business and it's going to be better." Lloyd looked at him. "You wouldn't consider borrowin' the money and buyin' in with me?"

Cy shook his head. "Thanks, but no. I have a hunch everything comes down to asking the right questions. I know enough answers to automobile engines."

"Well," Lloyd Tanser said, "you ever want a job, Cy, there's a job here."

Dr. Tanser would close no hospitals to him. "How's to take that week after trout and sagehens?"

"A nice idea," Lloyd said, a little wearily. "Later, maybe."

On Saturday afternoon he took one of Joe Bates's six-months-old tan cocker spaniel puppies under his arm and drove off to Orchard Street. He had supposed that Josephine would make it a fete and she had: there were nearly twenty little girls in white dresses, playing games with the decorousness of little girls that always seemed so odd to rowdy little boys. His foster-daughter was half princess and half gamine, electrically charged and sedate at the same time, and instantly she had wanted a puppy all her life and this one above all others. It stopped the party short for a space but presently its owner was willing to let it retire to a box with a pillow in it and went back to being the honored guest.

"You have to feed him, Butch," he said. "And brush his hair and teach him manners."

"Cy," she said, "I'll be his mother," and ran off to join a figure that Hattie was forming on the lawn. Sun glinted in her hair—but Josephine's hair in that same sun had its quality of luminescence. Josephine in net blouse and white skirt, undiminished by desert sun, vehemently lovely.

"You don't forget, do you, Cy? I was wondering if you'd come."

On the far side of finality there appeared to be no antagonism. She met him casually, as a neighbor dropping in, and that must be the key to the future. And birthdays had always been important at the Canedays'. Hattie in her best dress and Ase in professorial seersucker but with an aquiline offhandedness for Cy, the resentment which his daughter did not feel and he would not overtly express. The iceman arrived and hurried in to take a shower and reappear in white pants and play his saxophone for figures in Hattie's party games.

Early August in the Ophirs, with brown patches in the lawn and oakbrush burned brown halfway up the peaks, the smell of summer dust, no sign of the first slight blue mist that would promise autumn. The voices of children were a pleasant shrill-ness above Andy's sax, singing for Hattie and Josephine. Going to Jerusalem, London Bridge Is Falling Down, Oats, Pease, Beans. "Waiting for a partner, we're waiting for a partner. So open the ring and choose her in, And kiss her when you get her in." A dozen of them were shrieking for they had trapped Cy and Hattie. They screamed "Kiss her!" and he kissed the plump cheek, and Hattie blushed like a girl. Presently another con-figuration had Cy and Josephine paying forfeits and redeeming them. At the edge of shade from the box elder they stood in a ring of white dresses. Their touching shoulders set up no field. Her eyes were deep with reminiscent happiness. On a birthday her daughter was playing the same games on the same lawn, in-closed by the same love. A continuity had been achieved and for Josephine it was bedrock.

"I was wrong," Cy said. "Some of it can be got back."

She smiled. "But store ice cream! It really isn't a birthday un-less you get the dasher all to yourself."

"We're a decadent generation."

"And we always used to push the piano out on the porch and Nancy would play it. Or Mrs. Sargent. It generally turned out to be a party for grown-ups before it was over. Lots of people came. The kids loved them to because then they'd forget about us and we could raise Cain.'

"Deborah's having as good a time as you ever did."

"You are too. I like that, Cy."

She took his arm and led him to the deck chairs in the shade and they sat there watching. Why, she was without thorns. She had no urge to remind him of the contempt and repudiation of their last evening. Simply, she was under no pressure. She bore his gaze with awareness and assent.

"I'll have a new job next month. I'm the new music teacher at High."

He wondered. "Is that particularly bright?"

"Why not?"

"Music means too much to you. You'll wear a lot of rough edges on it teaching it to adolescents."

She smiled but not pointedly. "I haven't got your feeling about the pure amateur."

Deborah rushed up with a chaplet of withered flowers, left it in Jo's lap, and whirled away. "She's pretty high," Cy said. "When the shooting's over, take one of those sleeping pills I gave you and dissolve it in some water and give her half."

"I've been expecting some tantrums but there haven't been any. Sam was here last week."

"Sam?" Startled, Cy scrutinized her inscrutable eyes, the free color flowing in her cheeks. "In Custis? Just out of the blue? What was he doing here?"

"He said his publisher was entertaining some blue-ribbon authors at a dude ranch outside of Denver. He said he wanted to see Deborah."

"So how did Deborah take it?"

"Like a lamb. She treated him like a guest, and then she was enraptured, and now she's forgotten about him."

And how did Mummy take it? At least without a hangover. If she had been angered or distressed, no sign of it remained. Hattie called her and Andy was setting up tables on the porch. "Party time. And we hope no stomach upsets." She stood up and walked across the lawn in a flat light that made her white skirt blaze. Easy, relaxed, untroubled, lyric in hip and shoulder.

A taxi deposited Gid Huntoon at the curb and his cowboy yell brought Ase down from the porch. The Old West was a pounding of shoulders. Just in from his damn dam, Gid said, in a voice that published it to all Custis. "Hi, Cy—hi, Andy." With a war cry, "Hello, Hattie!" And the Old West never forgot: he had a big doll under his arm.

262

"Child's goin' to have more daughters than Brigham Young," Ase said, handing it to Andy to deliver.

So the Enchanted Mesa was validated by the arrival of at least one family friend for a birthday. The four males sat under the box elder and Ase and Cy accepted cigars but Andy's refusal outraged the Old West's morality.

"Say I sold the junk man things the neighbors didn't know they lost," Gid said. "Say I had eatin' tobacco on my chin before I got my second teeth. Say I hung round saloons when I'd ought to of been in school and knew too many whores for my own good. But by God, I never smoked cigarettes."

Andy laughed. "You mean cigareets, don't you, Gid?"

"Roll them with one hand and they'll be moral, Andy," Cy said.

But it turned out not to be a grown-up party after all, for when the guests began to be called for amid flurries of contention and a few tears, Gid announced that he didn't want no salad, he wanted a man's meal and would take Cy along to share it. Sunset began to color the lawn. The air became alive. And Josephine said, "I'm sorry. I was hoping you'd stay for supper, Cy." She swayed a little and he caught a faint perfume from her hair, and there was disappointment in her face. She really had wanted him to stay. Why? Cy was puzzled, driving Gid downtown. His mind darkened: nothing is ever said completely, you always try again, there is always more to come. And worse.

It was a man's and a cattleman's meal. "And I don't want that steak so raw I have to listen to it moaning," Gid directed the waiter at the Gallatin House. Four inches thick, platter-size, and finally approved by Gid, who probably owned the hotel or perhaps sold it its beef. A relaxed evening in Gid's room, with the usual plenitude of whiskey and a succession of bellboys bringing ice, and the night breeze cooling the desert outside the open windows.

"Come September," Cy said, "I'll take you up on that hunting trip."

"September? Too early for deer. Well, we could camp near

a sheep wagon and say it was mutton. Nothing to shoot but sage-hens. I got it!" Gid's face kindled. "My place on the edge of Snowy Mountains Forest—I let an old-timer think he ranches it and he's got a pack of dogs. We'll get some lions maybe."

It should be ducks. Out in the tule marshes. "I'll be moving on, pretty soon," Cy said.

"Where you headin' for?"

"Just on. I'll let you know."

It was a good evening, man to man and no requirements, in a way his own continuity with the past. Gid Huntoon was doubtless not too fastidious in the ethics of turning a dollar, a wildcatter from more spacious days. But life burned in him, he was foursquare with the world, and his friends were his friends. Cy's mind fell away into the peace of that night with the storm outside and the darkness of the box car lightened by the red-hot stove. Gid snoring in his blankets, the walls creaking when gusts hit them, sound of frantic water, sound of fury overhead and quiet in his heart. It must have been, he thought, that I felt safe.

Gid made his standard complaint: Cy was not sufficiently a drinking man. "I couldn't possibly keep up with you," Cy said. "You're a damned old rum pot. You've tanned your interior with aldehydes till we could ship sulphuric in you. Your liver turned to stone years ago."

"It ain't that. You just ain't a man to celebrate when you get a chance."

"Show me something to celebrate," he said, faintly resentful, "and I'll match any orgy you want to put on."

"You let me know and I'll come a-runnin'. Man like you ought to throw a heller when he throws one."

"It talks about you in the book. You're elder vice. So surfeit-swelled and so profane."

"By God, I sure used up a barrel of red paint in my time. At that," Gid said with relish, "the drunkest I ever got was the night my old man died."

"I never knew your father."

"Sure you did."

"Not to remember. What was he like, Gid?"

An exceedingly odd expression—part mirth, part anger, part surprise. "You kiddin', Cy? Well, I'll be damned! Let it go. He was just one of Old Doc's friends. Anyway, I sure as hell liquored up to see him out of town."

And Gid was one of Wes Kinsman's friends too and if you looked close enough you ought to be able to find out why he was the only one who was Cy's friend too. Maybe because he was the only one who had no reproach for him in Old Doc's name.

At midnight he had had enough. They shook hands, Gid's balding forehead rosy, his voice unthickened by the sum total of whiskey, and promised each other to get some mountain lions in September. With a rope if we're good, Gid said. Cy drove to the barn, wondering what was mysterious about Gid's father and why he had got drunk the night he died. Ask somebody who he was.

It could not be Josephine, he thought instantly when the telephone rang and had him on his feet in early sunrise. It wasn't, it was Lloyd Tanser. "We got some trouble, Cy."

"Yes?"

"Art Ricco's got a bullet in him."

"Where?"

"In the shoulder. Oh, he ain't dyin'."

"Bring him over. No, I'll come and get him. Is he bleeding badly? Tie a towel on it as tight as you can. Where are you?"

"My place."

Emmy and Myrt were there too—Art had gone to their place first. They had Art's shirt off and had tied the shoulder with a towel, as directed. An ugly, deep wound that ran down the arm almost to the elbow and it began to hemorrhage again as soon as Cy released the pressure. He replaced the towel.

"Hospital," he said. "I'll phone Rulon Williams."

"No, by God," Art said. "They'll be looking for me there."

Emmy, already hysterical, burst into fresh tears. Myrt was

pale and controlled and hard. "Art thinks it was a sheriff or the marshal," Lloyd said.

"Okay, my place. Know a druggist you can wake up?"

"If I have to."

He listed antiseptics, surgical needles, silk, tetanus antitoxin. He had enough sponges and dressings. "Get these," he said. "Go with him, Myrt, and bring them to me. Have Lloyd take Emmy home. . . . Behave yourself, Emmy."

He bound Art's arm to his chest, wrapped a coat around his shoulders, and supported him to the Ford. Simple enough, as Art told it jerkily, beginning to shake. He had been a few miles from town when, toward three o'clock, somebody wanted to stop him. He didn't stop to ask who. He breezed past and whoever it was let go. He got off the truck and lit out. Got away in some brush and kept going. Ought to have come right to Cy but he wasn't thinking straight. Excited, he guessed. Went to Emmy's house instead, like a damn fool.

Cy set up a dispensary and put instruments to boil. Silent, even paler than she had been, Myrt came in with the supplies and Cy directed her to scrub her hands and forearms as she never had before. "Can you take it, Myrt?"

"I can take what I got to."

He sat Art at his table and unbound the arm. He examined the wound minutely. He had Art flex and unflex his muscles, work his fingers, rotate the wrist, make various movements. Myrt wasn't taking the blood very well.

"Ain't you going to stop it bleeding, Cy?"

"I'm trying to see how lucky he was. You see, I might have to suture a nerve."

He got sensation wherever he used a pinpoint. "Pretty lucky, I'd say. Let's go. I'm not going to put you out, Art. You'll have to take it."

"Go ahead, Cy."

Traumatic surgery, Captain Kinsman at an old specialty, gunshot wounds. He worked slowly, doing a careful job. There was some muscular tissue to debride and Myrt said once, "Oh, God, it sounds like tearing silk," and Cy wondered what she would do if Art proved sensitive to horse serum. But it was a simple job; all it took was care and thoroughness. "Hold these things by the end when I give them to you," he instructed Myrt, when he prepared to close the wound. "This would be a bad time to get sick, too."

She wasn't quite sick when he finished the last stitch but she was weak and dizzy. He had some aromatic ammonia, which would have to do, and stopped working long enough to force some on her and put her in the office chair. He put a dressing on the wound and prepared fifteen hundred units of tetanus antitoxin.

"Normally the sergeant does this," he said. "Normally it goes in the tail too, but we'd better not shock the nurse's sensibility." He put it in the small of Art's back and made a sling for the arm. "That does it. I always wondered what I had a pair of pajamas for."

He put the pajama coat on Art, who was weak, dizzy, and feverish. Couldn't put him to bed here. Better not take him to his own room—he might have been recognized or known. That made it Lloyd's.

"Yeah," Myrt said. "All his friends—we'll take care of him. So next time he can get shot through his thick head."

The patient, stretched out on Cy's cot under a blanket and beginning to feel everything to the full, protested. "A guy fixes me up and you put on an act. I'm ashamed of you."

"Maybe I should bawl and kiss Cy because he fixed you up. Maybe you can get Emmy to kiss him."

"Maybe I'd better give you both a sedative. Stick with it, Myrt, we've only got one more lap."

They got him to Lloyd's house and put him to bed under many blankets and he went right to sleep. Lloyd came in, very depressed—it was a depressed trio altogether. But Myrt looked ghastly.

"I'm pretty sure there's no nerve damage," Cy said. "That was the real risk, the rest is simple. He'll feel like hell when he wakes up. If he feels too bad, phone me and I'll put him out. He'll come out of the shock fast. I think there won't be any infection—I learned that one from Uncle Sam. I'll look in this evening. Stick round and read the funny papers."

Church bells were ringing when he drove Myrt home, and she looked in worse shape than Art—exhausted, chilled, despairing. She was worried about explaining to her parents but Emmy had taken care of that, explaining that Art had been in an automobile accident. Emmy was recuperating—Myrt wasn't, she was sunk. He and Emmy put her to bed and he knocked her out with morphine. Call on her this evening too.

He drove downtown for breakfast, hungrier than he could remember having been for years. Also restless and rebellious, though on the whole less so than he would have expected. Did it on the Somme often enough. It was odd, it was damned odd.

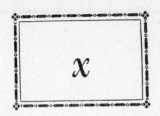

*X*

THE MORNING after Deborah's party was full August heat, a dry burning. Josephine sent her out to play in just a pair of underpants, with orders to stay in the shade. Hattie was dressing for church and no, Ase would not go with her—how often had Josephine heard that mild refusal that could not be budged? "I'll go with you, Mother," she said, and it was at once an excellent idea and charmed her as much as it pleased Hattie. She too dressed in her best but with a good many fewer garments than Hattie and they walked the stark sidewalks through light made all but insupportable. Yet the First Congregational Church was shadowy and cool—and cooler still with remembrance of that girlhood peace. She sank into a reverie that was all perfume— girls whispering and giggling, Bible class, getting ready for Easter music, the voices of the Canedays, and the socials and the rummages and all the splendid sureness that this could never change.

They stood up for a hymn and Josephine sent her voice toward the far wall, rich and full. "Ten thousand times ten thousand, In sparkling raiment bright . . ." It was a magnificent hymn and she had never sung like this for the Schurz Street Presbyterian. The churchly rustling when the congregation sat down, and the minister went to the pulpit and read a text and began to speak. But Josephine was thinking of Cy.

But he's in prison and what a shrew I've been. And what a fool, what fools we both are. Yesterday with an arm round Deborah, so many times with an arm round Deborah, so many times with me clinging to him as if the world would slip away if I let go, and it would have. There must be an end to fighting sometime. And right now.

There was a loathsome but still intoxicating knowledge: the will might be unlovely but it would suffice, she had enough. She had mastered Sam and if Cy were harder, still she could master him. The whole year pointed it out. Let us simply stop murdering each other. Last round, for she could do it and she would.

At the door the minister asked her if she would agree to sing for him sometimes. "I'll be glad to," she said but had no space or time for thought. "You go home, Mother. I'll be along later."

The sun was a heavy hand on her hat, blinding gold to walk through. Whirling sprinklers could do nothing for brown lawns. The peaks were flat planes against a flat sky whose blue diminished upward till the zenith was steel gray. But walk the town with your head up at last.

A couple of blocks before she reached the barn, Cy's Ford eased up to the curb and he said, "Going my way?" That's right, she hadn't for some time but she was now. "Let's get out of the sun," she said and got in beside him. Something irresolute showed in his face. Or defensive.

"Place is pretty messy, I guess."

An aromatic coolness as she went through the door and for a moment the dimness kept her from seeing. Messy! There were surgical instruments on Cy's desk. Gauze swabs hideous with blood were in the wastebasket and scattered on the floor. There were half-used bandages, rolls of medical tape, cans of antiseptic, a basin of bloody water, a blood-soaked towel.

"What happened?" she asked, mystified and alarmed.

"I haven't had time to clean up—sorry. This is an emergency ward. One of the boys got hurt."

Cy began to pick up the bloody swabs and put them in his stove. "Too hot to burn them now." He put things away but talked away from the point, while a quiver of apprehension broke out along her nerves. Well, Lloyd Tanser had phoned him and Art Ricco had been shot in the shoulder and the upper arm. He had been driving a load of liquor. Presumably something had gone wrong with the arrangements. Nobody knew. And girls named Myrt and Emmy. A long raking wound, not serious but he had lost a lot of blood. He was okay.

Josephine was shaking. She was sick. She closed her eyes against giddiness. She had never been so weak. "The state hasn't licensed you to practice medicine," she managed to say.

"I couldn't let him bleed, could I?"

"Aunt Mary Heath could go to Dr. Williams. But not this thug."

"He isn't a thug, Jo. He's a friend of mine."

"And running from the cops. Dr. Williams would have had to tell the police, wouldn't he? But you were safe. Just make Dr. Kinsman's barn and he'll sew you up and we're all thugs together."

"Yes, it was an illegal operation."

"He runs liquor—so do you. He gets shot—and there you are at hand. I think I see. You're the boy that had to grow up to be an outlaw."

She was staring at him, a big chunky man with a face that had been refined by failure. A big man who might have been a great man. She was beginning to see. But her last word had brought a startled expression to his face, as if she had shone a light somewhere.

Cy said, slowly, "And maybe that's right."

So far it had been shock and giddiness and nausea. But now it was wrath. It rose in her and spread and billowed, shaking her far worse, blinding her. "That's what you've been trying to do. Kick decency out and you'll be safe. You won't have to live up to a talent or be a great man or be anything. Doing the dishonorable thing, that means there's no obligation, you're free of obligation. That's what you've been trying to do. Shut the door and lock it tight. And too pure a soul to look at Aunt Mary because that would soil your purity."

Say what you would, they were twinned and married souls, and any emotion one of them felt immediately set up the same emotion in the other by induction. Cy was just as mad as she

271

was at once, if his voice was steadier, and he struck hard at her least defended point. "I'd better not write my novel. I'd better do what you want me to. Because, of course, you know, you're the right one, you're so strong and sure."

Her treacherous ego betrayed the hurt and her cheeks went violently hot. But she nodded. "Yes, you're quite a bit like Sam. You've got a noble soul and you think up pretty pictures. You're nobler than he is, and you've been wounded much more deeply. So deeply that surely we will all weep. Your Paris is Tanser's Garage—"

"I'm leaving Tanser's—"

"I'm sure you are. You wouldn't mean even that—it would be unsafe to mean it. All right, let's say you really did have to throw it all away, all the years of work, all the skill you feel so noble and regretful about. Say you did. Say it really didn't have that splendid integrity that would be almost as noble as you need. All right, throw it away—but shut up—forget about it—work at Tanser's but for heaven's sake, mean it—"

She choked on rage, not tears. Cy said, "All right, you tell me what I've been doing."

"You and your flaming sword! Remember telling me about Old Doc wishing you could learn all he never knew? And that pitiful line that something kept you back—you didn't know what."

"But you know."

"So do you. You've been exhibiting your heartbreak and asking us to cry. You've been begging for pity. You've been—oh, you've been a little two-by-four Greenwich Village genius. Except that they're harmless and rather sweet and appealing, but you're rotten, Cy, how soft and rotten you are!"

She was getting it said. The underlying darkness had been cleared up. It was simple enough why love and the sharing of fear had got them nowhere, why the hope of living their lives out had been illusion, why there could be no peace between them. Nobody else can walk it for you! Before this she had thought they had reached the end and now they had. This was

272

their final hour. It was worth a gentle sadness, for that hope too had been clean. But it was best to know.

By now Sam would have been looking like a stricken little boy. Cy was listening but he did not look at all rebuked. He said, "Or there's the hypothesis of luck. Pete Estey had it, I didn't."

"What luck did Pete Estey have?"

"Maybe to be born an honest man. Maybe to be inside and believe it. Maybe to have no one saying no."

"Nothing happened to you! You just found out you weren't God and it broke your heart. You thought you were the king on a white horse. You thought you were the little Jesus of all the world. You thought—oh, I think you thought you were Douglas Fairbanks. It turned out you aren't and that's more than you can bear."

She had not found a crack; he was all armor. He was not even defending himself; he was solidly set and unshakable, no matter if inside he might be shaken by a rage as great as hers. "Or another hypothesis," he said. "Maybe you're not wise to be sure."

But repudiation headed up and broke free. "Poor Mary Heath has got cancer. Sam just had adolescence—he was a nice boy who lacked the sinews to grow up. I was trying to be something I couldn't be and so I had a breakdown. But those are clean diseases. You're—Cy, you're rotten with the disease of greatness, you had to be a great man, the greatest man of all, or else you wouldn't—"

Cy broke in on the torrent, "All I've ever wanted to find out was what was saying no."

"That isn't true. You've told me a thousand times, don't kid yourself, Jo, kidding yourself is the worst of all, but you're kidding yourself. You had a little setback. You took a stand and it got you fired—"

"I went out to kill something—"

"No, you just had to be a great romantic hero that fate betrayed."

Her breath caught hard but she plunged on. "It's ham, Cy,

it's too hammy to be borne. You can't have what's noble enough for you, so you won't have anything. You won't practice medicine, you won't even repair cars in earnest. We'll all be aghast and wring our hands and say, it's pitiful, isn't it?—poor Cy, what a waste, what a tragedy! And you won't have to accept any obligation at all. You'll be free."

Her breath caught again, still harder, and her breast rose in a long sigh. Cy was going to say something but she raised a hand. "No, I'm talking. I came here today—you wouldn't believe what I still believed. Yes, and I can talk about what you've done to me."

She closed her eyes and trembled some more. But oh, get it said. "All those months in New York when my world was breaking up. You were the man who could do what he was meant to. The man who could make order of his life. Who wasn't licked by rough going. The man I had to respect. I lived among silly little egos that made me sick—but you were running Mercy Hospital. I adored you then, Cy. I knew life was decent just because it had you in it. . . . Then those months out here after I came home."

She had suddenly lost the tempo and her voice was out of control. But go on, get it said. "You were gentle. You were kind. You knew me through and through and there you were, always. I couldn't understand what had gone wrong for you but you were, oh, strong. I believed it still. Even at my blackest I had that blind knowledge that we were going to make something of our lives. Even when I was just a crawling fear. And when the damned fear would go for a while I'd think, the world does make sense—Cy and I are going to live together all our lives—it is going to happen, we can grow old together, I can have kids for him. . . ."

She slumped in her chair and covered her face with her hands. It had seemed so clean a hope. In cold to feel a warmth and in darkness to see the light ahead. And now known to have been just a delusion. "And why doesn't he take what was his long ago, why does he always go home and leave me, he knows we're one

274

flesh, but some time he will. I found out why." Proved a delusion and a damned silly one. She sobbed once and straightened up. Cy had nothing to say. But she did.

Tired, spent, slack. "You closed all the doors. You built the walls up high. You're safe. You're free as air. You haven't got a wife to love. You haven't got a kid to raise. You haven't got a job to do. You haven't even got a mistress to sleep with. I might have been nicer in bed than your little tarts. But no, I was in love with you and that implied something, and it would have implied something to be in love with me. You couldn't just hand me two dollars and feel no responsibility."

Don't let me bawl! "You fixed it up the way you want. You've worked out how to have that splendid integrity of nothing and at no cost. You don't have to pay a thing. There isn't anything you have to do. Nobody can hold you to anything. And you're a beautiful soul—how noble and how hurt."

She stood up. It was said. She had swept away the mirages. The world was clear as winter sunlight and August Sunday was as cold as the night beyond the stars. She said, "I was rid of being in love with Sam when I laughed at him at last. I was rid of being in love with you when I found I had to despise you. This is the year I've been divorced twice."

Cy met her eyes. "I guess that says it."

"Yes. All of it. Most of it. Well, there's this."

She looked at him for a long moment, then sat down again and had turned to stone. "That was a fine joke a long time ago when you told me to cut my hair. And when you told me to bandage my breasts so that I'd look as if I didn't have any. Two men have shown me now that I'm not a whole hell of a lot of a woman."

She had felt so much that the overloaded nerve could carry no more feeling. "I'm not fond of being that way but there it is. Well, I'm twenty-six and I've got Deborah. Maybe there can be more in her life than I've had—it's worth trying. Maybe I can even get more for myself than I've had so far. I don't want the sun and moon—I can't be God, I don't want to be, I don't want the sun and the moon. But maybe there's something. Something more. Maybe I won't always be thinking, is this all I can have? I'm going to try. Try with clipped hair and one breast maybe, but I'm not dead anyway, and I'm not in love with death. I'm going to work at a job. And I'm done with you. Go be nobly wounded. But keep out of my way."

She got out of the barn somehow and divorce was the right word. Her marriage to Cy Kinsman was over.

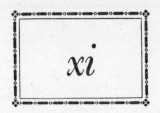

*xi*

THEY HAD TO PROMOTE Lonny, the adolescent
helper, to the temporary status of mechanic and the boss himself sometimes had to come out of the salesroom and put on a
grease suit and get to work. After a couple of days Art came down
and lounged round unhappily, his arm in a sling. It was a strenu-
ous place when it was short one man, and just as well. If you
kept busy there was a certain anesthetic effect. But Cy listened
to the familiar sounds in a knowledge that this too had run out.
The obscenities of Tomcat Jones, the arguments with Joe Bates,
the good salt cynicism of Lloyd Tanser, the jokes and derision of
an equal fellowship—these were the last days of it. He had had
to shorten the radius still more.

He had had his nose rubbed in it. There is this convenience
about the way things are: if you go on refusing to look at it,
eventually someone will make you look at it. Josephine was an
accomplished operator, a good surgeon; her dissection and de-
bridement could not be criticized. She had exposed the field and
there the growth was.

Except that you must doubt still. She had probed deep enough
to satisfy herself. Cy was not satisfied that the factors were all
stated.

He himself had set a term to Tanser's. He had told Tanser he
was quitting, he had told Gid Huntoon that he was moving on,
he didn't know where. It was not he who had somehow cut him
off from fellowship: that was Jo's surgery. So that he was now a
bystander while the boys talked, a bystander who worked with

277

them but had lost his part in their fraternity. They had some sense of it, a rough affection, even a solicitude showing in their treatment of him.

Saturday afternoon he called Art to the barn and took out the stitches. A good scar; the wound had healed perfectly. He manipulated the arm in the right movements and positions, checked the fingers separately, took the reflexes. There was really no need; he had known when he sewed it that it was all right. He put a fresh, unnecessary dressing over it with tape.

"Throw away the sling. You won't get much use out of that arm for a week and you won't get full use out of it for several weeks, but it's okay, it will be as good as ever. You picked a good M.D. But the seat of your pants was full of horseshoes and all the good fairies had their fingers crossed."

"You're telling me! You'd ought to hear Emmy. Or, Myrt—my God, you ought to hear Myrt."

"That's not what I mean. The point is, the law severed no nerves that count and missed every sinew. Arms no worse shot up that I worked out on in my Mobile Unit are still in the hospital, twisted or half-paralyzed, and never will be much good."

"Makes you think," Art said. "You wouldn't want to take my run over?"

Cy laughed. "I ran my last load two months ago. I mean my last."

"I don't know whether I have or not."

"It's not worth it, Art. Maybe we'd better be reformed characters."

"It ain't that." Art had a black scowl, a man pulled several ways and resentful of it, for he had had no experience of indecision or frustration.

"What is it then?"

"I don't think no man ought to let a woman tell him what to do."

A superficial delusion of males and Art would lose it pretty soon. The first sensible word from either him or Emmy would dissolve their simple, their altogether trivial frustration. They would have no final frustrations.

Cy broiled a dinner steak, ate it, policed the quarters. His evening was a long reverie in Paupers' House. Quite literally, there was nothing he cared to do. The "Second Hungarian Rhapsody" was without impulse. The self-taught mathematician? No, he had proved that the moons of Jupiter were not habitable. His favorite novelist, Mr. Willard, would have no new book out for a year or so. There was nothing to be learned from the file on Mr. Willard's daughter and the file on Mr. Willard's former wife had been closed.

Paupers' House was an odd blend of the forcibly self-contained. It was a blend of two Dr. Kinsmans, two army surgeons, two dead medical men. How little was left of Wesley Wales Kinsman, a house where a bemused daughter labored in commemoration of a mad philosopher, a barn where his freemartin son proved unable to recover from the delusion that he had been Douglas Fairbanks or the king on a white horse, some office furniture which the son had converted into household furniture, some old books, some old instruments. Of course, the bemused daughter and the infertile son. And a diminishing memory in his home town.

And a pile of notebooks. Cy leafed through some of them but not attentively. He found that he pretty well knew them by heart. The jotted memoranda of a good GP and they had come to nothing. They came to nothing. And at that they were too redolent of the living Doc Kinsman, the vitality of a man who had lived coarsely and with a gusto that could not be stayed.

You've got the sex wrong, he thought, going to bed. The freemartin is the infertile female calf. Well, let it ride. For some nights now he had lain awake till dawn, who had been accustomed since the first week of his first internship to sleep instantly when he lay down. He had tried to be a number of people in his time. Unsuccessfully. Maybe he was trying to be Josephine now; maybe it was not the first time he had tried. Well, tonight's lying awake had the theme of moving on. Retire

Wes Kinsman's furniture to the loft he had exhumed it from. Let the smell of leather and harness soap and horses and oats regain their former fee simple. For this experiment too, Dr. Bartlett, we must report a negative result.

That would be a specimen of what Josephine meant by how wounded and how pure.

But certainly he was Josephine. As soon as she had found the Enchanted Mesa was merely the western town of Custis she had at once begun wondering about Mount Caneday.

Late Sunday afternoon he analyzed the values of cooking his own or going to Timmy's. Timmy's won on the ground that Myrt had the nightshift this week. Some friendly words without tension, a momentary meeting of personalities after a void and before a void. He put on a tie and an automobile came up the alley and stopped at his door. Old Frank Bramwell got out of it.

"Come in, Dr. Bramwell," he called before Frank could knock, and Dr. Bramwell came in. His first visit and what now?

"Cy," he said, "I want you to come to the hospital. I want you to look at Mary Heath."

The automatic refusal did not get uttered. The look in Frank Bramwell's face would not brook refusal and, a confusing jangling beginning to set up in him, Cy said, "All right," and went out and got in Frank's car.

"Rulon operated her Thursday morning," the old man said. "Radical mastectomy."

Cy nodded. Unseen, it had been diagnosable. But there was the sound of a high wind in his ears. "Much involvement?" he asked.

"Some. From what Rulon says, not too much. But she didn't get along very well. I've kept an eye on her. I'd have thought she'd rally all right. She just sort of marked time. This morning she fainted."

Delayed shock. The kind we understand least, the kind we do not understand at all, if you're honest. I called it an irreversible reaction. There's no point in a consultation: she's dying.

"Rulon transfused her right away. Hasn't done any good."

It was called the Custis Hospital, the name given it by its founder, Wesley Wales Kinsman. It should be called Kinsman Memorial. Wes's original two-story frame building, with a wide lawn in front of it, was now flanked by two three-story brick wings and must be mostly offices and files and consulting rooms or clinics—were there clinics here? Outpatient, maybe, OPD.

How is it I didn't say no? The question was neutral curiosity but as he went up the cement walk at Frank Bramwell's side curiosity turned to fear and it became Why didn't I say no? Going through the wide door he stumbled and staggered and the hospital smell took him full in the nostrils and he could see nothing at all. They were in an elevator that mounted an inch an hour and Cy was blown downwind like a shred of paper. It was violence, an interior hurricane, and half of it was a nuptial violence like Josephine in his arms, and half of it was terror.

A door opening on a room with a lot of beds in it. "No, not here," Frank Bramwell said. It was a ward and Cy had turned into it, making his rounds.

He put a hand against the wall of the corridor. But Rulon Williams was at the desk, and two nurses. A quiet world came out of the hurricane. Rulon shook his hand and said thanks. The three medical men and a nurse went into the room and looked down together at the unconscious woman, whose face was leached of all humanity but sleep. The intricate process of the total mind and nervous system that is beyond consciousness— Little Mac had called it skill. It would have been impossible to separate out the minute observations of Mary Heath that were instantly checked against nine years of what Cy had seen and done and analyzed and thought out. She was dying.

"Take off the dressing, will you, Rulon?"

He intently examined what he saw, the area involved; he estimated the metastasis, the blood loss. He pictured it step by step. He jerked a thumb and Rulon replaced the dressing, the nurse skillful in assistance. He read the chart. He asked a few questions, knowing the answers in advance. All this was perfunctory, a convention, the ritual that the analytical part of the mind insists on after the instantaneous act of skill. He raised one shoulder in the immemorial acknowledgment and they went out into the corridor and closed the door.

"She'll die about one o'clock," Cy said. "They like to die after midnight."

They knew that. They had not wanted to hear him say anything. They knew there was nothing to be said. Why had they brought him here?

"What went wrong, Cy?" Rulon asked. "I've done half a dozen mastectomies and no trouble. I don't think I did anything wrong. Where did I get off the track? Where did she get off the track?"

Cy shrugged and was shrugging away the Central Pathological Conference at Mercy and the question. "You can't save them all, Rulon." He turned away and the clarity of his mind was beginning to be fogged again.

"Stay with her, Rulon," Bramwell said. "I'll be back."

Cy was making for the main entrance. The Pregnant Auk should have been here, but this was not Mercy, it was Wes Kinsman's hospital, and here was Frank Bramwell, its proprietor, standing with Cy in sunset light. Frank sighed and bit off the smallest possible piece of cut plug, which was exactly what Wes Kinsman would have done. Bramwell was old issue, he was the family doctor, he was out of the vanished time. It was Polly who wired me at Harvard but it was Frank who saw him through. I got here before he died but too late; the old man never recognized me.

"I've watched Mary since Rulon operated her," Frank said. "Rulon's a careful man. He knows his job. I'd have said she was all right. She didn't have any right to die."

He looked at Cy, waiting for some comment, and had said that she had no right to die. Someone else had said that. "You know she's dying of shock, Frank."

"Sure. Two days later than you'd think if she was going to."

"Delayed shock."

"Sure. Why?"

"Maybe Rulon didn't watch his sponge rack. Maybe he didn't

282

realize how much blood she was losing and let her lose too much. Maybe she had less than her share of comeback and drifted past Painted Post before he knew. He ought to have transfused her right there in the OR, not this morning." Cy heard his voice leap up. "Transfuse them again and again till we find out why. Will you never understand?"

Bramwell was staring at him. He said, "She didn't seem to need it. I wouldn't have transfused her and I didn't tell Rulon to. I didn't think she needed blood."

I did not kill her! He flung that into the wind, at someone who had accused him. Whirling sprinklers on the lawn of Kinsman Memorial and their spray fell straight down like lead in no wind, but there was a third person on these steps in the sunset. That is not one question but many. I do not know. Why do you not inquire? Slight and stooped person with a scrawny beard that had faded to the color of rope long in water. Cy shook his head to clear it of what amounted to a hallucination.

"We don't know what shock is, Frank. We judge and assume. Some of them come out of it. Some of them can be brought out of it. Some of them can't no matter what. We just guess, we just kid ourselves. We just kid ourselves. Into guessing lives away. The Jesus factor is the name we give to human ignorance."

He couldn't do anything about it. This was hallucination. He shook his head again, a diver freeing his ear of water. "I don't know. You don't know, Frank. What Bartlett wanted me to do was investigate."

Frank Bramwell said, "I don't think we'll ever be able to put a needle into a nerve and read on a dial when mortal man is going under."

Frank was a character part in hallucination. Typed: the old GP voicing wisdom from a lifetime in which too many lives he had fought for had slipped through his fingers. Ain't no pain nor shame nor mortification in the world like seein' a man or a child die because you don't know enough, because nobody don't know enough.

It was past midnight and raining outside. Polly was sobbing

and Frank was trying to do something for her; I should have too. They carried that damn basket downstairs and slanted it round the newel post and took it through the door. I went outside into the rain and watched them drive away. I thought, I'm free to love him at last. It wasn't love I meant and I wasn't free.

That day McAllister grew a beard. In sunset light Frank Bramwell had horribly become Wes Kinsman. Wes Kinsman at Mahoney's family saloon, with the foam of beer on his thick brown beard, rumbling basso profundo, "You owe God one death and there ain't no way of knowin' when He's goin' to call your note of hand."

It wasn't Little Mac, it wasn't the healing art, what I've got is gerontophobia, what I've got is orchidatrophia, what I've got is a god damned endless series of old men with beards, what I've got is a radical testectomy.

He had started down the walk. "Cy!" Voice of Frank Bramwell, eventually. Cy stopped, hitching a shoulder as if for defense. "You move into my office tomorrow, Cy. I'll have no more of this."

Cy turned away and knew he was not running though he seemed to be, into the wind, away from the succession to the successor. What he said or yelled was, "It was the old man who said no." It was walking, all right, but it was walking into the wind.

He wrestled with the Lord through an evening and half the night and all the next morning. He had finished putting on a manifold when he added another name. Paraplegia. Paraplegia, and that does it. You can know and knowledge can still be helpless. You can name the nerve that is destroyed and still be unable to move the limb. You can want knowledge and hunt for it and get it, and if the original destruction was vital, what good has it done to find out?

Also, you can quit right now, no point in waiting till the end of the month, Art will be coming back. Certainly, right now. He checked off the work sheet, wrote in the time, initialed it, and went to take it to Lloyd. Lloyd wasn't there. He laid it on his desk. His eye caught a small pasteboard box that was half out of a pigeonhole. Pills.

He picked it up, then shot a quick glance at the bookkeeper, who was frowning at some invoices. He put it in his pocket and went looking for Lloyd. Lloyd was at the big rear door, talking to a customer who was taking a car away. When he had finished Cy went up to him and took the pillbox from his pocket.

"Better not pin your hopes on this, Lloyd," he said.

Lloyd seized his arm and rushed him through the door, into the big lot. "Cy, for God's sake, not in front of the boys. Well, tell me."

"Sucker stuff. Dr. Finley's Regularizer is nothing but senna and cascara. It's just a physic. No physic has ever brought a girl round yet unless she was coming round anyway."

Lloyd Tanser squatted on his heels. He picked up a handful of dust and let it trickle through his fingers. A self-sufficient man, skillful, honest, a confident untroubled mind, proof against erosion, on top of his life. A man. But now a man in the toils.

Carefully, "All right, what will?"

"You've got to make up your mind to it. Nothing will."

"At that, you must be right. She took everything the women talk about. She's scrubbed the floor. She took hot baths till she's parboiled. She run up and down more damn stairs. My God, I took her out to Riverside and rode her on the merry-go-round till I shot my lunch. We went damn near halfway up Mount Gallatin and run all the way down. No go."

"It doesn't work that way. That's just folklore."

"You must be right."

The noon whistle blew at the railroad shops. Cy and Lloyd sat with their backs against the stucco of the walls, light narrowing their eyes. Against the whine of an electric motor rising in pitch as the load went on, this was a good man, Lloyd Tanser, a man who met circumstance head on and had now met circumstance he could not deal with.

"It's something a girl can easily be mistaken about for a while, Lloyd. Are you sure she's pregnant?"

"She is. So are two docs."

"Who?"

"Williams—you know him, he was at High. And this old codger named Patman, over in the First National."

"They won't take care of her?"

"Uh-uh."

Naturally not. Lloyd Tanser, on his way up, had not yet climbed quite high enough; his girl would not have crossed the meridian into the ethics of Park Avenue. Whatever stood for Park Avenue in Custis. Here was another undetermined point, the point where the predictable effect of motherhood on a woman's health would be so disastrous that the oath of Hippocrates clearly could not apply. Hell, on any crosstown street off Park Avenue, a small, perfectly appointed private hospital.

"Abortion mill is a crude word. Tough luck Custis isn't metropolitan enough to have the right kind of hospital. For primiparas of fragile constitution."

"Tough luck anyway. Tough luck all around."

Or impulsive, frightened, or desperate girls, girls capable of creating a situation that enabled medicine to understand the larger good, to understand the relativity of things. That circumstances alter cases as much as bank accounts. Cy laughed with sudden brutality.

"I don't get that one," Lloyd said.

"Just that if she had been considerate enough of medical ethics to endanger her own life. That's the phrase the books use. Rulon Williams or this Patman—I don't know him—or anyone else on earth. Hell, if she had only offered ethics a decent bluff. But you mustn't be honest before the fact."

He perceived that Lloyd Tanser had the quality of Pete Estey. They were one more than one. He said, "You can always cross the state line. Put this place in someone else's name—Joe Bates's maybe."

"Uh-uh."

Flight being an idea that would not occur to Pete Estey. It was an extraneous necessity, an unintended one, but Lloyd intended to meet it. This is what is called the refusal of illusion. It is what is called reality.

"A guy don't always know the right way to act," Lloyd said. "Maybe I was a bastard to one woman. My wife said so to the judge, anyway. I don't want to be no more a bastard than you got to be."

"How old is it? How far gone is she?"

"Two months and she says a day or two."

Easy. Cy had no hesitation. He was a member of no profession. "Who is she, Lloyd?"

Lloyd spat in the dust. Honor's stern command. "I'm being the doctor," Cy said. "It's safe—the doctor never tells. Who is she?"

"Well . . ." Lloyd shook his head. Gazed out across the lot where metal blazed in sunlight. A jaw-muscle twitched. "Well . . . Oh, hell, it's Myrt."

Myrt! Cy sickened with the sheer dross of life. Myrt, brave, hard, kind as your aunt, wholesome as life itself—far more wholesome than life. "My God, Lloyd, you haven't got any problem. Why, you complete fool! Marry her today. And damn lucky, a damned sight luckier than you've earned any right to."

"It's an idea. Trouble is, you see, Myrt's married."

"Married? Myrt?"

"I thought you knew. Chuck Barnes, you knew him, he played second base. Master mechanic at the P. F. & W. The railroad said he lifted some brass and I guess he did. Two years in stir—he'll be out in November. How he'll like findin' Myrt five months gone I don't know."

"Is he a good guy?"

"I never thought so. Myrt did, I guess."

And Myrt, how would she like living with a man who had a record? That fierce, that fanatical pride in honesty. That abhorrence of Emmy's bootlegger.

Lloyd said, "She's a damn fine girl. I guess you get lonesome when your guy's in jail. I get damn lonesome right in my own shack. I even get crazy enough to think I could live with that wench that trimmed me again."

"And maybe she'd divorce him?"

"You think of everything, don't you?" Lloyd had a hard bitterness. "My God, have I argued that! She won't even talk about it. It wouldn't be square. He's in jail. Crazy—my God! Square!"

Full stop. Lloyd and Myrt tangled in the irrationalities and the undesigned. Tangled in what they were and what they set themselves to be.

"Nothing to do." Lloyd stood up. "Myrt has to go ahead with it. When they parole Chuck, well, me and him will have it out between us."

That was Lloyd Tanser. You do not often encounter reality and honor.

"She doesn't have to go through with it," Cy said.

You can clear the extraneous circumstance. You can make sure that out of the past there will be no future. You can remove necessity and restore the original terms. The two of you can be cleared to deal with your lives as you see fit.

"If Myrt isn't afraid of me, I'll take care of her. If she'll trust me."

She would trust him. She came that evening to the barn whose title was getting to be Kinsman Memorial Hospital, and he examined her and made sure. He explained to the full exactly what the risks were. And Joe Bates's wife, told enough and no more, would take her in for a few days, the sisterhood inclosing them. There were no risks and he prepared his case with absolute care and the next morning he performed an abortion on Myrtle Hill. He spent most of the next three days at Joe Bates's house, a full day more than there was any need for the most scrupulous anxiety.

They were three days of a calm which he knew was deceptive and of a friendship which he hoped was not. Far more easily, he had done for Myrt what he had done for Josephine, he had healed her of terror. You could say that the independent practice of Dr. Kinsman had consisted of three cases, or it might be fair to add Deborah and make it four. And was now closed. If he had been seeking to lock the door, it was clear now that the door was barred and triply locked. And both he and Josephine appeared to have used the wrong words. It was neither anarchy nor outlawry.

So he sat by Myrt's bed and they talked as friends. Her pretty face against the pillow, and he was the entire staff of Mercy Hospital, and she had a hard mind and wisdom. It made no difference what the idiom was, of Mercy Hospital, of Timmy's Diner, of Tanser's garage, of Orchard Street, the unconstrained talk of friends dealt with the light of the stars and the destiny of man and the nature of ignorance and truth, the influences of the Pleiades and how the sparks fly upward. Arcturus and his sons, the treasures of the snow, and why the light is withholden. It did not matter in which room the stove burned red.

On the third day he understood how deceptive his calm had been. And on that day he told her that there was now no doubt that she would be all right. "I never had no idea I wouldn't be, Cy," she said. Medically, his patients always trusted him absolutely. Mrs. Bates would be competent to take care of her unassisted for the remaining few days. He told her so, and she said, Why? was he going away? Myrt was brushing her short blond hair and make-up materials were ready on the little table. She put down the brush and said, "Sure he is."

"How do you know, Myrt?"

"You sit right here and I won't know there's an earthquake?"

His word when he came down the walk from Custis Hospital had been hurricane. He was a book which women read easily, any woman, Rose or Josephine or Myrt or conceivably Mrs. Bates. Up to a point.

"All right, tell me why."

She shook her head. "I wouldn't know. You tell me."

He wouldn't know either at the moment, except that the gale which had been blowing at Bramwell's hospital had begun to blow again. It could certainly not be called panic, as some gales he had seen this year were, and if it was compulsion he could not say what the objective was, nor would he call it guilt or shame or any of the other emotions which the year had uncovered in him. Call it erosion; it was taking away consciousness bit by bit; his mind was guttering. Not too much of it was left when Joe and his wife and Lloyd Tanser were sitting in Private Wing after supper and Cy stood up, realized that he had overturned his chair, and said "I think I need a drink."

Lloyd said, "I'll say you do. Let's go."

It eroded more in the bacchanalian facilities of the Custis underworld. There came a point when Lloyd said, "Do you want that many?" and a point when he stopped asking the question. And another point when Cy was trying to locate Gid Huntoon by phone. It proved difficult and without protest Lloyd took over the job. There were ellipses and lacunae, growing darker and Lloyd patiently using the phone. Till he said, "He's in Nevada."

"Tell him to join us."

"In the first place, I'm not talkin' to him, I just found out where he is. In the second place, he couldn't get here before tomorrow night."

"Tell him I want him along."

"Look, Cy, why do you want him?"

"It's his party."

"I can't get him on the phone."

"Tell him it isn't paraplegia."

"Cy, you need a drink."

"Tell him it's the damnedest drunk he was ever on."

"He ain't on it, Cy. He ain't goin' to be. I'd say you need a drink."

"Tell him."

Tell Gid something, he couldn't quite make out what. But he had the drink, and the ellipses grew longer and a form of violence seemed to be coming into them, till it was all ellipsis and black.

*xii*

WHEN HE WOKE he was free and in jail. It was clear that this was a cell and this was he in·it. Custis jail smelled bad. Doubtless he did too. As he began to remember fragments of the night, scattered, discontinuous fragments, he felt his soul turn gray. Yet it was a neutral color; if this was degradation, if it was appropriate, all right. His mind was clear; also it was completely quiet. The cool windless morning that followed a hurricane.

At eight o'clock a warden gave him a tin pan of mush and milk. No thanks. The cell contained a bucket of water and what purported to be a towel. He made himself as neat as the facilities permitted. At nine o'clock a sergeant of police came in. He was out of Custis High in Cy's time and he was both mad and apologetic.

"You damn fool! We tried to take you home. Lloyd Tanser tried to help us. No, you wouldn't go, you had to put up a fight. We done our best. We threw you out, we carried you out, we done everything, but you had to keep coming back for more. Damn it, Cy, I had to run you in. I didn't want to. You just made me."

"You did exactly right."

At ten o'clock they marched the petty criminals into municipal court. There was the same fat bailiff of fifteen years ago. They sat down and waited for society to deal with its offenders. A few spectators were on the chaste side of the railing. Two of them were Lloyd Tanser and—Josephine. Side by side in the front row, and Josephine with a hand on Lloyd's arm. She looked stricken, Lloyd wrathful. Cy turned his gaze away.

The alumni of Custis High were gathered together, for when the city attorney came in he was from Cy's class. Named Dutton. On the political belt line. The bailiff wheezed an order for the prisoners to stand up and old Keogh came in—Custis had been re-electing him to this job ever since Wes Kinsman's time. He embodied the peace and decency of the city of Custis.

He worked fast. He disposed of a vagrancy, a theft of garden hose, another vagrancy. The bailiff handed Cy a slip of paper and the city attorney of the class of Naughty-Six had written, "Plead guilty and wait for me outside." An assault and battery. Prisoner had counsel—also from Custis High—and after some wrangling with the city attorney counsel demanded a jury trial and was granted an adjournment. The bailiff called "Cyrus Kinsman."

Cy stood up. The bailiff panted through a charge of drunk and disorderly. The peace and decency of the city of Custis had to find a symbol and this was it. But the law Cyrus Kinsman had broken had no bearing on drunkenness or disorderliness. In Keogh's mind it would be the respectabilities of the ruling class he had broken, and Keogh was wrong too.

"How do you plead?" the bailiff asked.

"Guilty."

"Anything to say?" Keogh asked.

"No, your honor." If the court please, it was not an ordinance I broke last night.

"Where did you get it?"

"Your honor, I haven't remembered yet."

The old man looked at Cy. It was clearly his duty to reprimand Wes Kinsman's wayward son, in the name of Custis whose laws and expectations he had equally flouted and in the name of Wes Kinsman whom he had begun disgracing long ago. Wes's son was out of relation to Wes's society and the embodiment of its statutory and moral law had a double obligation.

But your honor is wrong too. The words are wrong, not

292

anarchy, not outlawry, not man's relation to the world but only to himself. It is merely that I was seeing a man out of town.

"I sentence you to ten days in jail," Judge Keogh said. A smothered exclamation from across the railing was identifiable as Lloyd Tanser, outraged by injustice. A protest spurted in Cy too but lapsed at once. The court in the name of its society and its old friend was entitled to assess a penalty—or a fee—according to its understanding.

But Keogh added, "Sentence suspended during good behavior. Next case."

But, if suspended, still passed and Cy had a record now. And yet it was an admirable resolution of the pressures working on the court. Wes Kinsman and his son had both been taken care of, and the peace and decency of Custis, and the judgments and the misconception.

The city attorney looked as if he had been ready to protest too. In answer to Cy's glance he nodded and Cy went out to the desk sergeant's office and was given his money, watch, and keys. Lloyd and Josephine were waiting for him in the corridor. She took his arm; she had been crying. They went out into sunlight that was like a blow and Lloyd cursed.

"The old bastard! I brought fifty dollars. They never do anything but fine a drunk. Five for a drunk, ten for a brawl."

Cy laughed. "He wasn't thinking of me as a drunk."

Lloyd nodded. "And I don't think you were. Cy, damned if I knew what to do. I did my best to get you to go home. You were off your nut. What was a man to do? When the cops sat in and you wouldn't see it their way either, I didn't put up no fight. I thought I'd let them take care of you—damn if I didn't think it was safest that way. What should I of done?"

"There wasn't anything you could do, Lloyd. And thanks."

"You don't need to thank me. Comin' to the garage?"

"No."

"I brought the Ford," Josephine said. "It's parked on Bannock Avenue."

They went to it across the parched grass of the City Hall park,

293

Josephine still holding him by the arm, Lloyd in step with him. "What are you going to do?" Lloyd asked.

"I think I'll go be born a second time."

"Yeah?"

"You won't go camping with me. Gid Huntoon won't—"

Lloyd looked amused at last. "You sure did your best to deal him in last night."

"Well, I think I'll go by myself."

"Want a good car?"

"No, the Ford will do. But if you'll lend me a trout rod and some flies."

"What I've got, you got. Just go take what you want." Lloyd shook hands with him, a hard, firm grip. "So long, Cy. I'll be seeing you."

"Drive me to the office," Josephine said. She was wearing a yellow dress, the same color as Deborah's best, brilliant in this August sun. She was grave, subdued, intent.

"You've lost the morning," he said as he drove off. "Who told you I was laid by the heels?"

"Mr. Tanser of course. I like him, Cy."

"You were prepared to pay my fine too." She nodded but he could not make her smile. He stopped at the sugar company and she got out, stood looking at him a moment still solemn and stricken, and turned away. He watched her cross the sidewalk. He drove to the barn and made some coffee, bathed, shaved, and got to work. He tested the Ford's spark plugs and changed one and began to assemble an outfit for camping. He got out Captain Kinsman's sleeping bag and rolled his blankets in it. All his blankets.

Josephine was standing in a slanting beam of light from the door that made the yellow dress luminous. "I took the day off," she said. "I'm quitting at the end of next week anyway, to get ready to be a teacher."

Cy said, "I'm not mourning, Jo, I don't even have to repent."

"Of course not. What's a college boy drunk?"

She sat down and the edge of that beam of light crossed her

ankles. The barn was as peaceful as his mind. There was no flurry of anger, no clash of confused wills, no conflict. She watched him complete his outfit. Small, functional outfit: army outfit, Captain Kinsman's. It was like packing when his Mobile Unit was moving on.

"Why is there a crown on your bedroll?" she asked.

"It's the King's. I was his officer first."

"I always forget that. Is that Mr. Tanser's shotgun?"

"Young Kit Carson's. I'd forgotten I had one. But Kit had put it away in grease—it's in perfect condition. I'll get some shells."

He stowed everything in the rear seat of the Ford and sat down to list supplies. Finishing, he said, "You'll have to change that dress."

"Why?"

"It's a nice dress but it won't do for the mountains."

He saw color go out of her cheeks, she would not meet his eyes, she was distraught. "I hadn't counted on that."

"Some old clothes and shoes. A heavy sweater anyway."

"Ase and Hattie?"

"You don't need to ask permission."

"I suppose not. Nor the superintendent of schools. Oh!" her breast rose, "there aren't any drawn battles! We've got to fight it out to the end. It just means a licking for both of us, but honor says you go on fighting as long as you can fight."

He nodded. "Till they count ten on you."

"I suppose so. There's no way out. There is too!" She stood up and was simmering. "I don't have to. I don't have to go through it all again. I won't. I'm not going."

"You're going."

"I am not."

"Jo," he said, "this isn't a case of being asked. You can go in good humor or you can go raising hell. That much is up to you."

"Why?"

"What did you just say about honor?"

He could see her go through the cycle from raising hell to something that, if it fell short of being good nature, was assent.

"Damn you, Cy!" Fight went out of her. "Do you insist on taking Deborah?"

"Deborah stays home."

"Call for me when you've done your shopping. Do you want me to bring my axe?"

"Bring your brass knuckles. Bring anything you think will help."

The first canyon had a fair road. Beyond that was a wide valley with ranches in it and a final gas station, then canyons leading to other canyons with the road degenerating to ruts that deepened steadily and had high weeds growing between them. And by midafternoon it was clear that the battle had been postponed. Probably that was what started him talking about Armistice Day.

They operated steadily, two teams in one room and other teams elsewhere in the Base that was mostly the Château. All day Toul was noisy with the gunfire of peace and as the afternoon wore on the Base began to be noisy too. They quit work at last and he and Little Mac went out through the wards, where all the orderlies seemed drunk and all the nurses were crying and all the beds shouting, to the garden back of the Château. Trench coats over stained white ducks in a rain that was cold and miserable. But Mac was wearing his French cavalry boots—he was the commandant, by God, and there was talk that he wore them to bed, with spurs. Mac knew better than to try to quiet the wards. So they walked up and down between ilex hedges smoking many cigarettes and the rain ran down Cy's forehead.

"We didn't need liquor. We were drunk on peace."

Cy was feeling an overmastering regret because he was sure that what was ended now was the deepest thing that could ever happen to him, but he was also feeling an overmastering joy because the tide had turned lifeward. "That was the feeling I've kept wanting to get back." He couldn't think very well, he was emotion on the loose and whirling, hoping for an anchorage. Tonight was as far as he could think. He would put on a uniform and go down to Toul and sip a frugal cognac and find some poilus to talk French with. So Little Mac offered him the residency of Mercy and he said yes, and they started back to bind the agreement with some champagne that Mac had stowed away. Then they were stopped short in the rain. For above the noises of the town and the Château one was dominating the rest, a heart-pulverizing sound that opened your soul down its length. The convalescent wards were singing.

"What were they singing?"

"About the only song a nice girl would ever have heard was 'Hinky Dinky.'"

"There was a mezzo on a balcony above Fifth Avenue. She sang 'Praise God from Whom All Blessings Flow.' I bawled till I couldn't see. Thousands of people in the streets with their hats off and all of us bawling. It took me from nine-thirty to six to get home from Vesey Street to Twenty-Third Street. I got carried north of the Public Library. But Sam wouldn't ever be drafted now, and we could plan our lives, and nothing else mattered for the war was over." Josephine turned toward him, her mouth strained. "Cy, maybe there are drawn battles after all."

The cliffs began to turn violet and carmine. They came over a divide and by switchbacks dropped down a sheer canyon that was filling with shadow. About as far as was safe, considering the gas tank. A hundred-odd miles from Custis. Probably not even cattle or sheep men passed here for months at a time. He turned the Ford up a side canyon with a creek that was big for August brawling down it and bumped over the remnants of a logging trail for a mile farther. Across the creek there was a cove walled off at the end by a vertical cliff, willows and cottonwoods at each side. You could cross from stone to stone, so he drove the Ford under some willows and they started to carry the stuff across.

By full dark they had made a camp, broiled and eaten a steak, scrubbed their dishes with sand, and stretched out by the fire. Night gathered them in its hand. Solitude was emphasized by the fire, which turned the lower leaves of cottonwoods red and made the black beyond them blacker. Existence was pin-pointed in a void that was black and had mass. Night had made the creek louder.

Her hip was uncomfortable and he showed her how to make a shallow hole for it. Stretched out in firelight, tan skirt, tan blouse, and her face peaceful. "That long word about us and the dark? I never can remember."

"Not phobia."

"Not any more. It never was altogether."

She had said that before: we're afraid of the dark but we love it, too, we hold it to our breast. She was holding it to her breast now. Certainly, both of us, all the time. Nyctophilia.

There was no pressure of talk. Occasionally he was saying something about the Medical Corps in France. He decided that he was cherishing France because it meant the last time he had been whole.

And with dependable clairvoyance Josephine spoke from the far side of the fire. "Poor Sam. He never will. I mean, he's spent his life trying to make himself complete and it can't be done. I wasn't hating him when he was here. I even liked him. Maybe that's the cruelest thing of all to say."

On his back Cy watched a star poise at the tip of a fir that stood up above a ridge. He waited but she did not follow up. It was Sam again when she spoke after a while, but down another path. "He thinks his paternal heart is yearning for Deborah."

"He can't have her if you say no."

"He'll have to have her sometimes. Not now—she wouldn't profit from a European tour. But we mustn't forget he's her father after all."

How long ago. Twenty-Third Street. A different era, the era of Mercy Hospital, in so many ways an era of innocence. Cy got up to put a log on the fire. Flames snapped in a light wind and beyond them was the rush of the creek. A wall of heat pressed outward, as hypnotic as the water. You find out. You try not to but you get marched up to it and then you know.

The fire burned down. Josephine slipped into the dark, then came back and stood above the embers. "I don't know the accepted nightwear for the wilds."

"Take off your shoes and stockings but take them into bed

with you—there's dew in the canyons. Put on a sweater and sleep in your clothes."

"I'm appalled when I think of bathing in that creek."

His sleeping bag had an air mattress, so she would use it. A few feet away he had made a bed of interfolded blankets; tomorrow he could chop spruce boughs and give it a cushion. Josephine buckled the sleeping bag up to her chin. He sat by the embers for a long time. The past was a thousand years.

He thought she had been long asleep when he turned in but presently she said out of the darkness, "What is that occasional low boom in the creek?"

"Big stones slide down underwater and hit other stones."

"It sounds like fate offstage in a Village play. And yet this is the most complete silence I've ever heard. Will there be animals?"

"Porcupines probably—you'll hear them sniffing. Maybe a skunk. He'll be harmless. If you hear a thrashing in the bushes it will be a deer scared and getting away. It will sound like a buffalo but it won't be."

"I suppose that's a coyote howling down the canyon."

"Yes."

"And I can hear the trees. But it's absolutely silent."

"If you wake late you may hear stones coming down the cliff. The rock cools off and cracks and the fragments come down."

"What have they done with the world?"

Yes, the trees overhead and a generalized sound of wind among the pines higher up the mountainside. And he had wanted to hear her rich contralto voice speaking to him out of the dark, and now he had heard it.

"About Sam," she said quietly.

He waited. "I try to write novels but I just can't," she went on. "Fiction seems to be beyond me. If it's a pain you can get rid of by thinking how wise and sad we are and how divorce has taught us understanding and a stronger love, I'll have to stay uncompleted."

The end of Sam. Cy turned it over and over. "That was what he came for?"

"It was ungenerous of me not to be on hand when Cassie failed him. But we could build a life out of forgiveness. That will be Chapter One. Or maybe his touch would wake me to fire. It will be a good book."

"Why do you tell me?"

"I have that habit. Good night, Cy."

Pale gold slanting through cottonwoods woke him to dew on the grass, streamers of mist rising from the creek, and a stratum of smoke motionless above the dead fire. Her nose, an eye, and her tumbled hair were above the canvas. She slept forthrightly; the curve of her body had frailty. Cy stood looking at that abandoned, open slightness, counting one more night they had spent together in a different set of improbabilities. Then he made a fire and put coffee on to boil, shaved in icy water, and went looking for a pool deep enough to duck into.

"Can you make me a fisherman?" she asked when the after-breakfast policing of camp had been completed.

He spent the morning teaching her to cast a fly. Toward noon she dropped it where a ripple carried it under an overhanging stump and, improbably, a trout struck. She managed to land it and her cheeks flushed with excited pride.

She watched him gut it for the pan. "Now show me a grouse. Show me a buffalo. Heck, show me an Indian!"

"Sure. Being primitive with a good outfit is great stuff. You're a silk-stocking savage."

Breeze died with the noon and the canyon radiated heat. High up the peaks aspens had turned gold and patches of scarlet were showing in the oakbrush but at camp it was midsummer. Josephine braved the sun with her blouse off for a few minutes but came back to the blue shade of cottonwoods. They were sun-drugged, too lethargic to talk. But he became aware of a tendency not to look at her. The movement of a wrist, her head turning, the dipping of her shoulder were to be glanced away from. Her sleeve opened to show a white arm, there was a color without name where her hair made a shadow along her forehead, her skirt fell away from her calf: these were to be avoided. When the

300

shadow of late afternoon brought coolness and they strolled down their canyon to the larger one it opened off he was under pressure to go ahead of her, lest he see her walking.

When it was her mood to sing that evening, for once he was out of sympathy. Those too simple songs were mannered. They suggested that she ought to go barefoot, swinging a sunbonnet; there was too much earthy American sentiment. The lacquer of firelight on her cheeks and forearms, this whole carmine splotch against the dark—it was theatrical, a tableau.

"Have I lost my audience?" she demanded.

"That's the Stephen Foster theme and this is 1920. I don't think he's a clue."

"Are we looking for clues? Then tell me about the army."

He looked up, his breath indrawn and suspended, then he released it. No, there was no clue in the army. For a period you had proved yourself, you had acquired mastery. In another period, mastery turned out to be an illusion. You saw good men die, you learned that men have courage and are staunch. Then when the terms changed you learned that the man who faced upstream into death most carelessly might have no bowels for action later on. What you had learned proved not to apply.

I will have to make up not only ten years but another ten, and do it as I go along. What you learn from surgery may help you not at all in a laboratory. I will have to accept a ten years' handicap and make it up. From now on it must be my insomnia, sitting up till dawn to learn what I should have begun learning ten years ago. But if you fight back, it gives ground before you.

Josephine too had fallen into reverie and there was nothing to say while the fire sank. Presently she went to bed. And once more, after a half-hour of silence, there was that deep, quiet voice speaking in the dark. "I knew once, I think. Cy, down the canyon, those five stars in a zigzag, close down to the rim. What are they?"

He located them. "Really there are seven, though you can't be asked to make them out. That's the Ethiop Queen. Cassiopeia in her chair. She's turning upside down."

"Why?"

"She goes on turning round the pole—she's immortal so she never sets. But she was too proud of Deborah, so the gods humiliate her half the night. It teaches you not to brag about your daughter."

"I thought Deborah was your brag."

"Cassiopeia is where time begins."

"What does that mean? How can time begin?"

"Better just take my word for it."

"Try me."

"Well, it involves the ecliptic, and the equinox, and the celestial equator. And revolving round the pole."

"You were right—I'll take it on faith. Has it got anything to do with the moons of Jupiter?"

"No," he said. "Not a thing. Time is calculated from there. It's called the first point in Aries."

"What a fine education you have, Doctor. . . . I haven't called you Doctor since Twenty-Third Street. That wasn't a bad time, Cy."

"East Side, West Side."

"I think we used to laugh more then."

"It was before we set out to kill each other."

"I suppose we did."

Or someone else. It turned out not to be you I had to murder.

"I was wrong again," he said. "No one can choose death."

"There has to be an end of getting hurt. I think that's over, Cy. Forever and ever."

"World without end."

"Amen. Good night, my dear."

There was a mild hallucination that her voice lingered on in the dark. He was still staring into the fire when he realized to the full that the interdict had been broken. His excitement was not so much nuptial as conjugal, and he and Josephine had been married some time ago. When was the wedding day? Wes Kinsman was dead at last.

Josephine knew it too. After breakfast, sitting on her heels, she was arranging cans in the grub box and he saw that her lips had a new, a different line. They were softer, newly informed. She was—bridelike. She had come into knowledge while she slept.

The morning was full of broken sentences and sudden abstractions and became intolerable. "Can you do without lunch?" he asked in desperation.

"Why?"

"Let's climb to the ridge."

"Couldn't we take sandwiches?"

Kit Carson had not thought of sandwiches. He watched her make them and it was true that her smile was nuptial. There were parts of old logging trails on the mountainside, stretches of brush, outcrops of shale, rimrock. Part way up they found the shaft of an old mine, caved in and choked with boulders, where someone had hoped for bonanza fifty years ago. They pressed on up steeper slopes and came at last, breasts bursting and muscles quivering, to the shoulder of the peak, with a cold wind sweeping over it and the world falling away in chaos below. They dropped down a few feet on the other side out of the wind and sprawled on bare rock till breath came back.

"This must be the roof of the world," she said.

"Just one of the gables."

Far below them firs and spruce and pine spread through three-quarters of the compass, climbing mountainsides half a mile lower. Beyond the forests the side of the bowl rose to another ridge, back of which a row of peaks stood up in a blue blur, with a vast hidden valley between. Cy set up two fragments of stone and sighted them toward one of those blurred blue cones. "See which one I'm pointing at?" Josephine stretched out to squint across the sights. "Those peaks are part of the Snowy Mountains and that one is Mount Caneday. Beyond them is the forest."

"Third highest of five," she counted. "The Canedays run average."

They ate the sandwiches and silence came upon them. This was a narrow shelf of rock, with a slope dropping from it, and then a cliff. Josephine was leaning back against the rock, her eyes remote with distance and dream, and he was free to look at her. "This must be the uttermost," she said after a while. "Nothing at all but us. But you kept your promise—you showed me my Pop's peak. And no thanks. It's beautiful and nobody could live with beauty."

She had regained the faculty of quiet he had believed in long ago, all of it. Leaning back against the rock, in this moment and no more. His hour struck suddenly.

"Jo, it was my father I was afraid of."

She touched his hand. "I don't have to know, Cy, there isn't anything I want to be told."

"You were right. I was afraid of Old Doc Kinsman. I didn't dare be the better man. I don't dare now. Surgery is finished."

She turned to meet his eyes. With gravity. "Cy, I don't have to know. I want you to know. I want to stop hurting each other."

"I'll have to start from scratch. Ten years late."

Her gaze moved away. We've learned rebelliously, against our wills, maybe altogether at random, maybe by pure chance, but we have learned. Pain suffered without reason, grief experienced uselessly—for the love of God there must have been some purpose in it.

"That drunk of mine," he said. Her eyes came back to his and he came close to not saying it but the purpose was that it must be said. "It was pure cliché. Story book stuff by Sam Willard. You see, I had performed an abortion."

Her eyes did not turn away but were in crisis. "Was it . . . your girl?"

"No. She's a friend of mine. But she's a friend's girl."

"Is she . . . all right?"

"Of course."

She lay back against the sloping rock and closed her eyes. Lines showed on her forehead, a single tear appeared on one cheek, he could see the pulse in her throat. They had got beyond judgment, to the far side. There has to be an end of getting hurt, she had said last night.

Josephine said, "It might have been me. I made you promise you would take care of me."

304

The far side of judgment. Blue space and molten sun lapped them round and it had been said. It seemed a long time before she spoke again, her voice faintly tinged with weariness and compassion. "Cy, how we've always had to tell each other the truth! But I don't quite see—are you thinking that makes it final?"

"I don't know. It was the right thing to do. Anyway, the thing I had to do."

"I hope it is. I hope you're out of bondage now."

It was not that they always had to tell the truth but that in the end they always found it impossible to hide from each other.

"If the door is closed, I don't know if I'll find another door."

She smiled and exigence and urgency were gone out of them. After an indefinite time they started down the mountain. They walked slowly, not talking.

They reached rimrock. Cy was ahead of her. He stepped to the top of a boulder and as he stepped down there was an unmistakable dry whirring. Instantly he turned back. Josephine was stepping down from the same rock. The snake struck as her foot touched the ground, coiled again, and Cy crushed it with a fragment of rock. Josephine clung to him. He stripped off her shoe and stocking, examined her ankle minutely.

"Thank God!"

"Of course it didn't," she said. "Not by two feet at least."

Her cheeks were white and she was gripping his hand hard. "Sorry! I don't think I'm scared exactly—but what a thing to happen."

Cy kicked the writhing coils under a rock, then stooped to cut off the rattles. Josephine put her hands behind her when he held them out to her. "Thanks, no. Cy, don't be a savage!" Color came back to her cheeks, then they flushed scarlet.

Five minutes later she stopped short, so mirthful that she had to sit on a boulder. "That snake's instinct misfired and he paid for it. Nature is not so damn infallible! Why make a rattlesnake that can miss when it strikes? If it misses, then it's a bum rattlesnake. Nature has muffed the job. That should make us all feel better about ourselves, brethren."

"Sure. Poke a stick at a hornet and it will pass you up to let fly at the stick."

Her mouth was soft; it had a bride's reminiscence. "And that teaches us not to mourn our misconceptions too much." She was riotous with laughter. "That's a good snake!" She was ribald. "And not an apple tree for fifty miles."

Now she was wholly open to the sun. She went ahead of him down the mountainside. He watched the movement of her shoulders and hips, watched her skirt loosen and draw tight across thigh and calf, watched her knees bend and her arms brush past the swell of her breasts. She intended him to. She had gone ahead of him for that sole purpose. Rightly.

She said without looking back, "Why, pleasant thighs if you think so, Cy." There you had it again; speech was something they could dispense with. "You called them abnormal on Twenty-Third Street but you'd keep on leering at them, just the same. Don't you suppose I can feel you looking?"

They cooked dinner, Cy compounding a stew from cans, Josephine making biscuits in a tin reflector. They ate, they policed camp, they built up the fire, night settled into the canyon, and silence walled them in. There was nothing to say: words lack meaning on your wedding night. Except that silence was ravished by knowledge. Josephine got the pneumatic pillow from her bed and then, holding it forgotten in her hand, stood looking into the fire. She was savoring the last moments of her maidenhood.

"I wish you'd sing."

"I've sung too much."

Well, then, the rush and whisper of the creek. She stretched out with an elbow in the cushion, cheek in her hand. She turned her reverie toward the fire for a long time, then faced outward toward the dark.

The fire burned low and at last Cy got up to put another log on it. He didn't. He stood watching the embers quiver. Lines of garnet ran down the char, zigzags and whorls picked out momentarily and extinguished.

Josephine said, "We could always go back to Custis."

He made a curt gesture. "The voice that breathed o'er Eden
—either we thought . . ."

He turned toward her and she said frantically, "Give me a
cigarette."

"Jo, take down your hair."

"No."

"I can, then."

She said with spent breath, in his arms, "Oh, can you, why
have you never? . . ." His hands shook in her hair, her arms
inclosed him, her mouth crushed against his, and the world
broke up. When time came into reality again darkness was absolute and there was the sound of the creek. Josephine sat up at
last, then bent down to kiss his mouth, and her hair fell over his
face, and he saw the stars through her hair.

At noon five days later Josephine turned from the grub box.
"Two cans beans. One can sardines. One jar Vienna sausages.
Darling, God knows His orchestration but we seem to have
reached the coda. Unless you can shoot a buffalo this honeymoon
is over."

"I guess it adds up to Custis."

She nodded. And now she would watch the world come back,
little bit by little bit. And just which world?

When they had eaten they packed everything with military
precision and stowed the outfit in the Ford. They policed the
camp site, burned the last papers, made sure that every can was
buried, poured water on the fire, threw the charred sticks into
the bushes, swept the ashes into the grass. A good pair of Kit
Carsons.

"The colonel will be pleased," Cy said. "We can get a week-
end pass."

But they were still sitting by the creek when late afternoon
began to fill with color, their legs in the sun, the silver lacework
of cottonwoods overhead. In a week autumn had dropped far
down the peaks; oakbrush was vermilion and aspens were stippled
with gold. A clump of poplar saplings was altogether gold but

the true mark of autumn was the powder blue mist that lay along the ridges. Why did they go on sitting here? Why didn't they go home?

Cy's mind took the thought from hers. "We can come back any time," he said.

"Not to this place. Never. The moment we leave it, it won't exist. That's why we haven't budged."

"There are other places."

She looked at him. That was not only the right thing for a lover to say, it was true, world without end. Her heart was full, her eyes stung, she dissolved in tenderness, then she was molten.

"Jo! What grotesque whim made you put on all those clothes?" She glanced over her shoulder toward the willows where the little cove ended. "Why, for that matter, why, Cy, why, darling —it's a condition we could deal with. . . ." So sun was beating on her eyelids and when she opened her eyes there was the movement of leaves across blue sky and it was blurred by Cy's shoulder and now they could go home.

Hours after dark they came out to the open valleys and saw lighted farmhouses and then the lights going out in little towns. Remember all they had said in each other's arms, remember all there had been no need to say. But remember too that that was honeymoon, God's orchestration, and the music had reached its end. Every mile they drove was the disregarded world coming closer to necessity again. The pain she was prepared to feel had begun to make itself felt, for everything was settled but nothing was.

It was past midnight when Cy stopped the car at her dark house, carried her stuff to the porch, and took her in his arms. They stood embraced forever, then he said, "I'll come in the morning," and left her. She went noiselessly upstairs and into Deborah's room. Deborah's unlocked room, and the little body motionless under a single sheet, and no terror here, no terror of death or of herself. She picked the child up and Deborah murmured and clung to her, a tenth part awake. Josephine kissed her till she slept in her arms, covered her, knelt with one arm

308

over her. Nothing here but the two of them, nothing at all, or ever again.

She went to her own room and undressed in the dark, warming as she thought, how odd to be putting on a nightgown. She lay awake, and lying awake had also once been in fear.

For a while you've got to forget what his hand and lips can do to you, forget you've been on a honeymoon. For a while. You've got to think more clearly than you've ever thought in your life. Don't let a honeymoon clutter up your thinking.

Fate is just what you've got and what you let yourself do with it. God has only got your character to write his music with.

Cross out the years with Sam as failure. Now a better music had been partly written but only partly. She herself would have to finish out the phrase from where it broke off. Cy had brought it this far but he could not finish it. He had broken through into freedom, she had the best reasons for knowing he had achieved a honeymoon, but his utmost would not be enough to achieve a right marriage unassisted. A right marriage had to be achieved and the rest was up to her.

No symphony is ever written to climax, you do not achieve completeness ever in this world, but they were more nearly whole than they could ever be apart. Proved. I'll have to be in some part a man for both our sakes, I'm the woman with one breast after all. When I said that first it was in anger but it's true in— oh, hell, in all the happiness there is. I thought I had to be more. Don't try to be more.

There it was, the reality. You take what you can, you make of it what you're able to, and a minute or two before midnight it turned out that we would both fight back. It has started, she thought with immeasurable rejoicing, it's under way at last. And as she fell asleep there was the high-voltage thought that at night anyway she was a complete woman. She murmured, Yes, Josephine, we agree on that.

Andy's departure for his ice wagon woke her to fresh and vital morning. She bathed ecstatically and went to wake Deborah. Deborah was out of bed putting on a pair of white underpants.

"You've got them on backwards, snooks," Josephine said and reversed them for her. "How brown you are! They'll all want you for the county fair."

"Mummy, what a pretty dress!"

You've seen it often enough and you really mean, what a pretty woman. "That's Cy's doing," she said and picked up Deborah and raised her to her shoulders. "Ten thousand times ten thousand, In sparkling raiment bright," she sang suddenly. "The armies of the ransomed saints Throng up the steeps of light."

She came into the dining room singing, "Fling open wide the golden gates, And let the victors in." Ase was at the table, Hattie just coming from the kitchen. Their faces blazed, they were both going to begin, and she stopped them with, "Cy and I are going to get married."

Ase was wrought upon. "I hope to God!" he said under forced draft. Much more of that would have exploded at once but Hattie silenced him, for Jo's announcement made the world altogether different and brought everything out right. Reproach and rejoicing so mingled in Hattie that she was incoherent. The Caneday family had a fine breakfast.

Ase permitted himself one remark before leaving for the U. "I think you're a fool. You ought to have taken the other one back. Anyway you wouldn't have to support him."

You can't possibly know how I'd have to support him. She said demurely, "Maybe you're wrong about Cy. I found out I was."

She put Deborah out to play with her multitude of dolls and went into the kitchen to help with the dishes. Hattie looked square into her eyes and Josephine laughed.

"Well, yes, if you come right down to it," she said. "But only very recently, no matter what you've thought. In fact, only this last week. It's a wicked, wicked world, Mother." She kept wise eyes leveled at that wise face. "You've seen a lot of it. You know what women sometimes have to do to get their men. Pity I didn't know it long ago."

A completely idiotic discussion followed. Josephine found

every detail of it absorbing, downright spellbinding. They were two women who had a wedding coming up. Talk wandered along exalted planes like the nature of man and woman, dropped to fascinating questions of costume, ministers, and possible brothers and sisters for Deborah. Yes, and possibly right now. I hope so. They worked up the bliss of a good cry and a fierce current of energy was running in Josephine.

A thought of awe presented itself. "I've lost a fetish," she said. "There is no reason whatever why I shouldn't bob my hair. I'm going to." Noonday sunlight overspread her mind. "Mother! I couldn't tell you what that means."

"All the girls are doing it," Hattie agreed. There could be no flaw in a daughter who was getting married.

Josephine telephoned a beauty shop for an appointment, then changed her dress. She did her hair up for the last time, not quite black hair, of a color there was no name for, of mysterious effect on Cy, of exactly the best effect on Cy. The woman in the mirror would do. Now to go on from here.

She was thinking, maybe I'd better let the bridegroom know he's going to be a bridegroom sooner than he's counting on, when Hattie called from downstairs, "Josephine, Cyrus is here."

He certainly was! Pressed suit, the suit she had made him buy, presentable tie, a scrubbed, carefully shaved man. And Lloyd Tanser with him, dressed much better than he, shaking hands with Josephine, all grin. "I brought Lloyd to lend a hand," Cy said. "That's a nice dress. Put one on Deborah and get your hat and let's go."

"Where are we going?"

"Downtown and get married." He turned to Hattie. "I suppose you'll want a hand in this, Mother. Better take off that apron."

Josephine's heart was thumping. "One of us has got his lines wrong and I don't know which. I think you stole my speech. Cy, you come here."

She dragged him up to her room and shut the door. Control had passed out of her hands; she hadn't been consulted. She was breathing as if she had fallen in love.

"I've had a busy morning," Cy said. "A man can get a lot done when he ties into it." He took a slip of paper from his pocket. "The state says it's legal, we can be man and wife. Pick any minister you like. My choice would be Judge Keogh. Damn! I forgot about Ase. We'd better phone him."

She was trembling more uncontrollably than she had ever trembled with fear, frustration, marriage, or adultery. An only self-respecting defiance flared in her. "You mean, phone Ase he's got to take on another mouth to feed?"

"Look," Cy said. "Arguing won't get us anywhere. And you've got it wrong. Ase is losing dependents. You and Deborah are moving into the barn. You'll both like it a lot."

"Who said I'd marry you? I didn't."

"I didn't ask you. And another thing. I went round to see the superintendent of schools. I told him he was ut one music teacher. Damned if I'll marry a schoolmarm."

Josephine sat down on the bed, her knees bucklin . Don't be such a fool! Stop wanting to bawl, stop shaking, yo. 're not a schoolgirl, you're not a young bride, and God is my witne s you're no virgin, either. She said, weakly enough, "Even if you weren't a jailbird, damned if I'd marry a bootlegger."

"Why, if it came to it, yes," Cy said sunnily. "It doesn't come to it, though. Who are you to be choosier than a State University?"

"Where does the U come in?"

"I told you it's been a busy morning. A prison record does not stymie President Warren and he hadn't been able to fill his job. You're not the schoolmarm, I am. I'm going to teach physiology."

The self-respecting defiance had only a few grains left. "You made that bitter, bitter speech. You don't know any physiology."

"That's right. It can be learned."

There was a moment when for the first time in her experience Cy looked sheepish. It was only a moment. The room was still, quiet, motionless. This was Dr. Kinsman.

"Let's find your daughter," he said. "We've got to tell her she's got another papa on the Salt Lake Line."

She thought, I was wrong, it was the best time I was ever wrong. I was wrong, we can be complete. I was wrong, time begins right here. She thought, it doesn't matter whether I cut my hair, that's all foolishness. Her thoughts whirled into a chaos of things lost and things wasted and things snatched from the fire in time, and she was crying in Cy's arms.

He said, "That's a hell of a way to enter the holy estate of matrimony."

She halted his knowing, wandering hand. "That's a hell of a way to act before you enter it." She sobbed once more and it became a shout of laughter that scattered the past. "Darling, it has been all week."